ROOT ROT ACADEMY

TERM 2

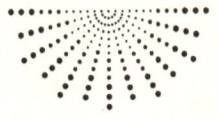

RHEA WATSON

Cover Art: Anika @ Ravenborn Covers
Proofreader: One Love Editing

CONTENT WARNING

Please note that the Root Rot trilogy includes content that may not be suitable for all readers. Across all three full-length novels, you'll find a Why Choose romance, graphic violence, coarse language, and detailed steamy, steamy steam.

CONTENTS

Dedicated to snowy sunsets and candlelit Yules.

BJORN

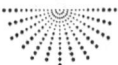

A lifetime ago, I was the one to wield the axe.

The sword.

The daggers.

My bare fucking hands.

As a human raider and an orphaned vampire, I had spilled oceans of blood—painted this whole island red time and time again. Every sin imaginable, I reveled in. Every. Last. One. I laughed and sang and strung men up by their bowels just to watch them squirm.

Centuries crawled by. Humanity turned civil—and slowly, painfully, I had as well. Not quite the tamed dog everyone hoped us rogue vampires might eventually become, but I set aside my axe, my sword, my daggers, my bare hands. Embraced a more cultured way of life. Learned philosophies and psychology. Studied humanity. Studied emotion and thought and *needs*.

I came around eventually.

Dedicated my new life to helping young supernatural beings, shifters on the cusp of destruction and orphan vampires who want to burn the world. Teach them that the bloodlust, the war cries in their hearts, didn't control them. *They* had power over themselves, something that had taken me ages to learn—and above all, accept.

Yet I seldom considered those who had survived my brutality.

Did they crawl into their beds after the assault, after the loss of their beloved, after the burning of their homes and never want to leave, too?

Did they wallow in their own weaknesses?

Did they mourn?

Did they flinch at the creak of a floorboard and the squeak of a doorknob?

Two days after Samhain, nearly halfway through our weeklong break between terms, I still couldn't decide if I was pathetic or not. After all, I had survived the attempt on my life. Leroy and his gang had been expelled with black marks to their names. The security that had stood by as they levitated my incapacitated body through the back gate had been fired with charges pending against them from the high council of academies.

All in all, we were on the right track.

Alecto and Gavriel had found me—taken the time to *look* for me on a night meant for debauchery and celebration.

Jack had stood up for me, taking swift and severe action against all who wronged me... *hurt* me.

The rest...

No one had come to check on me besides head healer Seamus, and the warlock had just been doing his job. No one asked after me. No one... cared.

And that was fine.

Just as I had curbed my savagery, I had accepted that most of the supernatural community wished vampires would one day cease to exist. My kind had legions around the world, ancient monarchs who wielded more power than anyone cared to admit. They despised us for our strengths and our failings, our effortless immortality *and* our inability to do something as simple as stand in the sun.

I knew that.

My colleagues' disinterest had never bothered me before.

But I had never come so close to the end before.

Never feared I wouldn't wake up.

Never felt Death's cold hand on my shoulder. Never hallucinated a reaper behind my closed lids.

A reaper wouldn't come for me in my final moments.

My soul had left long ago—as soon as the vampiric disease killed me and reanimated my corpse, I was gone.

And I had almost been gone for good that night. Crucified. Staked. They had all avoided my heart, either intentionally or because they had no fucking idea where it actually sat. Perhaps they had wanted to see the fear in my eyes at sunrise.

I couldn't sleep.

While a vampire could push himself three, maybe four days without dozing off, it wasn't ideal. We were solid matter. Flesh and bone. Thick, cold blood and a barely beating heart. The corpse needed sustenance—and it needed sleep. Just a little, here and there, to recharge the battery that fueled the superhuman body this sickness gave us.

But I couldn't... close my eyes.

Not without feeling the pain of the stakes, the iron nails in my palms.

It had all healed within the hour. Wounds closed. Flesh regenerated. Internal muscle and tissue and viscera mended. If someone *didn't* know a bunch of wayward teenagers had nearly murdered a seven-hundred-year-old Viking vampire, they wouldn't be able to tell by looking at me today.

But I still felt it—*them*, every last stake, every pinprick of

3

wood. All of it. Over and over again. Heard the laughter. Endured the agony. Tasted death.

It was karma.

I had centuries of it stacked on top of me, held up by a few flimsy boards and rusty screws, precarious and ready to crumble at any moment. I had done all that and worse to humans in my lifetime. To shifters. To witches and warlocks and all sorts. Anyone I could get my hands on. Anyone who caught my eye. I had played the butcher and *liked* it, and no matter how many new leaves I turned over, I could never fully erase that.

The last few decades, I'd been a good boy. I taught the dregs of supernatural society, the children offloaded by their parents because their darkness ran too deep. I gave to charity. Sponsored animal rescues. Signed petitions. Protested inhumane conditions and laws. Saved some poor girl from a vampire attack in Essex a few years back on a term break just like this one. Heard her squealing. Smelled the blood. Ripped him away and tore him apart.

Modified her memory. Got her home. Even watched her for a few days after, just to be sure she was all right.

I had started to pay back a lifetime of carnage, one brick at a time—but it wasn't enough.

If the scales of the universe had anything to say about it, many more encounters just like Samhain loomed on a dark horizon.

And if I couldn't handle *this*—couldn't get out of bed, couldn't sleep, couldn't *speak* to those who did bother to check on me—then I was in for a rough fucking ride.

A floorboard creaked outside my closed door.

She did it on purpose. Alecto usually avoided the more talkative wood panels around our flat, but since Samhain, she stepped on each one, announcing her arrival before she reached my door. Exhaling sharply and shrouded in shadow,

I pushed up from my slumped position on the bed, neck stiff from the odd angle it had been bent at for… well, *hours*.

Pathetic or not.

Still unsure.

Her knuckles rapped on my door just as I drew my knees up and slung an arm around them—casual, *totally* normal, seated in a dark room, alone, exhausted and sulking.

"Yes?" I croaked. As the knob squeaked, I went for the little lamp on my bedside table, bathing the space in a yellow glow that cast shadows across her face when she poked her head in.

"Hey."

I offered a limp smile in return. "Hey."

That was permission enough: Alecto slipped into my bedroom, bringing her vanilla-infused scent with her, the kind that clung to my sheets and muddied up the walls. Even long after she left, she was still *here*, still hovering.

When I came to, it was there—vanilla. That charged through the fog first. Then shimmering pools of amber. *Plop.* A hot, wet tear on my cheek. Her voice all high and frantic as she dragged me off Death's door.

She had seen to me a few times a day since then, always seeming mildly disappointed when she tiptoed in and found me awake. Sometimes she knocked. Sometimes she didn't.

Most of the time, however, she came to me dressed down. Loose trousers and thick sweaters. Wool and cotton and fleece, her hair in a sloppy bun on top of her head, sometimes dangling down her back.

Things should have been different between us by now.

I should have kissed her come midnight on Samhain, somewhere private and soft and secret.

Today—tonight, this morning, whenever—Alecto appeared dressed *up*, looking lovely for someone else, not me. Gone were the ill-fitting slacks and the staticky sweatshirts. In their place, leather pants that clung to her shapely calves and thighs. Faux leather, actually, given the smell. Ankle boots with a low heel. A pine-green long-sleeved shirt that, while slouchy, somehow highlighted her physique as if it were flush to her curves. An attempt at casual *and* sexy. Even her curls had been tamed into a perky, bouncy ponytail, a few loose tendrils coiled around her face.

And... makeup?

She had somewhere else to be but first had to check on her ward.

"I made you something."

Blinking hard, my gaze dropped to her hands. So focused on her outfit, I hadn't even noticed the pint glass, the liquid inside a red ombre like some fancy cocktail.

"Oh?"

"It's a sleeping aid," she insisted, padding over to my bedside and setting it on the table. "I'm sure you can smell the lavender, but there's a touch of valerian root and some blue skullcap, plus—"

"I don't have trouble sleeping."

Her full mouth snapped shut, then twisted into a frown at the outright lie we both saw through. Sniffling softly, Alecto fidgeted with the cuffed sleeves snug around her wrists, the fabric hugging her forearms and flaring at her elbow.

"Right. Sure. I just—"

Really, like I *deserved* her pity. "It's a nice sentiment, but—"

"I had a shitty thing happen to me when I was little," the witch blurted, her cheeks suddenly flaming, her eyes everywhere but me. "And back then, I had trouble sleeping... for a long time."

Lost for words, I sat up straighter. "Alecto—"

"So, I thought—"

"This is very kind of you—"

If we could figure out how to speak to each other again,

that would be fucking swell. It was all my doing, the awkwardness between us, the tension in the air. She had found me at my most vulnerable. Rescued me. Brought me back to life and tucked me into bed. I was the wounded animal here, and *I* was the one who kept throwing off our rhythm.

"It's a blood base," Alecto told me after a reset pause, fidgeting with her fingers—oh. Look. She had done her nails at some point, the tips even and glossy, not a speck of soil to be found. Rare, given her daily routine. "Type O. It's all they had in the kitchen. I know regular food..." She trailed off, mouth snapped shut again, and then cleared her throat. "Er, I mean, human food—"

"It's fine." I dismissed her embarrassment with a wave, the flush in her cheeks lovely but unnecessary. She fiddled distractedly with the loose wispy curls around her face, alternating between tucking them behind her ears and dragging them back out.

"Anyway, I know it can make you a little nauseous, so I kept the herb dosage low." As if to still her fidgety fingers, she finally folded her arms, then offered a smile that didn't quite reach her eyes. Not because she couldn't smile at me— but like she wasn't sure *how* to anymore. Alecto seemed to struggle between playing caretaker and friend, overly nurturing one moment and sarcastically blasé the next. She couldn't figure out how to take care of me—a creature far older and far, far stronger—but I still appreciated her efforts.

If anything, they made me want her more.

Which was a problem. Samhain had ruined everything, the buildup broken, the bond between us splintering apart and weaving back together different.

"Plus, you know," she rambled on, "a little magic to help with sleep... People always say my potions are smooth. I've

7

never made one specifically for a vampire before, so I'm sorry if—"

"Thank you, Alecto." Taking the glass from the table, mindful not to slosh any of her hard work over the rim, I tried to inject my grin into my words, desperate for our easy conversations again. Desperate for *us* again. "This is too kind of you."

Frustration knit her brow. "It's not... It's... Too kind isn't..." Huffing softly, she backpedaled, her smile strained and stretched too wide. "You're welcome. When and if you want to talk, I'm here."

Right. Pathetic it was, then. Any other vampire would have bounced back after this within the night, but here I was, moping, still wounded days later.

Traumatized.

Definitely pathetic—and in front of the woman I wanted to impress. I had taught Alecto to *waltz*. Soothed her concerns about Samhain. Shouldered the burdens, the bulk of the work, because it seemed to make her less stressed. Made her laugh night after night on the couch out there. Picked up toothpaste for both of us in the village when she was running low. Let her paint my toenails—*once*—because it made her giggle-squeal and snort, which then made her blush the loveliest crimson hue.

And now...

Now the dynamic was off.

Because of me.

Silence dragged on again, the pint glass clutched in both hands and sitting on my lap, and I finally managed a nod. "I know."

She would listen to me. Share words of wisdom— apparently she had trauma of her own.

And I'd hate every second of it, becoming less and less of

8

a man in her eyes the more I shared. No. Never. These anxieties, this trauma, stayed with me.

After a brief hesitation, Alecto drifted to my bed, knees nudging the wooden frame, then leaned over and kissed my temple. Braced on my shoulder for balance, her hand was an inferno compared to my icy flesh, and without meaning to, my eyes fluttered shut, all of me enveloped in vanilla and *her*.

Our first kiss.

If only I had the stones to turn my head and claim her mouth, transform this chaste peck into something more.

But I was broken. Pathetic. Lost.

No sense infecting her as well.

In my mind, it lasted forever. In reality, the kiss went on maybe five whole seconds before she withdrew, smoothing a hand down her flirty sweater thing before flashing a farewell grin and heading for my bedroom door.

"Where are you headed dressed like that?" It took effort, but the question *almost* sounded like the me of three days ago —before it all went to shit.

"Oh." Alecto turned back, still ambling for the door, and motioned to her outfit with a shrug. "I have an appointment with Jack. Figured I shouldn't go in my pajamas."

Curious. Jack was currently drowning in the aftermath of Samhain, much of his security decimated, Iris Prewett on her yearly retreat with the entire admin team, the high council no doubt breathing down his neck after a professor was nearly murdered on his watch. Strange that he would make time for anything *but* damage control. "About what?"

Another hapless shrug—as if that would deafen the sudden thunder in her chest. "No idea. He scheduled it."

For the first time in days, genuine amusement fluttered through me. It died fast, but at least it was there... At least I could feel something beyond this tedious, unwelcome tangle of emotions.

Smirking, I watched her go, head bobbing at her little wave, then waited until she *almost* had the door shut to add, "Liar."

Her breath hitched, the door a hair off from closed, and she then dragged it the rest of the way a beat later. Not quite a slam, but firm enough to make a point: *mind your own business, Bjorn.*

So be it. Chuckling, I brought her potion up for a sniff, the blood strong, the lavender stronger, teeny bits of greenery floating on top.

Right.

I plugged my nose and gulped the entire thing down in a single go—for her. For her efforts.

Two minutes later, I was dead to the world, snoring away in a dreamless sleep.

The pain forgotten.

For now.

2

JACK

A tentative knock on my closed office door startled me out of the mountain of paperwork stacked so high around my desk that I could barely see over it. Frowning, I glanced at my laptop, then down to the little clock in the corner of the screen, and... Oh. *Bollocks.* Completely lost track of time. How was it three o'clock already?

Ignoring the sudden flash of panic, I hastily shut the laptop and shifted things around to create an opening wide enough to see the twin chairs on the other side of my desk. With that sorted, I buttoned the top clasp on my dress shirt, then adjusted my tie and rolled down the sleeves. Given the circumstances, it was best to look professional despite my monumental failure in that arena just a few short days ago.

"Come in, Miss Clarke."

This was the absolute *last* thing I ought to deal with amidst all the other fires snapping at my heels, but I had done the crime. I had broken professional boundaries —*touched* her, almost kissed her.

And what a kiss it would have been, all forceful and

11

domineering to make an already plump lower lip beautifully swollen.

I'd come so close.

The flames ought to consume me. I deserved to burn.

If she accepted my offer today, I *would* burn, brightly and very publicly, her harassment report the nail in my career's coffin. The high council was already furious over the Bjorn incident, and with Mabon still fresh in everyone's minds, I had two rather serious strikes against me—along with one pending, Fiona Simpson's death still a secret I'd only shared with Bjorn. Throw in some inappropriate conduct with a young professor and I was finished.

But this was the right thing to do.

The door whooshed open soundlessly, and Alecto Clarke poked her head inside, bringing with her a waft of freshly brewed french roast courtesy of Marigold, the only admin girl Iris had left me for the week.

"Hello, Headmaster."

I waved her in, catching a flash of Marigold's golden curls in passing as the witch blitzed around the administration wing all by her lonesome. Honestly. Absolutely *ridiculous* that under these circumstances, Iris still thought it appropriate to take her staff retreat in Barcelona. Yes, she went every year, scooping up almost all her girls and whisking them away to the Spanish coast for... work, supposedly. Training. Whatever they did out there, I wasn't privy to it; Iris came with an established reputation at the academy, and even though I outranked her, I'd always felt I couldn't pry into her private matters with *her* underlings.

Which was absurd, but that was the dynamic we had set for ourselves since I started, and thus far, it had kept conflict to a minimum.

So, here I was, *alone*, dealing with one bloody crisis after another, poor Marigold barely shouldering the burden alongside me. Not only had we expelled every student involved in Bjorn Asulf's kidnapping and attempted murder, but I now had the parents raising hell, their covens and clans demanding answers. The high council had their collective foot shoved so far up my ass that every time I swallowed I tasted leather. Then there was the matter of hiring all new security after such a disastrous breach...

Marigold was stuck sifting through applications today while I contended with the rest. With *everything*. Without my assistant headmistress.

And now... Alecto Clarke had walked into my office, as requested. Shut the door behind her. Barricaded us inside, the air thick and her aura especially buzzy. Distracting. Beautiful as always, the young witch settled into the chair I gestured to in front of my desk, a little fidgety, cheeks already a delectable shade of pink.

My preferences erred toward darker hues, red and tearstained my all-time favorite, but never mind. It was that kind of thinking that got me into this mess in the first place.

That and my own personal failings. *Really*. Grabbing her like that, pinning her to the wall as she stared up at me with wide, wanting eyes. After that breach in control, I no longer deserved to carry the Dom title.

"Alecto..." I threaded my hands together and tapped them on my desk, wishing I had gone with the *Miss Clarke* I'd practiced for the sake of propriety. "I owe it to you not to mince words."

The height difference between us was purposeful, one of the few things I did to establish a power imbalance with those called into my office, usually students who needed a more serious talking to, occasionally professors and staff who overstepped their bounds. Here, having Alecto blink up at me, brow furrowed, lower lip snagged between her teeth, all deliciously submissive and lost—*fuck*, she was perfection.

I should have called Marigold in too, but there wasn't a chance in hell I'd let anyone know what had transpired between us unless Alecto filed a report.

Which... a part of me almost hoped she did.

I should be punished for—

"Sir?"

For loving the way that *word* tumbled from her lips, all light and airy, innocent and full of promise.

"What happened between us in the stairwell on Samhain..." With stress at an all-time high now, the siren song of Dominant-submissive play had been much harder to resist. The promise of complete release—the disconnect it offered from all your problems—was such a *gift*. Some sadists entered the lifestyle because they lusted after pain, desperate to let loose on someone who would gladly take it. I fell into it because of my own proclivities, yes, but when I realized I could finally just *be*, just exist without a million thoughts and concerns whizzing around my brain... I never looked back. But now it had screwed me in the worst way possible, and if karma had its day, I'd never play out a scene again. "First, let me apologize—"

"Headmaster—"

"It was wildly inappropriate," I insisted, lifting my voice just enough to quiet her but not so loud that an undoubtedly eavesdropping Marigold would hear. Clearing my throat, I leaned forward and stared into those amber gemstones with all the sincerity I could muster. "I'm so sorry, Miss Clarke." Better than *Alecto*, even if it left a strange taste in my mouth to shirk that intimacy. "If you wish to file a report with the high council about the incident, you have my full support. Please know that I won't stand in your way, nor will you face any repercussions for doing so."

She shook her head frantically, shifting to the edge of her seat. "No, no, I would never—"

"Please don't feel frightened of me." Women seldom reported incidents like these, especially against their professional superiors, because they feared the fallout. They feared ruining their career, their reputation—everything. Just the thought of Alecto trudging through that sort of inner turmoil made me physically ill. "The last thing I want is for you to—"

"I'm not afraid of you."

She might have gulped after, but she sounded so bloody frank that I found myself at a rare loss for words. Oh, and a little hard, too. Shit.

Alecto licked her lips, then tugged her chair up to my desk so she could plop her elbows on it, sandwiched between the stacks of endless paperwork, her cheeks on fire but her expression adorably serious, like she was gearing up for something. When coherent thought *did* trickle back into my brain, I kept it to myself, allowing her a beat of quiet to think, possibly even to *re*think.

"What happened... I..." Her blush sharpened, unmistakable now as her eyes danced around my office. Gods, what was she about to say? No. No. *Please don't look at me like that.* "I... I liked it."

Fuck.

"It *was* inappropriate," she added slowly, thoughtfully, drumming her fingers on my desk with a frown, "given our professional relationship."

"*Very* inappropriate." The correction came out all stern and Dom-like, which seemed to make her squirm. Sighing, I tried my best to sound softer. "I can assure you, it will never happen again—"

"But I can't stop thinking about it," Alecto told me, risking a quick glance up to my eyes, meeting them for a moment before hers fell to my unusually cluttered desk. "About your... your..." She motioned halfheartedly to my hand, as if

I needed the reminder of how it felt to cuff her delicate throat and *squeeze*. "I-I don't really understand what I'm... feeling, but..."

Trailing off with a sigh, she looked to me like so many submissives looked to their Dom for guidance. Not because they depended on us for everything. Not because they were worthless or useless without us, but because they liked the security we provided, the comfort found in our response, in our care.

And we liked giving all that and more.

"We..." Right. Okay. Although once again we veered dangerously close to scandal, I could be upstanding and professional in the way I handled this. If anything, giving her the full picture, making her understand all of it by being clear and open, could very well protect her in the end. "We seem to have fallen into a Dominant-submissive courtship... quite unexpectedly, I might add, and certainly not intentionally on my part."

She opened and closed her mouth a few times, soundless, until: "A *what?*"

Her innocence would be my downfall. Honestly. "Well, dominance and submission are subsects of the BDSM community—"

"No, no, I know what they are." Cheeks still flaming, Alecto clapped her hands to them to block the redness, possibly even to remove her blushes from the interaction. Smart. "I didn't grow up under a rock. I just... What do you mean by *courtship?*"

It had been years since I fell so seamlessly into one. It seemed a shame to sully it with all the behind-the-scenes technicalities, but she deserved to know what had been brewing between us, if only for her own peace of mind.

"Sometimes..." I hesitated. Once again, here I was, steamrolling professional boundaries, propriety miles behind and a public spectacle at the cost of my career ahead. Screw it. This was my doing. No sense abandoning her in a sea of unanswered questions. "Sometimes potential pairings feel each other out beforehand—see if it's a good fit."

Alecto's eyebrows shot up. "Romantically?"

"Not necessarily," I said swiftly. Best shoot down the notion of *romance* before a whole new set of issues sprang up between us. "I've played with many submissives over the years outside of romantic relationships. We were just, er, consenting adults who dug the same kink, as it were."

Hard to believe I was having *this* particular conversation —out loud, in real life—with one of my professors.

And she hadn't run out of here screaming. Nor did she stare up at me now with eyes that screamed *Bloody pervert!*

I knew the look. I'd seen it before when trying to introduce my preferences into a rare and usually fleeting relationship. The society witches my family deemed appropriate to inherit the Clemonte name had always been so scandalized at the *mention* of dominance. Submission never factored into the conversation after that, and it was vanilla sex, lovely but boring, until the inevitable breakup.

It had been easier to play with subs who knew the rules— who weren't looking for more than a very specific type of friendship.

Alecto showed no signs of past paramours' discomfort. No fear. No disgust. Caution, perhaps, as she settled back in the chair, hands off my desk and folded together on her lap. Curiosity, certainly, given the nibbling of her lower lip, the blush on her cheeks a tell that her mind was working through more salacious topics.

Although I enjoyed watching her most of the time, this afternoon I did so with more intensity than usual. If I caught even a flicker of distress, this conversation ended. Period.

Mind you, it was rather disconcerting to have a man,

your boss, stare you down, all calculating and silent. So, I stood, always keeping her in the corner of my eye or studying her in the windowpanes, the grey outdoors offering a clearer reflection than usual. Snatching my wand from the top of a precarious parchment stack, I drifted over to the tiny coffee bar under one of the windows, then tapped the pot while uttering a simple heating charm. Seconds later, the water started to boil inside, bubbling away as I readied two cups for some afternoon tea.

Damn. No cream or sugar in the snack cupboard. Yet another thing Iris had dumped on me before she flitted off to Spain.

"I hope chamomile is all right. I've just got the bag—"

"I've always been interested in it," Alecto blurted as though she hadn't heard a thing I'd said, something that would have earned her a chastising smack to the backside in another life. Not this one. Never this one. She frowned down at her clasped hands, making it difficult to tell if she was sharing with me or just thinking out loud. "The lifestyle, I guess... Nothing too over-the-top."

Back to her but still watching in the window, I tipped boiling water into two china teacups, each white with blue-and-gold filigree around the rim. "I'm afraid my brand isn't exactly for beginners."

"No?"

"I suppose that's a bit dismissive of beginner submissives," I said as I doubled up on tea bags, one in each hand, dunking them nine times—my preference for the perfect flavor—before discarding them. "But I indulge in sadism play." Bags tossed in the bin, I carefully picked up the little china saucers, then returned to my desk and passed Alecto's over. She accepted, as I knew she would, with a silent nod, eyes unfocused, lost in thought. Once I was back in my chair, a newfound buoyancy grew in my chest at the fact that finally

—*finally*—someone was willing to have a frank, open, nonjudgmental conversation about this. Just the thought gave me the courage to add, "I like to inflict pain."

"*Oh.* Sure." Alecto's eyes rounded, cradling the saucer with one hand, the other with a dainty finger curled around the teacup's handle. "Like, uhm…"

"Physical pain," I said smoothly—confidently, almost, like this really *was* an earnest Dom-sub courtship and we had already sprinted through the first lap. Dangerous territory, thoughts like that, but a part of me couldn't help it. I spent all my life being careful, cautious, thoughtful. Annoyingly meticulous. With her, in this moment, it was just… natural. Free-flowing. Easy. Simple. I liked pain. I liked tearstained cheeks and squeaky cries and hoarse begging and red marks that would last for days.

And then I liked to end it by giving my submissive a screaming orgasm amidst all that pain.

Some called it sick. Twisted. *Fucked*-up.

I found it relaxing. Distracting. A healthy, and dare I say, *fun* way to disconnect from the burdens of the real world—if only for an hour or two.

"Not mental or emotional pain," I clarified after a tentative sip of tea, Alecto still gawking at me from across the desk. In my experience, the pain I inflicted on the physical body was nowhere near as brutal—damage-wise—as that done by Doms who tormented mentally or emotionally. Perhaps I just wasn't skilled enough to do it, but it wasn't my *thing*. No lasting damage. No scars. Nothing a submissive would carry with them outside of a scene… Well, no longer than a week, tops, even less so if they let me use a magical balm during aftercare. "Some Doms only indulge in that— mental and emotional torture. Not my scene, I'm afraid."

Alecto finally risked a big sip, grimacing: still too hot, little one. "Why?"

19

"Well, they—"

"No." She set her tea on her lap rather primly, her posture perfect for play. "Why do *you* like pain?"

Why did anyone like *anything* they did for sexual gratification? While there were probably countless studies out there on the specifics, I'd never bothered to psychoanalyze myself. I liked what I liked, and everyone else could just piss off.

"I only like delivering pain, not experiencing it." Though I had, in the early years, asked a few Dominant friends to do to me what I did to subs. It was only fair that I knew precisely what they felt—and when to stop, even with the stubborn ones who refused to use their safeword.

Unfortunately, that didn't seem to be the answer she was looking for, and when Alecto's full lips parted again, perhaps to press harder, perhaps to clarify her intentions, I cleared my throat and tapped my finger on the desk. Loud. Hard. Centering her focus to *that* and not her curiosity.

"I'm not exactly comfortable delving into my sexual preferences in greater detail—"

"Oh, *gods*, of course," she babbled, cheeks flaming once more, tea sloshing dangerously close to the cup's curled lip as she shifted about in her seat. "No, no, of course, I'm so sorry—"

"I just find playing with a consensual partner relaxing," I told her, hand up to stop her rambling apology in its tracks. Curiosity ought to be encouraged in all things, but I had no problem politely curbing it when it cut a little too deep for comfort.

Her eyebrows shot up at that, perhaps at just the thought of relaxation while physically hurting another person, but in theory, the other person *wanted* it. That was the thrill. That was the game.

"It sounds ridiculous, I know, but that's the honest truth."

As much as I was willing to give, anyway. After another sip, the water's temperature more palatable, I eased back into my chair—something I seldom did with someone else in the office. This wasn't a place to slump and slouch and relax. This room, this desk, this very chair, was the heart of authority at Root Rot, but it felt wrong to lord over her for this. Just for a moment, we were *almost* equals, Alecto and me. "I've made a career of dealing in stress. Every job, every step—stressful. I carry a lot, always have..." The Clemonte name promised no less, most of us barely functioning disasters behind closed doors, addiction, anxiety, and depression rampant throughout the family tree. "If I can find something to alleviate that, just for a little while, why not embrace it? I find all of it a comforting release."

That one little word—*release*—triggered a blush of epic proportions, but I pretended not to notice, allowing her a moment to compose herself by taking an unnecessarily long gulp of tea. By the time I set the cup down, Alecto seemed more centered, no longer fidgeting or shuffling or overtly avoiding eye contact. Comfortable as she might come across with the subject matter, she still didn't understand. None of them did until the first strike of the whip, the first swing of a flogger—the first cruel bite of a nipple clamp.

And by then, they had handed over all the power.

That was part of the game, too.

The panic in their eyes upon realizing *precisely* what they had signed up for. *Exquisite.*

"Can I say something..." She paused, then set her teacup on the desk, removing all possible distractions. "...off the record?"

Panic lanced through *me* now, and I did my best to keep the surface calm as I nodded and motioned for her to speak. "Of course. If you don't mind, I'd prefer all discussion of *kink* with one of my professors to be off the record."

Her little giggle settled the maelstrom brewing below these still waters. "Absolutely."

But then the shine in her eyes dimmed, humor gone, replaced with—fear. Uncertainty. Her throat bobbed ever so slightly through a gulp, and I allowed her a moment to lick and nibble at her lower lip—a habit I would stamp out if I were her Dom. Too obvious. Too revealing. All that fidgeting told the world she wasn't sure of herself, and darker predators than me would take advantage of that.

"I…" Her gaze shot skyward for a moment, and she took a deep breath before continuing. "I… kind of like rough sex. It's taken a while to clue into it, but… I like being, you know, *controlled*. I like… when it hurts a little."

I stiffened. Like catnip, her omission. Her surrender. Her secret. *Fuck.*

"Do you think I would like pain?" Alecto carried on. She sat straight and sure, hands still, and I admired her bravery— even if she wouldn't meet my eye anymore. "You know, receiving it… Maybe as a stress relief, just like you?"

When those amber gems glanced up, they knocked the wind out of me. So open. So raw. Looking for guidance in all the wrong places.

It could have been so *right*, this dynamic twining around us fluid and natural, easier than any submissive I had met in the past.

But…

But she was one of my professors.

An employee.

An underling.

I… couldn't.

Right?

If it were up to my cock, I *certainly* could. Already it had stiffened to half-mast, thickening with interest the longer she looked at me with that overtly submissive expression—

"Alecto." I cleared my throat and leaned forward, adopting a tone I might use on a troublesome student—then instantly backtracking. Because it only made my cock harder to imagine her as a student in need of both guidance and discipline, and *that* was just so unacceptable I ought to be tarred and feathered this very second. "I'm happy to discuss this with you. I would obviously ask that you keep these conversations to yourself—" That had her nodding frantically like such a very, very good girl. "—but for the sake of our professional situation, I think we should leave it at that... *talking*."

"Oh. Yes, of course." She deflated right then and there, schooling her features as she stammered, "Definitely. I wasn't... I... You... I wasn't trying to, or, or insinuating—"

"No need to be embarrassed," I insisted, hating the thought of a rejection I didn't want to give making her clam up. "Although... I'm a little embarrassed myself. I don't usually discuss sadism over afternoon tea."

That and I officially couldn't stand up anymore—not if I wanted to maintain some level of decorum. Still, that didn't seem to make her feel better, her blushes shameful now, no longer pricked with an excited pink. Gods, this had taken a turn.

Pain.

I hadn't meant to inflict it, yet I'd done so without laying a hand on her.

"Why don't we circle back to this another day?" I offered. Let her breathe. Let her *think*. And let me get rid of this blasted erection. "Tell me about your lesson plans for the upcoming term while we finish our tea."

Clearing her throat, Alecto planted her hands on the chair arms and pushed up. "Oh, no, I won't take up your time with that. I can go—"

"*Sit.*" Out barked an order from a man who wasn't her

Dom but sure as hell *sounded* like him. She stilled, eyes snapping to mine, and then slowly sank into the chair. I nudged her tea toward the edge of my desk, a flicker of my brow encouraging her to take it. And she did. Held it close. Took a tiny sip, gaze trapped in mine, focused. Excellent. Best to end this in a safe place, to not let her mind spiral after dashing out of my office. Picking up my cup, I gave her a small approving nod. "Good. Now, tell me your lesson plans."

Like everything taught at Root Rot, I possessed vague knowledge of the herbalism and potions curriculum, but Alecto immediately delved into *such* exquisite detail that I'd never forget it if I tried.

And that only made things worse.

Because she responded to my request flawlessly, in depth and without skipping a beat.

But this was for the best. She relaxed in time, passion for her profession obvious—and the main reason I'd hired her without bothering to check with all fifteen of the references on her application. Alecto Clarke was *good*. A treasure for any academy.

A treasure I could tarnish if I wasn't careful.

So I listened deeply and spoke sparingly. I let her take charge, steer the conversation, get intense about specific flora that caught her interest.

All the while trying to get rid of the hard-on straining against my trousers. Usually shop talk was the furthest thing from arousing, but it didn't go away. Didn't lessen. Stayed proud and firm and stiff, the sound of her voice spurring it on.

Hell, the stubborn bastard remained long after she left, the appointment concluded on good, safe terms, and wouldn't disappear until I took care of it.

Once again disappointed in myself.

Unable to think of anything *but* Alecto until I chugged a dreamless sleep aid later that night.

Fully aware that even though we had set boundaries, she was going to be a problem.

A problem that, honestly, I didn't want to solve.

And only when I acknowledged that, just before the potion dragged me into the black, did I realize I was well and truly *fucked*.

3
ALECTO

Yesterday's conversation with Jack had been... *illuminating*, to say the least.

And I'd been thinking about it ever since he dismissed me, three cups of tea later and my lessons for the next four months nitpicked apart by a warlock who definitely knew what he was talking about.

It had taken a lot of balls to share that side of himself with me, someone who, for all he knew, could shout it to the world. Write a letter to the high council. File a report like he'd suggested. None of those thoughts ever crossed my mind, of course. He had been there for me without judgment, without criticism—except when it came to my lesson plans. For those, he had a few thoughts and tactful suggestions that sent me scurrying back to the drawing board today. Sure, I had a curriculum guidelines to adhere to and content that needed to be covered in the second term, but the way I delivered it was always up to me.

And my delivery could use some work, apparently. Jack constantly framed it as *to make things stronger, why not...*

I appreciated that.

He handled me with kid gloves, just a little, and usually I hated that approach from my boss.

But I liked it with him.

I found myself hanging on his every word, desperate for him to never stop talking, to lull me into a stupor with that ridiculously deep, rich voice of his.

Only I wished he had talked more about sadism.

About pain and distraction, relaxation and release.

I'd tried just about everything else in my twenty-nine years. Sex and alcohol and the odd hit of pot or pills. Memories stayed with me, fire and smoke and my shrill cries drowned out by splintering wood and crumbling walls. Articles written about the fire, about my parents and their scattered parts. Growing up without them, with grandparents who did the bare necessities to raise me but always treated me like an adult—as if trauma had aged me a few decades when, really, I had regressed.

No one saw that.

No one saw that I was still a little girl on the inside, frozen in fear, desperate for a hug and a cuddle and soothing words to make the nightmares go away.

They thought I had matured.

I was just angry. And scared. And alone.

There were so many shitty things out there to make me forget for a little while, but pain had never been one of them. I'd always thought I had enough pain in my world. Sex made me feel good, but its thrall became less and less effective as the years went on, as the connections between me and the guy—or guys—in my bed felt thinner and more superficial.

Maybe I needed to take things to the next level.

Change it up.

Really disconnect.

I'd been thinking about it since I tiptoed out of his office, pushing the conversation deep down and praying that no one could read our secret on my face. Last night, my hand had crept between my thighs while Bjorn slept soundlessly in the other room, Jack's voice whispering across my flesh, rumbling in my ear, and I came harder than I had in *ages*.

So *good*—just from the memory of him, of our private talk that would never leave his office.

Today, however, I needed to focus. Even in an almost empty castle, most students gone home for the break, a few professors vacationing around Europe while they had the chance, the job never stopped. My chat with Jack had opened my eyes to more than I cared to admit, so much so that I tried spanking myself with a hairbrush after my shower— just one smack, which didn't really do much, honestly. But our discussion had also shined glaring spotlights on a few holes in my plans for the term, and before I forgot all the points he raised, I had to fix them.

I... *needed* to fix them.

Because he had told me to.

And it felt good, another of our dirty secrets, to do as he instructed.

All that had led me to the staffroom. With colleagues scattered around the main table, working and chatting and drinking gallons of coffee, I had opted for the couch, forcing myself to sit near the low fire in the hearth, the flames tinted purple and only occasionally snapping—only *occasionally* launching my heart into my throat.

Pen in hand, I'd been at it for the better part of an hour, and as the clock chimed the three-o'clock toll, I moved on to midterm study outlines.

I hadn't bothered to give them last term, and most of my first and second years had flopped. While they performed marginally better on my end-of-term exams, I decided to throw them a bone this time around—as per Jack's suggestion—and guide them through the specifics to get a passing grade.

Massaging the knot at the back of my neck, I glanced toward the main table, to my colleagues and the chandeliers and the hazy sunlight streaming through the many arched windows. All of it reminded me of Bjorn, who had been out cold since yesterday, my entire potion consumed by the time I poked my head in to check on him at sunset. Fear that I had dosed the medicinal properties too high reared its ugly head between all the Jack thoughts today, but even distracted, I could nail that potion in my sleep.

And I *hadn't* been distracted brewing it for him—unless concern counted as a distraction, then maybe. He might have been a tough former Viking, a vampire warrior born in a more violent time, but that wasn't *him* now. Bjorn was sweet. Empathetic. Thoughtful. Hilarious and snarky and more than capable of calling me on my crap. Of all the people in this castle, I'd always suspected my roommate would be the one to sniff out my fraught connection with Benedict Hammond long before I ever considered sharing it.

The thought of losing him that night...

Gutted me.

Terrified me to the bone.

Since starting at Root Rot, I might have developed an inappropriate crush on Jack Clemonte and still occasionally lusted after Gavriel, the sex too good to forget, but I valued Bjorn above all the rest. He was my friend and then some, and I dreaded the trauma waiting for him to deal with when he finally woke up, rested and healed but still just a little bit broken.

Or, like me, a lot broken.

Because I was a fucking expert at trauma, unfortunately, and something like that—being crucified, threatened by the sun, weak and helpless and afraid—stuck with you.

Pen to parchment, I scribbled a few bullet points about the midterm outlines, head down and brow knitted—when a body suddenly plopped onto the couch next to mine, forceful enough to send me bouncing and make my pen jump. Usually Bjorn was the only one who literally hopped onto the couches with me, but there were a few other professors I clicked with who might try to up the friendship ante on our mini holiday.

Only the figure in the corner of my eye sat taller than any of the ladies I'd drunkenly belted Spice Girls tunes with back in July.

Dark and big, imposing, he smelled like sandalwood and cedar—

My blood ran cold.

Why the *fuck* was Benedict Hammond—aka Ash *Cedar*—sitting next to me?

Slowly, I glanced to my left, willing it to be anyone else.

But nope.

Patrician nose. Thin lips. Trimmed stubble. Salt-and-pepper sideburns and tousled faded brown waves that always looked finger-combed and artfully sideswept. Same old stupid traditional warlock robes, this time in a rich mahogany, his shoes a polished leather. Purple flames glinted off their sharp pointed tips, and I swallowed a wave of nausea, heart thundering at the sight—at the heat crawling up my spine, the fire closing in.

Exhaling sharply, I shuffled over as far as the couch would allow, but that only put *maybe* an extra half foot of space between us, his body directly in my personal bubble and triggering every internal alarm.

"I thought you were hiking in Switzerland," I said as lightly as I could manage. Even in hiding, Benedict must have had the backing of the Hammond coven fortune behind him. His clothes, his shoes, his snobby air all screamed money, and the fact that everyone knew he took lavish vacations any chance he got, usually with some twiggy aristocrat descended from French or Austrian witch royalty, was telling.

But he was here.

Beside me.

Breathing the same air, his arm outstretched along the back of the couch and his body angled toward mine.

"No, I... Things are a little messy on the home front." He adjusted his robes so they fell open just enough to reveal a crisp white dress shirt beneath. "Thought it best to stay and support the headmaster during this... trying time."

I nodded, unable to look at him this close after those *words* he had casually tossed my way, drunk and invasive and dangerous to the core.

Do you ever think this Samhain will be your last Samhain?

What the fuck had that even meant, anyway?

A threat?

Had he figured me out? Or was he just rambling—just feeling wistful on a sabbat that really meant something in our little sect of the supernatural world.

Parchment in my lap and scattered on the armrest like flags to stake my claim on the couch, I death-gripped my pen to my chest. If he exhaled that spearmint breath on me one more time, the tip was going right in his eye. "Ah. That's nice of you, I guess."

Cue a strained silence that threatened to go on until the end of fucking time—

"Alecto, I'd like to apologize for Samhain."

Ignoring the stab of panic at the sound of him saying my name, murmuring it like he had the right to make it sound so intimate, I frowned and slowly lowered my pen-shank. "What?"

"I only have a hazy recollection of our talk," Benedict

31

insisted, sweeping a hand through his hair with a huff, like he was just *so* disappointed in himself, "but I know it upset you —whatever I did say, anyway. And please know that was not my intention." He shuffled closer, steering me under his arm, and my hand leapt to my throat when I felt the airways constricting. "I'm so sorry. After the night you had with Asulf, the last thing you needed was me—"

"You don't have to apologize." *I never* need *you, you murderous fucker.*

"But I do." With an elegant snap of his fingers and a murmured summoning spell, a coffee materialized in his free hand, and he offered the steaming mug with a smile so sugary sweet that it could make your teeth rot from the proximity alone. "Consider this an olive branch."

Uh. What.

"One cream, one sugar, and a splash of vanilla."

Oh *gods*, he knew my coffee order.

"Just the way you like it."

"Oh. Uhm..." I swallowed hard, bile sizzling up my esophagus, and then accepted his stupid peace offering with a shaky hand. "Thanks."

Liquid fire spilled over the rim and dribbled down the sides, and as Benedict chuckled and swiped at the droplets with his knuckles, I resisted the urge to chuck the whole thing in his face and be done with it. Instead, juggling my pen, the mug, and all the papers piled high around me, I awkwardly maneuvered things so I could set the coffee I had zero intention of drinking down on the flat armrest.

Classic inconsiderate nice guy schtick—look like you're doing a kind thing, all the while making it inconvenient and terrible for the woman in question.

"We were all out of sorts that night," I told him, unable to take his expectant silence a second longer—like he was waiting for me to trip over myself thanking him for the coffee and the apology and the handsome smiles he kept casually tossing out there.

"Yes, but I don't want *us* to stay out of sorts."

Alarm bells shrieking an octave higher and louder than usual, my head snapped his way, pen falling and rolling into the cushion dip between us. What... the *fuck* was that supposed to mean?

"You're a very brave witch, Alecto," Benedict mused, easing closer and staring into my eyes as if he hadn't already memorized every fleck of color. Honestly, this guy and my eyes. Seldom blinking. Always *staring*. How didn't the world know this freak was a psychopath slasher killer? He went for one of my curls, perhaps to stroke it or tuck it behind my ear, but I shifted just out of reach with a sniff, pretending not to notice.

"Uh, thanks—"

"Doing what you did that night for him, for some... *vampire*," he sneered, his disgusting husky rumble bulldozing clear through my objections. "It was very admirable for someone so young, and I... I'd like to get to know you a little better."

"Oh." *Do not stab him in the eye. Do not throw the coffee in his face. Be cool. It's not the time. Not the place. Not the day for him to suffer.* "Okay."

His charcoal-black gaze swept up and down my figure almost... suggestively. "Lovely."

Oh.

Oh *gods*.

Was he... hitting on me?

Just the thought made my skin crawl.

"Going over lesson plans, are we?" Benedict went for the top parchment on my lap, and at this point I was practically crawling up and over the back of the couch to get away from him. Read the fucking room, asshole.

"When are we not?" I managed with a forced laugh, which triggered some big guffawing outburst from the warlock. Right in my face. Big ol' belly howls.

Fuck me.

It wasn't that funny.

"Exactly," he said through the chuckles, wiggling his eyebrows like this was the first of many private jokes between us. "Let me get my things… I'll join you."

I'd rather die.

As soon as he was off the couch, his back to me, I grabbed the coffee and tossed it in the fire. When he drifted to the main table and quickly became entangled in conversation, laughing with a few of the grey-haired warlocks—though nowhere near as obnoxiously as he'd just done with me—I gathered up my things and waited for the opportune moment to get out.

The second he leaned over, deeply engrossed in his monologue all of a sudden, his full attention elsewhere, I bolted, not looking back until I was out of sight, out of touch…

And *way* out of the castle.

4

ALECTO

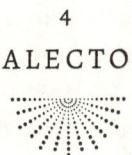

I kept walking until I reached the coast.

Walking, not running. Benedict would have had no idea where I'd gone, but I refused to run from him. Power walk? Sure. After ditching my stuff in the flat, Bjorn still conked out like a sleeping stone statue, I bailed on the castle. Zipped through the back gate, eyeing the walls that suddenly had barbed wire coils along the top. Followed familiar paths at a steady clip and just kept going, going, going.

Surprisingly, walking actually helped more than running. Even though I had become a seasoned runner over the last ten years, I was still out of shape, Root Rot's demanding routine always edging out my runs in the first term. My body still wasn't conditioned enough for it, and while I could have tried, pushed and then hated myself for failing, I held back.

By the time I stumbled down a rocky coastline and into the sand, a dark Atlantic lapping at the shore, I still hurt. The highlands were both beautiful and unforgiving, full of scraggly shrubs and thick grasses and hills on hills on hills. No telling how long I'd been walking in all that, but the even drumbeat of my feet on solid ground had, for the first time, kept me out of my head. No longer midafternoon, the barely there sun had wandered across a hazy sky, and when I eventually plopped down in the damp sand, exhausted and sweaty and cold and sore, sunset wasn't far off.

Now, a good hour later, darkness slowly descending here at the end of the world, I was mostly just cold. The shimmering gold orb at my side offered light, not heat. It hummed with my magic, ancient and earthbound and comforting, but if it could mysteriously turn into a furnace, that would be *awesome*.

I knew the spell to produce a floating fire—quite useful when there was no kindling around.

Still too chickenshit to use it, unfortunately.

At least this little guy would eventually light the way home; it would be a pitch-black march through a landscape hungry to snap my ankle at every turn, so that should be fun.

Sighing, I toed at the sand, legs folded into my chest, arms wrapped around them, and then set my chin in the dip between my knees. The distance from the castle, from *him*, should have given me room to think, but I'd been thinking for months now. Sifting through the same thoughts, the same scenarios, over and over again. Nothing new. Just the same plans and considerations, the same pros and cons lists. At this point, the thoughts raced by at warp speed, my mind primed to whip through what it had already dissected a thousand times before.

I just needed to decide what to do with Benedict and commit. Pick a plan and execute.

But I couldn't.

And that pissed me off.

Left me frustrated and tired and anxious—exhausted. Today, disgust joined the ranks, still totally grossed out that Benedict Hammond knew my coffee order, right down to the vanilla I splashed in at the end.

I turned my head to the side, cheek on my knees, and closed my eyes with a shudder. He had tried to *touch* me. Stroke a curl, maybe eventually tuck it behind my ear.

Or... I dunno, grab it?

Ugh. My gut roiled at the thought, and I swallowed down the flood of bile, his peppermint breath carrying on the next gentle gust that swept across the empty beach.

He wanted to *know* me.

Groaning, I sat up and stretched my legs out, jeans rigid from the November chill, my massive black wool coat peppered with sand and dry grass bits and the odd thorn that had hung on for the ride. Scrubbing at my cheeks, then massaging up to my forehead, my skull, all my curls wild and free as black water crashed along the shoreline, I stared out to a shadowy horizon, water and sky eventually merging into darkness.

What the fuck do I do about Benedict Hammond?

Seduce and destroy? He wanted to know me anyway, so maybe—

I'd vomit. The first time I had to kiss him, embrace him, stroke my hand up his thigh, I'd hurl. That was out. As much as I wanted to be that girl, to pretend I could throw on any mask and get the job done, I just wasn't.

Not yet, anyway.

Maybe time would force my hand.

Maybe—

A voice suddenly rose above the waves.

A high, clear soprano, sweet as a tinkling bell and gentle as a spring mist.

Frowning, I twisted around to scan the slope at the cusp of the beach. The same rocks and brambles and darkening sky stared back—but no source of that *voice*. So hauntingly beautiful, its melody blanketed me, sank into my skin and settled in my bones.

Siren song.

My heart skipped a beat, and I whipped around when I realized I'd been looking the wrong way. A song so lovely, so pure and enchanting, all the way up here—in a land where fae portals dotted the coast, selkie lived in abundance, and siren clans called home… I needed to look to the sea.

And there she was, perched on a rock like this was a fairy tale, gorgeous from tip to tail. Shamrock-green hair trailed down her back, slick from the water, her skin a creamy ivory and stamped with shells. Bare breasts, full and weighted. A taut torso met her scaly tail, green and blue, shimmering in the sunset, beautiful.

Dangerous, too.

Sirens sang to lure their prey, to coax unwitting humans into their arms so they could drag them down and consume every last morsel.

Fortunately, their song had no sway on supers or shifters. It was just a pretty melody, wordless and lovely. As breathtaking as she was perched on that black rock, all sharp edges and cruel angles hoisting her above the water, she must have been young—inexperienced. Why else would she continue to sing at me? I tipped my head to the side and smiled, willing her to realize I wouldn't come, that I only appreciated her song.

That it didn't call to my heart.

Move on to easier prey, girl.

Not that I encouraged the active hunting of humans, but not every supernatural society felt the same, nor did they obey our laws. Sirens were wilder than shifters in that regard, throwing caution to the wind, separate from the rest of us in their underwater societies.

She wanted to eat me. Feast on the flesh of this lone land-dweller seated halfway up the beach. She risked a lot choosing a rock so close to shore—exposure, capture.

Maybe she was starving.

Hardly a thriving human population up here—

A splash interrupted both my train of thought and her song. It erupted at the base of the siren's rock, water jutting up and sprinkling her tail. We both frowned at each other— and then a rock pelted her in the face.

Hard.

A rock from the shoreline, *bam*, right in the forehead, splitting her flawless skin and unleashing a spray of dark green blood. Instantly, the siren went from breathtaking to monstrous, her mouth elongating in a shriek, spear-like teeth exposed, her eyes flashing to pure black. Little angry fins popped out of her neck, flailing rigidly, and she leapt into the water with a snarl, gone in a flash.

Who the hell had...? I guided the floating orb aside with my wand, scowling down the beach, and then exhaled a long, irritated huff when I spotted the culprit.

Of *course.*

Gavriel stood about a foot out of the ocean's reach, the water charging up the sand and retreating *just* before it grazed his feet. Garbed in black from head to toe, he reminded me of Jack for a moment with a formfitting dress shirt, in pants with an ironed line cutting down the front, then a pair of leather oxfords hardly made for the beach.

His hair as wild as mine, thick and luscious, the silver highlights in all the rich dark brown catching the fading light like whitecaps on the water. Smirking, he turned away from the rocky perch, but as soon as that grey gaze settled on me, his mirth flatlined to nothing, his pinched brow mirroring mine.

Neither of us were thrilled to see the other, apparently.

While I hadn't seen him since Samhain, I'd heard he was still somewhere around the castle, not the type to take vacations. Until now, I hadn't wondered if he was avoiding me, but the longer he stood there, both of us locked in the glaring match that could last until the end of time, I half expected him to wheel around and storm up the beach without saying a word.

Instead, he scrunched his dress shirtsleeves up to his elbows, then shoved his hands in his pockets and meandered my way.

Took his sweet-ass time, too, plodding along through the sand, until eventually he plopped down next to me, never once asking if I wanted company.

I didn't.

But I didn't have it in me to tell him to fuck off, either.

As snippy as we'd been that night, Gavriel and I were a *team* on Samhain. We saved Bjorn together, and that kind of, sort of, *maybe* made me dislike him a little less after the theft incident in the greenhouse.

Still hot as sin, of course, which didn't help matters, my body tingling with interest, perking up at the closeness and shaking off the cold. But hot didn't override douchebag—not anymore, at least.

And definitely not when I was sober.

At the next whoosh of the bitter breeze, I drew my knees to my chest again, teeth on the verge of chattering. Out of the corner of my eye, Gavriel nudged at the floating light orb.

"Right. Why the fuck isn't this thing on fire?" he demanded, voice all rough and scratchy, oddly thick when it usually dripped like velvet. "Freezing my tits off out here..."

"Okay. Dramatic." I held up a hand to silence him when his head snapped my way, mouth open and ready to argue. "It's not that cold."

Rolling his eyes, Gavriel snatched the orb with both hands, and when he released it, it burst into purple fae fire. Heart in my throat, I scrambled away from the flames, only to have Gavriel scoff and shake his head.

"Relax. She doesn't bite."

Asshole. Scowling, I inched closer, drawn to the warmth and the fact that this fire looked nothing like the stuff that haunted my nightmares.

"What are you even doing out here?" Both of us bathed in magenta, I stretched my legs out again, then crossed them, rearranging the baggy wool jacket so that it covered as much of me as it could. Gavriel, meanwhile, drew his legs up, arms wrapped around his bent knees, that lean jaw set in a scowl.

"There's a portal to the Otherworld in a cave up the way," he muttered, tipping his cheek toward the floating fire like a cat rolling into a sunbeam. After a beat of awkward silence, his narrowed gaze slid to me. "What are *you* doing here?"

Facing the choppy waters ahead, I shrugged. "Thinking."

"Thought I smelled smoke—"

Too far away to smack, I flicked a bit of sand at him, which the fae repelled with a thigh block and a lukewarm chuckle. In the quiet that followed, I let the annoyance of his sudden appearance on *my* beach of solitude fade away. The longer he watched the water, the tide sweeping up and down, back and forth, the hardness seemed to ease out of him, too. Still all angular and lean and subtle fae sexuality, Gavriel softened just a little on the other side of the purple flames.

"Were you going home for the holiday?" I asked, and just like that, he closed up—turned into a diamond right before my eyes. "Or… coming back?"

Jaw clenched again, he fidgeted with his sleeves, dragging them down his muscly forearms before ripping them back up. "No."

"Oh."

When the hovering flames drifted too close to me, carrying on the wind, I steered them out in front of us, all the while hoping he missed the way my wand trembled, palms slick with nervous sweat.

"I... like to visit the portal sometimes," Gavriel admitted, totally oblivious to my discomfort as he glanced down the beach toward the rockier sections, hills rising in the distance. "Just to feel home... To feel true fae magic again."

I blinked back at him. That... was unexpected. He caught me staring almost immediately, no doubt taking my shocked expression for something it wasn't. Something crueler. His silvery eyes thinned to defensive slits.

"What?"

"That's just... kind of nice," I told him, still thrown by his reasoning—by the notion that beneath the snark and sass and general assholery, Gavriel *might* just be a man with actual feelings. "And sad."

A fae who missed home.

Who felt out of place here.

Lonely. Maybe even a little lost.

Something I should have recognized sooner, because, *hello*, kindred spirits.

Gavriel studied me briefly, then flipped me off, turning his glare on the water.

"No, I didn't mean..." I floundered a little, searching for the right words and sighing as I smoothed my curls away from my face. "I'm seriously not being a dick about it. You just... You're not a very genuine person most of the time."

I mean, was his shit attitude supposed to be a secret?

He chuckled coolly. "What an incredibly rude thing to say."

"Well—" I shrugged when he faced me, still battling with my hair, the wind deciding this was the moment to really screw with me. "—that's your vibe and you know it."

The fae's brows shot up, lips twisting into a snide grin. "You want to know *your* vibe?"

"Nope," I said curtly. Wrangling as many curls as I could

into one hand, I tugged up my jacket collar and tried to stuff them under. "Not even a little."

I braced for a venomous comeback.

Nothing.

Huh. Strange.

Out of the corner of my eye, I caught him staring at the water again, all quiet and pensive, distant and hard. Even the magenta glow highlighting the attractive lines of his face did nothing to soften him, all traces of that oozing fae sexuality I had come to expect from Gavriel gone.

Maybe his visits to the portal between my world and his weren't for pleasure. Maybe that had been a lie, one of many he told on a daily basis, to hide the real reason.

Because the truth made him vulnerable.

Maybe he and I—

"So, we're alone out here."

Gods. I bit back a smirk, fully aware of where this was headed. "Yup."

"Want to fuck?" And there it was. He wiggled his eyebrows when I glared in his direction, the corners of his mouth kicked up to reveal just a hint of the fae I thought I had all figured out before today. "Warm you right to the core, fury."

"No."

I mean, I could have gone for a tumble in the sand, no one around for miles to catch us. It probably would have been all brooding and angsty, rough, a battle to the very end—until he trapped my wrists above my head, pinned them to the sand, and pounded me into oblivion.

Unfortunately, my conversation with Jack hadn't just triggered the depraved warm and fuzzies that had always been there—it got me thinking about my coping mechanisms. Over the years, I had absolutely used liquor and sex to distract myself, to forget the horrors of my past, the murky possibilities of the future, the end of a legacy—the Corwin name eventually dying with me, a witch who desperately craved to be the center of someone's whole world but was too stubborn to let anyone below the surface.

I liked sex. Even if I wasn't using it to forget, I *liked* all of it. The physical sensations. The wild abandonment, losing yourself to the moment—in another person. Nothing beat a good climax, but all things considered, screwing around with Gavriel, a fae who could and *had* made me feel shit about myself when it was all over, probably wasn't the healthiest thing to do.

Plus, you know, the theft and him thinking he was smarter than me—blah, blah, blah, it wasn't always about *him*. I had to consider myself, too, *my* self-worth, my self-esteem, my feelings when all was said and done.

"Smoke?"

I flinched when his voice cut through the racing thoughts, that lofty fae accent quieting the storm, all rich and seductive as he offered what looked like a hand-rolled cigarette. I scowled down at it for a moment, then turned my fury on him.

"Are those *my* herbs?"

"Partially," he admitted, arm still outstretched between us. "No telling what's in the blend at this point, but this one's really chill. Mostly lemon—like a palate cleanser between courses."

For a man who clearly enjoyed smoking, his pipe a permanent fixture after meals, he sounded pretty bitter as he explained the nuances.

What the hell had happened at that portal?

Was this pretty playboy more layered than I gave him credit for?

A part of me wanted to pry, to push and wheedle because he seemed vulnerable enough to share something that he normally wouldn't.

But that was a shitty thing to do.

I'd never forgive someone if they did that to me.

"Sure," I said, hesitant, reaching for it and then withdrawing. After a few seconds of staring, I collapsed in on myself, wilting under Gavriel's slightly impatient gaze. "Can you... Can you light it for me?"

Gods, why did he still look so fucking attractive even with a judgmental frown? Once again I steeled myself for whatever he had to say to that, no doubt something cruel and teasing, something mean after what I'd said about him not being genuine.

And once again he surprised me.

With a sniff, Gavriel folded forward and held the end of the cigarette in the floating purple flames, giving it a moment before retreating and blowing on the end. He then handed it over without a word, and I took it, no stranger to smoking the odd joint, albeit a few years out of practice.

As advertised, lemon stood out the strongest after the first inhale. Lemony, citrusy, a strong palate cleanser, smooth like sorbet.

"Fly you back to the castle if you give me a blowjob."

Exhaling a generous gust of smoke, nowhere near as talented as this fae at making shapes and patterns, I turned on him with an unimpressed scowl.

Which made him laugh.

Actually laugh, the skin around his eyes crinkling, mouth open, expression briefly—gorgeously—carefree. I giggled, unable to take another pull until we both settled.

The heavy quiet returned faster than I would have liked, all the bullshit from before resurfacing, racing around my skull and demanding answers. But there was something comforting about experiencing it alongside another person, someone else who seemed trapped inside their own head, same as me. So, we smoked and watched the water together, the clouds eventually clearing just enough to catch the sun vanish below the horizon.

And when the fae fire couldn't warm us anymore, our teeth chattering but both of us too stubborn to cuddle, Gavriel flew me back to Root Rot Academy, dropped me off at the back gate, and—

"I'll take a rain check on that blowjob, fury."

Even as I flipped him off and tried to slam the gate in his face while he shouldered through halfheartedly from the other side, our laughter echoed through the empty grounds.

Stayed with me for the rest of the night, even, an unexpected shield against everything else.

And for the first time in days, I slept through until dawn, not a nightmare to be found.

5

BJORN

With the last of the third years flitting out my classroom door, the first week of the second term came to a close. I watched as the wood panel slowly swung halfway shut behind them, then pivoted around and went for the chalkboard. Eraser in hand, I cleared the notes from this evening's lecture, tensed, senses on high alert for any errant footsteps creeping into the room—any sudden whiffs of cologne that ought not be there.

Pathetic, really, to be checking over my shoulder.

To carry Leroy and Malorie and all those little fuckers with me after that night. As soon as Alecto had tucked me into bed, Gavriel hovering awkwardly over her shoulder, it should have been over. Done. Dusted. On to the next disaster.

I preached self-care in this very room. Patience and love and understanding. Awareness of one's flaws—*acceptance* of them.

Only I couldn't apply any of that to myself.

Perhaps *that* was the pathetic thing here. Not the fear, not the paranoia, but my unwillingness to accept that I might need time to heal.

Chalkboard clean, milky-white dust floating around me, fusing up my nostrils and down my dry throat, I moved on to the desks, gathering the reflection essays I had given my kids the last hour to work on. They could be as short or as long as they desired, but they needed to reflect on the past term— whether they were here at Root Rot or some other academy —and then set some goals for the upcoming four months. Reasonable goals. Something they could confidently conquer.

The first sheet of parchment was two sentences. Right. And then—oh, six pages. Biting back a grin, I quickly grabbed the rest for some four-o'clock reading long after Alecto had gone to sleep.

Sleep—the gift my flatmate had given me, along with her kindness, her attentiveness, and her *slight* hovering during my recovery. Whatever she had done to that draught worked like a charm: I had slept for three days and nights, and when I finally came to—slowly, peacefully, not jolting awake from a night terror—I felt refreshed.

Most of all, I felt like myself again.

Or, at least 80 percent of the way there.

The rest would come with time. Term had gotten off to a shaky start, the swarm of uniforms and the influx of body odor, laughter, and activity more of an assault than usual. Fortunately, none of the students knew about Samhain. Unlike my colleagues, there were no stares or whispers, no pitying glances or awkward attempts to express shallow condolences. The kids were just… kids. Moody and withdrawn and angry. Snooty and disruptive and lost. I found myself amongst them, and as the first week wrapped, Friday-night curfew fifteen minutes out, my confidence was *just* about back.

Maybe.

No telling what tomorrow might bring.

After stacking the essays, I tidied around the room: tucked in chairs, straightened the rows of desks, locked all my things in drawers. I fell into familiar busywork until the nine-o'clock bells tolled through the castle, curfew in effect —and Alecto and my movie night officially underway.

While she had been babying me since Samhain, I hadn't the heart to stop her. Outsiders fretted when people they cared about struggled; they just wanted to *do* something, anything, to make it better. And after all she had done for me, I owed Alecto that much. Let her fuss and coddle. Let her wear the odd low-cut top because men and their simple brains liked cleavage. She was *trying*.

No one had ever tried for me before.

I hailed from a culture of warriors. The men in my raiding party might have been brothers on the battlefield, partners in the shieldwall, but they would never provide a shoulder to cry on, never lend an ear just to *talk*. Alecto had offered both in the last two weeks with no strings attached, and while I'd refused them, not about to cry in front of the witch who, despite our friendship, still made my dead heart dance, I appreciated the sentiment.

Classroom organized, I grabbed the pile of essays and headed for the door.

Only to stop just shy of it, anxiety tickling my insides, a reminder that I had once been *human*—and that I couldn't escape feeling like one every now and again. Along with all the other shit that had hounded me since the incident, I'd been checking doors almost obsessively. Scrutinizing their handles and knobs, poking at them and retreating, waiting for the spikes to flare.

No credence behind the behavior. No reason for it.

I did the same tonight, hesitating before prodding at the copper ball, rearing back a second later and waiting.

Nothing.

Teeth gritted, fangs cutting into my lower lip, I shouldered into the hall with a scowl. Ridiculous. Totally nonsensical—but that was the way with fear.

With trauma.

Fucking *fuck*—

Footsteps whispered in the shadowy stone corridor. I stilled, not exactly afraid but on higher alert than I would have been before Samhain. Had it been a roving security guard, the footfalls would have continued in one direction or the other, tromping along like always, their boots heavy and authoritative. Purposeful.

Gone now, the echoes fading off.

Followed by a *whump*, then a muffled cry.

Clutching the reflection essays tight, I blitzed down the hall, silent and clinging to the shadows. A racing heartbeat to my immediate left stopped me in front of an alcove near the northwest tower stairwell, a small circular space students occasionally loitered in. I'd even caught a few snogging at the foot of Clíodhna's statue along the exterior wall.

No surprise there: queen of the banshees *and* love, that goddess. Smitten teens flocked to her, this remnant of the old world trapped underground.

Tonight, however, a heartbeat drummed behind her towering figure. Beautiful, even in stone, the immortalized goddess loomed tall with her hands outstretched, reminiscent of the Virgin Mary—except for the lack of clothing, one breast exposed, the rest barely covered by a slip of fabric, while a trio of stone songbirds perched daintily on her shoulders. Face serene, nothing like the horrible screams of her banshee children, she stood on guard in the bowels of the castle, watching over all the tiny witches and warlocks who might still worship her, her hair wild and curly.

Savage, all the old Celtic deities. Utterly wild.

So like my own gods, the immortals I'd once spilled legions of blood to impress.

Just the one heartbeat behind her, breath hitching and falling—hard and heavy nostril gasps, if I heard it right.

"Come out," I urged, internal alarm bells falling silent. While I wasn't afraid to walk these corridors, lately anger nipped at my heels—anger that I'd been captured and strung up and staked. All my life, I had been the aggressor. I'd done the damage. I set the tone. Rarely had I felt helpless. So much of the last few decades was new to me: controlling the bloody beast within, chiding rogue vampires, being completely ignored and dismissed by other supernatural entities.

While it helped me understand and connect with the students here at Root Rot, the learning curve was steep after centuries of letting the monster run free.

"You're past curfew." While the heartbeat behind the statue had quickened to unsafe levels, she refused to show her face. From the very faint, almost sickeningly sweet rose perfume, I assumed it was a *she*, anyway. "I'm not going anywhere, so you might as well just come out." Nothing. "I also don't *really* need to sleep, so I can play this game all night."

Some thirty seconds later, a sniffling shadow emerged from behind the goddess's outstretched arm, and I softened as soon as the light hit her face.

Alice Jameson.

The witch who couldn't cast.

She crept shyly around Clíodhna, head down, arms crossed, bringing with her a rush of that saccharine sweet perfume and... salt water. Frowning, I looked her up and down. Not a speck of water anywhere, but the scent was unmistakable.

Maybe a body scrub, the salty brine tickling my nose, just as her defeated posture and her cowering stance plucked at my heartstrings. Poor thing: shipped off to Root Rot because she was the family shame, the one witch in her coven who couldn't summon an ounce of magic. Even here, on the isle of misfit toys, she struggled to find her place.

"Alice…" I beckoned her to me with a gentle smile. "What were you doing back there?"

"I… I heard you coming," she admitted, her dark bronze-brown curls manic tonight, looking as though she had tried to comb them straight and now they were giving her hell for it. "I thought… I didn't want to get in trouble."

The rose and salt water crashed together the nearer she came, melding into something rather unpleasant for my keen sense of smell. Fortunately, I towered over her by a few feet, and the air was always a bit clearer up here.

The height difference also showed the spots along her hairline where she hadn't properly spread her foundation, the makeup about two tones too dark against her naturally fair complexion. At this age, all the girls were experimenting with new looks, but from the bumps on her forehead and chin, someone had been trying to hide a surge of acne.

Makeup. Perfume. Brushed hair and her uniform skirt hitched a smidgen higher than acceptable… Was this little sparrow out here to meet someone?

"Come along." Whatever the reason, it was none of my business. Alice lacked a social circle now that the Samhain committee had disbanded, and according to Alecto, she excelled in the theoretical work of every class—just less so in the practical unless she was out in the gardens. All that considered, Alice Jameson was a good girl. A shitty witch, sure, but a child who did *not* belong at Root Rot Academy. "I'll escort you to your tower."

Shoulders slumped, she padded after me as I headed for the nearby stairwell. "I'm sorry, Professor. I really didn't mean to... I lost track of time—"

"It's all right." I paused and waited for her to catch up, reflection essays rolled in one hand, the other in my pocket. "We all make mistakes."

Especially in our youth.

Fuck—what if some devil had tricked her into waiting for him out here?

I bit the inside of my cheek, fighting a scowl. Honestly, I wouldn't put it past any of them.

In fact, it wouldn't have surprised me if there was a whole *group* waiting in the shadows somewhere to jump out and guffaw in her face.

Never mind.

I'd found her first, this little outcast, and I would see that no one made her feel worthless tonight.

"But let's not make a habit of it, shall we?" I mused as she fell in line beside me, her smile shy but her enthusiastic nod promising this wouldn't happen again. And unlike so many of the others in here, the ones who assured me they would try harder, do better, be kinder, I actually believed her. Alecto had an obvious soft spot for the girl, and perhaps I did, too. For weeks I had watched her flourish on the Samhain committee, but now here she was again—alone. No friends except the herbalism professor.

Difficult as it was *not* to intervene, it was best to let them figure it out on their own. Struggling through the dark and coming out the other side stronger built character.

Note to self, you ancient fuck.

"Right, let's go." I motioned toward the nearby door at the base of the northwest tower. While Alecto and I had agreed to meet outside my classroom to walk back to the flat together—just another sign of her babying me, escorting me through the very corridor I had been attacked in—she was a big girl. A grown witch. As soon as she realized I wasn't there, she could draw her own conclusions and meet me upstairs after I dropped Alice off at her dorm.

No way was I letting this girl who smelled like the sea go wandering by herself.

And I wouldn't have to.

Just before we reached the door, me going for it, about to prop it open and usher Alice and her slightly hitched skirt through, her full name hissed through the corridor.

We both rounded in place, Alice's eyes wide as saucers at the approach of Nadia, a bear shifter den mother with cropped strawberry blonde hair and murder in her eyes.

"Where have you *been?*" the shifter demanded, almost as tall as me and twice as imposing. Swathed in black from head to toe in standard den mother attire, her gaze bled from green to dark brown as she stalked toward Alice, her inner bear surging to the surface now that she had found her lost cub. "I've been looking everywhere for you!"

"I—"

"It's my fault," I interjected smoothly, placing a hand to my chest as the den mother slowed, nostrils flared like she was giving me a nasal once-over. Or, more likely, she too scented the salt water and was searching for its source. "Alice stopped by to help me tidy the classroom, and I'm afraid we lost track of time. I was just taking her back to the tower."

Heartbeat frantic, Alice nodded at my side so hard that it was a wonder she didn't snap her own neck. I frowned down at her.

Little mouse, what were *you doing down here?*

Nadia shot me an annoyed look, disbelief rippling across her features, then snapped at the stairwell door.

54

"Well, perhaps you could pay more attention to the clock next time, Professor," she growled, marching forth and snagging Alice by the shoulder. "Good night."

I scrambled out of the way so she didn't barrel clear through me. Honestly, bear shifters were the ideal den mothers; mess with their kids and they *will* tear you limb from limb, magic or no magic.

"Of course," I said with a nod, delicately grasping the stack of coiled essays in front of me as the pair rushed by. "Have a pleasant evening—both of you."

Alice peeked around her den mother, mouth open to say something, but the shifter's growl had those thin lips snapping back together, and in a blink, they were gone, footsteps echoing off the stone steps. Slowly, the wooden door eased shut, cutting off their departure and blanketing the corridor in a familiar bedtime quiet.

But the smell of the sea remained. Salty air and marine brine—

Jaw clenched, I peered around the corner into the little alcove again. Clíodhna remained, silent and lovely, arms outstretched like she was beckoning a lover into her embrace. That scent—unmistakable. I'd spent decades on the water as a human, sailing, raiding, swimming, transporting stolen goods to seedy markets...

The oceans of this world were in my blood. They lingered, even with this vampiric disease, and should I ever actually die one day, I hoped my loved ones would toss my ashes to the waves.

Perhaps I ought to write that in a will, just to be safe.

I'd never considered writing a will until now—until a band of children reminded me that even immortals weren't untouchable.

This goddess smelled like the sea. Loosely grasping the reflection essays, I blitzed to Clíodhna's side. Nothing behind her. Nothing around her. While a faint magical aura pulsed in the alcove, that was expected in a place like this. Frowning, I leaned in close—and flinched at the crash of water. From the statue's heart, I swore I heard waves, sloshing and splashing. Eyes closed, I almost *felt* the salty spray—

"Bjorn?"

But there was nothing here. Just stone walls and hollow limestone eyes, Clíodhna's mouth carved in a seductive arc.

"*Bjorn?*" Alecto's voice pitched higher this time, her concern ricocheting through the underground corridors. I eased back from Clíodhna, giving her one last up-and-down sweep even as my mind wandered elsewhere, drawn like a moth to the flame at the lure of Alecto Clarke.

Strange, though, that smell. It started to fade as I padded away, but this was a Root Rot first.

A Root Rot mystery, at that.

But one to ponder another time.

From here on out, there would be no need to ponder or speculate.

With her, all I needed to do was *feel*.

And I for one very much welcomed that—a chance to switch off.

"I'm here, Alecto."

To smell vanilla instead of salt.

A welcome change indeed.

6

ALECTO

When the nine-o'clock bell chimed, the castle fell under a curfewed hush that lasted until sunrise. I'd always found it a little oppressive and creepy, almost punishing in the way the quiet bore down on you—a firm reminder for students to get back to bed where they belonged. From nine o'clock on, silence reigned supreme everywhere.

Everywhere but the kitchen.

Because the kitchens at Root Rot Academy were a kingdom unto themselves.

At the back of the dining hall, just beyond the staff table, stood a pair of swinging salon doors that opened to yet another dark stairwell. As soon as you shouldered through, you were smacked in the face with a cacophony of competing scents: freshly baked breads, slow-roast chickens, desserts that gave you a sugar high just by smelling them. Students weren't permitted down here without an escort, but staff like myself made use of the fact that the kitchen was a twenty-four-hour operation. If they weren't serving a meal, they were preparing for the next one—and the next one, and the next one, the bakery crew working the crack ass of dawn shift and the Italian head chef in the evening a total douche-canoe.

I rarely went deeper than the main entrance, loitering at a marble counter like everyone else who wasn't a citizen of this food republic after giving my order. Sometimes I placed it in the mornings for pickup in the evening; tonight, after a rare night class and then a long ninety minutes spent pruning in the conservatory, I'd stumbled in fifteen minutes ago and relayed my evening snack order to a flustered sous chef.

Drumming my fingers on the countertop, I cringed at the crash of glassware somewhere deep inside the bright space, obnoxious white counters and shiny stainless steel as far as the eye could see. Of course, I appreciated the fact that even though it *was* so white, the place looked spotless, but coming down here after navigating the castle's dark corridors was always such an assault.

"Professor Clarke?"

I perked up as one of the lesser chefs—evidenced by the spattered apron, the messy hair behind the net, and the huge bags under his eyes—marched out of the chaos with my order.

"Yes, hi," I babbled, straightening and reaching over the counter to relieve him. "Thank you."

"One thin-crust pepperoni pizza," he said flatly, his white cotton tee visibly stained around the pits. Yikes. Not quite as sparkly clean as all the stainless steel and marble implied, apparently. The nameless cook shoved the pizza box into my hands, almost with a *Didn't you eat at dinner?* glower in his eye. Just because we all made regular trips down here for after-hours nibbles didn't mean any of them liked having us in their space. "The ranch dip is inside."

My mouth watered at the first whiff of three different

kinds of melted cheese that wafted out during the handover. "Ugh, *yes.*"

"And… *this.*" Nose crinkled, the cook practically threw the thermos of blood at me, as if he couldn't stand to touch it a second longer. Balancing the pizza box on my forearm, I steadied the metal cylinder on top, all my previous friendliness gone. Same shit, different day with this crew. They prepped blood regularly for the castle's vampire inhabitants; it seriously shouldn't be such a big deal to heat a few cups and put it in a thermos. If it was *that* offensive, they could always pretend it was tomato soup. You know, just be an adult and get the fuck over it.

Warlock asshole.

His aura hinted at him being another magic-user, but the wand poking out of his apron's pocket was the dead giveaway. Hands planted on his hips, the cook lifted his eyebrows at me, wordlessly asking if I was done while also silently insisting I fuck off already. With a sniff, I gave him a nod of thanks, no longer in the mood to gush over my pizza no matter how delicious it smelled, then turned on my heel and stalked out.

Pizza box jabbing into my side like I was a seventeenth-century washerwoman lugging a basket of laundry around, I let my feet guide me up a floor to Bjorn's underground classroom, the Root Rot castle familiar enough by now that I could navigate it no matter how distracted.

And I was distracted—distracted cussing out that fucking cook in my head, belatedly coming up with all the clever and sassy things I could have sneered at him and his anti-vampirism attitude.

Only to stop, brain short-circuiting, at Bjorn's closed classroom door. Swallowing thickly, I glanced at the knob. So gross that those kids had hexed the copper to grow wooden spikes. Sometimes I questioned why Bjorn hadn't noticed them—but then remembered we all walked these halls on autopilot, a million other problems to think about in the meantime. With a shake of my head, I balanced everything with one arm and popped his door open.

And was greeted by an empty classroom on the other side.

"Bjorn?" I poked my head in, scanning the orderly bookshelves, the tidied desks, the dusty chalkboard. We had *promised* to meet here around this time, to walk back together and hang out tonight for a movie—no work, no shop talk, no nothing. Just me and him decompressing after surviving the first week of the second term. He wouldn't...

He wouldn't bail.

And he wouldn't just leave his classroom door unlocked.

Anxiety trickled down my spine like the first breath of winter frost. Annoying, really, to still be triggered by his empty classroom, but that night had stuck with me. Sure, Bjorn was the traumatized one—and rightly so—but seeing him up on that cross, hanging limp and slick with thick, dark blood, stakes buried deep...

That would stay with me for a while.

At the time, I'd thought I lost him, and my heart just... broke. Of course, I shoved all that aside and focused on getting him down. As soon as his eyes had fluttered open, something warm and welcome stitched my heart back together, whole again—for now.

No one answered my call. Blanketed in the castle's nighttime quiet, I marched deeper into the classroom for a more intense look, then jogged out to the corridor, panic making my throat tight.

"*Bjorn?*" Tight enough to turn my voice all squeaky. Awesome.

"I'm here, Alecto."

While I still couldn't see him, at least I had a direction, his voice carrying faintly from the left. Readjusting my grip on the pizza box and the metal thermos perched on top, I hurried down the hallway, around the corner, and then *bam* —nearly plowed straight into him.

"What are you doing down here?" Heart whumping loud enough that I just *knew* he heard every beat, I peeked around him at the alcove near the tower staircase. No one else around but a love goddess; I arched an eyebrow. "Clíodhna giving you that look?"

"Always," he said with a deliciously deep chuckle as he accepted the thermos, looking positively scrumptious in green and beige tweed tonight, the leather elbow patches always a nice touch. I used to think the look was stuffy, but now it... *did* things to me. Even worse, he had started wearing the odd pair of dark jeans to lectures lately—which just fit him *so* well. Bjorn Asulf had the hot professor vibe down better than anyone I'd met in my entire teaching career.

The vampire gave the thermos a little shake, still grinning as he said, "No, I was... Well, I found your Alice hiding behind her."

"What?" I dropped the teasing pretense with a frown, shifting the pizza box to my left hip so it wasn't jutting straight out at his torso. Nostrils flared, the greasy cheese-pepperoni combo probably an assault on his senses, Bjorn eased back slightly and shrugged.

"She was out after curfew and tried to hide from me."

"*What?*" Even though her family had hidden her away at a reform academy, Alice Jameson was the furthest thing from a rule breaker. A goody-goody and an overt people-pleaser, just the thought of her bending the rules *slightly* put me in a tailspin. What had triggered this? Had I read her wrong? We spent oodles of time together; given her coven's rejection, the witch who couldn't cast craved attention and lots of it. I did my best to ensure that she received *positive* attention for all her other talents, especially her green thumb, so my little awkward duckling wouldn't go looking for the wrong sort elsewhere.

"She's fine," Bjorn insisted, tapping his rolled stack of parchments against my arm, his grin nowhere near as reassuring as usual. Alice ignoring the rules was really out of character; she always left early so that she didn't risk missing curfew by a *second*. "I gave her a warning, then covered for her with the den mother."

And there was Bjorn, wildly *in* character, forever the shepherd to Root Rot's lost, stubborn, moody lambs. Seriously, I could always count on him to be the good guy. Smirking, I shoved at his arm, all steely and solid under the unassuming tweed.

"You old softie."

His icy blues narrowed, that handsome mouth twitching like he was fighting back a smile. "Little witch, I hail from warrior descent—"

"Yeah, yeah, whatever." I poked at his bicep a few times. "Not a warrior now, are you?"

Just a big ol' bear who would protect his cubs from everything—even themselves.

Bjorn cocked an eyebrow and tucked the thermos under his arm. "Depends on the circumstances."

Lightning fast, the vampire snatched my wrist and dragged me into him. I stumbled forward like a giggly schoolgirl, surrendering to the play fighting, to the push and pull and laughter. With him, I couldn't help it: this vampire was Forever material.

But he was my roommate.

And my friend.

And as fun as it was to flirt and giggle and tussle with each other in a dimly lit underground corridor, it probably shouldn't go beyond that. So, as always, I retreated first, stepping back to put some healthy distance between us, still chuckling as I scooped my curls behind my ears.

"Anyway." Cheeks a dull pink, Bjorn tossed his head toward the nearby stairwell. "How *is* Alice doing these days? Any magic?"

"Nope."

"Shame," he muttered as we ambled along. "She's quiet in my classes as well."

"Yeah, no friends yet, either," I told him, waiting while he nudged open the door and then ducking by while he held it, "but I'm working on it."

"I'll keep an eye out for the sane ones." Bjorn's honeyed baritone rumbled through the stairwell as we climbed together, me a few steps ahead and still only a few inches taller.

"'preciate that, bruh."

"Do you hear what comes out of your mouth sometimes?" The vampire snorted when I flipped him off over my shoulder. "What the fuck is a *bruh?*"

"You." I shouldered through the door at the first-floor landing and propped it open for him, pizza box gritted into my waist, its fresh-out-the-oven heat starting to get uncomfortable. "You're a *bruh.*"

"No, thanks," he said, breezing by with the thermos to his nose. He slowed, waiting for me to catch up with his long strides as we trekked through the open-air corridor around the main courtyard. "Is this AB-negative?"

I shot him a *duh* look, then rolled my eyes as he smiled thoughtfully.

"You know me so well, little witch."

"Well, after you went on that rant about the nuances of AB-negative, I kind of figured it was your brand."

"It wasn't a rant—more a reflective monologue about…"

He trailed off, chuckling again when I stabbed my elbow into his arm. I might have loved to listen to him talk, his velvety voice a siren song that *actually* did something to this witch, but I couldn't take another speech about the subtle wonders of AB-negative.

"So," I started, meandering along, forcing him to go at my pace when his much longer legs could outrun mine by a mile, "you still up for a movie night?"

"Always." Bjorn thrust his chin toward my extra-large pizza box. "You obviously are."

"Always," I said with a sniff, nose up, totally unfazed at the implication that I would, in fact, demolish all fourteen pieces of this nirvana before the movie was up. "Preference?"

"Your call," Bjorn told me as we drifted around a corner, a frigid breeze whipping through the courtyard and rustling the magically protected greenery inside. Although this hallway was just as chilly as the exterior, strategic charms would keep the elements out of the castle when the weather took a real nosedive in a few weeks.

Apparently. I still counted on wearing six layers to get from our flat to the greenhouse when winter finally struck.

"I'm in the mood for..." I nibbled my lower lip, not really needing those few seconds to consider my options but doing so anyway, reveling in the chill. Having lived on Canada's west coast for almost a decade, I so wasn't down for northern winters, but the frosty breath of the highlands always perked me up.

Made me feel alive.

Reminded me of Bjorn's icy touch.

"Oh, wait, let me guess—"

"Shitty horror," I finished for him. I knew his favorite blood type just like Bjorn knew the movie genre I'd campaign for when given the chance. He let out a knowing laugh and shook his head.

"When are you not in the mood for that?"

"Like..." I brought the pizza box to my other hip, giving the left side a break and putting a cardboard buffer between me and the vampire whose bones I *so* wanted to jump but *so* wasn't allowed to. "Like human teens go camping and are killed by a slasher psycho horror."

Bjorn's eyebrows shot up, and he tapped his nose with the rolled-up parchments. "Bit on the nose with that one. Slasher is *out*."

"Nosferatu?" I floated with an innocent flutter of my eyelashes. Bjorn's lips thinned, unimpressed, and I sighed dramatically. "Okay, swamp monster? Or—*oh*!" A little too excited for the night ahead, I did an embarrassing shimmy and hand-flap thing that had Bjorn grinning. "*Or*, like, ancient sea monster rises from the abyss after we drill too deep into the ocean floor, hell-bent on dominating the land *and* sea."

The vampire scoffed, trying to look all serious and failing by a mile. "No. Been done to death, that one."

"Oh my gods, *fussy*." I huffed, racking my mental database for human horror flicks we hadn't already watched. Many were supernatural in nature—and way off base. But I, like many, loved horror because the hero always made it. Tortured, tormented, beaten, whatever, the sole survivor defeated the Big Bad and went on to live their happily-ever-after, scarred but alive. It was kind of fucked, but I found the whole genre weirdly uplifting. And, you know, humans screwed up us supernatural folk *so* much that there were guaranteed laughs. "Family moves into a haunted house and at least one of them gets possessed?"

Bjorn shook his thermos at me, its contents sloshing around noisily. "That—that's the one."

"*Yessssssssss*." We bumped elbows, his hands too full for one of our usual high fives, and then descended back into the silly, flirty, giggly energy that I should have discouraged.

Instead, I ate it up just as hungrily as he did, conversation drifting toward our options now that we had narrowed down the horror subgenre. Passing by one of the arched doorways to the courtyard, however, someone else caught my eye.

Gavriel.

At least, I assumed it was Gavriel, half the figure's lean body hidden in the shadows of the gnarled old oak twisting and twining around the center of the courtyard. A telling puff of smoke whooshed from the darkness, confirming my suspicions, and I faltered when a little guilt-bomb detonated in my chest.

Seeing him sitting all alone—again—after our smidgen of bonding on the beach last week sort of... pulled at my stupid heartstrings.

The fae was always alone.

Or with someone he didn't really talk *to*, more like flirted *at*.

And from experience, that existence was a really depressing one.

If I were a better witch, I might have pointed him out to Bjorn; the pair seemed to get along, and with Bjorn's penchant for the lost and lonely, he probably wouldn't have objected to inviting him along for a movie night.

But a little shared misery on some cold beach wasn't enough to put Gavriel and me on overly friendly terms.

Besides, I coveted alone time with Bjorn like a dragon hoarded gold. If we weren't grading or lesson planning in front of the TV in silence, we were all laughter and underhanded compliments and subtle flirtations and the occasional lingering eye contact.

With everything else going on in my life, from Benedict

Hammond knowing my coffee order, wanting to know *me*, to my pet project Alice breaking the rules, all the way over to Jack Clemonte and I chatting BDSM at the risk of both our jobs...

I was *allowed* to be selfish occasionally and keep Root Rot's hidden gem all to myself.

So, I carried on without a backward glance, even as a certain silvery fae gaze scorched into my back, and tried my best to let everything else go. Forget the world existed outside the four soundproof walls of our flat.

Embrace a night of horror films and stupid jokes and snuggly blankets and pepperoni pizza.

And above all else: Bjorn.

My vampire. *Mine*.

Honestly, the rest of them had no idea what they were missing.

7

GAVRIEL

In a moment of weakness, I wanted *that*.

Them.

Bjorn and Alecto—what they had.

Laughter and carefree conversation and a constant companion and—

All of it. I wanted *all* of it, the good, the bad, and the sickeningly sweet.

With my evening pipe near its end, I watched them saunter down the exterior corridor from the shadows of the oak. Watched her bounce at his side, clutching a massive pizza box and sporting an even wider smile, all flirtatious and giggly. Watched Bjorn lap it up, standing tall when he usually hunched, moving slow and confident by her side— accommodating for her shorter legs, totally in her thrall.

The beginnings of love, perhaps.

Or, maybe I was just so fucking starved for a proper friendship that I had forgotten what one looked like. In fact, I could scarcely remember a time when I'd been *friends* with a woman, always diving headlong between her thighs when the opportunity presented itself.

And with my charm, my looks, my know-how, that opportunity came sooner and sooner with every conquest.

Then it was over.

Alone again.

Like all Root Rot staff—save Iris and Jack, naturally—I too had a roommate: Seamus Norman, head healer. Given his good bone structure and his somewhat smarmy charisma, outsiders might consider us quite the pair. We would clean up at any bar on this miserable island, yet he couldn't *stand* me. Absolutely despised the way I plowed through his nurses each year—something he could have done just as easily given he was a single, rich warlock with a prestigious job title. Instead, he constantly had a go at *me* about the string of broken hearts I left in my wake, perpetually unimpressed with my antics and *always* snippy.

Always.

Barely spoke more than two words to me in any given conversation, and they were forever laced with disdain.

Bjorn had been alone for the last six years of his tenure at Root Rot, but now he had *her*.

What I wouldn't give to shove my flatmate off the staff tower and trade places with the vampire.

I inhaled sharply at the thought, dragging in a much too big pull and hacking all the smoke out like a total amateur.

Trade places with him—for the *solitude*, of course, not to room with Alecto Clarke. Lovely as she was, immune to my advances now like she had taken a vaccine against me, she wasn't worth the trouble. That little witch, whose laughter echoed down the corridor even with the pair long gone, made me *feel* more than I cared to admit.

Made me... *consider* things.

Consider her.

Consider what it would be like *not* to navigate this dull realm totally alone, everyone kept at an arm's length.

After a swig from my silver flask, small enough to fit neatly and discreetly in my jacket pocket, I settled my throat enough to enjoy the last of my pipe before I had to dump its charred contents all over the courtyard. Fuck them. Fuck Bjorn and Alecto for looking so fucking *happy* and smitten. Fuck Seamus for not seeing the purpose behind my casual affairs. Fuck all of them—I wasn't here for friendship.

Pipe dangling from my lips, teeth anchoring it in place, I went for my *other* inner jacket pocket. Left side. Seldom used. A letter had arrived for me today, delivered straight to my desk by one of the admin ditzes while I'd been stuffing my face at lunch. Slowly, I pulled it out and flipped the aged parchment envelope over. No return address, of course, but the red wax stamp with its subtle 666 in ornate flourishes was telling. Biting down harder on my pipe, I slipped a finger under the top fold and carefully broke the seal.

Then waited.

Some envelopes could be hexed, capable of maiming the recipient the moment they opened them.

Nothing.

Exhaling a curt breath, I wrenched the letter out—and scowled at the glitter dust that came with it. Doused in little sparkles, I tossed the envelope aside and opened the folded paper within.

Ah.

As expected, the Darkwell Academy emblem saluted me from the letterhead, even more glitter inside the folded parchment.

DEAREST GAVRIEL OF THE ASH COURT...

My eyes narrowed as I deciphered the nearly illegible, beyond obnoxious cursive scrawl. While I'd almost thought this might be a handwritten note from Lucifer himself given the wax details, its origins lay in his dark academy's admissions office instead.

And contained a single snarky paragraph thanking me for the dozens of exceptional student candidates I had sent their way this year.

Snarling, I bit down so hard that my pipe's ebonite stem splintered.

Cracked right down to the bowl.

The bastards then had the nerve to sign off with:

ALL OUR LOVE, AFFECTION, AND GRATITUDE,
DARKWELL ACADEMY ADMISSIONS
XOXOXOXOXOXOXOXOXOXOXOXO

Along with a half-dozen hearts around the signatures of what appeared to be the entire admissions office. I stared at the big picture for a moment—the hearts, the emblem, the glitter—and then viciously crumpled the parchment into a ball. However, before I could hurl it across the courtyard or will it alight with fae fire, I stopped. Reconsidered. Smoothed it out, folded it over and over and over into a teeny rectangle, then shoved it back in my jacket pocket with trembling fingers. Fueled by fury, *humiliation*, it would have been easy to get rid of the evidence.

But I ought to keep it. Carry it around with me. Let it be an embarrassing reminder of my failings.

A reminder *not* to get swept into the affairs of those around me. To not covet what Alecto and Bjorn shared—but to covet a position in the Ash Court. That was what this had always been about: a lowly fae, once a great warrior, returning home like the prodigal son, beckoned into the king's embrace courtesy of Lucifer.

Nothing more. Nothing less.

But all the little urchins are shit this year—

71

Seething, I emptied my pipe one last time and kicked at the scattered black bits that settled between the grey cobblestones. Time to lock myself in my room so I didn't snap on the wrong person.

Time to drink until I passed out, honestly.

Again.

With a clenched jaw, I marched across the courtyard— and slammed right into another body marching *in* through the arched opening.

"Fuck's *sake.*"

Ash Cedar stumbled back on impact, leveling a curse at me with those hauntingly dark eyes, but neither of us said a word to each other. No apologies. He looked down slowly, however, to sneer at the glitter I'd transferred onto his stodgy warlock robes. Thankfully there wasn't anyone around to see the blunder, and we shouldered by each other —hard—to squish through the archway at the same time like a pair of stubborn children.

Fuck him.

Fuck the letter in my pocket.

Fuck Darkwell and Root Rot and Bjorn and Alecto and Ash fucking Cedar—

Fuck everything. I was officially *done* until sunrise tomorrow, and if anyone else got in my way, I'd put them through the fucking wall.

8

ALECTO

Tap, tap, tap.

Over the raging winds, someone was determined enough to make their knuckles heard on the door of the main greenhouse. Red pen in hand, the checkmark I'd just made all jerky from the shock of the noise, I slowly glared toward the door at the back. Lights on, greenhouse a beacon in the oppressive November darkness, seeing through the glass pane was a crapshoot, and given my mood, I was tempted to just ignore it.

Who the hell went outside in this weather, anyway?

Tap, tap.

I gritted my teeth, refocusing on the quiz, steadily blitzing through the multiple-choice questions with a check, check, check, huge X of my pen. If anything, I could blame the sound on the wind, because the last thing I wanted to do this gloomy Saturday night, my weekend office hours long since over, was talk to anyone.

Precisely twenty-six years ago, my parents had been brutally slaughtered in their own home.

Torn apart.

Butchered.

And I had been left there to burn in my bed.

In the past, I mourned their loss with my grandparents. We kept busy on the anniversary, lighting candles and holding rituals for the spirits of those long gone. I wrote letters to my parents individually, telling them about my year, all I had accomplished and all I still hoped to do.

Usually those letters ended with a vow, a promise to avenge their deaths and make the culprit *pay*.

I had him within reach—but he still hadn't paid.

And I was so miserable today, so heartbroken—just *broken*, period—that a part of me wondered if he ever would.

Wondered if I even had the courage to do what I needed to.

Probably not. I mean, I spent all day in bed, the last place I ever wanted to be on the anniversary of the night that changed my life. I cried and slept and grieved and pretended I couldn't feel the heat slithering across my skin, couldn't taste the smoke choking me from the inside.

Unfortunately, office hours were mandatory, and mine were on Saturdays this term. In an ideal world, that meant more students should have time to visit, and based on the end-of-term exams before Samhain, most of them *needed* to visit me during these off days. But no one showed, same as always, except Alice. The witch had hunkered down at the desk in front of mine to work on assignments that weren't even herbalism or potions related, overly meticulous in her research of wand woods for her spellwork term paper.

Then office hours ended. She left.

I stayed.

Skipped dinner, preferring the solitude, needing to be alone in my misery, my angst. No candles lit today—I was too much of a wuss to play with fire alone—and no letters written.

What could I say to Mom and Dad?

Hey, guys! Found your killer. He's been hitting on me a bunch lately, but Imma just let it slide while I drown in cowardice, indecision, and self-loathing. K, bye, have a great time in the spirit world! Say hey to Gram and Gramps for me! xoxo

Yeah. That about covered it. Pathetic.

From my list of coping mechanisms, I settled on one of the healthier strategies: work. No booze. No men. Just—boatloads of grading that kept me busy for as long as I could focus. Anytime my concentration wavered, I was gone, sinking hard and fast. Fortunately, as night took hold and my stomach roared, I had a week's worth of quizzes from all my classes to drudge through. Overall, these were a vast improvement from last term, which meant my kids had either realized what I wanted from them, or I had figured out how to speak to this particular bunch.

Either way—silver lining on a shitcake of a day.

Tap, tap, tap, wham.

Knuckles turned to a fist on the other side of my door, and I slammed my pen down with a huff. Fine. Couldn't exactly blame that on the wind anymore, even if it *was* screaming like an army of banshees out there.

I'd made it up, around my desk, and halfway down the aisle between student worktables when the door finally creaked open.

And Benedict Hammond poked his head inside.

My gut bottomed out. My knees buckled. I lilted to the left and barely managed to brace on a table before collapsing.

"Sorry, sorry," the warlock crooned, taking my silence as an invitation and darting in, battling to close the door against the wind. "I didn't want to frighten you by just barreling inside, so I thought I'd knock."

Mouth dry, throat suddenly thick and raw with unshed tears, I just stared at him. Blinked. Trembled. Panic flashed through me like lightning. All the immunity I had built up against his stupid fucking face, against his presence, the odd touch—accidental or not—up and died. I couldn't... I just...

You killed them today.

What were you wearing? Were you smiling like that? Did they invite you into the house, or did you force your way inside—just like this?

"Saw the light and knew you were burning the midnight oil," he insisted, cheery and oblivious to the meltdown tearing through me. "Thought I'd bring this." From behind his pack, he produced a to-go cup, presumably of coffee since that seemed like all he fucking knew about me, my stupid coffee order, and that was *more* than enough. "Just the way you like it."

With the anniversary creeping up, November 26 a permanent black mark in my yearly calendar, I'd gone out of my way to avoid him more than usual lately.

But he had found me.

Wasn't exactly difficult.

I should have made it difficult.

You should make him suffer, *you fucking coward.*

"Listen..." Benedict readjusted his dark grey warlock robes, heavy, almost oppressive material that still seemed tailored to his tall, lean figure. Another regal cloak-cigarette pants combination, along with a pair of polished loafers caked in fresh mud. "I was wondering if you'd like to go to the village tomorrow for a spot of lunch. It's a human pub, which—" He scoffed dramatically and rolled his eyes. "—I know, I know, but trust me, they do this amazing Sunday roast—"

"Appointment," I blurted, half croaking the word, half screaming it. He flinched, taken aback by the volume, and I cleared my throat, unable to force the smile I usually did for this murderer. "I-I have an appointment tomorrow. With Clemonte."

Benedict's dark, neatly trimmed brows shot up, nostrils flared as if to sniff out the lie, and I braced harder on the table, slowly losing control of my calm—of everything.

"To talk… lessons," I finished lamely.

"Right." He frowned for a moment, looking me up and down slowly. "Sure. Okay. How about next week, then? We could take a leisurely lunch hour, have a bit of wine…?"

You cut them into pieces twenty-six years ago.

And now he was asking me on a fucking lunch date.

Like I could share a casual Sunday roast with him without puking it all up a second after forcing it down.

A wave of light-headedness struck, more vicious than the screeching winds, and I popped a hip against the table, needing to lean almost all of me on it to get through this.

"I… will have to check my planner." Gods, that was painful. Rejecting him outright, screaming in his face, tearing off my mask and reminding him of the woman who had my eyes—who was his *sun*, apparently—felt… premature. Impulsive. Dangerous. Alone down here, just him and me, I had no plan, no exit strategy, no road map for the future. Sure, my wand sat in its holster up my sleeve, but he had one of those, too, and from the way I reacted to just the *sight* of him tonight, I wasn't in the proper headspace to duel.

He might even kill me.

Make it an anniversary to remember.

Bury yet another murderous secret.

Benedict studied me with a grin, eyes roving my body more suggestively this time, making his intentions crystal clear. "Splendid. Do let me know, and if you forget—I know just where to find you." He tapped at the to-go coffee as I gulped down a flood of bile. "Might need a warming charm for this… Got a bit distracted on the way here."

"Okay," I bit out. *I know just where to find you.* That sentence would haunt my dreams tonight, shrouded in fire and smoke.

Attack him.

Do it.

Move your fucking useless body and gouge his eyes out—

That was the fury in me, the little piece of the true Alecto I adopted when I took her title, when I chose it for myself at thirteen believing I could be a warrior, a woman of righteous —violent—justice just like her.

I didn't deserve her name.

I'd always be Hannah Corwin, the terrified little girl trapped in her bed who wet herself at the pop and sizzle of a raging fire.

"Good night, Alecto," Benedict purred, rapping his knuckles twice on the table in front of him, grinning like the cat who'd finally caught the canary. "Don't work too hard, now."

I nodded reflexively, laughed without hearing it, head still bobbing like some manic wooden puppet by the time Benedict was out the door. He struggled to shut it, really throwing his back into it and body shoved up against the pane, but then he was gone, fading into the black as a high-pitched whine blotted out the wind.

Sick to my stomach, every thought erupted in a maelstrom of *sound* whipping around my skull a hundred miles an hour. Accusations and protests and misery and insults and the odd *You're doing your best in a fucked-up situation* barely above a whisper. Couldn't think straight. Couldn't see straight. Couldn't speak, my throat closing, the heat of that horrible night creeping up my neck.

Dizzy. Too dizzy. Need—*air.*

Trembling, I managed to turn around and stumble two desks forward before collapsing. Agony ripped through me, grief shredding my lungs as I broke apart after months of keeping it together.

I hated him, but I hated myself more. What was the point of paying some djinn nearly everything I had to show up here and do *nothing* about Benedict motherfucking Hammond? Coward didn't even begin to describe it, but my inner self sure loved bellowing it as I curled over and wailed into my hands. Screamed and sobbed and—

Need air.

Need air or I'd pass out.

Gasping, I somehow got on my own two feet. Made it to the back door and out into the tempest. The clouds turned cruel suddenly, like they had been waiting for me, and misted the academy's grounds with a freezing damp. I'd forgotten my jacket, my sweater, my scarf. The air out here was too sharp, too bitter, too painful as I sucked it down by the lungful.

Torture. Can't take it anymore.

Trapped in my head, in a body that fought me for every step, I staggered to the stone stairs embedded in the hillside, then hauled myself up one at a time. Fell along the way. Slipped on the wet. Knocked around by the wind and lost in the dark.

Until I reached the top, the lanterns bolted around the castle doorways flickering but bright against the elements. Only it wasn't their warm orange glow that felt like a buoy in the tumultuous seas.

It was Jack Clemonte, lording over me at the crest of the staircase, that massive body layered in black and utterly unyielding against the wailing winds.

Cold and lost and desperate, I crumbled to my knees at his feet as the world went up in flames.

9

JACK

The storm wasn't supposed to hit until midnight.

But when had the weather ever done what it was *supposed* to?

It had been building since six o'clock this evening. Clouds darkening. Air thickening, cooling fast and furious enough to fog all my office windows. Although the reports might fail me again, the storm was predicted to last until Monday, battering the castle through the night, Sunday a complete wash—along with it, my morning run. No outlet tomorrow, no chance to really blow off steam, let loose the stress that built like stone towers on my shoulders.

As eleven o'clock crept closer, I had decided to abandon my work—for a little while, anyway—and see that my castle was sealed tight, then call security inside. Given the raging winds and the smattering of freezing rain on the windowpanes, it was unlikely students would risk it. Still, those on the outdoor detail could post up by the doors, just to keep an eye on things. This new batch of roving warlocks replaced those I nixed after Bjorn's kidnapping, but they were speedy hires—*just* adequate. Sufficient. Satisfactory.

Hardly the cream of the crop. Iris wouldn't shut up about their failings, and for once, my second-in-command and I were on the same page.

All these plans, all this storm preparation that I as headmaster didn't *need* to do but felt responsible for all the same...

They all vanished when I spotted the light in her greenhouse.

The thought of Alecto braving the tempest when it finally struck had a knot twisting and twining beyond reprieve in my chest. Unable to leave her to fend for herself, I took a sharp detour, stalking through the empty Root Rot corridors, footsteps falling like thunder, thick wool cloak thrown over my shoulders and a scarf looped around my neck for good measure.

Come inside, little one, before the storm gets you. That thought had quieted all the rest, everything else falling to the wayside until I ushered her safely indoors where she belonged. At this hour, weekend or not, she wasn't the only professor working into the night, but she was the only one with a classroom outside, and I couldn't stand the idea of her being thrown around in this gale as she tried to get back inside.

It was supposed to be a doozy, this storm.

And when I shouldered through a small door at the north end of the castle, the one closest to the hillside stairs that led down to the greenhouses, the highlands told me at least *that* prediction had been true. Met with screaming winds and a wall of cold, misty rain, I tucked my chin into my scarf and marched into the black, noting we should add a railing to those steps.

Steps where I found *her*, a drowned witch crawling over the stone, stumbling along without a coat, her curls stuck to her forehead and her eyes hauntingly broken. While I had

81

witnessed Alecto *off* before, this was something else entirely.

The moment she saw me, she sank to her knees in the cold and the wet, shivering almost violently. My chest tightened, fury detonating and going nuclear in a second: she looked as if someone had attacked her. Hair disheveled. Long dress shirt untucked and messy. Mud splashed up her leather knee-high boots.

Teeth gritted, I sprang into immediate action, straddling the razor-thin line between panic and rage as I dropped to her level and took her by the shoulders. The Dom side of me demanded I scoop her into my arms. Tuck her under my cloak—shield her from the world. Wrap my scarf around her head to blot out the mist.

But I *wasn't* her Dom, despite our previous conversation, and...

And it didn't matter what I *wanted*.

All that mattered was her.

Fixing *her*. Making it *right*.

So I clutched Alecto by her arms instead. Helped her to her feet. For the sake of balance and stability, I tucked her against my side, then marched my weak-kneed professor out of the wet and under the stone outcrop that extended over the doorway. Candlelight danced in the lamps on either side, each of us backlit by warmth, our faces marred with shadows.

My hand hovered an inch from the door handle when she came undone against me. Breathing hard and fast, Alecto collapsed in on herself like I wasn't even there, arms limp at her sides and shoulders rounded, seconds from plummeting back to the ground. Steely-eyed and focused, I situated myself directly in front of her, blocking out everything but me, and stooped to her eyeline.

"Alecto?"

She wasn't there—not really. Those amber orbs darted about, from the lamps to the awning to my forehead, but they were glazed over, lost, as though she wasn't processing a single thing.

I knew that look.

I *loathed* that I knew that look, but my anger didn't change the fact that I had seen it on Darcy's face before, my sister the victim of a brutal assault in our teens.

Father strung up the assailant by his guts— metaphorically at first, but then literally when the high council handed the bastard over for punishment.

An old friend.

An academy chum who thought he had the right to *touch* my baby sister.

And now here was that look again in Alecto's eyes, and I had to steel myself against it, remember that she wasn't Darcy—that I had no bloody idea what had happened to set her off like this, but it wasn't good.

"Alecto, look at me," I ordered, soft but firm in my delivery. When she refused, I grabbed her chin and cuffed it between us, jostling her just enough to bring back the light in her eyes. Her chest bobbed in uneven shudders. All the color had drained from her cheeks. She stood shivering before me, gasping, fighting for breath, sobbing without making a sound. "Alecto—*now.*"

There they were—*my good girl*—eyes like gold and flecked with sorrow. They latched onto mine like I was her only life preserver, and that certainly cemented things for me—finally settled on the decision my rational mind refused to even consider. Logically, I ought to usher Alecto to her flat and have Bjorn take care of her. Seven hells, maybe even the infirmary was the better choice. But my office was closer, just up a flight of nearby stairs, then down the hall to an empty admin wing.

No one could see her like this. She tried so hard to put on a good show—they all did. No one wanted a reputation, and people had been whispering about her, Bjorn, and Gavriel all month. No. I refused to add to that; when she sobered, just the thought of *me* witnessing this breakdown would likely be humiliating enough.

"What happened?" I whispered, a last-ditch effort to quash this before I had to take further action. Cheeks hollow, Alecto just shook her head furiously in response, then tried to twist out of my grasp. "Alecto. You're safe with me. Tell me—"

Her protesting whimper forced my hand. Keeping a firm but not bruising grip on her rain-slicked arm, I escorted her inside, then up the stairs, down the hall, and into the silent north-end administration wing. Curtains drawn back, a few desk lamps lighting the space, I walked the familiar path through to my office with Alecto's shuffling figure at my heels. In those thirty seconds, the skies shattered. Mist turned to fat, punishing drops of freezing rain, lashing the windows, pummeling the glass. Lightning split the black above, followed by a calamitous *boom* that made quill feathers shiver. Not a soul around, I had no qualms kicking open my office door and tossing Alecto inside rather than putting on a show of politely coaxing her along.

She needed a small, safe space to decompress.

She needed the quiet but also the *power* of the storm.

I closed the door soundly behind us but didn't lock it. In fact, when she shambled around, I made a point to open and close it so she knew she wasn't trapped inside. Escape was always an option, though I had a serious issue letting her leave in this state.

Arms wrapped around herself, curls flat, rainwater dripping off her clothes and muddy footprints on my floor, Alecto enjoyed a *brief* moment of calm. A few steady breaths, as if the change of scenery offered just enough to soothe whatever had her mind and body racing.

But the quiet never lasted.

Like the storm, she came undone again, quickly ramping up to hyperventilation, shaking, squeaky little sobs caught in her throat.

Fuck.

For an intense physical and emotional episode, I personally only had one cure.

Something I had put off and buried deep in my mind because it was too inappropriate for a headmaster to pick up the whip again.

But given our last conversation, her eagerness, the darling gleam in her eyes at the *thought* of pain, Alecto was, at the very least, open to all of it.

And in a moment like this, her wildly out of control and me perfectly in it, the burden fell to me—it was *my* responsibility to think clearly.

My responsibility to help her in any way possible.

All the while aware that she was compromised, that a lesser man would have taken advantage of it.

Clemonte men weren't *lesser*.

After peeling off my outer layers and tossing them onto one of the chairs in front of my desk, I undid my dress shirt cuffs and jerked my sleeves up to my elbows. From there, I made a beeline for my desk. Grabbed my forgotten black suit jacket off the back of the chair I had spent several years of my life in at this point, then placed it on my desk. Smoothed it out. Spread it wide enough to accommodate her. Everything else had been neatly set aside or put away before I left, which gave me a clear workspace.

"Alecto," I beckoned her with a crooked finger, speaking, just this once, as her Dom and not her boss, "come here."

Unlike before, she moved without hesitation, crossing

right to my side, still shaking, still battling with her breath. Exhaustion rimmed her eyes, all those tears shed making her look gaunt and worn—beaten down but still standing. With a soft exhale, I smoothed the slowly frizzing curls away from her face, then dried her cheeks and forehead with my thumbs. From there, I relied on magic to warm her—to make her feel as though every garment was fresh from the dryer.

"*Arfacio*." Wand tip grazing her arm, a soft whoosh of marigold yellow rid her of the rain that continued to pound the windows. For a moment, I thought—once again—that that was enough: a safe space, dry clothes, a firm touch. But then her eyes watered, and she tried to turn away from me.

Tried to leave without permission before it was time.

Wand set aside, both out in the open and out of reach, I blocked her escape with my body, herding her between my chair and my desk, and then motioned to the latter with a flick of my eyes and a snap of my fingers.

"Alecto, bend over."

Lips tumbling open, she blinked up at me, then down at the desk. Back and forth, the order processing in a mind that must have felt so scattered and frantic. The goal was to calm it—to center it on one sensation, *one* thought, not a thousand.

It shouldn't have surprised me that she followed orders unquestioningly. After all, she had done so ever since I'd known her, always complying with my requests, never arguing, never talking back or questioning me. But the moment she veered toward my desk, to my jacket splayed wide like a lover's embrace, I caught her again, first by her arm, then her chin, needing her to hear this clearly—needing to see understanding in the amber before I went any further.

"You say the word *rot*, and it stops," I told her. "You say the word *rot*, and I step back. Do you understand?"

Not exactly my most creative safeword, but given she

hadn't uttered a single thing since I'd found her, I wanted it to be simple and unmistakable, one syllable with hard sounds. Swallowing thickly, Alecto nodded up at me, slower this time. I almost made her say it, just to test how loud she could speak, get her accustomed to the word before it started, but those watery eyes, those pale cheeks, her shivering body had me releasing her and guiding her to the desk. No physical contact, of course. I couldn't bend her over myself—not in this situation, anyway—but my hand hovered at her lower back because...

Because not only did I delight in pain, but I had always craved the role of protector and guardian. By now, it came naturally, especially with her.

Without a word, Alecto eased over my desk, widening her stance just enough to accommodate. She went right into my jacket, hands flat over the fabric, thighs quivering under my scrutiny. Wearing a pinstriped dress that resembled a man's dress shirt, the thin cotton nipped at the waist and framed her figure perfectly, leading my eye down to black leggings and the leather boots that had muddied up my floor. Ordinarily, I preferred to play with a naked sub while I remained fully dressed—red, warm, worked flesh was just such a fucking turn-on. Goosebumps and pebbled nipples and telling blushes.

But that wasn't the point of tonight. I made no move to push her shirtdress up, nor drag her leggings down. Instead, I gently brushed the hair from her face, gathering that rebellious mane to one side, and then braced my left hand on the desk.

"Turn your head to the side," I urged, wanting her to be able to *breathe*, to look at something that wasn't the abyss of my black suit jacket. Alecto complied, the strain of holding her head up visible in her neck, her breath suddenly catching. "Cheek down. Relax into the desk."

87

Another order gobbled up by a woman *made* to submit. I angled my fingers so that the gold Clemonte family ring on my left index finger was obvious, a shiny token for her to focus on. And she did, eyes falling to it, locking onto it, hooded and bloodshot. Good.

Good girl.

A quick glance toward her backside was all I needed to ensure my right hand lined up for the big swing. Fingers slightly curved, hand cupped *just* so. Years of abstinence fell away, muscle memory kicking in. Had I less self-control, I might have faltered at the thought of this—of spanking a professor to calm her down, of realizing that this was the first time I had done this with anyone in far, *far* too long.

But I was lost, just like her. Lost to the moment, the scene, the storm battering the windows.

Calm swept through me, top to bottom and back again, glorious relaxation trickling through my limbs.

The first smack of my palm to her ass echoed through the room, followed swiftly by her startled gasp. Alecto's eyes shot open, shock and surprise obvious—but something else muddled the pair, too, like a light had been switched on back there and shone through now. Gods, whatever it was, it was bloody beautiful.

Hand firm on her backside to alleviate some of the sting, I waited. Gave her a moment to sift through the chaos in her own mind and digest what had just happened. Her headmaster had spanked her. Hard, too. Some submissives needed to be worked up to that pressure, but given her state, her predilections, our strange but impossible-to-ignore courtship in dominance and submission, I had gone for the jugular from the start. And while her mouth opened and closed, the little witch said nothing. She adjusted herself, rolling her hips as a lone tear swelled in the corner of her eye and dribbled over the bridge of her nose.

Nothing.

Still, I waited.

Waited until her breathing evened out *just* enough, a barely there calm slowing her panicked gasps, nudging her away from the ledge.

Only then did I strike again, this time to the other cheek, hard enough to slam her folded figure into my desk. To jerk her supple body forward. My cock twitched with interest, the sight so fucking mouthwatering, to see her maneuvered by my hand, and a languid, oozing desire throbbed in my low abdomen when her fingers curled over my jacket and twisted into the fabric.

Settling into my Dom second skin, I let loose. Spanked her, one side, then the other, back and forth. Never harder than the first time, but faster, totally fixated on her face as her body jerked back and forth on the desk, driven by my intensity. Alecto blinked hard, squeezed her eyes shut. She winced and grimaced, gasped and whimpered, fisted my sprawled jacket and bunched the fabric up around her face.

But she stayed put.

She *took* it—me, my firm hand pounding her rounded backside.

She took it until I decided she'd had enough. At no point did her lips even start to curve around her provided safeword, and a filthy, dark whisper at the back of my mind insisted she could have taken much, much more.

But this wasn't a scene, per se. We weren't here to have *fun*. I had always found calm in kink. Strength and focus and *power*. From my conversations with subs, they found much the same. If she was as naturally submissive as I'd always thought, this would help her.

Therefore, while my cock strained against my briefs, pulse pounding between my ears and every part of me quivering with a need to push on until we had found a mutually satisfying end, I withdrew. Backed away when it was obvious she had lost herself in *this*, not whatever had made her eyes look so terribly hollow before.

Unable to help myself, I smoothed both hands over her ass. Just a little sturdy pressure to will away the ache of the spanking, followed by an adjustment of her striped dress. Then, keeping a hand on her lower back so that she wouldn't stand—*not without permission, little one*—I ducked down and grabbed the half-drunk bourbon bottle from the back of my bottom desk drawer. I'd been nursing this since my first day, but its burn felt beyond appropriate for aftercare, especially when I couldn't—shouldn't—cuddle her like I wanted.

Patting her lower back, a silent reminder to *stay*, I eased around my desk and grabbed a china teacup, the same she had slurped her chamomile from during our rather telling conversation all those weeks back. After splashing in a shot of bourbon, I capped the bottle and left it on my tea tray, then hurried back, refusing to leave her like that for longer than necessary.

Submissives were so fragile after a session.

She wasn't *mine*, but what had just happened, her intense emotion leading up to it, left her ripe for another meltdown if I wasn't careful.

Behind her once more, my hand found the back of her neck and cuffed it firmly, but then guided her up gently, allowing her to set the pace. While I trusted she could stand on her own, I kept that hand there to hold her in place so that she didn't nudge back into my cock, into the erection to end *all* erections.

Still, she was close enough to feel my presence—close enough for me to feed her the shot of bourbon. Bringing the teacup to her mouth with my free hand and tipping it back when her lips parted, those amber eyes locked on mine over her shoulder, somehow felt more intimate than anything we had done up to this point.

After finishing her chaser, shuddering through the bourbon's bite, Alecto stood perfectly still, no longer shaking, gasping, or crying, as I set the cup aside and wrapped her in my jacket. Just around the shoulders, mind you, the sleeves much too long for her. I then steered her toward my high-backed chair, the leather worn but still padded enough for her tender backside.

Normally I'd make a sub sit on the floor, on her heels, just so she could really *feel* her Dom's claim on her body—that I *owned* her and her pain, just for a little while.

Again, not a scene, no matter how aroused I was, no matter how she looked at me—no matter how delightful the hot pink flush in her cheeks.

"Can you sit?" I asked, shifting my tone from stern and commanding to soft and warm. Still masterful—my voice had always possessed a natural richness to it, which worked well in scenes—yet comforting, too. Or so I'd been told, anyway.

Alecto's nod had me easing her into the chair, utterly enraptured with her slight wince as she settled, and I stooped to pull the jacket tighter around her. Even though she positively drowned in all that fabric, its embrace would help ease her back to the now.

My arms would always be better—ideal, really—but I had no idea how Alecto Clarke liked her aftercare, and smothering a new sub was such bad form.

Crouched in front of her, knees cracking angrily on the way down, I tipped my head to the side and scrutinized her expression. "Would you like some tea?"

Lower lip snagged between her teeth, she shook her head.

"Would you like to talk about it?"

Her eyebrow flicked up, and Alecto looked pointedly at

the desk with *the* brattiest little smirk. I bit back a grin of my own.

"No," I said with a lightly chastising tap on her knee. "Not that—about what put you in the state I found you in."

She deflated, her slight head shake a very resounding *no*. Right, then. I wouldn't push—tonight.

"Okay." Still crouched in front of her, as low as I could risk without kneeling at her feet, I pinched her chin and forced her back to me, catching her eyes as I said, "Are you all right? Did someone hurt you?"

The smirk returned with a vengeance, and once again she glanced slyly toward the desk. *Brat*. Brat times ten.

My grip tightened on her chin. *"Alecto."*

"No," she finally croaked, her first word all night. Her hands went for my forearm, perhaps to clutch at, maybe to remove, to shove it out of her orbit, but I was already on the retreat, our dance out of sync suddenly. So, she gathered up the jacket's empty sleeves instead, brought them to her nose, and took a deep, damning inhale that had *every* drop of blood in my body zooming for my cock.

Bloody *hell*.

Not good. Not good. *Redirect—*

"No one hurt me," she whispered after lowering the sleeves and clutching them to her chest. Her dark lashes painted her cheeks as she fidgeted with the fabric. "I'm sorry you found me like that... I'm sorry, Jack, for—" Her breath snagged, and she shot up as if jolted by a cattle prod. "Oh, no, *Headmaster*. I'm so sorry, Headmaster, for—"

"Please—Jack, I insist," I said with a chuckle, holding up a hand to stop that runaway train. "Really. I just spanked you... I can be Jack for tonight."

Alecto sank back into the chair, her little smile beyond endearing, stoking my protective side as no one ever had.

"Really though..." I brushed a curl from her face, then

another, then another, her hair made for distraction. "Given your state and our last, er, *discussion*, I thought this might help... I didn't hurt you, did I?"

Alecto gave me a long look, emotionless in a way that made me start to sweat, before another bratty smile split her face.

"Yes," she murmured. "You did." *Shit.* "But I liked it."

Double shit.

Swallowing a groan, I finally felt confident enough to leave her and perch on the edge of my desk. Gods, what a mess. Scrubbing at my face, I glanced at the clock through my fingers and then exhaled briskly. Nearing midnight— hardly a good look should anyone catch a professor exiting my office at this hour.

"Let me walk you back to your flat."

Fussing with her hair, Alecto frowned. "You don't have to."

"Yes," I rumbled, pinning her with a *don't question me* look that made past submissives quake in their boots. Alecto merely stared back, fearless and calm but still a bit bratty— just the headspace I had hoped to put her in. "I do."

And now I ought to see her home, make sure nothing else happened along the way to ruin our good work. Not only had this helped her, but as she stood and shrugged off my jacket, I found *myself* in a much better place than I had been even an hour ago. Sure, the stresses of this job remained, the uncertainty of my place at Root Rot, the pressure from the high council, but in Alecto's presence, having finally *played* again, I just...

I could draw a *real* deep breath for the first time in eons.

I hadn't climaxed—and was forced to tuck my erection into my belt when she turned her back—but as I escorted Alecto out of my office, relief felt even better. Relaxation. Warmth and contentment. Just being near her, this much too young witch who knew and kept my secret, who hadn't judged me, who leaned into my heavy hand without question, was heavenly.

Neither of us said a word on the walk to her flat, but the surrounding air stayed serene even as the elements battered the castle at every turn. Wind screamed through the corridors. Rain pounded the roof like war drums. Lightning illuminated the windows, and thunder cracked down to Root Rot's deepest foundations. Yet with her, I walked on *air*.

And she seemed much the same, ambling along at my side, forcing me to slow down to accommodate her shorter stride. Her gentle smile, her hooded eyes, her relaxed posture: whatever had hurt her earlier was gone—for now. I wasn't foolish enough to think a bit of spanking was the cure, but if it had helped her calm down enough to attack the problem with a clearer mind, then I had done my job as a Dominant.

All the while failing miserably as her headmaster.

We exchanged soft good-nights at her door, and as soon as it shut behind her, I sprinted out of there to avoid anyone catching me.

Only to slow in the stairwell and lean back against the wall, the minutiae of life outside of the scene creeping in bit by bit. With her, the world went quiet. My mind wasn't cluttered with a thousand racing thoughts—just her.

And that was... alarming.

Unhealthy, probably. I rarely engaged in an emotional connection with submissives beyond friendship, but Alecto Clarke had me yearning for something more.

I pinched the bridge of my nose and groaned. Like every Saturday night, I ought to retire to my office and resume work for at least another two hours.

Get a measly three or four hours of sleep, then up for a punishing run before dawn if the weather allowed it.

Instead, I pivoted and climbed all the way up to *my* flat. My empty, dark, silent flat in need of a woman's touch and a whiff of vanilla. While I usually rooted in the chair before the hearth, books and folders stacked high on either side, I veered into the bedroom. Stripped down. Climbed into bed thinking of her, of her fingers twisting my jacket, her shocked gasp, the lush fullness of her backside in my palm.

And for the first time—possibly *ever*—I fell asleep within minutes. No potions, no pills, no tricks, no magic. Just—out.

Out and dreaming of her.

No stress-induced nightmares.

Just Alecto Clarke…

And everything my heart wanted to do to her.

ALECTO

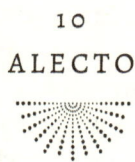

"Hello, Professor Clarke."

I gritted my teeth as yet another staple crunched through the thousandth midterm prep packet I had put together this afternoon. Of *course* she found me back here, tucked away in no-man's-land, the far corner of Root Rot's library quiet and relatively student-free: Alice was a little Alecto bloodhound, and I had no doubt she searched the greenhouse first before coming here for her usual Thursday afternoon study hall.

"Hello, Alice." Pretty standard procedure: if I had a free period that coincided with one of hers, she was *right* by my side. Two short, dark weeks into December, I found the greenhouse too chilly to work in most days and only bothered with heating charms if I had classes. The other two greenhouses and the conservatory had regulated heat orbs working around the clock to take care of the flora inside, but the main one, packed with students five days a week, needed more finesse to account for the fluctuating number of people present.

And without the twenty or so extra bodies in there this afternoon, I couldn't be bothered to finagle with the heat, the glass panes ice-dusted and temperatures supposed to take a nosedive this evening. So, I'd ventured inside with my mountain of work. Bjorn had started sleeping more regularly in the afternoons, which put him in a better overall mood most nights. Disturbing him, therefore, with the constant crunch of a stapler eating parchment was on the bottom of my to-do list.

Like the rest of the faculty, the staffroom was always at my disposal, but I had avoided it since the anniversary—since that awful night that ended in such a strange, wonderful way that I still couldn't stop thinking about it. That I couldn't stop *fantasizing* about, Jack's hand on my ass, the solid wood of his desk propping me up—keeping me in position, bent over and vulnerable. Helpless. Throw in a dash of pain and a dollop of hot headmaster who didn't press for too many details and I was *golden*.

In the fortnight that followed, I hadn't spent alone time with either Benedict—thank *fuck* for that—or Jack.

Which...

You know, made things a little weird. We hadn't found the time to talk or dissect what had happened in his office, but maybe that was for the best. Maybe it had been nothing more than a warlock helping a distraught witch in a way that was private, personal, and intimate to them. Because fuck *me*, it had helped. He had been so good about everything, so sweet in the aftermath, so thoughtful and tender but still... *gruff*. Manly. Masterful and powerful in a way that didn't make my hackles rise.

Fuck misogynist assholes. I saw a lot of them in my profession, and my patience for their bullshit had thinned to nonexistent over the years.

It hadn't been like that with Jack.

Even though he had spanked me, steered me around, fed me a shot of bourbon that burned bright in my belly, the interaction felt oddly... equal. Somehow. I still couldn't put my finger on the nuances, but Jack always looked like he was buried in work, hounded by the administration, then stuck dealing with truant students day in and day out—I didn't want to add to the load.

I owed him that.

Not only for what he had done for me that night, but for the trust he put in me while doing it. Our conversation at the start of term had been risky, but it was just talk. This had been action. I... I could have filed a report. Gotten him fired and ostracized in the academic community. Jack Clemonte, for all his power and prestige, for the heft his family name carried, put himself at *my* mercy.

He had trusted me, just like I'd trusted him not to hurt me, to take care of me, to drag me out of the depths as I slowly drowned.

I owed him however much space he needed.

At the very least, things weren't awkward at staff meetings. My heart raced, sure, but for an entirely different reason these days. Overall, I woke up the following morning —and every morning since—feeling better than I had before the anniversary of my parents' murder. Still not 100 percent sure what to do about Benedict Hammond, I had finally made a decision, at the very least...

Trust my gut.

Trust my intuition.

Trust the gods to shine a big, fat, blinding spotlight on the solution when it was finally ready to be seen.

I had been a survivor since that psycho tried to burn me in my bed: I needed to put more faith in myself. Trust that when it was time to make a move, I'd know.

Hopefully. As long as my anxiety and wavering self-worth didn't get in the way.

For now, I figured it was acceptable, for the sake of

vengeance, to string Benedict Hammond along as necessary. Put on that fake smile. Nod. Make polite chitchat about shallow crap.

But I couldn't—wouldn't—let him in. He wanted to *know* me, but that wasn't happening.

Nor would I *ever* find time to go for that stupid fucking lunch he kept trying to push on me. No dates. Nothing private. Just—stay in his good books to keep his suspicions low.

Maybe even let him trap himself.

Self-incrimination.

Wouldn't that be satisfying?

As Alice unpacked her massive backpack, spreading her things throughout mine so she could hunker down for the next hour, I twisted around in my chair and did a quick scan of the nearby stacks. Nothing and no one as far as I could see but books and wooden shelves, which was just how I liked it. Sure, I enjoyed chatting with my kids, but not when I needed to get shit done on an encroaching deadline.

"So, how are things?" Alice and I spent a *lot* of time together, in and out of work hours, and this was the question I had been dying to ask for weeks. Unfortunately, I couldn't phrase it how I wanted without her assuming Bjorn and I gossiped about the Clíodhna incident behind closed doors, and if she thought that, *poof*, there went her trust in me.

Still, breaking curfew wasn't her *thing*, and last week I could have sworn she had a hickey on her neck—or a bruise from something more nefarious; it was substantial enough to be either.

And no matter the cause, I did *not* approve.

Alice was a good girl, and if someone was hurting her, or messing with her, or trying to turn her into a bad girl, they'd have my foot shoved so far up their ass everyone would see my toes wiggle when they talked.

A hand-knit scarf in Root Rot's school colors—maroon, gold, and white—draped her neck today, blocking my scrutiny when I turned it back on her.

"Oh, you know," she said with a sigh, arranging her pens and highlighters in stick-straight rows, "same old."

"Made any new connections lately?" Friends or otherwise. Despite my best efforts, she remained a bit of a loner around campus. Alice shrugged, unfazed by the insinuation.

"Not really." She dug into her backpack and hauled out the massive alchemy textbook that probably gave these kids premature back problems. "Same as always, you know?"

Slowly taking a sheet from each stack of parchment piled around me, I compiled my test prep booklets without looking, focused on her and chomping down on the insides of my cheeks. I couldn't be her only friend. I just couldn't. It wasn't... professional. And it wasn't good for her development. At thirteen, Alice was in a precarious position: a witch unable to cast, a teenager sporting a fresh batch of pimples and no new friends. Not ideal.

"And how is, you know..." I looked pointedly at her hands as she flipped through her textbook. "How are you doing? Feeling any new tingles?"

Cheeks pink, Alice pushed her textbook to the side now that she'd found her page, then grabbed her notebook and shook her head.

"Well, that's okay," I insisted, tapping my parchment stack on the table before reaching for the stapler. "It'll come."

"But how do you *know* that?" she whispered, watching me staple the corner of the new packet and set it on the pile of completed ones. I pointed the stapler at her, then arched an eyebrow and grinned when she finally met my eyes.

"Because witches and warlocks don't make human babies. They just don't." Unless her mom slept with a human, then *maybe*, just maybe, she had missed the magic gene entirely. I didn't know the circumstances, nor would I ever float it as a possibility. "It's genetics, Alice. You're a witch. Your magic is in there. Sometimes it's just a bit stubborn. Mine, for like a month when I first went to the academy, turned everything green. Just… No matter what spell I cast, whatever my magic touched turned green. It was a *nightmare*, but it sorted itself out. Yours will, too."

No telling whether stories of my own failings helped, but as she tucked her chair closer to the table, Alice beamed up at me, then grabbed her preferred silky black pen.

Only to stop just shy of touching its tip to her notebook.

"Can I tell you… a secret?"

Hands flying from stack to stack, I prepped another booklet with a slow nod. "Uh, sure. Go for it."

After a quick check over both shoulders, Alice leaned across the table, all giddy and adorable, the aggressive whitehead between her brows glaring at me like a third eye. "I met someone."

I fumbled with the stapler, crunching the staple in wrong enough that I'd need that little metal remover to get it out. "You—"

"A boy," she clarified, her eyes bright and her smile toothy. She wanted me to be excited for her. She wanted me to squeal and demand *deets*, because that was what friends did.

But I wasn't that kind of friend.

And like 99 percent of the teenage boys here were the *worst*, so…

"A… boy?" So that was the best I could do, eyebrows up as I tore the warped staple out, my tone dubious. Ever the smitten kitten, Alice smiled dreamily as my skepticism zipped right over her head.

"He's just *so* awesome," she gushed, and with the next

deep breath, I braced for a wave of teenage girl word-vomit. "And funny and smart and kind. He listens to me for *hours* and never complains, always asks such thoughtful questions. He wants to *know* me... I can't believe I got so lucky."

My heart dropped at the *know me* bit, but hopefully that stemmed from my own insecurities and not her reality. "Who is it?"

She turned bright red as she fiddled with her rebellious mop of brown curls. "Uh, can that stay secret a little while longer?"

Right. The full boyfriend package—in a teenager at Root Rot Academy? Sure. Sounded *totally* legit. Still, Alice had never been the type to embellish before despite her circumstances. She was awkward, sure, but she owned her opinions, her stories, and her trauma.

In her own way, anyway.

"Sure," I told her gently as I stapled that test prep packet all over again, getting it right this time. "You can tell me when you're ready—or not at all. Your decision."

She straightened, smile blooming once more and gaze soaring over my head. "Oh, hello, Professor Cedar!"

Gods. The hairs on the back of my neck finally stood up, a delayed reaction to his approach, and I stiffened at the first hint of his cologne in the air. Sandalwood. Normally the smell didn't make my stomach turn; common in men's scent products, I didn't mind it. Hell, Bjorn had a sandalwood-infused cologne that was to *die* for, the perfect complement to the rogue, manly smell he seemed to exude naturally. Throw in a splash of his dryer-fresh tweed and leather and just *unf*.

Perfection.

Maybe my body just had an aversion to Benedict Hammond overall, because anytime I caught a whiff of *his* sandalwood cologne, my gut looped and mouth watered like

I was about to vomit. Something in the mix just wasn't right —like him. Playing the nice guy around campus, but rotten to the core.

"Hello, Miss Alice," he boomed. The man was Canadian, same as me, but he sprinkled in a weird high-brow English accent every now and again—as if that made him cultured. I locked up tighter when his hand found my shoulder, clamping down and squeezing. "Professor Clarke. What a nice little corner you two have here."

Alien as it still felt to smile at him, I did it, my facial features relying on muscle memory, just like my hands as I carried on making prep booklets. Alice, meanwhile, looked at up him with more earnest affection, which I couldn't understand; Benedict was a supernatural snob, a man who only entertained the opinions of fellow witches and warlocks. Alice was one of us, sure, but in the eyes of many in our community, she was defective. The thought of him giving her the time of day, or any other special attention that made her all bright and bubbly, was almost laughable.

With trembling fingers, I grabbed paper after paper, stacking and tapping them, even as the blood drained from my face and static whispered around my skull. Whatever they were talking about, Alice animate and Benedict chuckling, was just white noise—because his hand was still there, on my shoulder, pressing down like we had that sort of relationship.

Like he could just... *touch* me.

I fucked up another staple when his thumb started to stroke my arm, slowly, softly, *barely* moving to outsiders but all I could feel as my body shifted into panic mode. Fight or flight. I might have decided to indulge him, to trust my gut that the right plan would fall into place at the right time to expose him, but the rest of me hadn't caught up with that yet.

The rest of me wanted to fight *and* fly—staple the shit out of his hand and then *run*.

I took a settling breath instead, one and then another, sinking into the mundane rhythm of stapling packets—and the memory of Jack's firm hand on my ass. Weird, to fall back on a grown warlock spanking you as a coping mechanism, but that night, the blazing sting had shone brighter than anything else. Somehow it had grounded me, centered my scattered focus, reminded me that I was *alive* and not drowning in a sea of grief and fear.

The sound of a book sliding off a shelf had me snapping my head to the left suddenly, chin *almost* brushing Benedict's arm. Down the nearby aisle stood a glowering Gavriel, a massive tome in his hand, dressed to the nines in his standard professional attire.

Only this time his lavender suit jacket had tails, which was just... a lot.

But he had the looks and confidence to pull it off, to seem effortlessly fashionable with his sideswept silvery-brown hair and a jawline that could cut glass.

Cheekbones that could carve diamonds.

And a scowl that probably sent students scattering to the winds.

His layered grey gaze flicked between me and Benedict, back and forth, back and forth, before he snapped the huge, weathered book shut and stalked toward us.

Oh. *Gods.* I shot him a pleading look *not* to draw attention to the fact that I was absolutely dying under Benedict's hand.

"Oi," he snapped, motioning to our table with the book and instantly silencing Alice and Benedict's conversation, "chatterbirds."

Alice giggled as she swiveled in her chair to face him. "It's chatter*boxes*, sir."

Gavriel feigned a little laugh, then rolled his eyes. "Right.

Whatever. This is a *library*." He charged directly into my personal bubble, not stopping until he was basically on top of me and Benedict, who was then forced to step back. The second his hand left my shoulder, I could breathe again. Gavriel, meanwhile, continued to glare like we were a bunch of misbehaving teenagers. "Either talk at a respectable volume, preferably not at all, or get out."

Alice's smile shriveled up, and Benedict huffed behind me. "This is *quite* inappropriate—"

"My house," Gavriel sneered, "my rules."

A tense quiet followed, and while I didn't dare look back to see how the inevitable staring contest was going, Alice watched the pair for me, brow furrowed and pen gripped tightly.

"Well then," Benedict Hammond growled at long last, the nice-guy façade falling away for just a moment—at least in his tone. Then, after clearing his throat, it was back, and he patted the table with his index finger, his nonchalant smile crumbling around the edges. "Until next time, ladies."

"Bye, Professor," Alice squeaked. Over my shoulder, I watched the warlock dip into an unnecessary bow, like he and Gavriel had been in on this little display. His dark gaze slid to me, but I only offered a thin, fleeting smile, then my back, waiting, tensed, until his curt footsteps disappeared down a nearby aisle.

Shaking his head, Gavriel watched him go, then glanced down at me. Impossible to read, this fae, whenever something serious happened. Put him in a situation where he could flirt and schmooze and the guy was an open book. With Alice staring at us, however, I couldn't press the issue. Instead, I grinned up at him—genuine, this time—and fluttered my lashes, then made the motion of zipping my lips.

Which earned me another eye roll.

And a faint, *barely* there smirk.

The world became routine again when he left us, Alice sinking into her alchemy homework, me stapling test prep packets and organizing the massive stacks by year.

The rest of the day carried on as usual, too, dinner followed by my early evening class with fourth years, now a week into our new potions unit. It ended with the usual stroll back to the flat with Bjorn around curfew. Chats about our students, a brief indulgence in wine and reality TV drama.

I only deviated just before bed, opting for a shower.

A scalding hot shower, wherein I scrubbed the shoulder he had touched *raw*.

But even then, I could still feel him, still lugged Benedict fucking Hammond around with me.

Sore and exhausted, I went to bed hoping, praying, that the gods would show me some guidance soon—because the nonchalance, string-him-along thing was bound to take its toll.

One way or another.

GAVRIEL

Right. Easing back in my office chair, I closed my eyes and counted the bells chiming through the castle, each stroke designating the hour.

Seven.

Eight.

Nine.

My eyes snapped open. Nine. *Only* nine? Scowling, I lurched for my laptop and smacked the space bar, the screen flickering back to life. Sure enough, curfew had *just* come into effect.

Fuck *me*. Two bottles of pricey Merlot deep and it was only nine o'-fucking-clock.

Tipsy, alone, empty inside, I slammed my laptop shut and sighed, the exhale turning into a long, raging groan. All the little librarians outside my door would have gone by now, their shift ended a half hour ago. I usually stayed on until curfew, but good fucking luck to any of the urchins in need of bibliographic assistance at this late hour; if it really mattered, they would have gone to the information desk sooner.

I'd finished all my work for the day ages ago. Managed the budget and sent that off to Prewett. Skimmed employee evaluations that I'd had my crew perform on each other—rather savage, some of the reviews. Done my daily cataloguing. Tinkered with the back-end data for our online resources that a few of the more human-tech-savvy students relied on. Filed several boxes of new arrivals throughout the library. Monitored things. Told a few loudmouths to shut the fuck up already—kicked three of them out for hurling paper balls at a den mother while she tried to help a first year with the computer.

All in a fucking day's work here at Root Rot. Ordinarily, the *real* work began at night. Sure, I might indulge in a smoke after dinner. Drink to numb *everything*, but I could set aside all the mundane bullshit of the day—so much bitching among my underlings, like our job was *so* taxing—and invest my time, energy, and focus into what mattered: finding students worthy of Darkwell Academy.

Couldn't send them by force, mind you.

All about free will with that smug fallen angel.

Had to seduce and butter up and coax—

But I had returned the batch of files I'd nicked from the admin wing days ago because all the new arrivals this term were shit.

I mean. Shit for my purposes. Fewer black souls roaming the castle corridors these days now that Leroy and his girl had been dethroned. Thus far, no one came close to their level of cool-kid prestige.

Or Lucy's skill.

So, yeah. Just great. Just *fucking* great.

Blinking the blur out of my tired eyes, I stood and meandered over to the window. Ice gathered in the corners, December just as cold this year as it had been the last three.

Not a soul in the highlands tonight save the poor security bastards on perimeter detail—

A light stretched across the back grounds, warm and soft compared to the savagery of the surrounding landscape. Yellow and inviting, it stemmed from the greenhouses, strings of lightbulbs stretched around the enchanted outdoor vegetable and herb gardens.

Alecto must have been down there, braving the elements to tend to her flock.

With nothing else to do, pipe smoked and wine fridge empty, my mind drifted toward the next best distraction: fantastic sex. Even though Bjorn's rescue elevated my reputation around the academy, I just couldn't be bothered with the women who fawned over me.

To most of them, I was the hero—for however much longer was anyone's guess. But at first, I'd milked that for all its worth. Even the ones who were cross with me for one reason or another came crawling back, and I basked in the attention, the grabbers-on boosting my ego, my worth... albeit temporarily. Still, this was how it would feel as a noble fae one day in the Ash Court: creatures I could barely have a conversation with licking my boots—my cock—for a flicker of my attention.

But it got old.

In a few days, actually, I was over it, but I stretched it on longer than my patience allowed because *this* was the life I eventually wanted—wasn't it?

Tonight, when I thought of carnal distraction, I didn't want a simpering, mewling, hero-worshipping woman in my bed.

I craved a fight.

Passion.

Anger and brutality and a fury's nails raking up my chest,

down my back, her teeth on my neck until I eventually pinned her—

Right. Evening plans sorted, then.

Leaving my minimalistic office behind, I stumbled down to the outdoors in a haze. It took a lot more than two bottles of *human* wine to intoxicate a fae, but tonight the alcohol made me more honest than usual, more open to myself about my own wants and needs.

I'd have to get a grip on that before I kissed her.

Tuck it all away so she couldn't use it against me.

Assaulted by the bitter night air, I trundled all the way to the main greenhouse, steeling my emotions—only to find it empty. Lights on, nobody home. Scowling, I checked the other two, cupping my hands over the glass and peering inside. Greenery greeted me, the walls fogged with the temperature difference, and it wasn't until something clanked way to the left that I realized she was outside.

Quiet as a mouse but swift as a fae, I crept to the corner of the main greenhouse, next to which stretched rows of raised gardens—and in the thick of it, Alecto. Something in the fertilizer made the foliage immune to winter's kiss; it had rained this morning, which had turned to snow around noon, then back to freezing rain come supper. As the temperatures took their usual nightly plunge, ice built up, frost spread, but Alecto's vegetables thrived, her bunches of herbs and spices spilling over the sides of their wooden beds.

Looking a bit wild down here—someone needed to tame those things.

Which, to her credit, Alecto seemed to be doing, working her way through a lavender bush, snipping and pruning and gathering a bushel of the stalks. Bathed in the warm glow of the little lights strung around all the beds and up to the greenhouses, she looked rather... *cute* tonight.

Not a word I used often, nor one I associated with a

fury, but sporting an earthly autumnal color palette—oranges and browns and ruddy reds—and all those layers gave her this bundled-up, adorable sheen that I rarely appreciated. Usually she was quite fashionable, but this look was soft. Cozy. Layered with scarves that clamped her curls down around her ears like wild muffs. The fingerless gloves gave her an advantage with harvesting, maneuverable enough to manage the scissors, and her brown boots had this rustic buckle on them that really... *did* something to me.

What the actual fuck.

I wasn't here for sweet and cozy, for cheeks kissed by the chill and flyaway curls.

After cracking both sides of my neck, decidedly more sober in the cold but in no mood to retreat inside, I waited until she put down the clippers before I made my move. Gathering her harvested lavender to her chest, the witch turned *just* before I pounced, nostrils flaring, eyes wide, breath catching.

"Gavriel—"

I caught her parted lips in a kiss that made her moan, her lashes fluttering, her folded arms and precious lavender crushed between us. Snaking an arm around her waist, I dragged her to me, forced her up on her toes and kissed her deep—hard but desperately passionate, the rhythm coming far too easy.

And she kissed me back.

Stars above as my witness, she kissed me, lips pliant, tongue tangling and tussling and showing what fire she possessed beneath all those many *cute* layers. My free hand cupped her cheek, thumb stroking the chilled flesh. Just as my fingers wove into her mane, however, Alecto inhaled sharply—then tried to pull away. I held firm, enjoying the struggle, the fight, the push and pull between us, cock already swelling with interest at the thought of some rough and tumble in the conservatory.

Only she *really* fought, and with one sharp twist, she jammed her elbow into my chest, then staggered back—but only because I *let* her. My lips quirked at the sight of hers all red and plump, and I prowled after her retreating figure, ready to *take*—and perhaps give, just a little—when the witch shook her head and thrust her lavender harvest between us as she once had her wand.

"No," she said breathlessly, holding my gaze and shaking her head. My barking laugh echoed through the gardens, and I did a quick scan of our surroundings. Had she spotted someone watching? No. Not a soul to be found, not a single supernatural aura shimmering in the ether. Totally alone, us two.

"Come on—"

"*No*," she rasped, firmer this time as she marched backward to counteract my approach. She then stabbed the lavender at me, brandishing the bunch like a sword, and hurled this *look* that insisted she was serious. Really. Her. Serious—about *not* fucking? The witch who let me pound her into the courtyard wall all those months back after exchanging *maybe* five words total? The one who permitted me to bend her over the table inside her greenhouse and then screamed—literally shrieked—through an orgasm that had her clamping around my cock like a vise?

Right. Sure. "Look, I haven't pinched a single thing from you since—"

"It's not that." Lavender still drooped between us, Alecto brushed a few curls back with a huff that briefly fogged in front of her flushed face. Frowning, I crossed my arms and arched an eyebrow. Was this a new game for us? Did she want me to fight harder? Or... did she prefer that I beg?

Under the right circumstances, I'd consider it.

At least it was something different.

"Well, what is it, then?" I demanded. "You're attracted to me."

Her smirk gave me hope for a swift resolution to... *this*. "Yup."

"You want to fuck me." I cocked my head, making a show of looking her up and down, letting her feel *desired*. "And vice versa."

She finally dropped the lavender, arm falling to her side, then pinched the bridge of her nose. "Oh my *gods*, Gavriel." After taking a moment, perhaps to collect herself given the oddly resolute twinkle in her eye when she straightened, Alecto took yet another deep breath before squaring off with me. "Okay, so I've been thinking—"

"Didn't I tell you that was dangerous?"

Her cheeks might have hollowed and her eyes might have narrowed, but none of that detracted from her impish grin. Clearly my charms still worked on her—so, what the fuck was she doing?

"We're really similar," Alecto started, slow and cautious, like she was taking care with her word choice. Before she could get any further, however, I laughed. Not because I found the statement funny, but because it struck an uncomfortable chord in me that I wasn't sure how else to process. Alecto readjusted her massive reddish-brown scarf, waiting for my cool chuckles to fade, then added, "We use sex to cope with feeling like shit."

"That's..." True. Painfully true. "That's rubbish."

"No, it's not," she fired back without missing a beat. "We use sex and alcohol—*Mr. Merlot*, I can smell you from here— and a surly attitude to push people away when we feel bad about ourselves, and it's not... healthy."

This uppity little—

How *dare* she read me like an open book? Who gave her

the right to possess that sort of insight? "Well, that's not for you to decide."

"I decide for *me*." Alecto stepped back again to counter my third attempt to close the distance between us. "No more. It's... I can't keep doing the same old crap, and it's not good for you, either."

Everything inside me hardened to ice. "If I wanted a psych eval, I'd have an actual conversation with my roommate."

Honestly, Seamus would have a fucking field day picking around inside my brain. Psychology was his secret obsession, the bookshelves around our flat crawling with human tomes about manipulating the mind. Bit weird, actually.

"Just..." Alecto licked her lips, her pretty speech floundering a little. "If you want to talk, we can talk, but we shouldn't..." She gestured between us with the lavender. "You know. It's not healthy."

What she's really saying is that you *aren't healthy for* her.

You're a disease, Gavriel.

No one wanted you back home, and no one wants you here—

My jaw clenched as anger and hurt melded into something foul in my gut.

Fantastic.

Nothing like searching for comfort and walking away feeling worse than ever.

"Fine," I sneered as I looked her up and down again, this time with such venom that she blanched. Preferring to keep the final word for myself, I wheeled around and marched for the hillside staircase, ego in need of coddling somewhere private. Seconds later, her boots clomped across the damp cobblestone after me, and I slowed, just a touch, at the thought of Alecto seeing the error of her ways—charging after me, grabbing my arm, kissing me as I'd kissed her.

Deeply.

Passionately.

Two warped creatures finding each other—

"Gavriel, we can be friends." But that didn't happen. She had already given up, her chase halfhearted, and I stopped abruptly, *friends* sounding like nails on a chalkboard. She huffed again like I was being ridiculous—I most certainly was, but like fuck I'd ever admit to it—and then cleared her throat. "You're kind of a rude asshole sometimes, but that doesn't scare me. I don't care that you're a dick, because then it means *I* can be a dick too when I spend all my time... not being one to the people who deserve it."

What the fuck was that supposed to mean? Stiff as a board, I pivoted around, but only halfway, like I couldn't be bothered to give her my full attention.

Never mind that my traitorous heart was hanging on her every word, starved for friendship, acceptance, a bond that I hadn't had since—

"We can be friends." But I couldn't afford that sort of attachment here, not when the only purpose this realm and its inhabitants served was to further my own desires. No. I... *No.* Alecto rolled her eyes and threw her hands up, lavender whooshing through her dramatics. "Gavriel, *I* can be your friend."

Where was the cruel whisper now? Had that shut it up for good? Beneath the offer, beneath her simple words, lay the truth: Alecto Clarke was willing to accept me for me, for the moody bastard I had become over these many trying years, hardened by hurt and betrayal. She stood there, all cozy and cute, windswept with swollen lips, her vanilla scent fused to my suit, and offered me her hand.

I didn't *have* to do this alone.

But if I kept my heart to myself, no one could stomp all over it. I had no need for *friends*.

Bjorn was my friend.

Barely.

But we could part ways tonight and never speak again, and while I would remember the vampire fondly, I wouldn't grieve as I had for those who haunted my past.

"I don't want to be your *friend*," I said coldly. "I don't *need* friends."

Alecto hugged the lavender to her chest, olive branch on fire, and a sick part of me rejoiced. *Hurt them before they hurt you.* And I had hurt her, her golden gaze suddenly glossy, but a beat later her features hardened.

Just like me.

We were similar. *Too* similar, it seemed.

"Well," she fired back with a watery laugh, "that's really fucking sad."

It was.

Sadder still, my heart ached at the look in her eyes.

It hurt me to hurt her.

And… that was just unacceptable.

You fucking idiot.

Ah, there he was, that cruel whisper.

You selfish bastard.

Steeling myself, I turned and flipped her off over my shoulder, then blitzed back to the castle in a burst of fae speed, spirited along by unseen wings all the way up to my flat.

My empty flat.

Where I barricaded myself in my bedroom, door locked, and drank another two bottles of wine to fall asleep. To forget.

And to punish myself, because tomorrow's hangover was going to be an even bigger bitch than I was tonight.

BJORN

As a den mother escorted the last students out of the dining hall, someone finally mercy-killed the music. *Finally*, the classical drivel that had been tinkling from the speakers for the last three hours vanished, and as the main doors swung shut, Yule came to a booming end, the rest of us trapped inside until the mess was tidied. No one needed to be told what to do: we had been given our orders at last Sunday's staff meeting, led by Iris Prewett with a gaggle of smirking admin girls.

Frowning, I undid the top button of my dress shirt, then loosened my snowflake tie as I scanned the hall I'd been booted out of hours ago. My task for the evening had been to skulk in the shadows, on the lookout for students making good use of the darker underground corners. I'd found no one, security tighter than it had been on Samhain, not even a whiff of liquor in the air tonight.

Courtesy of me, apparently. Iris had implied as much when she first announced her role in organizing and executing this year's Yule gala. No one had said it in so many words, but all this—tonight's failure—linked back to me.

My kidnapping.

My crucifixion in the moors.

The subsequent firing of almost all our security boys, replaced by warlocks who were only half as good and nowhere near as friendly—but it was the best Jack could do on short notice, so of course no one blamed him.

Me.

I was at fault here, and I felt the accusatory stares even now as I meandered across the dining hall, lights up, party over, fun nowhere to be found.

The Yule sabbat took place on the twenty-first night of December every year, the darkest of the season. Even back in *my* day we did something to celebrate light in the darkness, us humans gathered around fires, exchanging tokens, decorating the odd tree to appease the forest spirits. In this century, witches and warlocks were the ones to make a big deal of it, but I could get behind the message. Even in our darkest hour, there was *light* worth celebrating. Goodness. Hope. Family and friends, humor and song.

It was supposed to be cheery.

The admin clique had decorated the dining hall in blue, silver, white, and black. Lots of ice motifs everywhere, all hard angles and jagged edges. Judging from the earlier spread, our pre-gala feast had been sumptuous as always—but subdued. There wasn't the excitement of Samhain. No music for the kids. No opening waltz or buffet tables of sweets.

Sugar cookies as far as the eye could see, mind you, which were rumored to be Iris's favorite.

But otherwise, it had been a bland, boring affair, and every time I poked my head in throughout the night, there were more students seated at tables than jumping around the dance floor. Lots of chins propped on fists, frowns, yawns, and tired eyes, just waiting for it to be over so they could go back to their dorms.

Hands in my pockets, I sauntered farther into the hall, zeroing in on my flatmate as she dusted snowflake confetti off the drinks table and into a garbage bin. Worst of all, every staff member had been given a job. We weren't allowed to enjoy the night but had to *work* it instead.

Kept us all accounted for, Iris had insisted, once again side-eyeing me like this was a favor.

So, even though I hadn't spoken to anyone in hours, the general mood of the castle tonight suggested Yule had *not* been a hit this year.

We could have planned something spectacular, Alecto and me. Samhain, despite its obvious hiccup, had been the talk of the student body for weeks after. I slowed near one of the swan ice sculptures, loitering behind it but tall enough to see over it—to admire the witch who had stolen bits and pieces of my heart for months now.

Despite this disaster of an evening, there was one shining light.

Her.

Alecto was... exquisite. Having taken a detour from her Samhain gown, my flatmate swapped gold for silver, perfectly on theme for the evening's event. Where the last dress had sat like armor, metallic and structured, the brocade cape heavy and the shoulders pointed, tonight's was all softness. Feminine. *Luscious.* A-line with a tulle skirt billowing to the ground like a waterfall made of clouds, even the fitted bodice seemed graceful. She had gone back to feathers, much to my original dismay, but these sat better than the black raven plumes on the dress I had once rejected. They curled over her breasts in a sweetheart neckline, then fit to the swell of her generous hips like a glove, reminiscent of the midnight sky on Yule, taking the dress's silver and turning it to a rich Aegean blue. Like her skirt, her sleeves moved freely, loosely, generous bells that tightened around her wrists, just sheer enough to add some interest.

Yikes.

I knew way too much about gowns for my own good.

My flatmate had spent the better part of an hour taming her curls with a hot styling glamor, and although they had some of their spring back now, they still rolled elegantly down her back, loose and soft. A glittery snowflake headband kept them off her face, cheekbones dotted with tiny faux diamonds.

She had been the goddess Freyja for Samhain, the sun in all its glory.

Tonight, she was Máni, supreme goddess of the moon, outshining all around her without even trying.

Actually. No. The whole look had taken a lot of effort. I had to credit her for that—for her patience, for her kindness of shyly asking me to zip her into that gown.

And it was a fucking shame she had been stuck behind a table all night. While I stalked the empty corridors for hours, Alecto had been relegated to the drinks table, and under her watch, nothing had been spiked this time. Still, she deserved to shine. In that dress, she ought to be the center of attention, whirling about on the dance floor with a crowd of adoring onlookers.

Although… Preferably not a crowd of teenage boys—

Never mind.

She looked beautiful, and this was what I had wanted for her on Samhain—for *us*. A dance floor. A special night. A waltz and a kiss in the moonlight.

Back then, I had a Plan B. If her body language pushed back against the idea, I would have respected that.

Tonight, there was only Plan A, sprouting out of nowhere the longer I watched her from behind the ice sculpture. Since my attack, we had grown closer. Spent more time together. Laughed more.

Allowed for lingering glances across a room.

Touched frequently, sometimes playful, sometimes not.

As smitten as I was with her, the first woman in centuries to snare my wandering heart, I had suspected the feeling was mutual ever since...

Well, ever since I came to and found her glossy-eyed with relief, stakes scattered around us and her fingers slick with my blood.

Forgetting the why-nots, the cons of changing the dynamic between us and sullying the sacred flatmate bond, I moved. Strolled toward her. Seized what had to be our second chance.

Partially bent over the table, Alecto had her back to me as I approached, reaching for empty cups and tossing them in the bin at her side. Weeks ago, I might have hesitated, but a flicker of my old self scorched through my veins tonight—a reminder that I was a warrior who *took*.

She jerked upright when I tapped between her shoulder blades, whirling around with wide eyes, heartbeat skyrocketing before settling into its beautiful, familiar rhythm. With a grin, I dropped into a dramatic bow, one arm outstretched toward the dance floor, and when my gaze flicked up to hers, I found her biting back a smile.

"I believe I owe you a waltz, Professor Clarke," I drawled, stuck in the bow, waiting, still as stone while she considered me. Nibbling at her lower lip, Alecto peered around the hall briefly before dropping her golden gaze back to me. Her heart pitter-pattered—for *me*. An expert in reading that precious organ, I could decipher the nuances between panic and interest.

Usually, she pitter-pattered for Jack.

Sometimes Gavriel, though more often than not that dance came with a scowl.

And I understand that: both men were handsome in their own right, with qualities that made many hearts pitter-patter around the castle.

But tonight, hers did so for me.

Alecto's lips spread into a lovely smile, and she nodded, finally putting me out of my misery. "I believe you do, Professor Asulf."

All around us, colleagues cleansed the dining hall of a failed Yule. With or without magic, they swept the floors, took down decorations, stacked empty plates and rearranged empty tables. Music off, lights on, the gala had lost its sparkle, and a dull roar carried through the space, weary conversations slowly replacing the classical piano that no teenager wanted to dance to—ever. A few looked our way, the rumor mill on fire. I'd heard whispers that Alecto and I fucked regularly, that we had pulled strings to share a flat together, that we were *lovers*, always said with a sneer.

Fuck them.

I didn't care about rumors.

I cared about *her*—and this was for her. Standing tall and proud in my black suit, my ridiculous skinny tie stamped with snowflakes similar to those on her headband, I offered Alecto my hand without a care who saw.

And she took it. This witch who had coaxed me out of the darkness, who helped me find my feet after drowning in doubt and self-loathing for weeks, accepted my hand. Touched me in front of the others, her fingers gliding over my palm, more graceful and delicate than they had ever been during our practice waltzes.

I owed her so much.

When I had doubted myself, my character, my strength, she had been there. That was all I needed—maybe all I had *ever* needed: someone who stood by my side, whether I thought myself worthy or not. Alecto didn't care that I had been kidnapped by a bunch of children. She cared that I had nearly *died*. She was happy to have me back.

At the end of the day, that was what mattered.

When my hand curled around hers, there was that sweet pitter-patter again.

That mattered, too.

Her smile subtle, her glances shy, her body gravitated toward mine, cleanup duty abandoned.

Smitten.

I felt it in my bones, and I saw it in her eyes.

"Uhm..." Alecto cleared her throat, suddenly searching for the corner speakers with a frown. "Actually, there's no music, so—"

"It's fine," I rumbled back, guiding her toward the dance floor. "I can still hear it."

"That's called insanity, mate." Gavriel breezed by out of nowhere, arms full of stacked, used plastic cups, carrying with him the scent of sticky eggnog and that strange virgin spiced rum everyone had avoided like the plague. Alecto glowered briefly at the fae's back, then refocused on me, cheeks rosy and her hand clutching at mine like she was afraid I'd slip away.

I gripped back in kind, assuring her I wouldn't—that I was here to stay.

As I steered her onto the dance floor, I imagined the music. Pretended it wasn't just the shallow piano that had accompanied tonight's failings, but a full orchestra to serenade us in the waltz we should have had on Samhain. Alecto followed my lead, falling into the familiar footwork that we had once practiced around the flat, her hand in mine, the other resting delicately on my shoulder.

My lips twitched, about to blossom into a massive teasing grin that would make her self-conscious, so I held back.

Because she was rusty.

Clumsy.

Head down, she stared at our feet for the first few gentle rounds, until my hand smoothed across her lower back and guided her closer. Her eyes snapped up, lips slightly parted, but then she inched closer and burrowed into my chest. The stance would have sent shock waves through the Victorian community that so loved their waltzes, our bodies too near, our gazes too soft and intimate. Not friends. *Decidedly* not just friends anymore—this proclaimed it to the world.

Something more.

She…

It wasn't just my imagination. It wasn't just a read on her heartbeat, a guessing game I had been playing with myself since the day I first laid eyes on her. Alecto couldn't fake this, the fluidity of our movements, the ease of each round, her fingers suddenly toying with my shirt collar.

She…

She couldn't.

Right?

Music whispered out of the speakers. No longer just in my head, something classical and layered started up out of nowhere, and on my next turn, I spied Jack seated at one of the few remaining round tables, fussing with the tablet that was both DJ and orchestra. Although the beats should have provided a better road map for us to follow, Alecto and I slowed together, the breezy waltz devolving into rather intimate rocking.

Our eyes locked.

Her heart beat slow and steady, colored by the odd pitter-patter that set my body on fire.

"I think we've paid our Yule dues," I murmured when the

song finally trailed off—then abruptly died. Over my shoulder, we found Iris stabbing at the tablet with a scowl, Jack nowhere to be found. Alecto ducked back around me, hiding behind my much broader frame with a giggle.

"Agreed," she whispered conspiratorially, cheeks a delectable pink, her hand still in mine as the other slid down my chest and settled over my dead heart. To keep *something* from the Root Rot grapevine, I didn't slide my fingers along her bodice as I wished, didn't follow the luscious curve of her hips, the slope in her waist, didn't walk them up to the dip of her throat.

I placed my hand over hers instead, fingers curling ever so slightly around it. "Do you want to get out of here?"

This was it.

That *moment*, the one to change everything.

Alecto's mischievous smirk disappeared, lower lip snagged between her teeth, and she glanced between our clasped hands, my lips, and my eyes before shooting a longing look to the main doors. Try as I might, I couldn't concentrate on her heartbeat—couldn't separate myself from the anxiety of waiting for a response.

Her bashful little nod set my frosty heart ablaze.

"Yeah," she whispered, fingers coiling around my tie, "let's get out of here…"

I didn't wait for her to second-guess herself. Sweeping her under my arm, I marched us both for the main doors, hand eventually settling on her back.

Head held high.

Heart happy.

More than smitten…

Falling.

Falling fast without a parachute.

And loving every second of it.

13

ALECTO

I had no idea where this was headed—or what had come over me in the dining hall. Tonight had just been such a shitshow, and not because anything went *wrong*, per se. All things considered, Yule had gone off without a hitch: solid speech from Jack, epic dinner with individual teeny Yule log cakes for dessert, then a dance in a transformed dining hall that looked like an ice queen's palace.

But the kids had been miserable, totally unimpressed with the music choices, the early curfew, and the grossly watered-down eggnog. From the moment Iris had announced she and her admin cronies would be organizing things, nixing the student council who usually put on the larger sabbat celebrations, I'd expected as much. Iris Prewett might have been the bitchiest witch I had ever met in a professional setting, but at least she stayed consistent— always ready to meet your expectations, good or bad.

Trapped behind the drinks table all night, I found no amount of smiling or joking with my kids made a difference. By the end of it, when the lights came up and the music died, I was just... exhausted. From the performance, pretending this was on par with Samhain when it was clearly a snoozefest. From the weather, the highlands drowning in frigid rain for the last three weeks. From midterms and a new batch of moody, surly, angry kids whose covens or packs hadn't wanted to deal with during the holidays.

From Benedict Hammond sniffing around me at every turn.

From pretending to be flattered at the attention, if only to keep him on the line.

Just—wiped out.

Then along came Bjorn and it all disappeared. This man trailing after me in the dimly lit staff tower stairwell, this vampire holding up my dress *not* so he could sneak a peek but so it didn't drag through the dust—he was everything I wanted at the end of a shit day. His smile. His warmth. The way his eyes still managed to be soft and cozy and welcoming despite being the iciest of blues.

At a time like this, I just wanted him to hold me.

Whisper in my ear. Crack a joke that only we were in on. Smile. *Look* at me like he always did when he thought I didn't notice.

He was the port in the storm, my constant safety net, my fuzzy, weighted blanket.

Most of all, in nothing more than a look, Bjorn made me feel like the center of the universe—the center of *his* universe.

No one had ever done that before. Not past flings. Not previous boyfriends. Not my grandparents, who loved me unconditionally but were never very warm.

They saw too much of my parents in me, maybe, having my mom's eyes and my dad's laugh. I never went without, but I never quite got what I needed emotionally, either.

Enter Bjorn—who looked at me like I was the sun, eyes full of wonder. Who waltzed without music, who swept me away from the dining hall with his hand snug on my lower back, our friendship on the backburner for something *more*.

I'd pushed it all down—the physical attraction, the soulmate potential I saw in him. Fought it. Pretended it wasn't there. Told myself over and over again that friendships were forever, while flings with your roommate screwed *everything* up.

But this didn't feel wrong.

It didn't feel like we were screwing everything up with our fingers loosely entwined, me leading the way up the winding staircase, a breathtaking vampire at my back.

There to catch me if I fell.

That was Bjorn.

I would never risk him, but as the air crackled all around us, tense with excitement and promise and anticipation...

This felt *right*.

So, fuck it.

Maybe we went back to the flat and cuddled on the couch until I fell asleep.

Maybe he kissed me up against the door.

Maybe I hauled him into my room and kept him all to myself until sunset tomorrow.

Whatever happened, happened.

Things had always come naturally to us. We hadn't said anything since leaving the dining hall, cleanup duties forgotten, and, frankly, we hadn't *needed* to say anything. Comfortable in the electricity, we had drifted to the staff tower together, our hands seeking each other out on the stairs.

And now we were almost at the fourth floor, almost home, and gone were the fears of the past, the anxieties about the future. He put me in the now; it was one of the greatest gifts this vampire could ever give—and he had no fucking clue how much it meant to me.

Heart in my throat, I led him slowly around the final turn, the soft click of my heels echoing off the stone. Anytime I glanced back, just a little peek over my shoulder, I found his gaze on my ass.

Fair enough.

Despite the flouncy tulle, I *was* adding an extra sway in my hips—because that was where this night had taken us.

Up these stairs, right onto the landing, and—

Oh, *fuck*.

I staggered to a sudden stop, one foot caught on the last step, eyes wide and heart hammering.

Benedict Hammond leaned on our flat door, swathed in a fitted white suit that felt strangely modern for his traditional tastes, clutching a bouquet of long-stemmed white roses.

Uh. *What*. The fuck.

His thin lips twitched into a sneer, and, glowering, he pushed off the door and marched straight for me.

And for the first time since I had stumbled into him in this very stairwell, I held my ground without *forcing* myself to, standing tall and wearing a confused, albeit startled, expression that only seemed to piss him off more.

"Where the hell have you been, Alecto?"

The accusation—because it sure as fuck wasn't a question, no matter the inflection at the end—threw me for a loop, and I jerked my hand out of Bjorn's as I climbed onto the landing. "W-what?"

"Tonight was supposed to be something *special*," Benedict snarled, jostling the roses as if to prove a point. "I thought we were finally on the same page."

"I… *What*?"

"I'll give you two a moment," Bjorn muttered as he sidestepped this farce and headed for the door. Head down. Back to me. Sounding weird and off and put out and *no*. Benedict did *not* get to ruin this for us.

"No, Bjorn," I sputtered, reaching out for him, "wait—"

But he was already inside, the door closing softly behind him. Fury thrummed through my veins with every raging beat of my heart, because how the *fuck* could he leave me out here with Benedict? How could he look at this absurd situation, assume the fucking *worst*, and walk away?

Bjorn was better than that.

Benedict, meanwhile, hadn't so much as glanced his way, and he didn't seem fazed by the vampire's absence. Instead, he stalked into my eyeline, *right* into my face, and shoved the rose bouquet into my numb hands. I instinctively grabbed hold of them, pleased that the stems had lost their thorns at some point.

"I waited all night for you," Benedict sneered. He swept a hand over his slicked-back hair, dark eyes darting around like he didn't want an audience for this particular conversation.

Same, asshole.

Also, it was barely pushing eleven o'clock.

Fucking chill.

"I..." *Want to slit your throat and watch you bleed out.* "I literally have no idea what is happening right now."

I mean, I hadn't been blackout drunk lately, so there was no way I would have forgotten a conversation about us meeting up privately for Yule.

Because drunk or not, I *never* would have agreed to it.

Not only was this warlock bigot a murdering psychopath, but he was a *delusional* murdering psychopath.

Great.

"You know what's happening between us," Benedict whispered heatedly as he shoved a trembling finger in my face. His mouth arced into a manic smile, but his black eyes burned bright and hot enough to make my knees wobble—to remind me that as much as I hated him, there was a reason to fear him, too. "Don't deny it. We've been dancing around this for weeks now, and here you are, holding some vampire's hand—"

"Please leave." It took every ounce of self-control I had not to scream it in his face. As desperate as I was to argue, to deny this ridiculous claim and state—for a fact—that we hadn't made plans of *any* kind for tonight, there was no point. He was too worked up, already foaming at the mouth, and nothing I said or did now would change that.

Well.

If I fell to my knees and begged for forgiveness, that would probably make all this stop.

Apologize profusely, maybe even *kiss* him.

But then I'd vomit up that slightly too-sweet Yule log dessert cake—and I liked this dress.

Bjorn was the only man I wanted to kiss tonight, and this scumbag had chased him away with his fucking psychosis.

Jaw clenched tight enough to make the muscles flare, Benedict just glared down at me. In the last five and a half months, I had learned a lot about the warlock who'd torn my world to shreds. Tonight, I could add another adjective to the list: bully. From the way he invaded my personal space, used his size to intimidate, chewed me out in front of my roommate for no reason other than his fragile ego had been bruised and his delusion shattered—Benedict Hammond was a fucking bully.

I didn't put up with bullies. Not in my classroom, and certainly not at my front door.

"Now," I said firmly, stepping aside and pointing to the shadowy stairwell beyond the landing. "Leave—*now*."

"We can be so much *more*, Alecto," he told me with a shake of his head and a patronizing sigh. His voice might have softened as he meandered toward the steps, but his aura sizzled out a warning like an electric barbed-wire fence.

Touch him and I was toast. "A warlock of my prestige, a witch of your talent and beauty—we could really *be* something."

A few steps down, he rounded in place and planted a hand on the wall, pausing as if giving me one last chance to realize my mistake. I might have started to shake, my insides a furious mess, but I held my ground, expression frosty and body itching for a fight. Ten painfully long seconds later, Benedict shook his head again and turned away.

"I'm so disappointed in you."

I stood there, trembling and listening to his footsteps on the stone, each one an assault. Misty-eyed with righteous *fury*, when I finally blinked, hot wet tracks sliced down my cheeks.

"*Fuck* you." Whether he heard that or not was anyone's guess, the curse leaving my lips like a wolf's low warning growl, but the footsteps stopped—briefly—then started up again. A moment later, the portrait door four floors down slammed shut.

Like he had any right to be angry at *me*, disappointed with *me*. If anything, I *owned* every drop of rage and disappointment with *both* the men involved in this interaction, and, still clutching the white roses, I stormed into our flat like a hurricane.

Silence and Bjorn's closed bedroom door greeted me. No lights in the bathroom. No glow of the TV. No socked feet dangling over the edge of the couch. Still shell-shocked, I went straight over and tapped my knuckles on his door.

Nothing. No response, not even a floorboard creak.

What the *fuck*?

Was there something in the air tonight that made Root Rot men behave irrationally? One that turned them into idiots who just refused to *listen*?

I knocked again, louder and firmer this time, but couldn't

bring myself to call his name. He knew it was me. He could probably hear my heartbeat whumping between my ears, pounding in my throat. Still shaking, I glared down at the roses, furious—but also suddenly terrified of what had just happened. Benedict's rage over nothing threw a wrench in my plans to string him along, because maybe all my tepid smiles and fake laughs had hooked him harder than I'd thought.

And Bjorn wasn't here to save me this time. No raft. No life preserver. No weighted blanket at the end of a shit day. He was just... gone.

As much as he gave me with his attention, he could take, too, and with a snap of his fingers, my world could fall apart.

Did he think Benedict and I were some secret couple?

As if I wouldn't have already told him—

Maybe the argument had given him the chance to rethink things. Maybe he was doing what I should have done in the dining hall: put a stop to this before we changed, before we chose the dead-end road to nowhere. Second thoughts, regrets, doubts, a desire not to ruin what we had—all valid. All things he was allowed to feel, of course.

There were so many logical, rational reasons *not* to push beyond our friendship.

If I lost him because of bullshit like this, I might never recover.

As a friend, he would always be there.

Crossing that line was a risk—one that didn't always pay off.

But he wasn't *just* a friend. Not anymore. I had never felt this way about my friends... Never *craved* them like I craved him.

And I'd thought he felt the same...

Maybe I had read it wrong.

Maybe he had wanted to give in to the physical attraction, then realized his mistake.

Maybe we were both just caught up in the magic of Yule.

So many maybes and nothing for certain.

I refused to knock a third time. Instead, I wanted to hurl this bouquet into the potbelly stove we never used and set it on fire.

But it wasn't the roses' fault—they'd just had the misfortune of being picked by a psychopath. So, angry, bitter tears still streaking silently down my face, I put them on the desk in my bedroom.

Then just stood there, again, chest starting to shudder through every breath, another meltdown on the horizon. So much pent-up emotion—jogging wasn't enough to leech out the poison. Neither was vodka or movie nights with Bjorn.

Sex with Gavriel wasn't healthy, but even if I went there tonight, it wouldn't be *enough* to shut it all off.

Make it stop.

So, I left the flat. Climbed up to the eleventh floor in my sparkly silver heels, taking yet another risk for the night. I needed a hard reset after—*that.*

Needed to center myself.

Find my bearings.

And…

Jack lived on the eleventh floor, right below the staffroom, him and Iris neighbors, and as I stood on the landing, glancing between two doors, Flat A and B, a little voice told me to walk away. We hadn't discussed the spanking. Hadn't agreed to meet again. Hadn't pushed professional boundaries.

But I couldn't take another breakdown. Couldn't sob in the shower or wail into my pillow, frustrated and furious and guilt-stricken and so horribly alone.

With his rough hand, I could skip all that. Find my normal again without the usual pain.

Or, more accurately, *with* pain.

I had no idea which apartment belonged to the headmaster, but it seemed odd that his assistant would get Flat A, rumored to be the larger of the two on every floor. So that was where I went. Briefly, I eyed the copper plate, like I needed to confirm over and over again that this was, in fact, Flat A, and slowly raised my fist…

Then threw caution to the wind and knocked.

14

JACK

For the first time in a dreadfully long time, I had called it a day before midnight.

Barely after eleven and I'd already changed out of my suit, folded and put it away, and completed my bedtime routine. Flossed, water-picked, and brushed my teeth. Washed my face and patted it dry with a fresh towel. Just moisturizing left to go and then... bed.

How I'd fall asleep after such a bloody awful night was beyond me, but I was determined to *try*. Iris had been so ridiculous about Yule in the weeks leading up to it, bragging about the night like it would be the event to put all others to shame. Her girls had even shirked most of their *actual* work all week to meet their mistress's demands, and then—*that*. A horrid night where no one looked happy, accompanied by piano and nothing but sugar cookies as far as the eye could see. Miserable students cloistered at the tables, very few willing to stand an arm's length apart and sway on an empty dance floor, while annoyed faculty manned the workstations as Iris flitted around nitpicking them all night.

And I had... watched.

And I *hated* that.

Unfortunately, Iris had nestled deep into the pockets of the high council long ago, which meant a power imbalance had slowly but surely blossomed between us since Samhain. Any slight step out of line and she could report me, add that final strike to my file and have me sacked by the new year.

In all other scenarios, of course I would overrule her, but I hadn't thought twice about giving her free rein over an equinox celebration. We were of the same supernatural tribe, after all, and initially I thought she would understand the significance of making tonight something *special*.

A brief spark in the darkness.

A shining light in the bleak, miserable days of winter in the highlands.

But no.

She had to screw it up royally enough that the student body would dread every future sabbat.

On top of everything, she had the *nerve* to strut around afterward like the night had been a roaring success.

Ridiculous.

I could barely hold my tongue at that point.

Yet that wasn't what had sent me off. Standing in front of my gilded en suite bathroom mirror now, I scooped a dollop of moisturizer from its tin, then got to work on massaging it into my face, my stubble, and my neck. Every so often, I caught my reflection's gaze in the mirror, and a white-hot jolt of shame flashed through me.

I had left the dining hall because of Bjorn and Alecto.

Watching them rock on the dance floor, knowing what a terrible little dancer that witch was after having personally led her through a waltz on Samhain—it had done something to me.

At first, a strange warm and fuzzy feeling swelled in my chest. As desperate as I was to put her on her knees at my

137

feet and rope a collar around her neck, I wasn't in a place to give her *that*: public affection, intimate glances, a protective embrace that frightened off potential suitors.

But Bjorn could. After all, there were no rules about interfaculty relationships.

He could give her what she needed and more.

I... I could give her nothing.

As a parting gift, I'd done what I realistically could: I gave them music.

But then the warm and fuzzy shriveled, replaced with a tight, bitter frost that made my chest ache.

While I had dabbled in relationships before, always to appease my parents, I had never felt the sting of heartache—and a part of me feared that was the feeling it was: *ache*. Longing. A yearning in my heart for *her*, to waltz with *her* on a whim, all eyes on us, all the impending gossip meaningless...

Not a detriment to either of our careers.

Pathetic, really. We knew so little about each other beyond our mutual interest in pain, yet here I was... aching.

Aching for what, exactly, still eluded me. It couldn't *just* be her I craved. Perhaps I desired the freedom she and Bjorn shared, the closeness and the connection. Lonely was the head that wore the crown, not just heavy.

With a sharp exhale, I finished up with my hands, smearing the leftover moisturizer up my arms, then stilled at the rap of knuckles on my front door.

No. I was done for the night, locked in, dressed down, ready for bed.

But it wasn't in my nature to ignore anyone under my charge, and as I left the bathroom and strode through the suite's master bedroom, then out into the formal sitting room, I could only *hope* it wasn't Iris on the other side here to gloat.

Because that was coming; tonight or tomorrow, my second-in-command would corner me and brag about what a *brilliant* Yule she had hosted.

And I hadn't the stomach for it, not now, not with my heart still knotted in all that blasted yearning. Irritable and bogged down with tonight's failure, I wrenched open the front door, nothing about my expression suggesting I was up for *anything* from my assistant headmistress—

Oh.

Alecto.

The little witch must have been pressed right up against the door to knock, because she was just *there*, a breath away from me in her lovely Yule gown, her eyes watery and bloodshot again. The whoosh of my dramatic opening had her stumbling back, startling her enough to drop her skirts and cower.

Surely Bjorn hadn't caused the misery in her eyes. I couldn't fathom him breaking her heart; he might have been a warrior a lifetime ago, but I valued the vampire today for his gentle, patient temperament that worked wonders on our students.

All things considered, that ought to extend to Alecto. Hell, I had witnessed it with my own two eyes, the care and tenderness with which he handled her.

"Hi," she said in a small voice, all subdued and deliciously submissive. *Bloody hell.* It was like she did it without realizing, falling into the role I had lusted after for years, my needs never met, my wants unrequited. Clearing my throat, I peered around the landing, taking in the emptiness behind her and the dark silhouette around Iris's doorframe.

"Are you all right?"

Obviously not—why else would she be here? The shake of her head confirmed it, and the lower lip wobble was just torture. Gods above, *curse* my soft spot for lost, pining pain addicts desperate for a cruel hand and a good cuddle after.

Be professional. Right. Explore the proper channels first. "Do you want to talk about it?"

Alecto shook her head again, as expected, and my cock twitched with interest. Already the Dom in me was raring to go, wide-awake after scenting blood in the water. *No.* Eager as I was to formally play with the epitome of *my* perfect submissive, this was too complicated.

Too dangerous.

Arms crossed, I leaned against the doorway with a sigh. "Alecto, I know we didn't explicitly discuss this, but I thought it best to keep what happened before a onetime—"

"Is that what you really want?"

Her confidence threw me. Disheveled as she appeared after looking meticulous all night, like a winter goddess gracing us mere mortals with her presence, she sounded clear and firm now. *Strong.* No more quiet mewls, breathy croaks, anguished whispers. Without meeting my eye, Alecto challenged me directly.

Called me on my shit.

Bratty submissives could be *such* a chore. Unlike the good darlings who always did as they were told and never talked back, her kind knew precisely what their Doms desired above all else—and they weren't afraid to bring it to light.

This was a fork in the road, the moment that could change everything. Had this happened months ago, I could have sent her away, but something about *this* year in particular had weakened me. So many failings. So many losses. So many blows to my ego, my pride, and my job.

It had all beaten me down enough to force an honest answer.

"No," I admitted hoarsely. No, I didn't want a brief

spanking in my office to be the only time we tangled in kink together. "That's not what I want."

All my life, I had never gotten what *I* wanted. No matter the wealth, status, or prestige, Clemonte witches and warlocks did as family tradition dictated. Personal goals went out the window if they didn't further our legacy— didn't bring *power* to the lineage.

"Me neither," Alecto whispered, brushing her fingers under her eyes, catching the tears before they fell. *Fuck me*. Only a heartless bastard would leave her out there like this, but if I beckoned her inside, it wasn't a hot cup of tea and a good chat that either of us desired.

Hands fisted, I leaned forward and did a more thorough sweep of our surroundings. The darkest night of the year was also the most silent. No footsteps echoing through the stairwell, no voices carrying up to the eleventh floor.

With a shake of my head and a bristly sigh, I stepped aside and beckoned her in.

Weak. So bloody weak.

She made me weak.

And... I liked it. Just for tonight, I could admit to that.

Alecto padded in without a word, and I let her wander around the formal sitting room as I saw to the door. Instinct told me to lock it, but I left it open in case she suddenly decided to bolt. When I faced her again, I found her hands twined together behind her back, offering me her profile as she took in the space. Lovely, her outfit this evening, all silvery white and rich dark blues, a snow queen, a Yule treasure.

In another life, I'd rip that gown apart and fuck her on the shredded tulle.

For now, I let her revel in her surroundings, in the stark contrast they must have offered compared to the flat she shared with Bjorn. Like my office, the three-bedroom suite was a blend of traditional and modern with dark woods, hard angles, and updated furnishings. I had adopted a monochromatic color scheme throughout, black, white, and grey dominating the space. Not exactly the warmest place to bring a new submissive, but that wasn't the point.

In fact, there wasn't much of a point in having the largest flat on campus when I seldom used it. Sure, I slept each night in the bedroom's California king and made use of the bathroom, but I never entertained—so this formal sitting room with the twin couches, armchairs, and hearth was a waste. I never relaxed, so there went the informal living room through the closed door to the right, and I spent all day and many long nights in my actual office, so the small, private study behind yet another closed door remained untouched and useless.

In fact, Alecto was the first person I'd had in here besides Iris in about two years. Once, at the request of some of the older professors, I had hosted a wine and cigar night to better know my faculty, but that was a distant memory.

As she took in the overtly masculine landscape, the rugged corners and the varnished floors that offered no comfort for submissive knees, I studied her. Alecto hadn't said as much, but I knew precisely what she wanted—why she was here. She longed for what I had given last time: peace. A still mind and a quiet heart. She wished to feel better, to reset after something had clearly triggered her between waltzing with Bjorn and now.

"Alecto," I said roughly, "look at me."

Soundlessly, she turned in place, eyes on mine, open and vulnerable. Thank the gods she had found me and not a sadist with no morals: someone could really hurt her when she looked at them like that.

"This is... not how I ordinarily do *this*," I told her,

searching for the right words as I motioned between us, cautious of her feelings, "with a submissive."

Her eyebrows shot up, and gone was the open and vulnerable, replaced with an embarrassment that had her cheeks pink and her gaze downcast. Damn it. So much for caution.

"No, no…" I crossed over to her, fighting the instinct to pull her against me and tuck her under my chin. Instead, I threaded my hands together behind my back and stayed close. "I like to talk a great deal first. Everything done should *always* be consensual." Slowly, shyly, she glanced back up at me, and my smile seemed to reassure her. "Every Dominant and submissive is an individual, all with different limits, preferences, wants, needs… Ordinarily, I would like to know *everything* about you before going into this."

She gulped, the flicker in her throat telling. "I-I understand, but—"

"For the sake of helping you tonight, we can forgo that," I insisted. As much as I'd like to peel back the layers and root around, really grasp what made her tick—what made her cry —that just wasn't necessary to give her what she needed. "The safeword will remain as is… *Rot*. Say it."

"Rot," she parroted back to me, and I nodded, pleased.

"Good. If we are to… continue this, we will need to have another conversation. Something deeper and perhaps a bit uncomfortable."

I allowed her a moment to consider it, and Alecto fussed with her hair in the silence. Mahogany curls tamed to long waves, she swept it all to one side and coiled it, then brushed it out and twisted that mane again. Finally, when her head bobbed, it was like I could draw a full breath again.

"I… I'd like that," she told me softly. "Root Rot is stressful. Having a safe release with an experienced hand is actually really appealing."

Gods, she knew just what to say, didn't she? Blitzing by her confession that she desired *me* to be her Dom, I offered a thin smile and a hum of agreement. "Yes, the job demands a lot from—"

"It's not the job. Not really," she interjected with a wave of her hand. My jaw clenched; if she *did* intend to become my submissive, if I actually entertained the idea of making this underlying connection between us official, she would learn to never interrupt me in a scene. Tonight, I let it slide. With no rules discussed, it wasn't fair to chastise her, not when she was *finally* opening up.

"Then what?"

She smoothed her hands down her feathery bodice, as if desperate to keep them busy. "I don't really want to talk about it."

In a future conversation, we could discuss if this issue was a hard limit. If not, I could very easily—skillfully—whip it out of her.

But never mind.

"I can respect that." Respect it, but certainly not forget it. If something or some*one* in this castle was continuously upsetting her, I intended to make it or them—probably a *him* —stop.

By force, if necessary.

No one made my submissive cry but me.

"You seem better than you were the last time we met under these circumstances."

"I am." Alecto sniffled, the twist of her lips halfhearted. "Different scenario—kind of."

Right. On to the main event, then. "Would you like me to spank you again?"

She inhaled sharply at the offer, a beet-red blush skittering all the way down to her chest. Exquisite. My favorite color, that, especially when stripped raw across a submissive's backside. I let her sputter and flounder for a moment, eyebrow quirked as she tried to talk exclusively with her flailing hands. It was important for a sub to communicate what they wanted, after all, but this little one had no idea *what* she wanted.

Ugh. Like catnip for a tiger, honestly.

"Would you like to try something different?" I offered once she had suffered enough. The question seemed to reset her brain, and Alecto shrugged one shoulder, immediately more composed.

"Uh, sure?"

Now we were getting somewhere. There was so much more to our world than spanking. "Did you enjoy the pain last time? Or the surrender to me?"

Alecto nibbled her lower lip, fidgeting with her fingers and looking deliciously serious as she considered both options. "Both... kind of? I don't know."

"Well, little sub..." Smirking, I caught her by the chin, pinching it, loving her startled flinch. I hadn't called anyone *anything* in so long. Not slave. Not little one. Not filth. Not baby subby. *Nothing.* And never with anyone who wasn't either a professional in this fantasy or a longtime player with multiple partners. My grip tightened at the thought, shifting to engulf her lower jaw and down to her neck, tipping her head up so that she had no choice but to *look* at me. When I had her gaze trapped in mine, I grinned wolfishly, letting a glimmer of the darkness inside out. "Maybe we'll need to try a few things before we find your sweet spot..."

Her throat rippled beneath my palm, and she offered the tiniest of nods, seeming to melt at the thought.

So bad.

This—is so *fucking bad.*

Self-preservation demanded I retreat immediately.

Fear reminded me that my job was hanging by a precarious thread.

Logic insisted this would only end in catastrophe.

"Is that what you really want?" Her voice slithered around my skull in a confident whisper, and I surrendered to myself —to taking what *I* wanted, just this once.

"Right then." The moment I withdrew my hand, she stumbled after me, as if she had trusted me enough to just let go. Promising. I ducked down to meet her eyeline as I murmured, "Wait here." I then stalked toward the master bedroom, only to slow, a thought occurring: if we were going to do this, might as well do it *right*. "On your knees, Alecto."

Over my shoulder, I caught her sinking down, complying in a heartbeat. *Good girl*. Without another word, I strode into the bedroom, then tucked my slowly hardening cock into the waistline of my loose black slacks. No need to make her think she had to *do* something with the horny bastard, after all.

With that out of the way, I turned on the lamps on both bedside tables, then dug out one of my plain white tees from the walk-in closet, carefully selecting the perfect cotton blend from the built-in shelves. A twin to the one I wore now, I held it out for inspection, not expecting to find a stain or a blemish but needing to confirm all the same. Nothing. Clean, scented like the pine-fresh dryer sheets housecleaning used for all my things. No folds or stiff lines. Soft. *Much* too big for her, but that was the point.

Giddiness crackled through my veins like a lightning storm as I arranged the shirt on the bed, but I concealed it before returning to her, my excitement hidden beneath a stony mask and a rigid posture. As expected, Alecto sat at attention upon my return, but nothing could fix that sloppy kneel. Sure, she looked beautiful surrounded by a pool of silver tulle—no denying that. I just preferred a submissive to kneel a certain way: shoulders back, spine straight, head down, and eyes on the ground. Knees together, hands flat on her thighs.

We can work on that another day, little one.

Bloody hell—was this actually happening? Was I already preparing for another session? Crafting an agenda? Making a plan? Conflict ripped through me, but not enough to quash the thrill of the moment, my free fall into this night—our night—well and truly underway.

"Alecto," I said, soft but sharp. Subs had always enjoyed that about me: my ability to remain calm and composed as I tore them to pieces. I got off on it, too, of course, otherwise I wouldn't waste my time with it. When she looked up, hands nervously fussing with her dress, I motioned to the door behind me. "In my room there is a T-shirt on the bed. I'd like you to change into that, leaving your undergarments on, shoes off. Do you understand?"

Cheeks hollow, she nodded.

"Right, off you go, then." I stepped aside, creating a specific path for her to take from her spot on the floor to my door. She stood, navigating the volume of that dress gracefully, and then crossed the hardwood silently—like she was trying not to click around in her heels. Adorable. I threw down the toll gate just before she passed, stopping her with my arm and looking pointedly at the gown. "Do you need help getting out of that?"

She licked her lips, peeking over her shoulder briefly, then offered me her back. "Just the zipper."

I found it at the top of the dark, feathery blue bodice, and I gripped the material firmly as I slid it open, making it a point to avoid skin-to-skin contact—for now. That was the game: leave them wanting. As soon as the bodice splayed open over her lower back, I shooed her off with a sharp throat clear.

Even though what I really wanted to do was peruse the indentations left on her skin from the bodice boning, the red lines as lovely on her bare flesh as I'd always imagined.

Another time.

With a squeak of thanks, Alecto shuffled into my bedroom—the first and only woman at Root Rot Academy to ever do so—and closed the door behind her. Only halfway, mind you, the bright white light still spilling into the formal sitting area, but I gritted my teeth all the same. Submissives couldn't—and, frankly, shouldn't—lock themselves away during a scene, and I would never have allowed it in the past. As soon as we began this dance, I was responsible for her.

Fortunately, there wasn't anything she could hurt herself with in there. No toys or tools. Nothing salacious, either, all private and personal documentation locked in my office safe, the damn thing triple charmed *and* hexed to keep out intruders.

Next time, Alecto would start to learn the rules—and the consequences of breaking them.

If... she wanted a next time.

If I didn't scare her away with what I had in mind for tonight.

Nothing quieted a frantic mind better than a bit of light caning.

In her absence, I ducked into my study and went straight for the aged traveling trunk under the window. While I spelled most of my things shut, this had a simple combination lock with a numerical code: the year of my youngest sister's birth. After rolling that in, I popped it open and brushed my fingers along the tools inside.

Instruments of pain.

All my toys.

Head cocked, I carefully sifted through the relics of an age gone by until I found the one I needed for tonight.

Rattan cane. Light wood with a glistening finish and a mahogany handle. Springy, lightweight, flexible under the right hand, it was a cane that left marks—not bruises. There were far heavier, angrier instruments inside the trunk for that.

Not wanting to keep her waiting, I locked up my old friends again, then returned to the formal sitting room.

And there she was, loitering in the bedroom doorway, slightly disheveled without her gown and glittering snowflake headband. Alecto stood before me pared down, hair loose and starting to frizz, drowning in my T-shirt.

Desire throbbed low and rough in my gut at the thought —*my* shirt hanging over her figure, consuming her, claiming her. That gown must have come with a built-in bra; two pebbled nipples poked through the cotton, determined to make themselves known. I bit down sharply on the inside of my cheek as a reminder not to stare. As the brandisher of pain and control, I set the tone.

Ogling her like this was just poor form.

At the slight arch of my eyebrow, Alecto hastily sank into another sloppy kneel, knees not touching, shoulders slightly rounded. I resisted the urge to march over there and forcefully correct her, maneuver her luscious body to fit my standards.

Instead, I grinned.

She was a fast learner.

"I'm going to cane you, Alecto," I told her, holding up the instrument in question, allowing her wide eyes to wander back and forth warily. "It's for sharp, sudden pain. Submissives I've worked with in the past tell me they enjoy that it's twofold—the initial sting, then the burn after." Given I had no intention of warming her up, this would be a short session, whether she liked it or not. "You can stop after the first blow—or any thereafter. I leave that to you."

But *I* would stop every three strikes, just to check on her. After all, I knew nothing about her tolerances, preferences, or limits. It might be overkill to be so cautious, but I'd never played with such a baby submissive before. Alecto *deserved* my caution.

"I will *not* strike as hard as I would on more experienced submissives," I added, the statement meant to both reassure and inflict a little fear. Let her know I was being careful—and that I could go much, *much* harder. "Do you understand?"

After a tense beat, Alecto nodded slowly, still eyeing the cane.

"I will only cane your thighs tonight." I much preferred leaving red, raw marks along a bratty sub's backside, but the area was intimate, something carefully negotiated between partners. To push her with zero experience and limited knowledge would be beyond taking advantage. I allowed her a moment to consider everything, and when she finally lifted her gaze up to my face, I arched an eyebrow. "I need to hear your consent, Alecto. You can of course rescind it now, or at any time—"

"Okay," she croaked, nodding again and fidgeting with the hem of my shirt, which stretched all the way down to her knees. "I consent—caning on the thighs. Heard. Withdraw at any time. *Rot*. Understood."

Fuck me. This was it. The point of no return. I could stop it right here and retain what little professional boundaries we had left—

"Please face the wall." Well. Point of no return—crossed. I pointed the thin cane precisely where I wanted her. "There." Next to a massive landscape painting of the raging Atlantic, dark silhouettes of sirens cut into the layers of blue ink that made up the waves. "And brace with your hands."

Alecto did as she was told, once again without question. She tiptoed over to the exact spot, then slowly offered her back to me. Planted her hands flat to the wall, then leaned over.

"Bend a little more," I instructed, battling for the first time in decades as a Dom to keep my voice even, "to expose your thighs."

She readjusted her stance, inching her feet out on either side, adding a slight arch to her back—ass out. Oh, if only, little one. If only. Taking a steadying breath, I crossed over to her and placed a firm hand on her lower back, then hiked up the white tee *just* enough to bare her strong, full thighs to me. Carefully, almost clinically, I tucked the cotton into her panties, of which I barely noted, the pair nude and practical. Not that I had any intention of prying beyond that. Just need to… keep the shirt in place.

"Are you ready?" I whispered. Her stance here was far better than her attempts at a submissive kneel, posing her now like the perfect offering—the best way to wrap up such a bloody awful Yule.

"Yes," Alecto murmured back, all throaty and hoarse. The slight tremble in her thighs gave her away—fear and excitement.

An exquisite elixir.

Nodding, I stepped back into my usual stance behind a bent-over submissive, close enough for them to feel my presence but far enough that they were alone in their painful little bubble. Worried I might be rusty, I played with the cane's grip, then allowed myself a few practice swings. All in the wrist, sadism play. Precision assured no lasting damage. The correct tempo and pressure promised a satisfying session.

When I couldn't procrastinate a second longer, no matter how I enjoyed just *looking* at her like this, willing and ready, I swung. Reared back and struck the middle of her thighs —*lightly*, practically gifting her with an angel's kiss.

Still she yelped.

Alecto jumped and broke her position, hands falling to the pink line that matched the color in her cheeks.

"Are you all right?" I moved in fast, out of practice enough for insecurity to creep in.

But then she giggled, eyes alight and lips spread wide.

"Yeah, fine," she insisted brightly. "Just surprised me. Sorry."

"No need to apologize," I told her as she resumed her post. "You just tell me when to stop... No need for martyrs —yet."

I struck just as she started to nod again, catching her a few inches above the last mark. After the next blow, I pounced, stalking forward and examining her skin. Hot and burning, no doubt, the pain already blooming deliciously.

Alecto flinched when I smoothed a hand over all the marks—just a light caress to ease the scorch for this little pain novice.

I then returned to my spot and struck thrice more, delighting in her whimpers, her gasps, her jumps.

"Shall I continue?" I asked after the sixth line seared across her flesh. Nothing too deep. No blood drawn this evening. Nothing worse than a fussy sunburn for my girl tonight.

Alecto's head bobbed frantically, her fingers curling over the wall. "Yes... sir."

Teeth gritted, cock aching, I gave her a much harder strike for that one—because she must have known what that *word* did to me.

Cane in hand, the rest of the world faded away until it was just her and me in the darkness, a landscape of peaceful black. The high council, Iris Prewett, Samhain, a failed Yule, Fiona Simpson, Bjorn, the awful new security team we had hired on short notice—gone. Expectations, the family legacy, my father's hard voice—quashed. I could be me, just for a little while, even if I still wasn't confident in who *me* was supposed to be with all the rest gone.

At the very least, I could *breathe.*

After the twelfth strike, this one falling onto a red line I'd been shaping into something lovely, I heard it.

"*Rot.*"

And then it was over. Tossing the cane on a nearby armchair, I swooped in, concern bubbling in my chest rather than disappointment, and steadied Alecto with one hand on her hip and the other bracing her outstretched—trembling —arm.

"Was that too much?" My voice kept its gravely Dominant edge even as I transitioned into aftercare mode: pain off, cuddles on, *slow her nervous system down.* Alecto sucked in a wavering breath, then peeked up at me through watery lashes, her face rosy and her grin cheekier than I'd expected.

"Just enough," she whispered conspiratorially, "for now."

"Understood." From a simple five-minute session, I had a feel for her likes and her limits. Next time, I would know more—feel more confident in my handling of her. "Stand up and lean on me."

She eased off the wall, letting me clutch her forearm and steady her by her lower back. Briefly, I gave her space to breathe, to come down from the physical high of pain and pleasure.

Because where there was one, there was always the other for creatures such as we.

"How do you feel?"

"Better," she admitted, sweeping her hair over her shoulders, lost in the painting of the furious Atlantic to her right. "Distracted... Which I guess is the point."

"Sometimes," I mused as I removed my hand from her back, leaving its heat behind, her body's response to pain and adrenaline beautiful. "Not always." Ideally, pain was for *fun*, not necessarily a desperate escape. When she glanced back at me, I steered her toward the half-closed bedroom door. "Now, go change into your dress."

I held on for as long as I thought necessary, walking her to the doorway and allowing her to close it behind her—just for tonight. As soon as she disappeared, I saw to the cane, setting it on my office desk to disinfect later; even though I hadn't drawn blood, good Doms cleaned their toys between sessions. Back in the sitting room, I fetched a dark silky blanket from the back of the charcoal-grey couch, then stood waiting.

Hard as a rock and ignoring my cock as best I could.

A task made *infinitely* more difficult when Alecto limped out, the cane's bite probably starting to really sting now that she was moving around, tulle brushing the marks. My heart skipped a beat at the sight, just a little bit smitten with *her*—and not because she fit the submissive mold I'd searched for my whole adult life.

But because she looked *alive*, fresh-faced and young, shiny and new.

Reborn in my darkness.

Wordlessly, she turned in place and offered me her exposed back. Blanket hanging over one arm, I moved in to do up her zipper again.

"Headmaster?"

"Please," I said with a soft chuckle, "*Jack*. Outside of a scene, and away from the others, just Jack."

"Jack…" She rotated in place once I stepped back, looking very much like she was tasting my name on her tongue, adjusting to how it felt to say it. Little did she realize her newfound privilege: no other submissive had even been granted first-name status before. Just before I threw the silky blanket I never used around her shoulders, her eyebrows crinkled, and she looked up at me, confused. "Did you... enjoy yourself?"

"I did." My grin had her flushing scarlet, and I resisted the urge to drink in her body unchecked like I owned it— because it *felt* like I owned it, from this night forward, but things still weren't so cut-and-dry between us. "Your skin is lovely under the cane."

She opened and closed her mouth a few times, fumbling over her words as she fussed with her hair. *Magnifique.* Tongue-tied subs were such a treat.

Given we had shifted into aftercare, I culled the suffering fast, throwing the blanket around her and using it to steer her into me. Alecto came with stiff steps, all rigid and startled by the turn of events, until I tucked her under my chin. Wrapped her in the blanket and my arms, pressing down from all sides. Human studies had shown pressure calmed a frantic nervous system, and I had found that translated well into aftercare; so long as the submissive accepted physical contact, they *all* got hugs.

I'd never... sniffed past submissives' hair, mind you.

Never reveled in their scent.

In the way their bodies molded ever so perfectly to mine, small but strong.

Alecto stayed tense and silent for a little while, her arms folded between us, until eventually all the hardness gave way —and she just *melted*.

Well then. Bratty little pain sub liked cuddly aftercare.

Noted.

When I peeked down, I found her eyes closed, and something warm and fuzzy once again flared in my chest, all soft and cozy and *not* how I felt after scenes in the past.

Bloody hell.

Not good.

Not good.

Ruin the moment. *Save yourself—*

"Are you sure you don't want to talk about it?"

The little witch nodded, eyes still closed, and let out a long, luxurious sigh, her head turned to the side and cheek to my chest.

Right. So much for killing the intimacy.

I carried on holding her, deep pressure working its magic on her body, but made an effort to stand taller—stay above the cloud of vanilla that followed her around and *not* bury my nose in her hair. For now, I also let the catalyst of tonight go, just as I had the last time, but I couldn't keep quiet on the issue much longer. Twice now she had come to me in tears, heartbroken and lost, and the thought of someone in this castle *doing* that to her threatened to tip me into a rage...

A rage from which there might be no return.

Which was also a problem.

Sniffing her hair? Problem.

Wanting to tear some faceless bastard limb from limb for upsetting her? *Major* problem.

"Thank you, Jack," she said, her sleepy words cutting through the noise. Second by second, the chaos I lived with every day had trickled back in, thoughts racing, mind whirling, self-loathing and the cruel voices who always told me I wasn't good enough all reared their ugly heads.

Then three little words silenced them.

"You're welcome," I rumbled back, stomping out the urge to stroke her hair, rub her back, nuzzle in deeper to keep my brain quiet for a few more blissful minutes.

"I really appreciate... you," she added, then inhaled sharply. "*Oh.*" Her eyes snapped open, and she dug her folded arms into my chest to push back and look up at me. "I mean, no. A sadist doesn't want to hear that. You really *hurt* me—"

"It's what *this* sadist wants to hear," I assured her with a tired grin, surrendering to the moment as I tucked her hair behind her ears, then brought her back to my chest with a hand on the back of her head.

Where it stayed, cradling her to me, until her third yawn forced me to do the right thing.

"Right, off to bed with you," I ordered as I pulled back and found her looking as exhausted on the outside as I suddenly felt on the inside. Another sleepy, sweet nod from Alecto was all I needed to walk her to my door, savoring her slight limp, her barely there wince whenever her dress brushed the backs of her thighs. A part of me didn't want to let her go. No, it yearned to peel her dress away, put her back in my T-shirt, then tuck her into my bed in *my* room.

"Good night, Headmaster."

I cut her loose instead. I had to. There was no room in my life for anything beyond a carefully constructed scene—a play session negotiated between two consenting adults, with a start, middle, and very clear end. When that time came, we had to go our separate ways; there was no other choice.

I was her headmaster. She was my professor. My job hung by a thread. Her career had only just started.

I couldn't... ruin her.

Couldn't entangle her in anything deeper than this.

She smiled at me from the grey-stone landing outside my flat, a little rumpled but otherwise unassuming. No one would look at her and think someone had just caned her thighs *red*.

Lingering in the doorway, I leaned a shoulder against the frame and folded my arms. "Good night, Miss Clarke. Sleep well."

"You too," Alecto murmured, and for once the sentiment sounded genuine. All my staff thanked me, wished me well, told me good morning and good night—but they said it because they had to. Because I was their *boss*.

Not her. Not now. We spoke as equals.

Until it all came crashing down.

As soon as Alecto turned toward the stairwell, there was Iris emerging like a bony phoenix from the ashes, dripping with silver feathers, her face painted white like some Elizabethan queen. My heart stopped, then plunged into my gut. Alecto paled. Iris slowed at the top of the steps, eyeing us slowly, thoroughly. For me, she offered a smirk, thin lips twisted knowingly, while Alecto was given a scathing once-over and a dismissive *sniff.*

Without a word, my perfect submissive ducked her head and practically sprinted for the stairs, vanishing down them in a flurry of tulle and frantic *click-click-click*s of her heels.

Greying blonde hair swept in an impressively tall beehive, Iris strode onto the landing like the royalty she so obviously coveted in that gown: regal bodice, a dramatic silhouette exaggerated at the hips, a shimmering icy tail stretching behind. Silvery blue like Alecto, but my girl had made it work. Somehow, she had made the frosts warm. Iris was an ice queen through and through, complete with what appeared to be an authentic silver tiara coiled around that upstart hairdo.

I'd seen many like her in my time, strutting into my social circle in outfits that reeked of *new* money, all flash and no substance.

"Careful, Headmaster," she crooned as she floated to her door.

"Of what?" I growled, mindful of my tone, my posture, my expression—*everything*—as she plucked her wand from her towering, overly teased hair and tapped it on her door. "A late-night talk with an upset professor? Hardly something to be *careful* of—and I resent the implication."

As her flat door popped open, my assistant headmistress fluttered her fake lashes at me innocently, the ends of those long black wisps tipped with faux sapphires. Then, halfway in, her schoolgirl façade fell away, shifting from innocent to viper in a heartbeat.

"Of course." She pressed her wand hand to her chest, to the rigid corset that flattened every curve, her frail figure laced in tight and straight. "My mistake, naturally. Apologies, Jack."

Still smirking, she made her eyelashes dance again, then slipped inside, the subsequent *slam* of her door nowhere near loud enough to muffle her cackles.

Shit.

Shaking my head, I did the same, locking the door and heading straight to bed. If Alecto and I were to continue this, we couldn't do it here. Too risky. Too many eyes in this castle, including the portraits of my judgmental predecessors. I mean, seven *hells*, she had left her snowflake headband on my nightstand; we *had* to be more careful than that.

After admiring its sparkly details, I tucked the band in the little table's drawer almost reverently, handling it like a precious artifact, and made a mental note to return it later.

Maybe.

It seemed rather at home beside my bed.

While I had a few places in mind that could provide privacy and safety for Alecto and me, I didn't descend into my usual racing thoughts as soon as the lights cut out. No pros and cons list. No this or that. No admonishments, and certainly no ruminating over the failures of the day.

Not the usual routine at all.

Instead, as soon as my head hit the pillow, the T-shirt Alecto had worn draped over my ornate headboard, I was out.

Snoring like a chainsaw.

Dead to the world... with a smile on my face.

15

BJORN

Eleven long bells chimed from the staffroom's grandfather clock.

But you'd need a vampire's supersonic hearing to detect them over the cacophony of this year's New Year's Eve party.

Eleven o'clock—one hour to midnight. It had been chaos since things started at nine, and even though it was just a Tuesday and we all had classes tomorrow, no holidays permitted midway through the second term like other academies, I had a feeling no one would be calling it a night anytime soon.

Instead, tomorrow morning they would be forced to drag their hungover, exhausted shells down to the dining hall for breakfast, or maybe lunch at the rate some of my colleagues were drinking. Little did any of the students know, but tomorrow was a guaranteed easy day—a write-off of epic proportions for everyone but me.

And Jack, actually, who was still nursing the same bourbon in his usual crystal tumbler, circulating the fringes of tonight's party with a look in his eye that suggested he would rather be anywhere but here.

Anywhere *but* surrounded by pissed, sloppy professors who had turned our sacred table into an epic—and very much ongoing—beer pong tournament.

Like Jack, I clung to the outskirts, leaning against a cool windowpane and watching it all unfold at a distance. This term had really cemented the cavernous pit between myself and the rest of them, and not even the spirit of December 31, the promise of a new year, new me, could change that.

While Samhain was the supernatural new year for many witches and warlocks, the rest of us still recognized the last night of December as *the* night to party before another year rolled in. Drinking, feasting, and dancing now plagued the staffroom, along with shrieking laughter and boisterous arguments that fell like artillery fire on my ears.

In an age gone by, this had been my *scene*.

Replace the stone walls and beautiful glass windows for wooden halls and raging fires and furs scattered across the floor and this would have been a typical night in my ancestral village.

And I'd have been in the thick of it, drunk and merry, singing and fighting and gambling.

Centuries later, I stood off to the side—watching.

After a quick sip from my thermos, a tepid AB-negative trickling down my throat and warming my belly, I glanced to the far right of the room—to the one witch I had been trying *not* to watch all night.

Alecto looked magnificent in green. While sequins and glittery embellishments had become the norm for New Year's Eve attire, hers stood out as the most original. A lot of gold and silver around here, whereas my flatmate strode confidently amongst them in a shimmery pine-green dress that cut off around her upper thighs, the hemline tastefully jagged for visual interest. That asymmetry also appeared on the ends of her sleeves, which crept down to her delicate forearms. Formfitting, this outfit was unlike all the others she had worn this year: short, stylish, youthful. Rigid squared-off shoulders and a high neckline up to the hollow of her throat. All legs in that, hers made ever longer by the black heels.

Hair wild and free, curls flying everywhere, unfettered and untamed.

A smoky eye and a nude lip.

She was exquisite.

And she hadn't looked at me. Not once.

Things had been off between us since Yule, the rhythm around our flat unnatural and forced. Worst of all, it was my doing. No denial here—no pointing the finger at her. *I* was the one acting like a child. Me. *My* fault. But I couldn't help it: seeing her with Cedar that night, the night I intended to change *everything*, had made me question things. Try as I might, the two of them together, bickering, him with flowers and her yanking her hand out of mine, brought the insecurities of the last century into startling focus.

I had always been a confident man, even more sure of myself as a vampire.

Until the last few decades. Until vampire prejudice really took its toll. Until colleagues shunned me and students tried to kill me and everyone snickered about my innate weaknesses behind closed doors.

I could handle it.

For the sake of my orphaned vampire students, I *had* to take the bullshit in stride.

But throw Alecto into the mix, a witch whose absence rocked my whole world, and I was fucked.

Clueless and fumbling through things like I was just a teenager myself.

We stumbled around in this relationship purgatory together, her and me, and I *hated* it. No other woman had set me off like this before, made me spiral and question everything.

A deeply insecure part of me had decided she was just entertaining me that night.

Trying to keep the peace in our flat.

Maybe. Maybe not. Maybe she *had* planned to kiss me despite her dalliance with Cedar—

I glared up at my forehead, lost in thought, and then blinked down at my thermos when the metal warped under my slowly tightening fist. Right. *This* was reason enough not to change our dynamic, because I couldn't fucking stand this —the not knowing, the questions, the festering sore that oozed all over our relationship.

One that hurt worse with every day I acted like a twat.

Usually I could swallow my pride and push down the hurt.

But it was like Alecto Clarke had changed my brain chemistry.

Bewitched me with all that vanilla and laughter, cozy conversations and movie marathons…

With her constant presence, her willingness, her *eagerness*, to stand by my side and glare down the haters.

I felt so deeply at this point—*too* deeply—that one wrong move and I was lost.

I—

"Isn't she beautiful?"

Speak of the fucking devil. Ash Cedar strolled into the corner of my eye, blocking Alecto entirely, and I pushed off the window to rise to my full height. Draped in traditional robes, from the heavy brocade cloak to the stupid creased trousers that laced in the front, he radiated warlock snobbery in garnet, black, and gold, all the while reeking of butterscotch ale.

Nauseating, really.

163

"Green certainly is her color," he mused, head cocked as he stared openly at my flatmate, not bothering to hide the way his coal-black eyes swept along her figure. Across the party, Alecto was in the midst of being dragged into another round of tequila shots; from the strained smile and the wave of her hands, she didn't *want* to partake, but one of the nurses shoved a shot glass into her hand anyway, protests falling on deaf ears.

Ash Cedar never talked to me. *Never.* Rarely ever acknowledged me, even if we were the only two in the room, but tonight he addressed me like we were fucking *friends*. Everything about his stance implied he basked in my discomfort, from the easy smile to the obvious leer, diving into my personal bubble and practically shoving his drink in my face. Stiff from top to bottom, I merely took a long sip of my own, the slosh of blood making the warlock grimace.

"Tonight is a really big night for us," he remarked with a wistful sigh.

"What?" Fuck's sake. I should have walked away—clearly he was doing this to rile me up, the fucking prick, but apparently I was a glutton for punishment these days.

"First kisses..." Cedar toasted me with his half-drunk mug. "You remember them for the rest of your life."

Jaw clenched, I busied myself with the rest of the room, frosting over at the insinuation and doing nothing to hide it.

"We've been dancing around this for months now," the warlock carried on, "but tonight is perfect. At midnight, Alecto and I will make it official in front of *everyone*."

I sank my fangs into my tongue, hard enough to draw spurts of thick, cold blood, and said nothing.

"As her friend, I do hope we have your support."

Then the fucker clapped me on the arm and *waited*, gripping my bicep, grinning up at me like he knew he had finally won the war. Once again, doubt reared its ugly head.

Alecto had never mentioned Ash Cedar before, and we talked about everything. From students to her escapades with Gavriel, we shared our lives on the flat's couch with no holds barred.

Open dialogue came naturally.

I should just ask her.

But maybe she had sensed my feelings ages ago and kept her truer affections—not just passing flings in the greenhouse—to herself.

Maybe she still had secrets.

I had no qualms that she'd slept with Gavriel—or that she remained attracted to him, her heart pounding whenever he was around, her temper rising, the spark between them deadly but exhilarating. Throw in Jack Clemonte, a warlock she seemed to share some strange, unspoken connection with, and we had quite the lovely little harem of males developing around Alecto Clarke. Both men had their pros and cons, but when I thought about it—the rare time I bothered, because her interest in them had never affected me before—Jack and Gavriel could do her some good.

And she could offer them the same.

A different perspective. A spot of growth. A fearless voice to call them on their haughty shit.

She did it with me all the time.

Ash Cedar offered her nothing but traditional values and prejudices and boring one-sided prattling...

They just didn't make sense.

He had always rubbed me the wrong way, his pleasant façade in public just a mask that he peeled off in private around those he considered lesser.

Frankly, the thought of her *wanting* him made me question not only her character, but her judgment.

Which wasn't fair—but here we were.

Cedar's smile stretched wider, all teeth, a male trying to

warn a rival away from his mate, and he then clapped me on the arm. He might have tried to make this one a hard hit, swinging fast and slapping firm, but it felt like nothing.

Like a toddler swatting ineffectually at a full-grown man, desperate to prove he too was *strong*.

"Thank you," the warlock crooned. "Your silence speaks volumes, old man."

As suddenly as he appeared, Ash Cedar left, drifting back to the party, sauntering through the throngs with his head held high.

"What the fuck was that about?" And cue Gavriel to take Cedar's place at my side, popping into my personal space just as abruptly and bringing with him a whiskey cloud to smother the lingering syrupy butterscotch in the air. I glanced down, the fae and warlock roughly the same height, and then shook my head.

"Nothing." My growl had Gavriel smirking. "Just Cedar being a cock like always."

We both watched him guffaw with some of the aging warlock professors in the sitting area, lording over them on the couch and lapping up all the attention. Gavriel scoffed, arms crossed, his plum suit immaculate, right down to the snug vest, the silver tie, the polished oxfords, and the squared-off shoulders—but his expression gave away just how shit-faced he was already. Glossy, unfocused eyes. Flushed cheeks. Disdain out in the open for everyone tonight.

"Fucking wanker," he muttered. If I didn't watch him, things could take a messy turn. No idea what had set him off, but when he flicked those bleary eyes to the door, then up to the ceiling, I had a feeling I'd hear all about it—in excruciating detail—very soon.

As the distance between me and Alecto grew in the last ten days, so too had a routine I now shared with Gavriel:

drinking and smoking on the staff tower roof. The night after Yule, I'd caught him clumsily climbing through the window on the top-floor landing, and while I stopped him, literally wrestled his drunk ass back inside, worried he was too pissed to remember to flap those black fae wings should he fall, I eventually agreed to accompany him out and up.

At first, I'd just wanted to keep him alive.

But then we started talking.

Talking turned to grousing, and suddenly I was up there nightly with him, usually around one in the morning, for a bitchfest that went on a good hour before we called it. It was our little secret, the first I shared with a colleague who wasn't Alecto, and I... liked it.

The fae and I had a lot in common: two ancient warriors stuck in the present, trapped in the modern world where no one wielded a sword anymore to settle their problems. Not only that, but we old oaks were surrounded by saplings who didn't understand us, couldn't connect with us, and rarely made an effort to *try*.

Venting with someone who wasn't Alecto had felt freeing.

I'd even started to look forward to it.

I just hadn't expected he would bail on tonight's festivities so early, but as he crudely loosened his tie and scowled at everyone in a five-foot radius, something told me he needed a little space and a nonjudgmental ear.

No telling what the problem was beyond the standard frustrations, but when I caught the fae studying Alecto, lingering on her face, her curves, her bare legs, I suddenly wondered if we shared more than our warrior past.

"Yes," I told him, capping my thermos with its twisting lid and motioning to the door. "You good to fly?"

Usually the fae spirited me to the tower's top, but if he was too out of it—or had beat me to it—I could climb up there, too.

Rather not damage the suit though, midnight black and impeccably tailored, one the few pieces in my collection that had cost a pretty penny.

"Yeah, yeah, 'm fine," Gavriel rasped. Uh-huh. Sure. Definitely going to be a climbing night, what with him stinking of whiskey and swiping a full bottle from the bar table on his way to the door. I followed with a shake of my head, not caring if we missed the midnight celebrations in forty minutes.

I had no desire to watch Alecto kiss someone else tonight as twelve bells thundered through the party, Ash Cedar or otherwise, and from the glare Gavriel hurled at her over his shoulder before we left, he didn't either.

16

ALECTO

"Oh my *gods*... Is Gavriel talking to that painting?"

By two in the morning on the first of January, the shenanigans had finally dipped from a boil to a simmer. Music lowered, straight liquor switched to mixed drinks and water, we had crossed the threshold into the new year—and still had classes in the morning. If it had been a Friday or Saturday, the Root Rot staffroom would have been *howling* at this hour, but many had trickled out after midnight, leaving only the die-hard partiers behind.

And me.

Because... Well, Bjorn had bailed on midnight. No New Year's Eve hugs or kisses on the cheek—nothing. And he had been super standoffish since the run-in with Benedict on Yule. Which sucked. The vampire was basically my best friend at this point, the one I'd been searching for all my life without ever realizing it, and now it just... It sucked.

The heart complicated everything. Because I was smitten with my best friend, and now he was ignoring me, and I didn't want to go back to the flat where I knew he'd be awake and we would have yet another awkward run-in of us faking it until I went to bed.

Worst of all, I had no idea how to fix it. I might have shared everything with him, but Benedict Hammond was still a secret just for me. If I couldn't tell Bjorn the truth, I refused to tell him a lie. So, we would stay stuck in this stupid fucking limbo until he got over whatever had set him off in the first place, or until I found a way to tell him without actually *telling* him and just—

Ugh. Gods. Coming down from tequila shots and champagne was the worst. I'd stopped drinking two hours ago and already the hangover headache was scratching behind my eyes. Those who had stayed behind nursed drinks to taper off, a bunch of us—nurses and faculty, the younger generation who out-partied the oldies at the last rager—currently slumped around the table we used for meetings and grading.

Tonight, it had hosted a beer pong tournament.

And was now sticky with dried beer, red plastic cups scattered everywhere, upturned and on their sides and way too reminiscent of my post-grad academy days.

While most of us were at the table, a few of the sophisticated bunch sat on the couches by the hearth. A flirty pair whispered at the window. Jack had just gone to bed, exchanging a lingering, heated look with me on the way out that almost made me moan out loud.

Almost.

I wasn't *that* drunk anymore.

Just tipsy.

And headachy.

And tired.

And annoyed that Benedict fucking Hammond wouldn't stop trying to get my attention. Seated amongst the conversationalists on the couches, he glanced my way every so often, pointed and obvious, trying to catch and hold my gaze like he had earned that right. During the midnight countdown, he had shouldered toward me as everyone cloistered together to ring in the new year, but I had grabbed Sonia, one of my nurse friends and a failed conquest of Gavriel's, and kissed her before he could even *try*.

Just a silly peck, one we both giggled through and shotgunned our champagne flutes after.

Meanwhile, Benedict had had that determined twinkle in his eye I'd seen on drunk men at bars, like they were being *subtle* as they stumbled along and slobbered all over me, sloppy, breath reeking of booze.

Nope.

Nope.

Not on my darkest day would I let that happen, Hammond.

"Oh, he *is*—he's talking to the painting."

Giggles erupted around me, dragging me out of my thoughts.

"What a messy drunk."

"He's messy *everything* tonight."

More giggles and snickers, whispers rising about Gavriel this and Gavriel that, more than half the women around me notches on his bedpost—myself included. Guzzling down the last of my water, I twisted in my seat, eyes heavy, head pounding, and found the source of their amusement.

I exhaled sharply. *For fuck's sake, bro.* Across the room and to the left of the main door, there was Gavriel—messy, shit-faced Gavriel—talking to a fucking painting. As if the rest of us didn't exist, he carried on an animated conversation with the abstract canvas, art that if you squinted, you could *maybe* make out a face. If he had smoked as much as he drank tonight, the fae *definitely* saw something in all the colors and squiggles. Laughing, tossing his hands about, swaying side to side, he looked deep in conversation...

Much to the cruel delight of everyone around me.

And it would be easy to let him go on like that, making a fool of himself and totally ruining his campus seduction cred. I mean, the last time we talked, he had told me he didn't want to be *friends*, then flipped me off. The guy could be *such* an asshole. He used liquor and herbs to keep others at a distance, exuding a devil-may-care attitude while peering down his nose at the rest of us just because he was fae.

But I couldn't leave him like that.

Couldn't turn my back.

Because seven or so years ago, that had been me talking to a portrait, drunk off my face—broken inside. Hurting, deeply scarred and desperately wounded, in a way no one else could see or understand. I'd done all the same shit: drank, partied, slept around to numb the ache in my soul.

Back then, I'd had friends—*true* friends—who refused to let me face-plant when I self-medicated too hard. Friends who I shared a dorm with, who were in my herbalism classes, who had their own childhood traumas following them into higher education.

They hadn't let me permanently ruin my reputation around the academy—and I guess I wasn't about to let Gavriel do that either. When he was sober, if he wanted to be a fucking douchebag or make a fool of himself in front of everyone, fine.

But this little show was *over*.

I left the cackling peanut gallery without a word, steadier on my feet now than two hours ago—but still ghosting my fingers along the backs of the chairs, refusing to give the rest of them *two* hot messes to criticize at once. Sure enough, Gavriel was, in fact, deep in conversation with the artwork, enraptured enough with whatever story he was babbling that he didn't even notice my approach.

"Hey." I went for his arm, grabbing tight to bolster his swaying ass when he swung toward me, eyes wild and a million miles away. Hair staticky and finger-combed to death. Tie loose. Suit vest misbuttoned. Someone had either mugged him or fooled around with him at some point this evening—hard to tell. Given his state, neither would have been consensual acts. The fae slurred something at me, fluttering his dark lashes, mouth kicked in a flirtatious smirk, and my brows shot up in response. Yeah, that definitely wasn't English. I forced a smile and squeezed his arm, nodding just enough not to enrage my steadily sharpening headache. "Okay, cool." I then looked pointedly toward the door. "Come on, time for bed."

"*Bed*," he repeated, lilting forward and crashing into me before I could stop him. I grunted, bracing for the dead weight of a shit-faced fae, and pushed him upright with my shoulder.

"Yup, bed."

He wiggled his eyebrows. "*Bed*, fury."

"Oh my gods," I muttered, marching us around in a circle and dragging him toward the door. "Can you not be a horndog for like two seconds?"

While Gavriel wasn't the biggest guy on campus, he was solid as a rock, all sinewy muscle and long, elegant limbs that had zero coordination tonight. Fortunately, he must have been almost blackout drunk, because as heavy as he was, as strong as he *usually* was, he was easy to manipulate; I had him out the door and onto the landing in twenty seconds flat.

As soon as the door swung shut behind us, the party vanished, replaced by a cool, heavy quiet that fell like a ton of bricks. Dim lighting gave way to shadowy stonework, the

173

darkness really highlighting the exhaustion in my bones—
and I *dreaded* the thought of waking up in three, maybe four
hours for a full day of classes.

Gavriel would probably sleep the day away. I had seen
him intoxicated before, but as he lolled to the side and out of
my grasp, crashing onto the wall with a groan, this was the
absolute *worst* episode in our shared history.

Not good.

Something must have happened.

Something that wasn't my responsibility to fix.

He didn't *want* to be my friend, the stubborn fucker, so I
just needed to get him safely to bed. That was it.

"Okay…" Hands planted on my hips, I gave him a quick
once-over. "What's your flat number?"

Slouched against the wall, Gavriel tipped his head to the
side and grinned. "Fury…" His velvety growl had the hairs on
the back of my neck rising. "Fury…" He beckoned me to him
with a crooked finger, tongue flicking across his laughing
mouth. "*Fury.*"

The last one came out all singsongy and sloppy, seduction
botched by booze. Shaking my head, I moved in and shoved
his hands away when he tried to grope me—straight for the
boobs, of course—then quickly patted him down. After
digging his flat's skeleton key out of his breast pocket, I
tucked it up my sleeve, one step closer to wrapping up this
ordeal in a pretty bow, and then huffed at him.

Slapped his hand from my waist.

Watched as he struggled to flail off the wall.

Gods, what a mess.

Been there, buddy.

"Gavriel," I said slowly, grabbing his face and cradling it
between my palms. Skin hot and sweaty, he could have done
with a cold shower, but that was a step too far: like fuck I'd
bathe him on top of everything. With a deep breath, I gave

him a playful little jostle, redirecting his gaze to mine, and smiled. "Tell me your flat number so we can fuck in an actual bed, okay?"

His eyes dipped to my lips, and there they stayed, oddly focused and intense. "Nine A, *furyyyyyyyyyyyyyyyyyy...*"

Ugh, this guy.

Why did I have such a fucking soft spot for him?

Because he's you.

And he's broken, too.

Ughhhhh. Stupid... self-awareness.

After dragging his arm around my shoulder, I managed to get him moving, though I relied on the support of the wall to march him down the staircase without losing my grip—and Gavriel inevitably falling flat on his face. By the time we reached the ninth floor, his hand had found a way to cup my boob, but I let it slide if it meant we maintained this forward momentum, his feet disastrously uncoordinated and his eyes blinking at different speeds, seeming heavier and heavier with every step.

Door unlocked, I slipped his key in his pants pocket, then hauled his stumbling ass inside a flat that looked identical to mine and Bjorn's, only instead of the TV setup, the common area had a two-seater couch, two armchairs, a fur rug, and a massive bookshelf drowning in books between the two windows. The place smelled like dude, like wood and leather and spicy aftershave, and as I kicked the door shut behind us, Gavriel's boob-cup more of a death grip for balance at this point, I barely had time to process how weird it was to be in his home—his personal space. To the right were the same bedroom doors that I saw every day in *my* home, and with one shut, I figured Seamus had already gone to bed, which had me guiding Gavriel to the open one beside it.

Passing over the threshold into his private domain sparked another drunken attempt at seduction, only the purrs spilling from his lips were all slurred and incoherent, his head drooping and eyes hooded.

"Right, right, sure," I muttered, finally twisting out from under his arm and hurrying for the bedside table, the same make and model as mine, on top of which was an identical lamp—same fussy little knob to turn it on, too. Warm yellow filled the room after the *click*, and Gavriel staggered to the side, slamming into his desk suddenly with a hand up to shield his eyes.

"Oww*www*."

Gods. My academy friends were *saints* for putting up with my drunk self all those years. Ten minutes with Gavriel and my patience was already wearing thin.

Same as his library office, Gavriel's bedroom didn't have the lived-in feel you'd expect for a guy who had been here for, what, four years? Minimal clutter, academy-issued furniture, no wall art, no clothes out of place. Besides the neatly organized stacks of books on his desk and a few file folders on his bedside table, the room looked brand-new— like he had moved in yesterday and was still waiting for his stuff to arrive. He could take a casual five minutes to clear out and it would be like he was never here.

Which… Maybe that was the point. Maybe he, like the me of ten years ago, struggled to form attachments.

Struggled to identify and claim *home*.

"Okay." I planted my hands on my hips and rounded on him. "Let's get you ready for bed."

And there he was, sprawled across his desk, legs wide, tie somewhat looser, hooded eyes surveying me like he thought he was *king* of sexual conquest. Gods. Spearing a hand through his ashy brown locks, the fae smirked, cocked an eyebrow, and crooned something that sounded like a lyrical foreign dialect—or drunken nonsense.

Probably the latter.

"Yeah, sounds great, man," I said, striding over and attacking that tie once and for all. "Let's get this show on the road."

Undressing a drunk fae was like dealing with a squirmy toddler. Gavriel was all hands—as usual, honestly—but he lacked coordination and depth perception. No tantalizing caresses. No toe-curling roughness. No masterful grip on my throat, in my hair. Just... a mess. And a lot of flirtatious mumbling that I smiled and nodded at, cataloguing any snippets I *might* make use of later if we ever got back on speaking terms.

After all, he didn't want *friends*.

He had no use for people like me.

I rolled my eyes at the thought, then grabbed his arm and hauled him off the desk. Down to a pair of black silk boxers, his erection halfhearted, his skin like moonlight, Gavriel swayed at my side as I motioned toward his bed—which had been made up with near militant precision at some point, the linens tucked in tight, not a hair out of place.

"Time for sleep, buddy."

It almost seemed a shame to ruin his hard work, but there was something ridiculously gratifying about ripping the blankets back.

And it wasn't just ruining his OCD linen tucking that felt satisfying.

It was...

It was the smell of them that made *me* feel good, the cloud of Gavriel that whooshed up with the rustling of sheets. Unlike his delicious colognes, this was... earthly. Nothing manufactured. Nothing tailored to what women liked. Natural. Soft. Subtle.

Cozy.

Like a forest at dawn, the remnants of a long-dead campfire still in the air and fresh dew on the grass.

Safe.

Which was laughable.

Gavriel was the furthest thing from *safe*.

Of all the men in my orbit, that inner circle few had ever been welcomed—Jack, Bjorn, and Gavriel, apparently—this drunk idiot had the capacity to do serious damage.

Because tonight had confirmed it: he was me from seven years ago.

And the me of today just wanted to help, but he knew *precisely* how to hurt. Where to fling the dagger for maximum impact.

"I'm ugly, Alecto."

He choked out the statement just as I lowered him onto the mattress, so clear and concise that I ended up dropping him the rest of the way.

"What?"

"I'm *ugly*," he whispered, suddenly coherent even with the odd slur curling around his vowels. Crouched by the bed, I looked him over—because this fae was nowhere near *ugly*. He was breathtaking, always had been, from the sinewy muscle to the sharp lines of his face, the layered grey hues in his eyes. Given this was my first time seeing him nearly naked despite screwing twice already, I noted scars on his torso, some rounded and irregular, others long and thin. Surprise trickled through my veins like ice: who knew fae could scar? Not me.

But we all had scars, and they certainly didn't make him ugly.

"Gavriel—"

"I'm petty," he whispered hoarsely, eyes closed and brows furrowed like he was in pain. The rest of him had that alcohol-induced looseness, muscles relaxed, arms limp, feet splayed, but he gritted his teeth hard, as if my cautious hand on his shoulder were a knife stabbing down to the bone. "I'm

178

petty and jealous. I covet w-what isn't m-mine." I withdrew, frowning, unsure what the fuck was happening, but my absence didn't make the pained expression go away. If anything, it seemed to make it worse. "I'm *ugly*."

"You're drunk," I told him frankly, careful not to sound like I pitied him.

Because I didn't.

If anything, I *empathized* with him. Not sympathized. I didn't need to pretend to know how he felt in this exact moment; I'd been there more times than I could count.

"I'm ugly..." He cracked an eye open, the grey orb whizzing around until it found my face. "And you're the only one who sees it."

Where was all this lucidity before? Definitely could have used it while I was literally wrestling him out of that suit. I sighed, then grabbed his wrist and squeezed.

"Stop. You're not—"

"Ugly on the *inside*," the fae snapped, wrenching his arm away, then seconds later clawing back at my fingers. I rolled my eyes and patted the top of his hand, then leaned down to share a little secret.

"Yes, shockingly," I whispered, grinning when he peeled open the other eye, "I understand the nuances of this meltdown." My chuckle made him wince, grimacing against the sound. "You're not ugly, Gavriel. You... You're like..." Not a fae dildo. I'd called him that once before and felt shit about it to this day. "You're a wounded animal."

Been there, done that. In fact, I *still* fell back on old coping mechanisms, even with all the growth and self-awareness I'd slogged through in my twenties. Benedict Hammond really triggered my bad habits, and while I could stand in front of him without panicking now, I was still recovering from coming face-to-face with my parents' murderer months later.

Maybe once a wounded animal, always a wounded animal.

Gavriel just seemed to be in the thick of it tonight, his wounds fresh and open, while mine had finally started to scab again.

"*Ugly*," he hissed. Slowly, his eyes drifted shut, followed by a deep, lung-filling breath and a long, dramatic exhale. I felt for him—really, I did—but why did he have to make being his friend so *fucking* difficult?

Unless he wanted to be more than friends.

I mean... Sometimes I could picture that, more so lately when I realized we were both broken inside, that our connection could easily go beyond the physical if we put a little work in.

But that would be a disaster, wouldn't it?

Not something I could do on my own, anyway. To *be* with Gavriel, I'd need backup to call him on his crap and a support system for when the wounded animals in us *both* started to howl and snarl and bare their teeth.

As soon as his grip loosened around my fingers, I carefully extracted my hand and shook it out to get the blood flowing again. It was then I caught it—the glint of a metal flask tucked behind his lamp. Frowning, I grabbed it, uncapped it, and risked a quick sniff.

Yup.

Whiskey.

It might take the edge off in the morning, but what kind of friend would I be if I left it here for him?

So, I tiptoed across the flat, in no mood to deal with Seamus's questions—his stare and smirk that were bound to be accusatory and all too knowing—and navigated their shared bathroom in the dark. After dumping the whiskey and rinsing both the sink and the flask, I filled the little metal jug to the brim with the cold water, then charmed it to stay cold throughout the night with a bit of wandless magic.

Back in his room, Gavriel was dead to the world, snoring softly with an arm thrown over his face.

And that worked just fine for me. Setting the flask on his nightstand, I was just about ready to go, hand ducking under the lampshade and fingers searching for that stubborn little switch, when I saw it.

Light reflecting off something *else* metallic, this time in his closet through the barely open twin french doors. I scoffed. Those had to be a personal upgrade, because my closet door was basic as hell and creaked whenever I opened it. Curiosity piqued, I crept closer and pushed one door to the side, just enough to sneak a peek...

At armor.

Literal *armor*, steel and pristine, on a heavy-duty wooden clothes hanger. Eyes wide, I nudged the doors open completely to get a proper look at a breastplate with fire engraved up its center, obscenely detailed flames surrounded by shooting stars and blazing comets.

So...

This was new.

At the sound of a loud, chainsaw-y snore, followed by a hiccup and a groan, I hastily shut the doors and stepped back as shame burned through me. Snooping through his things when he was this drunk was just bad manners, *definitely* taking advantage of a usually very tight-lipped fae when it came to personal matters, but straight-up *armor* hanging next to his—let's be honest—weirdly stylish, expensive, and metrosexual suit collection was the last thing I'd expected to find in Gavriel's bedroom.

Arms crossed, I faced him with a steadily deepening frown.

The front he put on for everyone else, me included, wasn't him at his core.

It was that armor, polished and spotless, lovingly stored alongside his prized wardrobe.

I'm ugly. That, too.

Gavriel was a fae warrior who hated himself.

Why?

Distant bells chimed through the castle, faint but present inside all the flats if you had an ear for them. Nearly three o'clock—*way* too tired for this mystery tonight.

So I tucked this mysterious, snoring warrior into bed, positioned the flask of water within reach, turned off the light, and left.

Only after I crawled into my own bed, I couldn't sleep, stuck staring at the ceiling instead, trapped in one persistent thought loop that refused to let me drift off...

Who are you, Gavriel?

And what are you actually doing here?

JACK

"Welcome to Fort Dàn, little one."

As per the terms set at our meeting this past Thursday, the use of a chosen nickname indicated the start of a scene. Two short days ago, Alecto had strolled into my office during her lunch hour for what was supposed to be a review of her first six months at Root Rot Academy; I had them scheduled for all staff now that the new year had begun, which meant no one batted an eye at our hour-long conversation behind a closed door.

No one but Iris, of course, but she had nothing concrete to pin on either of us—so *there*.

In said meeting, we *had* discussed her professional performance at the academy, but that had taken roughly ten minutes total. My new submissive was an exceptional educator. She attacked her job with vigor and was well liked by students. No formal complaints from her coworkers. No professional infractions. Never missed a staff meeting. Embraced my rehabilitation philosophy. Volunteered here and there to take on added responsibility. Huge success with the Samhain ball—despite how it ended.

My girl was leaps and bounds ahead of many of my new hires. Such an impressive creature, Alecto Clarke.

Her evaluation was but a drop in the ocean that day. For the rest of the hour, we discussed formalizing our kink relationship, for I couldn't carry on as we had lately. While scenes themselves were about letting go, it needed to be structured and regimented beforehand so no one got hurt— physically or emotionally. Soft and hard limits had been discussed and defined, then noted and categorized. We had considered appropriate levels of undress and set each of our safewords in stone.

Then there were the nicknames.

I had chosen *little one* for her—which, all things considered, was the sweetest, softest title I had ever given a submissive. Alecto in turn settled on *Sir*, something safe and easy, and agreed to refer to me as *Headmaster* elsewhere, then by my first name during aftercare.

As soon as she heard her new name now, she practically sprinted for me, soaked to the bone and legs splashed with mud. The skies had shattered some twenty minutes back, turning a grey, miserable January morning into a bleak, dark, wet affair. These were the stormy months, after all, and the rain came with a chill that never really lifted until late spring. While I had studied everything about this morning in excessive detail last night, from the predicted hour rain would fall to the temperature changes, even the anticipated wind speeds, Alecto appeared to have been caught off guard.

I had brought an umbrella large enough to fit half the student body.

She looked like she had crawled out of the loch to my right, soaked and shivering.

As soon as she stumbled under its reach, I dragged her close and tucked her trembling figure under my arm, using my body heat to warm her—for now. A simple drying charm would see to us both inside the fort...

Not that she would be in her running gear long enough to relish the cozy, fresh-out-the-dryer feel. We looked like quite the matching pair this morning, me in my black track pants, her in a pair of black wool leggings. Up top, she wore a cotton Root Rot sweater with the emblem across her chest, heather grey and provided at no cost to staff and students. I, meanwhile, wore a swishy black jacket, both waterproof *and* intimidating, then a plain grey tee beneath.

A morning jog was a simple excuse we had agreed wouldn't arouse suspicion around the castle, as it was something we had each partaken in separately since July. I had a regimented schedule other staff runners knew about, and while Alecto had been more erratic with her outings, she did so enough times to be lumped in with the rest of the cardio junkies. Although we were in the thick of winter, snow came and went in the highlands, which meant many still used the trails when they had the chance.

Alecto and I simply went west rather than north, along paths seldom trod these days—overgrown and slippery, steep and rocky.

Worth the effort for the guaranteed privacy.

I had arrived two hours ago to set up and ensure the fort was safe enough for this morning's scene.

Now huddled against me, shivering and pink in the cheeks, Alecto had rolled in at seven o'clock, right on time.

Which boded well for her backside: I would have *loved* to punish her for tardiness.

Another day.

With both of us shielded from the relentless downpour, I steered her around to give Alecto a better look at the grey stone fort that had once sent terror through Root Rot students. Built into the cliffside of a soaring great incline, the crumbling castle had been a part of the academy's property for centuries. Before my arrival, it was a threat, a place where students were dragged out to in restraints—a torture chamber where they would be whipped and broken and punished for poor behavior. Agony stained the walls of these ruins like a persistent black mold.

When I had taken over, I intended to use the three-story fort as a rehabilitation retreat—a reward to scrub the old reputation clean. Unfortunately, it was in such disrepair that I couldn't in good conscience bring my charges out here. Until we had the budget to repair the dilapidated stone structure, here it sat, carved into the mountain on its eastern side, overlooking the indigo-blue waters of Loch Dùdach to the west. Time had worn the place down, and past headmasters used its decay as just another scare tactic. Most of the wood doors had rotted away. Parts of the roof had caved in, the parapets had seen better days, and the sentry towers at all four corners were full of debris and open to the miserable skies.

But there were a few spots in which I could gleefully torment a new submissive with pain and pleasure—make her scream bloody murder and no one would ever hear it.

A few rooms still possessed four walls and a ceiling, along with solid, uncluttered floors that wouldn't give way under Alecto's feet.

I let her curious gaze wander for a few moments, taking in the ruins, the winterized ivy creeping up the towers and around the gaping arrow slits. Rainwater sloshed down the hillside toward the lake, and at the first distant crack of thunder, I finally eased us along, headed for the main arched doorway. It was there I left my umbrella to dry, the entry corridor still covered, then took a sharp right up a steep, dark, winding stairwell to the second level, Alecto at my heels, my fingers coiled tightly around her wrist.

Not her hand.

No romantic fingers entwined. Not a lover's embrace.

Her wrist—possessively cuffed in my much larger hand, my grip capable of such cruelty.

And that was the thrill... for *both* of us.

Shrouded in shadow, I marched us to the tight doorway of the room I had spent the last hour preparing. Once used as a dining hall—maybe—it stood at the southeastern end of the fort, all the windowpanes shattered but the roof intact. Long and narrow, it made for the perfect playroom, lit and warmed with floating golden orbs, each one giving off the heat of a small bonfire.

She'd need them for what I had in mind.

Muttering the simple spell under my breath, I dried us both off with a quick flick of my wand, then tucked it into my forearm holster as Alecto basked in the feel of my magic.

"Inside, little one," I told her, voice gruff but smile pleasant as I gestured for her to pass into our makeshift playroom. Hands threaded behind her back, she did so with a dip of her head as she tiptoed over the threshold. I trailed after, far enough that I couldn't touch no matter how desperately I wanted to, but close enough that she could feel my presence crowding her.

Once again, I allowed her a beat to map the space with her eyes: the long empty hall, the wandering golden orbs, the shattered windows—the zipped bags of toys I had left out in the open. Arms folded, I cocked my head to the side as she stared at them, then cleared my throat so that she flinched out of her thoughts.

"Are you ready to play?" I asked, still light and airy and *kind* in the way I addressed her. Nothing like making a sub feel safe before ripping that sense of security out from under them. Alecto pivoted around, lower lip snared between her teeth, and then nodded.

"Yes, Sir."

After the lengthy discussion of limitations and interests, we had signed a contract—a vow of secrecy. Even though I already had it drafted, Alecto had been the one to bring it up first, going so far as to suggest we commit to a blood oath.

Which had just... made my day.

And reminded me why I had chosen her, why I felt so drawn to her.

On the same wavelength, Alecto and I had signed the contract with a bloody fingerprint each, swearing ourselves to secrecy, protecting each other. Trust was paramount between any Dominant and submissive, but signing it knowing the risks should either of us blab—an explosion of painful, pustulating blood boils across our entire bodies—ensured neither of our careers or reputations would be tarnished in the process.

Before I'd filed it, I had charmed the document to obscure the text to everyone but Alecto and myself.

Just in case someone—Iris—went snooping.

"Tell me your safeword."

"Rot," Alecto whispered, the word drowned out by the next crack of thunder. It tickled me that she had kept the one I initially chose for her, the thought of her using it like a safety blanket rousing my cock.

Not that it needed any further prompting.

Planning this morning's scene had stuck me with *the* most stubborn erection from the time I woke up until I eventually fisted it to death in the shower. Since then, however, I'd navigated the world fluctuating between semi-hard and half-erect.

Bloody fantastic.

Such a brilliant display of self-control and discipline, wearing my desire out in the open. For now, it was tucked into my waistband where it belonged, though more than once I'd already caught her glancing down curiously, as if needing proof that this was as exciting for me as it was for her.

Trust me, little one. It's even better *for me.*

"Good girl," I rumbled, then flicked my gaze up and down her figure, purposefully dismissive of her outfit—like it offended me. "Now, strip down."

As per our negotiations, Alecto was comfortable peeling away everything—but I had insisted that she kept her panties, just for now. I still had my own personal, private issues to grapple with over the fact that I had swept a professor ten years too young into my kink-sphere, and as much as I would enjoy her totally bare before me, offering all the lovely bits for me to *hurt*, one step at a time.

Panties were a must, no matter how confident she was with her body.

And what a *body* at that.

Gods. I should have pushed for bra *and* panties—because her breasts were absolute perfection, a small handful, perky with a little heft, too, and adorable nipples the same dusty pink as her lips. My cock snapped to attention at the sight, her virginal white panties almost cruelly unhelpful in this situation. A smallish chest area led down to a cinched waist, then flared out to positively delicious hips that always looked so fetching in pencil skirts and fitted cigarette pants. Pear-shaped and beautiful, Alecto stood before me practically nude, then tugged out her hair tie to free her curls.

The attire of a bratty, eager little pain sub complete.

And that... *did* things to me.

Made me want to shirk all the carefully laid plans I'd crafted since Thursday and go rogue.

No. *Focus.*

I owed it to her to be meticulous.

Still, I swept my eyes over her appreciatively this time,

letting her know without saying a word that she had pleased me. Color warmed in her cheeks even as her skin prickled against the chill, rain battering the old fort from every side, and as I strolled down the long hall, I added another trio of warming orbs to help shield her from the cold.

Though nothing could shield her from me.

Not when I scooped up the restraints I'd embedded into the wall earlier. When I faced her again, I showed off a long chain that had blended into the grey stonework, then the thick leather cuff at its end for her delicate wrist. With nothing more than an arched brow, I brought her to me, pointedly ignoring the jiggle of her hips and breasts with every step. Once she was close enough, I snapped my fingers, the sound cracking through the space, and Alecto offered her arm like a very, very good girl.

Then jumped when I snatched it, lightning fast and no doubt harder than she expected, and attached the leather cuff around her wrist. Tight, but not tight enough to limit blood flow.

The other chain nestled on the opposite wall, and once I had that attached, Alecto was forced to stand in the middle of everything, the belle of the ball, with her arms outstretched and shackled. Pleased, I circled her once, just for show, as if checking my work, then left her to fetch my toy bag.

And she stood there in silence, gnawing at her lower lip, curling and uncurling her toes over the chilly stone floor. A strong gust of wind blew the storm in through the shattered windows, and her sharp inhale behind me suggested some of its wrath had brushed up her back. When I faced her again, I found those distracting nipples even more pebbled, the pair downright torturous to ignore.

In time, lovelies. I'll get to you.

During our lengthy discussion of personal preferences, Alecto had requested that I *not* walk her through a scene beforehand, nor did I overly handhold unless I had something intense in mind. She expressed that being left in the dark, totally at my mercy, was rather exciting.

And who was I to deny her a little excitement?

So, I set up for the scene in silence, totally focused on unpacking but still keeping an ear out for the rustling of chains, the catch of her breath.

Which shot up her nostrils sharply when I opened my bag, unfurled a small black blanket across the stone tiles—and christened it with a flogger. Then a pair of nipple clamps, connected with a thin rose-gold strand.

Lastly, a wand-shaped vibrator, fully charged and downright merciless in the right hands.

Crouched over the spread, I glanced up and arched an eyebrow again, waiting until her eyes lost themselves in mine.

"Are you ready to give me what I want, little one?"

My raspy growl had the color in her cheeks plummeting down to her chest, her breasts dancing with each shuddery breath. Without hesitation, Alecto nodded.

Not good enough.

Not for this Dom.

"*Say* it."

"Yes, Sir," she whispered. Whether it was with the chill or the eagerness—or, *please let it be the fear*—Alecto trembled as I picked up one of my beginner floggers, all soft leather tails meant to induce a thuddy pain rather than a vicious sting. She had done well with the cane, but now that we had made our partnership official, this little witch had much to explore. No sense in rushing when anticipation was so fucking exquisite.

I stood, the flogger's braided leather shaft held in a loose fist, comfortable and familiar against my palm, supple leather tresses hanging at my side. "What do I want, little one?"

"M-my pain," Alecto replied. *Gods, yes.* I flashed a feral grin.

"And?"

She gulped. "And..."

I slashed the tassels at the side of her left thigh, light enough for this baby pain sub but sharp enough to center her thoughts. Alecto squealed on impact, eyes clenched as she shot up onto her toes, then lowered herself back down, arms stretched wide and starting to shiver.

"And my screams," she gritted out, cracking one eye open to me, then the other, wearing a familiar *Is that what you want to hear, Sir?* look that made my heart *ache*. As much as she pleased me with just that expression, her flesh already warming to a dull pink, I kept my features neutral save for the unimpressed quirk of my brow.

The one that told her she wasn't anywhere *near* finished yet.

"And?"

"And, uh—"

I brought the flogger down on her other side, catching her right thigh hard enough to turn her squeal into a squeak.

"And..." Alecto blinked hard and looked around, searching for what I asked of her. "And... *And...*"

I mimicked her stammering as I ducked under the chain and got to work on the backs of her thighs, getting them both at once, bringing down the flogger this way and that, the tassels so responsive to the slightest flick of my wrist.

Missed you, old friend.

It had been far too long since he came out to play.

To make a subby shriek.

"Come on, little one," I teased, catching her left calf so that she hopped onto one foot, supported only by the tension in the chains. "You're a smart girl, aren't you? What *else* do I want?"

I drifted back to the tops of her thighs, then worked my way down, striking in rapid succession from top to bottom. When I reached her ankles, I snapped my fingers and ordered her to lift her feet one at a time. Shaking, Alecto *barely* managed to offer up enough for a proper hit—which earned her a punishing *whack* to her ass, those thin cotton panties useless at muffling pain.

She hopped onto her toes with a pitchy squeal, then did as she was told, lifting one foot and then the other for me to slash at.

"You w-want my tears," she managed, her words thick, choked, like she could barely get them out.

"Good girl." Meanwhile, my words were warm—but my strikes were harder, cycling back up, alternating between her legs before getting to work on the rounded globes of her ass. One cheek, then the other, back and forth, painting the fleshiest parts a glorious red.

"And r-red skin," Alecto cried, jostling about, shifting her weight, trying uselessly to twist out of my reach. I hadn't instructed her to remain still, but one day I would: if she moved so much as an *inch* during my assault, she would deeply, deeply regret it.

"*Excellent*," I hissed, letting the flogger rest for a moment as I ducked back under the taut chain and strolled into her eyeline again. Bloodshot, watery eyes greeted me. Flushed cheeks. Hard as fuck nipples screaming for my attention.

Circling my wrist, I made the tassels dance, forcing her gaze to drop—and in that moment of distraction, I flicked her right nipple. Alecto jerked back with a gasp, her back rounded as if trying to fold in on herself, to make herself smaller, finally realizing that she couldn't go *anywhere*.

That this was how it felt to be at a Dom's mercy.

Just as she wanted...

The fear glistening in her eyes had me wondering: Did she regret it?

Grinning, I flicked her other nipple just to hear her gasp again. *Fuck.* No better way to start one's day than by making a submissive *suffer.*

And suffer she did. Leaving her nipples be—for now— made more room for flogging, and I worked the safest parts of her luscious figure *hard*, making her red all over like a delectable little cherry tomato. While my preferences erred toward single brutal lines blazing across a sub's flesh, this was just as nice, Alecto all rosy and squirmy and whiny. She darted up on her toes with certain hits, danced around in place, squealed and cried out and tried to fold over or twist away from the lash.

To no avail, of course. I had my way with her until her head slumped forward and her breath came hard and fast; only then did I allow her a moment to find herself again, to come back down to earth and exist beyond the exquisite ache pulsing through her body.

And when she did, I was ready for her, standing there with the nipple clamps in hand, round two on the horizon. Head cocked, I held up the plier clamps for her to take in, then nodded at her perfectly pearled nipples.

"These are pretty," I mused. Alecto swallowed thickly, throat bobbing again, and then forced a trembling smile.

"Th-thank you, Sir."

Flogger temporarily set aside, I used my free hand to attack both breasts, pinching her nipples to make them even harder. When we had gone through the lengthy list of kinks and interests, Alecto had told me nipple play was a *go.*

Foolish girl.

"I'm going to hurt them," I said softly, reverently almost, "so they'll be even prettier."

"Yes, Sir," she choked out, shivering from top to bottom

even as her skin burned bright like my own personal inferno. "Thank you."

"You are most welcome, little one."

Connected by a thin rose-gold strand, each clamp had adjustable screws attached to really tighten around some poor thing's nipples. For today, I had no intention of squeezing beyond the base level; my girl had never done nipple play like this before, I could guarantee that.

Without warning, I attached the first clamp, mindful to pinch *only* her nipple and not the surrounding skin. Still, even with my tender loving care, Alecto's eyes bulged as soon as the clamp was in place, and she immediately tried to squirm away.

"W-wait, Sir, wait a second—"

Oh, I so loved when they *begged* for mercy without using their safeword.

Meant I could ignore them to my heart's content.

Her pleas triggered something feral inside, a part of me that had been dormant for too long, and I cupped her breast, pinched her nipple a few times while she squealed, then added the second clamp. A tear careened down her cheek the moment I stepped away to appraise what a pretty piece of art she was now, and I caught the droplet before it dribbled off her jaw. Let it hang from my finger until she lifted that bloodshot gaze to mine. Licked it away right before her eyes and groaned at the salty taste.

Although I had yet to pause the scene and check on her— as per her request—we were officially on a timer now. No Dom left anything precious clamped for more than twenty minutes, and there was still so much to do.

I left her to ruminate in her suffering, her sniffles and whimpers a symphony behind my turned back, and when I returned, I had the vibrator in hand. Activated its lowest setting. Trailed the tip along her parted lips so that she jerked and straightened, wincing through every movement. After all, *everything* jiggled those clamped breasts now, heightened the pain, centered her attention right *there*.

And here I was, ever the cruel sadist, to try and distract her with pleasure.

Moving in close enough that my chest brushed the chain, made her jerk and squeal, I fisted her wild hair and wrenched her head back so I could really lose myself in those amber pools. Then, without warning, I thrust the vibrator between her thighs, up against her clit, against cotton panties so damp with need I could practically smell it from here. Alecto's eyes rounded further, and she struggled against her shackles, lips falling open in a silent scream. Even though I had the vibrations at their lowest setting, it was an assault all the same, a full-on *attack* of pain and pleasure.

Her poor body probably had no idea what to do with itself.

Might as well just come, little one.

What other option do you have?

Struggling up onto her toes, Alecto's expression wavered between agony and ecstasy, that pained look threatening to punt me over the edge without warning. Beyond sublime, her struggles, fighting the chains at her wrists, my hand in her hair, the vibrator wand thrust ruthlessly between her thighs. In less than a minute, my new submissive devolved into a shuddering, squeaking mess, and I was about to call her a little piggy for all those squeals, when she choked out something that sounded like *stop*.

I slowed.

"*Stop*," she gasped, eyes wild and body flailing. And I did.

Smirking, I completely detached, left her hanging there with her nipples clamped and her body coated in a sweaty sheen. The storm raged all around us, but I barely felt it in here. Barely felt *anything* beyond the unfettered high of dominating again, my many, many problems miles away.

If she couldn't handle the vibrator, then she would take the flogger. Setting the instrument of pleasure aside, I picked up the tool for pain and got to work repainting her body red. Her screams came louder this time, every shift and squirm and wriggle upsetting her clamped nipples.

"Oh, I'm so sorry, little one," I drawled, flicking the leather tassels at her ass, one side and then the other. "I thought you didn't *want* pleasure?"

Head bowed, Alecto merely whined in response, then yelped when I struck both cotton-covered cheeks in a single blow. Always aware of the time, I alternated between the two, pain and pleasure, vibrator and flogger, one in each hand. Thirty seconds of pleasure humming in her clit, then a full minute of leather tails everywhere else. On and off, back and forth, pain and pleasure again and again until they melded into one.

Until I knew she couldn't take it anymore.

Tossing the flogger aside, cock dangerously erect under my waistband, I strode up to her and upped the vibrator's setting. A brat at heart, Alecto had tried widening her stance to make its rapid-fire licks less intense, but I pressed harder, easily finding her clit at the crest of her covered sex and massaging it in slow, torturous circles. Her glazed eyes finally drifted shut, mouth open, muscles tensing—and then I grabbed the strand dangling between the clamps.

Curled it around my finger.

And pulled.

Not as rough as I might have liked, but *just* enough to shove her into the black. Alecto's eyes snapped open as she shrieked, her pain echoing through the dilapidated fort, and with a simple click of a button, I upped the vibrations to their max setting.

She came with a choked breath and a full-body shudder, scarlet erupting across her skin. At this point, it was a miracle I was even upright; every last drop of blood had to be in my cock, her climax a work of fucking art that I would crave from now until our next playdate.

But one last thing.

One *final* insult to wrap up the session...

As my girl squirmed over the vibrator, its assault ceaseless and no doubt far too strong for her sensitive clit, I removed the clamps. One at a time, quick and to the point, and she screamed twice more for me, endorphins at their zenith, the rush of blood back into the pinched buds a delectable, awful pain in its own right.

Struggling to keep my breath even, fighting for control, I forced myself back, arm outstretched so I could hold the vibrator in place just a little while longer, and looked her over from top to bottom. Drooped head. Tearstained cheeks. Trembling lips and flushed chest. Abused nipples and a core twitching through the aftershocks of a nuclear orgasm. Thighs aquiver. Knees weak.

Perfect.

Fucking *perfect*.

And then there was me with the worst case of blue balls known to man.

But I refused to pull my cock out and fist it away, spill myself all over her poor nipples.

Not today, anyway. We needed more time together before I felt comfortable letting *myself* go in front of her. For now, Alecto relied on me—my experience, my guidance, and my support. As much as it pained me, I had to forgo my physical release for her comfort.

No telling how long that chivalry would last, of course.

But in a few hours, alone in my office or my flat or my

shower, I would likely blow my load to the thought of her clamped nipples.

For now, there was still work to do.

Despite the throbbing erection, I moved swiftly and efficiently to put all the toys in the leather carrier bag, out of which I also pulled a blanket. Back by her side in a flash, I uncuffed her wrists without any fanfare, then hurriedly wrapped the blanket around her shoulders and dragged her into my chest. I'd expected her to fall, totally weak and helpless, but Alecto stumbled forward, then grabbed at my shirt, my jacket, her eyes nowhere near sleepy and spent.

But alive and ravenous.

Stronger than I had anticipated, my new submissive was in full control of herself as she climbed me like a fucking tree, threw her arms around my neck, and then slammed her mouth to mine. Her kiss was all raw passion and desperate fire, hard and needy, and for just a moment, I gave in. Kissed back. Threaded my hand into her hair and claimed her mouth for my own. Branded her with my tongue and teeth, snapping at that lower lip, determined to make it all plump and sore.

Pathetic.

My eyes snapped open, and as much as it pained me, I hurriedly wrenched her back by the shoulders, both of us panting, the pull between almost impossible to deny.

But I had to.

"Alecto," I said firmly as my insides turned to mush, even more besotted with her now than I was a minute ago, "no." Taking a deep breath, I shrouded myself in control. Made everything about me hard. Assertive. To the point. "This is a limit of mine, and you need to respect that."

Eager as I had been to claim her mouth, fuck her with my tongue, I had set kissing as a hard limit back at that meeting. What we did in a session screamed intimacy, of course, but it was a negotiated intimacy—a fantasy and nothing more. Kissing her, even in aftercare, took it too far. After all, I came into this with... feelings.

Feelings I refused to acknowledge or investigate. Feelings I buried deep down below the mountain of other shit crushing me one stone at a time. Our connection was complicated enough without confusing a shared kink with romance.

I... I didn't have time for love.

I had *just* enough time for this.

And when it was over, the session done, aftercare wrapped, we needed to be able to go our separate ways and live two separate lives.

Blinking hard, Alecto stared up at me for a long moment, hurt and confused and gut-wrenchingly lost, then finally seemed to come back to herself.

"Oh, I-I..." She shook her head, trying desperately to pull away, looking mortified to have broken one of *my* limits when I had been so careful with all of hers this morning. "I'm so sorry—"

"It's fine," I assured her, soft again, protective and warm as I brought her back to me. She went begrudgingly, stiff, perhaps even craving space, until I cupped the back of her head and forced her cheek against my chest—made her listen to my steady heartbeat.

Well, maybe not so steady now, but the rhythm would calm her all the same.

And as she softened in my arms, I made a note to tell her later that it really *was* fine. Yes, she had overstepped her boundaries, but this had been her first *true* scene as a submissive. All things considered, Alecto Clarke had been more than sublime. She took orders well. Cried beautifully. Accepted everything I gave her and then some. Came like a *goddess*. A little stumble at the end when she was deep in subspace, lost to the world and wholly in my thrall, was almost expected. The pleasure she felt would have come from kissing and touching and fucking in the past; no shock that she went there to chase the sensation, to bring some normalcy and familiarity to the moment.

In time she would learn that the closeness she craved could come from ropes and chains and the sting of the lash.

The thunder had blown over when our little cuddle ended some five minutes on. Exhaustion ringed her eyes, weighed down her shoulders, made her steps slow and sluggish when I left her to stand on her own two feet, which allowed me to partake in some of my favorite aftercare rituals.

I dressed my new submissive, manhandling her tenderly, hoping she took it as the worship it was—as thanks for what *she* had given *me* in that scene with her surrender.

Her willingness to take my brutality.

To minimize further stimulation, I tied her hair back in a loose ponytail to keep it out of her face, then bundled her up in the blanket again and sat her on the floor. Fetched an additional blanket as the rain poured beyond our grey surroundings.

Then set up the breakfast picnic that I'd had prepared in total secrecy…

Eggs benedict on brioche, drizzled with a thick, lush hollandaise. Smoked salmon and fresh-cut strawberries. Coffees and teas and juices for options. Waffle fries. I had no clue what my new submissive preferred, but from the way she took it all in, stomach gurgling and lips stretched wide, Alecto was more than pleased with the spread.

And despite my own hunger, my lingering hard-on, I fed her. Prepared her plate. Portioned her bites. Let her snuggle against me while I plied her with doughy, sugar-dusted fries.

All in the name of aftercare, of course.

Not because it made me *feel*.

Not because this was like a date no one would ever know about—no one but us.

Not because all of this made me genuinely *happy* for the first time in... gods only knew how long.

No. This was just me doing my duty, like always.

Taking care of business.

Oh, fuck it.

Even *I* didn't believe that.

And neither would she, which meant I would have to correct course and establish *much* clearer boundaries in the future.

So, for now, might as well just enjoy it while it lasted.

18

ALECTO

Ughhhhhhhh.

Fuck you, uterus.

For eleven glorious months of the year, I escaped the unfettered bodily bullshit faced by women worldwide. With a single dose of just one potion, I avoided period cramps, aches, and pains. No hormonal breakouts or weight fluctuations. No bloating. No overly sensitive breasts. No mood swings. No unwanted pregnancies. No STDs.

Honestly, that potion was probably witchkind's greatest invention. Sure, it was expensive as hell and you had to baby it all year. I had spent my entire first Root Rot paycheck on a starter kit when I arrived back in July because I hadn't been able to keep the petulant thing simmering when I moved from Canada to Scotland.

Since then, it had been bubbling away in one of my cast-iron cauldrons in the smallest off-limits greenhouse, maintaining the perfect temperature, stirred thrice a day, babied beyond belief.

All so I could avoid *this*.

Unfortunately, the side effects of taking a potion that kept a woman's insane mechanics chill for an entire year took a toll. Cue *all* the standard period symptoms—without the intense bleeding, thank the gods, but the odd bit of spotting still dropped by to ruin your underwear at random. Throw in a migraine or two, followed by a flurry of flu-like symptoms, and it was a fucking *party*. Two weeks of hell for eleven and a half months of carefree sex and no periods or icky diseases?

I mean. I guess I'd take it.

Glowering at the stairwell ahead, Alice's dark brown curls bobbing with every step, I slurped my ginger tea, death-gripping the thermos and wishing I was more than two *fucking* days into the fourteen.

But nope.

Just two.

And already I felt like death.

The next twelve were going to *suck*.

With a bristly sigh, I trudged down the stairs after her, then slugged another mouthful. While all the ginger I grew normally went to the infirmary and the kitchens, I snagged a little for myself this month, relying on its anti-inflammatory properties to make whatever was clawing at my insides fuck right off. Besides that, however, I relished its bite, that spicy kick with every sip.

Same as I'd relished Jack's bite, *his* spicy kick with every strike on Saturday. Knowing I'd be taking my potion Sunday, I had specifically requested Saturday for our first scene, which had been a blast and a half. Hot. Painful. The most efficient distraction from real world problems I had ever experienced, led by a master at his craft, followed by a breakfast feast?

Best morning I'd had in ages.

We had another session tentatively scheduled in about three weeks, and already I was counting down the days.

Just... had to survive this crap first.

At least I'd had one day of fun beforehand, the chance to forget and selfishly let go.

Because even though I felt like garbage, work didn't stop. Students weren't going anywhere. Staff meetings happened every Sunday no matter how gross I felt *or* looked.

Please gods, let the layered look still be in; I had layered the shit out of myself today, all shawls and baggy shirts and weathered leggings hidden beneath. Maybe it looked *cool*, maybe it didn't, but I needed to fight the impending chills and I didn't want anything touching my sensitive skin—so, win-win.

"Alice, aren't we meeting him in the courtyard?"

As the end of the day dragged on, dinner conquered and night classes underway, I had become progressively more tired, grumpy, and antisocial. The *last* thing I wanted to do was haul this cranky body into the depths of the Root Rot castle, but I had promised Alice I'd formally meet this new beau she had been hinting at since November. All this time I thought he was a fake, but tonight could prove me wrong. Maybe there *was* a nice, kind, funny, attractive teenage boy *somewhere* in this castle who made her happy.

Still. As pleased as I was that Alice had either found a boyfriend in this cesspit of acne or at the very least made a really good friend, I wanted bed. *Now.* Wanted to sleep this body grump away for as many hours as I could before I had to wake up and do it all over again tomorrow.

"Uh, change of venue," she insisted as we rounded the stairwell's curve and traipsed down the last few steps. Given I knew just about every student her age, even the ones who had been trickling in since the new year started, this was bound to be anticlimactic. But Alice had taken to me just much as I had to her, and when she asked me to meet her guy, she sounded so hopeful and eager and *scared*—desperate for my approval, almost. So, my inner monologue might be an asshole for these two weeks, but I would *never* project that onto her.

So, you know, here I was, crazy hair and wearing a million layers and moody as hell, off to meet some kid I already knew from class.

But for Alice, I'd do it.

Holding the door open at the bottom of the stairs, Alice offered a grating smile as I shuffled by, her aura staticky with frantic energy. While I looked like I had put zero effort into my outfit—or maybe too much effort to really nail that chic homeless aesthetic—she wore her uniform meticulous for tonight, tie perfect and wool socks pulled up to her knees, skirt swaying with the crispest of pleats. After witnessing a few failed attempts before, her cat-eye liner was on point, and she had managed to *finally* not brush her curls but work *with* them. While mine stuck out in every direction on top of my head like a half-baked bird's nest, hers were... cute. Docile.

She must have really liked this guy.

Gods, please don't be one of the assholes. I chugged down another few gulps of ginger tea, wincing at the nose-clearing sting, and then slowed when Alice took a hard right behind me into Clíodhna's alcove.

"Alice—"

"Back here, Professor," she called, and I hurried after her into... an empty alcove. Nobody but us and the statue, her arms outstretched and her eyes warm, full mouth quirked seductively. Before I could get another word in, Alice climbed *behind* Clíodhna—

And vanished.

"Alice!"

Thermos crashing to ground, I sprinted after her, confirming that, yup, she was gone. Panic washed over me like a tidal wave, icy as the North Sea and strong enough to pull me under.

"What the fuck?" I hissed, surveying the empty space behind the statue. "Fuck, fuck, fuck, *fuck*."

With barely two feet between the wall and Clíodhna'a back, I had no idea what possessed Alice to go back here in the first place.

But Bjorn had found her hiding *right* here months ago.

She...

Shoving the fear aside, the potion side effects ripping at my insides dulled for now, I tugged out my wand, braced on Clíodhna's thigh, and climbed in after Alice.

Which was a tight squeeze for a kid, never mind a full-grown woman wearing her entire wardrobe—

"Oh!"

My elbow went clear through the stone wall—like someone had glamored over an open doorway.

Actually... When I poked a cautious hand at the stone, it disappeared inside the wall of grey, and I realized that was probably *exactly* what had happened. Either that or someone up to no good had cast a portal.

"Damn it, Alice," I grumbled, peering around Clíodhna at the empty alcove, the underground corridors dead silent during night classes. No time to summon security—not when a student was on the other side, gods only knew where, doing gods only knew what with who. *Shit.* Shoulders squared, I charged headlong through the wall with my wand drawn...

And came out the other side still underground. The landscape, however, had a more natural touch to it, no fire-forged stone bricks, all smooth grey rock that looked like it had been burrowed through centuries ago. Wand gripped tight, I stood at the top of three limestone steps, which led down to a stone walkway that stretched into an underground lake. Dark blue water sloshed against the path, the ceiling high and domed, the cavernous space lit by hundreds of tiny white orbs that floated along like starlight.

"*Alice*," I snapped, zeroing in on her at the end of the stone dock as I stormed down the too steep steps. "What—is —*happening?*"

This was *so* not where I had seen the night going. Still sporting an expression that straddled the line between giddy and terrified, Alice crouched at the edge of the water, then shoved her hand in. The second she withdrew, wiping her fingers on her skirt, a huge shape lurched out of the bottomless blue after her, clawing onto the pathway—

A man.

I stuttered to a halt.

A *gorgeous* man. Angular jawline and bright aquamarine eyes. A shock of black hair and smooth ivory skin. Broad shoulders. Defined pecs. Shredded torso—

Webbed fingers.

I raised my wand, alarm bells shrieking, heart racing.

Siren.

"Get away from the water," I barked, charging down the stone runway straight for her. Slowly, Alice rose, her hands up and eyes wide, protests on the horizon that I was *not* in the mood to hear. As soon as she was within reach, I grabbed her arm and hauled her away, a quick glance to the depths confirming my suspicions: no mistaking that tail. Mermaids, the gentler of the two species, lived in warm, sunny waters, and while mischievous like forest sprites, they were relatively harmless.

Sirens were all teeth and claws, webbing between their fingers and a tail powerful enough to break bone with one swish.

Bottomless pits with the appetite of a gluttony demon.

"No, no, no," Alice cried, feet skidding uselessly over the limestone as I dragged her along. "This is *him*. This is Brin!"

"My lady…" The rich, velvety-smooth voice of a Scotsman floated after us, followed by the sloshing of water against stone. Out of the corner of my eye, I caught the bastard swimming along the walkway, his hand to his heart. "I've heard so much about you—"

I stopped and stabbed my wand in his direction, eyes narrowed. "Can it, siren."

Then, shaking my head, I tried to pull Alice toward the stairs again, but my little herbalism-obsessed beanpole put up a better fight this time. I whirled around with a huff, fighting to keep my temper in check.

"Alice, this is beyond reckless," I snapped, anger-articulating every syllable. Seriously—this place was like a bad dream. How many other sirens were lurking below the surface, hoping to snag an easy supernatural snack? Just the thought had the hairs on the back of my neck shooting up, and I gripped my wand tighter. "Like, are you *kidding* me?"

"I didn't do it on purpose," she argued, getting squeakier by the word, her eyes already welling with tears. "I-I just needed a place to myself, and Clíodhna smelled like the sea, like how the air smells near our coven's summer house—then I fell through the wall when I went looking. I thought it was… maybe my magic at first." One blink and it all came crashing down, tears spilling over, her breath catching in a heartbreaking sob. "I was so scared, but then Brin came and helped me! He calmed me down enough to go back through the portal—I swear!"

Oh my *gods.* I pinched the bridge of my nose with my wand hand. A dashing hero was just the thing to make a teenage girl abandon every shred of smarts she had—and let her guard down. Nope. *Fuck* no. Not on my watch.

"We've been talking for months now," Alice told me in a pleading whisper. "Please, Professor Clarke..."

Talking. Right. Rage went off inside me like a bomb; I'd seen a hickey or two on her neck in the last few months, and after learning she had a guy in her life, I had assumed it came from a bit of awkward groping in the dorms. Not this. Never this.

"Alice—"

"Sirens come with a fierce reputation, Mistress Alecto." If this fucker said my name one more time, I'd hex him so he sunk to the bottom of this lake and stayed there. I wheeled around, wishing looks could kill, hating that he spoke slow and deliberate like I was some thick idiot who couldn't sort through the nuances of that accent. He tipped his head to the side, smile warm, eyes... not. "Of this I'm aware, but, Alecto, surely you understand matters of the heart—"

"Buddy—" I held up my hand. "—you're going to need to stop saying my name like you have any idea who I am. Because if you knew me, you would have hightailed it the fuck out of here—"

"But I feel as though I *do* know you," Brin insisted, pushing up and planting his elbows on the walkway, way too close for comfort. One quick strike and he'd have Alice's calf; I put myself between them, barely listening as the siren added, "My sweet Alice speaks of you often..." His eyes slid to her like he could see straight through me. "I feel like I've known you all my life."

"Okay then." I snorted as I rounded in place and put Alice ahead of me, then marched her toward the soaring stone wall, hoping that this perv didn't have the power to seal the portal before I could shove her back through.

"Wait, Professor, no—"

"I would never harm her," Brin proclaimed as he swam alongside us. He then had the *audacity* to reach for me, maybe to grab my maroon shawl, my baggy white long-sleeved shirt, my lace-up ankle boots—something. Whatever his intentions, he got the tip end of my wand a breath away from his nose and instantly backtracked, hands raised innocently. "Please. Alice has the kindest heart I've ever known. Thoughtful and considerate. Patient and lonely. I long for her when we're apart, and when we're together, I feel *whole*."

I blinked down at this handsome jackass, then groaned when Alice literally *swooned*. No. *Fuck* no.

"Alice..." Briefly, hope sparked in her eyes, her whole being lifting like I was about to tell her good news—like I had fallen for his *crap*. Sighing, I took her firmly by the shoulders, and the slight shake of my head had her deflating, the floating orbs nearby glinting in her tears. "I would have to be the *worst* professor on the planet if I let this go on." I squeezed her shoulders when she sucked in a deep breath, as if to give me some last-ditch speech—a solid closing argument that would make me change my mind. Every teen thought they had it in them. "I'm sorry, but no."

It *killed* me to see her upset. Of all the kids at Root Rot, Alice's story cut the deepest. Only just fourteen now and already abandoned by her family, shipped off to some reform school all because she had a little trouble with her magic. Throw in a lack of friends her own age, her burgeoning personhood, her rock-bottom self-esteem, and the tragic coincidence of stumbling on what had to be an illegal portal into the school—of *course* she fell for this. Of course she clung to the one creature here besides me who treated her like a normal witch.

Watching her break down physically hurt me even more than the side effects of this damn potion, but no amount of tears could persuade me to let this slide.

If this siren tried to touch her again, I'd kill him.

Period.

"Wait..." Brin pushed up on the walkway, half his cut torso out, a smattering of discreet gills carved into the peaks and valleys of his abdomen. "Let me prove myself to you... Mistress Alecto, let me prove my love."

"Bye, Brin," I said flatly, grabbing Alice's arm and beelining for the stairs. Try as she might to fight it, this lost little first year was stick-thin and weak. Not a chance in hell she could overpower me—and I'd die before I let go and gave her the chance to jump in the lake to be with her man. Nope. Nope, nope, nope, *nope.*

She sobbed as I hustled her up the three limestone stairs sculpted into the huge stone wall, all of it way too human soap opera for my taste, and then shrieked for Brin when I finally shouldered her through the portal. Shooting the bobbing siren a glare over my shoulder, I kept my wand on him, arm outstretched and a hex on the tip of my tongue, as I climbed through the false wall after her.

And collided hard with Clíodhna. I cursed under my breath as pain flared in my shoulder, having forgotten how tiny the space was back here, then stumbled out from behind her and into the alcove. The salty air faded, replaced by the familiar thick mustiness of the lower castle corridors, romantic mood light from the orbs exchanged for bright recessed electrical bulbs and enchanted torches.

Thank the *gods* we had ended up back here—that someone hadn't closed the portal behind us. Rubbing at my shoulder and tuning out Alice's simpering protests, I peeked behind Clíodhna and poked my wand at the wall.

Once again, the tip vanished into what should have been solid grey stone.

Definitely a portal.

But who cast it? Sirens were said to have *some* magic at their disposal, but nowhere near as complex as witches and warlocks. As far as I was aware, portal-casting didn't factor into their skill set.

Super concerning, especially after what had happened with Bjorn.

Seriously... What the hell was going on at Root Rot? Was this just a case of same shit, different day, or was someone intentionally screwing with the academy?

Either way, the secret doorway between here and the underground lake was a danger to every student in this castle, and it wouldn't survive another *hour* if I had anything to say about it.

"*Please*," Alice cried as I scooted out from behind the goddess's statue again, suddenly *right* in my personal space, close enough to give me a front-row seat to the snot bubble swelling in her left nostril. Taking her by the arms, I marched us farther into the alcove, then wiped her tearstained face with my shawl.

"Alice, listen to me..." As furious as I was that she had put herself in danger time and time again, I couldn't stay mad at *her*. Alice was the child, Brin the pervy adult. Teen love came fast and furious, while heartbreak cut even deeper. If I could spare any of my students that, I would, but it was a part of growing up—feeling your heart splinter as the ground fell out from under you.

Then in a few days, weeks, months, that broken kid would put themselves back together. They would learn the heart could heal. *That* was the lesson behind all the pain.

Hard to understand when you're in the thick of it, of course. Right now, it was just needless suffering.

"Brin is very handsome," I acknowledged, because, yeah, the guy was a smoke-show. Like, descended from the gods *hot*. "Maybe he isn't like every other siren, but he's still too dangerous for you—and way, *way* too old."

And fucking gross for seducing a teenager; I left that part out of it, refusing to drive another knife in her back.

"But he loves me," Alice whispered shakily.

"Alice—"

"And sirens only eat *humans*."

"Sirens eat flesh." I pointed a finger at her to drive the fact home. "They're straight up carnivores. Humans are the only ones lured by their song."

"So he can't seduce me against my will," she fired back, her fight fading with every word, like she finally sensed defeat on the horizon. No argument would sway me here, and Alice slowly folded in on herself, arms crossed, head ducked, shoulders rounded—snot suddenly and violently snorted back. "I fell in love with him on my own."

"Oh, honey, no..." Ugh, my *heart*. Sighing, I pulled her close and tucked her against me. Jack had done it time and time again, using the strength of his body to calm mine, and I only hoped mine, while nowhere near as solid, had the soothing impact on Alice that his always did on me. "Okay, this—" I gestured back to the statue. "—ends tonight. I'm sorry, but I'll have to tell Headmaster Clemonte."

Alice gasped and twisted away, eyes like watery, bloodshot saucers. "No, *please* don't. What if he hurts Brin?"

Sensing an opportunity, I patted the air like I was calming a terrified fawn—because, really, that was *exactly* what I was doing here. "Fine. If you swear to never see him again, I'll keep your secret."

A little white lie never hurt anyone, right? Just because I didn't run straight to Jack tonight didn't mean I'd let it go. Not only did I plan to speak with her den mother and ask the shifter to keep a closer eye on her flock, but once I got Alice back to the dorms, I was headed straight to security to have that fucking portal sealed for good.

Anything less was just reckless.

And if I filed an official security breach with the dude bros patrolling this place, a copy would *have* to go to Jack. Well, probably Iris, then Jack, but whatever. Two birds, one stone.

While it took a little more coaxing, Alice eventually agreed. After, she bawled the whole way back to her tower, hiding her face and whimpering under her breath like she didn't want me to see or hear her heartbreak. No dice, kid—I could *feel* it. Having had my heart broken more times than I could count in my academy days, I knew the damage this night would cause.

But it was for the best.

And one day she would see that, after her heart healed and her spirit bounced back.

Until then, I'd keep her close.

Make sure that siren song didn't call her back to him.

As soon as I marched Alice into her room, I flagged down the nearest security warlock so we could get this shit sorted, still feeling like absolute crap, potion symptoms flaring even harder as the adrenaline subsided...

And then conceded that it would probably be a long, frustrating few hours before I dragged this grumpy, bloated, cramping body of mine to bed.

Ugh, for real though.

Fuck you, uterus.

19

BJORN

Fingers an inch away from the 4B doorknob, I stilled at the sound of an overly dramatic *Hell's Kitchen* elimination sequence blaring from the other side. She was in there—of course she was in there. Over halfway through the academic year, this was Alecto's home as much as mine. I hesitated and considered carrying on north with my satchel of student reflection essays, a hefty tome on Stoicism tucked under my arm.

But the staffroom had never been my safe haven.

And Alecto knew my class schedule inside and out, just as I knew hers.

She would be expecting me soon, camped out in the common area on her side of the couch, drowning in blankets as she trudged through the side effects of that awful potion.

No point in hiding upstairs; Gavriel had a budget meeting tonight with Iris and Jack, so I'd be stuck up there with the rest of them. With supers who dismissed me, ignored me, and would have preferred me and my fangs found work elsewhere.

So, with a shake of my head, I slipped inside lightning

fast, silent as a shadow and determined to get to my room with as minimal a disruption to her television-watching as possible.

Usually I'd join her.

Throw my stuff aside and plop down on the couch, in *my* corner, then demand a play-by-play for what I had missed.

But that wasn't the way with us lately, and as I crossed toward my bedroom without a word, barely glancing in her direction, I feared it never would be again.

I'd fucked it up.

Six years without a flatmate, and I went and ruined it by acting like child who hadn't gotten his way. The Yule weirdness had extended into January, made worse by Cedar's declaration that he and Alecto would share a midnight kiss on the thirty-first. I hadn't asked. She hadn't told me. In fact, we barely spoke at all lately, both of us busy with work, sure, but it didn't help that I holed up in my room anytime we were in the flat together.

Fucking it up. Again and again. Day after day, *sulking*.

She wasn't mine.

I had no right to mourn the loss.

A part of me thought that by giving her space, we could hit the refresh button and start over again in a few weeks.

But that was just an excuse—a temporary reprieve from the guilt I felt for how utterly and terribly and *royally* I had fucked this all straight to hell.

The music swelled, reaching a crescendo before Ramsay laid down his verdict about which poor chef was about to have his dreams shattered. Blue Team defeat again, apparently.

Maybe this was for the best. If a few choice words from another man had shattered our friendship, ruined what could have been, and turned me into *the* most insecure prat on the planet, then maybe space was what we needed. *Maybe*

I ought to foster my connection with Gavriel instead, two miserable souls drinking on the Root Rot rooftops, purposefully alienating ourselves from everyone else.

It didn't matter that I missed her.

That I *hated* myself for what I was doing.

If it spared us heartache down the road, our bond clearly fragile, then maybe it was a good thing this had happened now rather than later.

I glanced over my shoulder and found Alecto exactly where I'd imagined: bundled up on the far end of the couch, hair an absolute beehive, her sweatshirt's hood half-up in a sad attempt to contain all those angry curls. Drowning in blankets, the tiny, miserable, surly little witch was coming to the end of the first week of her yearly potion's side effects.

A pizza box sat on the coffee table, and from the excessive scent of melted cheese in the air, she hadn't touched a slice.

Troubling, that.

My traitorous heart demanded I swoop in and fix it—feed her slice after slice like a lowly servant plying his divine mistress with grapes.

Instead, I went for my bedroom with enough work in hand to keep me busy until midnight.

"Hey…" I stilled, dead heart pounding at the sound of her croaky rasp, anxiety's cruel talons stroking my rib cage, up and down, up and down. Behind me, Alecto shuffled around, perhaps to face me, her arm on the back of the couch for support, hand gripping the fabric. She cleared her throat. I closed my eyes, dreading her next few words, knowing what was about to come out of that beautiful mouth before she even said it.

"Bjorn, are we okay?"

I offered her my profile over my shoulder and a thin smile. "Yeah, of course."

Alecto muted the TV as I pushed my bedroom door open.

"*Liar.*"

I stiffened, aflame with her scrutiny—with her ability to see right through me.

"Can you just talk to me already?" she demanded, her words all wobbly and thick. "I hate it when you don't... Did I do something wrong?"

Fuck. The way she choked out the question *destroyed* me.

"*No.*" I dumped my bag in the doorway, followed by the massive tome I had read to my very disinterested fifth years this evening. "No, not at all." This time I gave her all of me, wheeling around and motioning to myself—to the guilty party in all this. "It's... It's my fault. It's me."

Every past fight with a woman—lover or otherwise—suggested an explosion was imminent. Let the countdown begin to shrieking and accusations and contempt. I braced for the inevitable, but she surprised me, as always, by sitting up and pushing the coffee table out in front of her. She set the still very full pizza box on the floor, then patted the table for me to sit.

Strange woman.

That's why you're such a fool for her, you ancient bastard.

True.

Scratching the back of my neck, eyes down almost sheepishly, I crossed the space and perched on the table before her, elbows on my knees and hands hanging between us. Only then did I get a true, proper look at the witch I had gone out of my way to avoid for almost a month now.

And she was *exhausted.*

Dark circles surrounded her eyes, those amber pools somehow heavy and hollow at the same time. Her skin creased and crinkled with lack of sleep, and her aura reminded me of a laptop battery display with only a dwindling percentage left.

Here I was, a centuries-old vampire who had banked a

hundred lifetimes of experience, behaving like a moody schoolboy. Pouting in my room. Miserable and *pathetic*.

There *she* was, suffering for *real* reasons—and I had just left her to it. Time and time again, Alecto had been there for me: Fiona's death, my crucifixion... She had stepped up for all of it, warm and helpful, keeping my head above water in her own way—the only way that made sense to me in the fog —and I had abandoned her.

Disloyal fucker. That wasn't me. Even the bloodthirsty monster who had haunted the English countryside stayed true to his friends.

I had so much to atone for—and that journey started with the ugly truth.

"The night of the Yule ball—"

"When fucking Ash Cedar was waiting at our door?"

My eyebrows shot up at her venom. "Yeah."

"Yeah," Alecto muttered, shifting about under her mountain of tawny blankets as if to cross, then recross her legs. Huh. Hardly the tone to take with one's lover. Gaze slightly narrowed, I cleared my throat and scratched at the back of my neck again, humiliated to even *admit* to any of this, let alone experience it for the last month.

"I... I got it in my head that you were just humoring me."

Alecto stilled with a sharp breath. "What?"

"I thought he... was the one you wanted to see. That I was just in the way. And I..." *Out with it.* No sense in telling only half-truths tonight, not when she looked so aghast that I'd never be able to lie to her again. "I regretted trying to change things between us. I felt like a fool, and I... I've acted like one ever since."

Again I braced for the fallout, and again Alecto cut me off at the knees. She cocked her head to the side and frowned, dragging the topmost blanket up to her chin. "Is that it?"

Her tone insisted this was a nonissue, but it *wasn't* just that, of course.

"Cedar told me on New Year's that you two have been getting…" I could barely stand to say it, never mind think it. "That you two are close, and that he planned to kiss you at midnight like some public declaration, and I… I couldn't…"

Words had never fallen like molasses before, everything a sticky, tedious effort. Quiet blanketed the room, the TV ongoing behind me, occasionally splashing the dimly lit space with color. Alecto's gaze drifted toward it over my shoulder, allowing me the time to find what I needed to say.

"I've been an ass," I muttered, rolling my eyes. "And I'm sorry. I'm not usually… With women in the past, I…" *Fuck.* What was *wrong* with me? My whole profession this century revolved around talking. I could chat up a storm if necessary, with anyone about anything, my mind a vault of experience. All who came before Alecto fucking Clarke—I could sweet-talk. Charm. Be blunt and honest, not caring whether they stayed or left once I had said my piece.

Well, no. Of course I *cared*, but they had a choice: accept me or not. Should their free will guide them out of my life, my heart ached for a few days…

But then it was on to the next. The next lover, the next city, the next victim, the next adventure.

I never feared the breakdown.

Words came easy before her.

Feelings came easy before her.

With her, it was all one earth-shattering storm, calamitous and unrepentant.

"I'm not usually like this, I swear," I managed at long last, my halfhearted grin met with her deep, damning frown. *Shit.* "I'm so sorry, Alecto, for ruining everything—"

I had enough sense to shut up when she dug her hand out from under the blankets and reached for me. Alecto went for my dangling fingers, her hand dwarfed by mine but her grip like steel. She held hard, our hands dangling between us, the tether finally physical again.

"I *hate* Ash Cedar," she growled, and I blinked back a wave of icy shock at the sound. Alecto had always struck me as a strong woman—shieldmaiden, a warrior worthy of standing by my side in the shield wall—but here, now, she was a wild thing, her ferocity a siren song to the beast inside.

But seconds later, her heartbeat quickened with panic, not rage, and I twisted my hand around so I could hold hers, easily engulfing her fingers and finding my strength again. What the fuck had the bastard done now? I'd always suspected nonsense went on behind the scenes with the warlock, but no one had ever come forward to prove it.

Until now.

Until Alecto's fear mingled with fury—and I swallowed the urge to ask if she'd like me to rip his head from his shoulders.

It would be *easy*. Warlock bones were sturdier than humans, but he wouldn't be the first magical fuck I'd torn apart over the centuries.

And if he hurt her somehow, I would take great pleasure in hearing him beg for mercy before the telltale *pop* of his skull dislocating from his spine.

"Ow, Bjorn..."

I loosened my grip, unsure of when I had gone from supportive to bone-crushing, and Alecto flexed her too-white fingers, blood slowly circulating again.

"Ash Cedar is a liar and a bigot," she said shakily, all the color draining from her cheeks. Even still, her eyes narrowed; maybe Alecto would prefer to tear his head off herself. "He's so much more than that. He's been hitting on me for ages, and it's like he's in this delusion that I'm... flirting back? Like if he aggressively compliments me enough, I'll just get with the program one day, but I barely talk to him."

Red mist settled over my vision at her forced chuckle, and I concentrated on my grip, on not crushing her bones to dust at the thought of that *fucker* making her feel so obviously uncomfortable in such an uncouth manner...

For making her cry in front of me.

Alecto's eyes shimmered with unshed tears, and she retreated, once again taking her hand from mine because of Ash Cedar, to wipe under her eyelids before any of those glistening diamonds fell.

A stake to the heart, the sight of her tears.

Twisted in deeper at the sound of her uncomfortable laughter.

Wedged in permanently—because I had been the unbelievable asshole who left her to deal with this alone, lost in my own trauma, in my own delusional world where I had thought *distance* was what we needed.

"He's, like, a legit psychopath," she insisted, her giggle more genuine, her eye roll coaxing a smirk out of me. "And no one seems to see it, which is fucking infuriating."

I see it. Never liked the bastard—never would now.

"Alecto, I—"

"But that doesn't excuse you freezing me out like you did —over *nothing*," she added fiercely, pink flaring in her cheeks like the snap of wildfire. Alecto wove her hands together on her lap and glared me down, making me feel about two inches tall—and rightly so. "This has been such a crappy month with, you know..." She gestured to herself, up and down, a wordless reminder of the potion's less than subtle impact. "And I kept thinking I'd done something—"

"I'm sorry—for all of it. Truly." What else was there to say? No excuses. No stories. No charm, no jokes, no diversion. I had fucked up—let jealousy take me down dark and stupid roads—and there was no getting around it.

Lips pursed, Alecto looked me over, then lifted her chin with a sniff, spine ramrod straight and head tilted to the side as she drawled, "You'd better be."

Seconds later, the snobby façade shattered with another giggle, her eyes glossy again, cheeks an exquisite rose.

"I swear it." I pressed a hand to my chest and dove headlong into those beautiful amber pools, smitten with the sound of her quickening pulse. "My sincerest apologies for my boorish, ridiculous behavior, Alecto Clarke. It will never happen again as long as I live."

"Bit dramatic," the delectable little witch muttered, suddenly fussing with her hair, eyes everywhere but me as her blush sharpened, "but okay. I accept."

"My dead heart beats easier, then."

She snorted. "Gross."

Our gazes collided almost accidentally, and bathed in the television's glow, we both grinned, the tension that had strangled us for weeks finally gone. Briefly, it felt good to revel in the cozy quiet that followed, the flat *home* again. Alecto's gaze even drifted to the TV behind me, watching the next episode on mute over my shoulder, and I let her, content to just *be* with her again.

My own curiosity ruined it a few minutes later.

"Alecto," I started, jolting her out of that intense way she scrutinized the show's ridiculous intro, "what are we?" She blinked back at me, and I shuffled to the very edge of the coffee table to block out the screen. "Friends?"

She swallowed thickly, the dance of her throat as noticeable as the skip of her heart, and she drew her knees up to her chest, then wrapped her arms around them beneath the blankets.

"More than friends, I think," she admitted in an adorably

small voice, and if it wouldn't totally destroy the moment, I would have leapt onto the coffee table and done my best Chandler-dance impression to make her *howl* with laughter —again. Instead, I played it cool, waiting, watching her lips part and press as she muddled through her thoughts, sinking deeper into the couch. "But I don't want to lose our friendship, either, you know? You're like... my best friend, which is *so* cheesy, but you kind of came out of nowhere."

Throat suddenly too raw with emotion to risk speaking, I just nodded. Of course I understood that: Alecto had come out of nowhere as well. I valued her above everyone, and she had stolen my heart without either of us noticing.

Little *thief*.

"But if we're more than friends, you need to know..." Alecto tucked her chin on her knees, nuzzling into the blanket. "I don't do jealous men."

And just like that, I was two inches tall again.

Smaller, even.

Justifiably gnat-sized.

"I've never really been a monogamy kind of witch," she told me with an unapologetic shrug, "and I know that's acceptable in some circles but not in others—"

"I see the way you look at Jack." She needed to know —*immediately*—that I didn't care if she took other lovers, if she shared her heart around. So long as I had an uncompromised piece of it, as long as what we had belonged to each other, so be it. Alecto went beet red at the statement, mouth hanging open and heart roaring, and I leaned closer with a smirk. "And *Gavriel*, naughty girl." Cue an even louder drumbeat as Alecto dragged the blanket up to cover her face. Chuckling, I grabbed at the fuzzy material and tugged it down, infatuated with her blushes. "I only ever cared when I thought it was Cedar."

Because he was a prick who was no good for her.

She and Jack shared an obvious passion for their jobs, obsessive in similar ways, dedicated to the work.

Gavriel could be a scoundrel, sure, but all our rooftop drinking and bitching had proven there was more to him than I'd ever known. Layers upon layers—and at the core, a wounded warrior who was capable of doing the right thing when the stakes were high.

Same as Alecto—wounded deep down but masking it well.

Ash Cedar had no redeeming qualities, nothing to offer but the chance to make a full-blooded witch or warlock baby, along with all the traditional bullshit values that entailed.

Alecto crinkled her nose at the mention of him. "I'd literally rather die."

My snort made her giggle, and she tucked the blanket up to her chin, sobering somewhat as she said, "For real though, jealousy in a relationship doesn't make me feel safe." She nibbled her lower lip, looking briefly worried—like I'd bolt at any moment. "I don't put up with it from the men in my life."

"And you shouldn't have to." *Never again. I swear it.* "I don't... I'm not that man. I've never been before, but you..." I shook my head, quashing that train of thought before it derailed everything. "No, that sounds like you're to blame. You're not. It's me. It's my issue. Consider it dead and buried."

"Don't be so hard on yourself," Alecto said, poking me from beneath the blanket, jabbing her toes at my knee. "Next time just talk to me. We're pretty good at talking, if you hadn't noticed."

"I had." A rare thing: open, honest communication. The level of trust it necessitated made my chest painfully tight, and I stabbed my knuckles into its center, massaging away the ache. "I like that about us."

Alecto grinned and nodded. "Me too."

We left it at that, one door closed and another wide open.

"Movie night?" Alecto offered, and the thought of cuddling crossed my mind until I remembered she might prefer not to be touched right now. Still, *more than friends* implied *some* closeness, at the very least, even if it was just an arm along the back of the couch.

"Sounds perfect."

Her belly celebrated our first movie night of the new year with a victorious gurgle, and Alecto eyed the pizza box on the ground beside the coffee table like she had suddenly found her appetite again.

"Give me a moment to unpack," I told her, jerking my chin toward my room. "Go pick some options—your choice tonight."

And probably every Friday night for the next few months after the stunt I had pulled; I predicated a great deal of melodramatic B-grade horror in the near future.

After swiping at her toes under the blankets, I went back to my things, about to scoop them up and then change into something more comfortable than my tweed teaching suit. One foot into my bedroom and—

"Hey?"

I nearly dropped everything again at that tiny wobble, the slight crack of her voice, and when I looked back, I found her eyes glistening.

"Missed you," Alecto whispered, and this time I *did* drop everything. Without a care, I hurled my shit in the general direction of my bed and blitzed back to the couch. Kicked the coffee table well away, heart breaking for her, *hating* myself far more than I did Ash Cedar for making her cry, and then dropped to my knees in front of her. Cheeks hollow, Alecto shuffled around under the blankets to the edge of the cushion, and when that lone tear finally fell, I pounced.

My heart yearned to kiss her.

I hugged her instead. Snaked my arms along her legs and around to her back, and Alecto fell into me with a shuddering sigh. A lesser man might have rejoiced that she came chest-first, pillowy breasts suddenly in my face, but I turned to the side so I could rest my ear over her heart. Tentative fingers worked into my hair, one hand cupping the back of my head, the other toying with the soft wisps at the nape of my neck. Eyes closed, I hugged her tight, dragging her bundled, crumpled, sore body to me as she huffed a giggle into the side of my head.

While I so loved to hear her heart race, *pounding* through every pulse point, tonight I realized there was something even better: listening to it slow.

And knowing she felt safe in my arms again.

That she, like me, was finally home.

20

ALECTO

"Hello, Professor Cedar!"

I stilled at the front of the main greenhouse, eraser in hand, my slack-jawed reflection captured in the whiteboard between my step-by-step potion recipe. Behind me, the general hubbub of students filing out at the end of a lesson continued as usual, but that fucking *name* rose above the din —and for a second I thought I was dreaming.

Because… why the *fuck* would Benedict Hammond be in *my* greenhouse in the middle of the afternoon? Not only had I just finished a ninety-minute sprint with my most scatterbrained first and second years, but I now had another ninety long minutes with my fourth years in no time at all. These kids had less than five minutes to bolt between classes throughout the day, and I had just as much time to clear down and set up for the next block.

"Hello, Montgomery—you all right?"

Gods. This wasn't a dream. White-knuckling the eraser, I slashed through the recipe for a really basic brew—just a simple headache cure. Not a migraine: headache, preferably a tension ache. I always started my babies off with this one because at the academy, whether it was good ol' Root Rot or preppy Glencrest, they were all due for a good headache.

And now, apparently one had just waltzed into my greenhouse.

I kept my back to him, refusing to even glance to the side to watch for his reflection in the glass windows. Teeth gritted, I hurriedly wiped away the recipe and did a mental walkthrough of my next lesson.

Thursday afternoon with my fourth years.

Usually I had something a little more intense planned for my elective students—the ones who actually *wanted* to study herbalism—but today was a free day to work on their ongoing projects. Fourth and fifth years had flora grimoires to create during the second term: they would put together their very own encyclopedia of all the plant life found in a chosen region, including lists of their magical and medicinal properties.

Plus diagrams—bonus points for accuracy.

So, really, my next block was pretty chill.

Benedict's presence, however, had just drop-kicked my stress up to an eleven.

Peeping over my shoulder, standard faux-friendly smile strained today, I caught him sauntering toward me with a hand behind his back, stuffy warlock robes fluttering like massive mauve bat wings. In the distance, beneath a painfully sunny and clear winter sky, my fourth years trundled down the hillside steps in a giant herd, a lone den mother bringing up the rear.

"Alecto—"

"This really isn't a good time," I said curtly, back to clearing the whiteboard, body language screaming *fuck off* as politely as I could manage. "I have another class literally at the door."

"Of course. I'll be quick."

I rolled my eyes. Of course he would say that—he'd be quick instead of doing the reasonable thing and clearing out. Exhaling sharply, I slammed my eraser into the little metal tray at the bottom of the whiteboard, then wheeled around with my arms crossed, eyebrows up.

All this attitude wasn't great for my end goal. I decided weeks ago to get a taped confession and had already come to terms with the fact that the best way to do so would be to flirt information out of the bastard. Yeah, just the thought triggered my gag reflex, but I could suck it up for an hour if it meant getting all the evidence I needed to present to a high council—

To eventually watch him *burn* for what he had done.

So, really, I should be nicer.

Maybe next time.

"I've been trying to find the time to apologize for a little while now," Benedict mused, finally stopping with only my desk between us. He brushed his fingers over the top, then tapped at it, all huffy and contrite, eyes down like I might fall for his sheepish charm.

Fuck off, dude. You're like fifty. It's not a good look.

Still mindful of my fourth years, I schooled my features and fluttered my lashes, hoping the hate didn't bleed from my eyes to my expression.

"What, for Yule? It's fine." I waved him off with a terse chuckle. "We all probably had a little too much to drink that night—I barely remember it. People were passing around stuff behind Iris's back, so, you know…"

Benedict stared at me for a moment.

And then his eye twitched.

Like I had said something wrong—*annoyed* him. My heart skipped a beat, and as the silence stretched on, it was like my ears slowly and steadily filled with cotton, muffling the rest of the world, until—

"No," the warlock remarked slowly, really drawing it out as if to purposefully waste my time. "Not quite."

I gestured to the bundled-up teens meandering toward the greenhouse behind him. "Sorry, but I really need to set up for my next class."

I didn't, and I definitely wasn't sorry, but his presence in my space—the slightly murderous glint in his eye because, what, I wasn't paying enough attention to his dogshit apology?—had me flustered. Made my neck hot and my heart pound.

Ugh. Flirting a confession out of him might require booze —a lot of booze. While I was still working on the specifics, I had finally decided to get things rolling during the next weeklong term break. Fewer kids on campus seemed ideal, but I was still debating whether or not to bring Jack in on the plan. After all, this fucker was one of his model employees, and if I had my way, he would be gone—preferably in chains —before third term started.

Unfortunately, while I trusted Jack with kink, our preferences aligned, my heart always happy to see him, *feel* him, this was another issue completely. This was... my soul. It went deeper than a bit of delicious flogging and cuddly aftercare.

During one of my recent midnight musings, as I lay awake tortured by my indecisiveness, I briefly considered asking Bjorn to just beat a confession out of him. No doubt a former Viking could do it like a total pro, but the thought of sharing my *own* confession with him made my skin crawl.

I mean, I had been all *just talk to me*, blah, blah, blah, the other week. Sure, it had fixed things—we were back to normal and then some, all stolen glances and thighs brushing under the dinner table, getting closer and closer on the couch with passing each night. But then here I was, lying, keeping something *huge* from him when I preached open and honest communication.

With Bjorn, I was... scared.

Scared to lose him when he learned the truth, that I wasn't Alecto *Clarke*, that the last surviving Corwin witch came here with ulterior motives when his sole purpose at Root Rot was to heal the broken.

Irrational as it was, I feared his judgment, his rejection, and his hurt upon realizing that I had pulled the wool over his eyes for our entire relationship.

The sting would be even sharper when he clued in to the fact that I was still doing it now as we tiptoed out of the friend zone and into something more serious.

Guh.

And then *this* piece of shit goes and produces a rose from behind his back. Benedict offered it to me with flourish, a perfectly red long-stemmed rose—one that looked suspiciously like those me and my student gardening club had babied since August.

Seriously, what was it with this warlock and roses? Did he just lack imagination—or was it really all about tradition? The white ones he shoved at me on Yule were still alive in my bedroom, but that was because I didn't have the heart to let them die.

Not on my watch.

Not out of spite, anyway.

"Give me a chance, Alecto," Benedict drawled, bowing a little as he thrust the rose across my desk. Behind him, my fourth years were close enough to make out the details in their faces, to hear the chatter as they crossed the cobblestone courtyard toward the greenhouses. His face suddenly popped into my line of sight, blocking them, his smile wavering somewhat as he added, "Let me prove to you that I'm *better* than any warlock you've ever known."

What the actual fuck.

I bit the insides of my cheeks so I didn't guffaw directly into his smug face. This whole spiel must have worked on so many witches in the past: Benedict *was* a good-looking warlock, worldly and well traveled with a stable career, and there had to be women out there who dug this whole... controlling, intrusive thing.

Right?

Hating the thought of my students walking in on me being offered a rose from another professor, I snatched it by the stem and let it hang at my side, hidden behind the desk.

"Look, uh, this is very sweet." Oh gods: I'd nearly said *Benedict*. Panic burned in my cheeks, and I did my best to distract from it with a dazzling smile. "I just..." *Don't fuck this up for future entrapment opportunities.* "I really try not to date colleagues. I made that rule for myself when I first started teaching... Things get so complicated, you know?"

Another eye twitch. Benedict straightened and smoothed out his mauve robes, his already much larger figure doubled in size courtesy of all that rigid brocade. "Is that so?"

I gulped, hyperaware of my wand in its forearm holster.

That sounded like a threat.

Surprise, surprise: Benedict Hammond couldn't handle rejection.

The door creaked open at the far end of the greenhouse, cold, dry air gusting over the herb gardens on the shelves to the left, conversations flooding in with the arrival of my fourth years. Knowing his pride, his *ego*, I expected Benedict to march out of here with his head held high—and then I would have to *really* sweet-talk him later to get back in his good graces.

Instead, he blinked, and up came the mask of normalcy, anger gone but no less threatening. He then lashed out and snagged my hand, yanked it across the desk between us, and planted his lips firmly to the top.

I dropped the rose.

Everything inside went cold as soon as his mouth touched my skin. Some of the chatter died down, and one student—fucking Rebecca Martin—had the audacity to *gasp*, a few of her friends pointing and whispering.

"I'll find a way to change your mind," Benedict whispered with a wink, words skittering up my arm like cockroaches. My hand flopped onto the desk as soon as he let go, fight-or-flight in reboot mode, my mouth hanging open.

And from the cruel twinkle in his eye, the saccharine twist of his lips, that was *exactly* what he wanted.

To shock me into submission—in front of my students and a very disapproving den mother. Radiating a haughty victory, Benedict flicked an eyebrow up before strolling out of the greenhouse.

Taking his time, once again, so that everyone got their fill of him, like he was king of his own warped, twisted court.

My eyes narrowed. *Finally*, things clicked back into place, and I wrenched my hand away from the desk, arms crossed, and tucked it out of sight.

That fucking *asshole*.

Every time he had hit on me had been about *power*—power over me, over Bjorn when he tried to stake his claim on New Year's Eve, and then now, back onto me and my kids. It wasn't about flirting with some pretty witch like he said: his dance was about intimidation, control, and force.

How many other witches had he bullied into a relationship before me?

Fuck him—so hard.

Shaking, battling to keep my cool when every instinct demanded I go hex him into oblivion, I went left and ducked out the seldom-used side door between the greenhouses.

Behind me, my fourth years settled into their seats, whispers and giggles chasing after me.

Once inside the secondary greenhouse, door shut hard enough to make the windows tremble, I stalked down the aisle and dropped to my knees in front of a pile of folded burlap under one of the long tables. Seething, I yanked out two scratchy brown fabric sheets, something we used for the plants not enchanted to withstand the winter frost, then shoved my face into them...

And *screamed*.

Screamed as loud and hard as I could.

Screamed until I stripped my throat raw.

Until I had nothing left.

Then, adrenaline fading, I folded both burlap blankets and put them away, smoothed my frizzy flyaways along the sides of my head, readjusted my ponytail, and wiped under my eyes.

Not a tear shed this time.

Just a drained body and a bloody throat.

I could work with that.

Shoulders back and knees dusted clean, I returned to the main greenhouse and started the next ninety-minute block like nothing had happened.

Even as humiliation scorched through my veins.

And Benedict's kiss became just another scar.

21

GAVRIEL

No.

No.

Definitely not.

Never.

Fuck no.

I tossed the final new arrival's file aside with a groan, then slumped in my office chair and scrubbed at my face. Five new little shits had walked through Root Rot's doors since the start of the year, and with February only a few days away, you'd think at least *one* might have shown some dark aptitude.

But no.

They lacked the grades. No noted special skills. Petty crimes and bullshit charges.

Nothing to impress the admissions board at Darkwell.

No one to fill my quota, which, lately, had felt more and more impossible to conquer.

And maybe that was the point.

Maybe this was some torturous lesson from the head

fallen angel himself—something about patience and tenacity and fortitude.

Fuck him.

I had plenty of all that; these fucking *kids* were the unexceptional ones. What I wouldn't do for an army of Lucy Eastwicks to parade through the front doors, all gangly and pimply and awkward little swans waiting to blossom, destined for dark espionage and war against the Silver City.

Instead I had *this* lot, painfully unremarkable and depressingly ordinary. Eyes like slits, I glowered at the folders as if the names taped across the tabs could *feel* my frustration, then lunged for the bottom right drawer of my desk to grab the mini bottle of bourbon inside. After all, I had finished the double Irish coffee whipped up by one of the lovely chef trainees ages ago, and with that depressing read over with, I required another boost to just... exist.

A firm knock stopped me on the cusp of the drawer handle, and I straightened with a frown, eyes flicking to the tiny clock at the top corner of my laptop screen. Nearly midnight now, all my underlings dismissed, the library a silent cavern on the other side of that door.

Who the fuck...?

I stood with a bristly exhale, then marched to the door and wrenched it open—

Ah.

Of course.

And found Alecto loitering on the other side, hair wild, eyes shrouded in dark, exhausted circles. A slight frown touched that full, luscious mouth of hers, and I cocked my head to the side, unsure if she was actually annoyed or if that was just the expression she wore around me these days.

The quick up-and-down scan of her figure showed a remarkably put-together Alecto Clarke given the late hour. Ordinarily she retreated into sweats after curfew, but she stood before me now in a silky white blouse, the material soft and fragile with a droopy bow crowning the high neckline, her cuffs buttoned with pearls and the tails tucked in to a tight, high-waisted black pencil skirt. Tartan stockings and low heels. She looked ready for a day in the classroom—not for me and my office in some shadowy faraway corner.

Still. Fucking scrumptious, the combination of a put-together outfit, prim and proper, and those wild, untamed curls begging for a fist.

My fist.

"What?" I demanded, eyebrows up as I braced an arm on either side of the doorway. If I could remember what had happened on New Year's Eve, perhaps I might be embarrassed around her. As it stood, the night was one hazy blur, and the only reason I knew Alecto had any part in it was the fact that I woke up the following morning to her vanilla scent on my sheets and pillow.

That and someone had replaced my bedtime flask's booze with water, and who else would be presumptuous enough to tinker with a fae's alcohol?

At one point in the last two weeks I had considered asking her about it, but every time I saw her she looked ready to decapitate anyone who dared *glance* her way.

So. You know. Yeah.

I'd steered clear of her—and a number of the female Root Rot species who had taken that damn potion recently. Loved the stuff—totally covered my ass from any accidental heirs who would go on to inherit all my nothing in the Ash Court —but, stars above, did it ever turn the sweetest of womenkind into terrifying swamp monsters.

Just... a whole castle of raging Medusas for most of January.

Fantastic stuff, really.

"You busy?"

From her tone, she had finally tamed the rage within. Good.

"Always," I crooned. Eyebrows lifted in a *Are you fucking serious?* sort of way, Alecto pushed up on her toes to peer over my shoulder, then glanced back for a sweep of the nearby stacks. Empty, of course, every last one of them, the library beyond closed for the night, all the lights dimmed and the highland stars twinkling through the glass ceiling.

Naturally, I knew what she wanted.

What other reason was there to approach a man's door at midnight *but* sex?

And I was more than happy to give it to her, to scratch an itch that had been more and more difficult to satisfy as of late, but she had to beg for it. *Beg.* Preferably on her knees with my cock in her mouth; she had turned me down once already—and now she ought to suffer a little before I rocked her world.

Playing the part, I leaned out to scan our surroundings as well, then retreated into my office with a scowl, hands on the doorframe and body barring her entrance.

"What can I help you with, Professor Clarke?"

Lower lip snagged between her teeth, Alecto went soft and silky as that blouse, sidling close enough to march her fingers up my torso and coil them around my tie. In contrast to her prim and proper, I was pared back and rumpled, my jacket and vest gone, sleeves scrunched to my elbows and tie loose. Mustard-yellow slacks that paired with a grey top instantly started to tent, the traitorous bastard desperate for her touch, and I slowly lowered my hands along the doorframe, as if bending to her will, to her cozy, sweet but not too sweet scent that lingered in my linens to this day.

Conflict tore across her features, but just briefly—a flash

and nothing more, as if to remind me she wasn't here because she had fallen for my charms.

This little fury craved release, same as me.

As soon as my finger found her chin, she let me tip her head back, let me guide her to my lips for a tender kiss—

"Oh my *gods*," I rasped, eyes open and boring deep into hers when they flared, those thick black lashes fluttering, "it's so *unhealthy*. We can't keep doing the same old *crap*."

A shuddering breath washed over my lips, and Alecto retreated seconds later, offended, wearing her hurt out in the open. She turned away in a hurry, about to scramble into the night with her tail between her legs.

I wouldn't let her.

After all, I didn't *want* her to go.

She just needed to feel rejection's bite, sharp and cutting, perhaps even a little insulting.

Feel what I'd felt that day in the gardens.

Only I didn't *pity* her as she had pitied me—that was the difference.

But this was good enough. Cruel enough.

Grinning, I skipped after her and snagged her crooked elbow before she reached the nearest stack.

"Come on, fury," I teased, wheeling her around, fully prepared for a smack. She came easily, stumbling into my chest like she was relieved, almost *happy* to let me lead. I wiggled my brows at her, refusing to read into it. "We can be unhealthy together."

I hooked an arm around her cinched waist and hauled her in, forcing her onto her toes for a kiss that had her squealing indignantly, all hard and furious, lips parted on impact and tongues tangling like old foes.

A kiss so distinctly *ours* that it made my chest tight and my knees weak.

But ever the pro at masking anything *real*, I walked us

241

backward into my office, then slammed the door and locked it. *You're in for the night, fury.* The threat carried in my rough caress, hands everywhere, cupping everything, pinching and yanking at her flimsy silk blouse and rigid black skirt that clung so perfectly to her generous hips.

Consistent to a fault, Alecto gave as good as she got, ripping my tucked shirt out by the middle, slashing her nails up my neck and into my hair. She matched my every flash of teeth with a nip and snap of her own, coming apart in my arms, trapped between a fae and a locked door, a wild thing backed into a corner.

Bizarrely enough, there was comfort in the storm, security in the savagery. Sure, lovers had surrendered to my brutality before, but they did so meekly, willingly—all without a fight. Alecto had always been fists and ferocity, from the first time to tonight, her touch electric and her kiss a maelstrom.

More than a worthy rival, my fury.

Exciting. Brutal.

But soft, too.

She always *let* me win—Alecto Clarke offered the best of both worlds, hard and soft, a beautiful dichotomy, a lover who kept me guessing.

I had started to need that.

Need *her.*

Never before had I revisited a woman this many times, but kissing her now, shoving her up against the door and greedily stealing her moans, felt like coming home.

Like this was where I—we—belonged.

For I was no stranger to the battlefield, and this fury was every inch a warrior.

My hands roamed far and wide, planting a flag on her every curve, until eventually landing on the thin zipper at the back of her skirt. As my teeth blazed along her jaw and down to her throat, I yanked at the little clasp and peeled the fabric open so it spilled along her thighs. I followed shortly after, questing down her figure, taking a pearled nipple into my mouth through the blouse and her brassiere, making her squeal so deliciously when I added some bite.

The moment my knees touched the hardwood, the rest of it didn't stand a chance. The stockings rolled down easily, and Alecto had stepped out of her kitten heels by the time I reached her ankles. Panties came next, just a boring pair of black cotton that told me she hadn't landed on my doorstep intentionally—hadn't come prepared to seduce me by any means.

Her thighs trembled long before my lips reached them, and I kissed my way north again, slow and steady, taking my time to nip and bite and suck, hoping to mark her up in the most inopportune places—

"*Gavriel.*" Until she snarled my name, her fingers suddenly twisting into my hair. Alecto's stance widened as she hauled me toward her center, and I smirked, hands curving around the backs of her knees and forcing her legs farther apart. *Greedy vixen. Demanding brat.*

Who knew that did it for me?

I found her neatly trimmed at the crux of her thighs, a smattering of mahogany to match her unruly curls. It had been a fucking *eternity* since I'd gone down on anyone, since I licked a lover from front to back, between the folds and up around her clit. Alecto shivered and moaned when I did it to her now, when I tasted divine femininity in its purest form and lapped at her altar.

In an age gone by, I loved to lick a woman's cunt until she screamed.

Lately, I'd just been so fucking miserable that I hadn't bothered with much foreplay in general, nothing beyond kissing and a bit of fingering anyway. Just enough to make sure they were ready for me—me, a selfish, miserable, drunk old fae teetering on the brink of a breakdown, the nightmares returning and the guilt giving me a constant stomachache.

Word had spread: the fae dildo wasn't much fun lately. Fewer fell into my bed, even less for my charming smiles and whispered innuendos. Had it not been for Bjorn keeping me company on the staff tower rooftop several nights a week, the pair of us gossiping like teenage girls and swapping war stories like brothers, I would have been totally alone.

And then there was Alecto—who had the sweetest pussy I'd ever eaten.

So much so that a lot of the shit outside this room and inside my skull faded away, leaving only her musk, her slick folds and swollen clit. Her quivering thighs and her insistent fingers. The moment her knees buckled, I threw them over my shoulders, propping her up against the door and spreading her ass cheeks so that I could dive deep and forget the world.

My thumb on her clit was her undoing. Press, press, swipe back and forth, circle over and over again—*gone*. She came with a sob, thighs clamping around my face and hips writhing over my laughing mouth. My fury rode me through the rise and fall of her climax, to the point that if she wriggled and mewled any longer, she might just suffocate me.

Maybe *that* had been the plan.

The ultimate revenge for my thievery, my rakish ways, the trail of broken hearts left in my wake—smothered to death by a woman's cunt.

Sounds about right.

Only when I eased her legs open and reared back to draw a full breath, Alecto let me, slumped against the door with flushed cheeks, her breath dancing in uneven beats. Pride swelled in my chest—need swelled in my cock. *Urgently.* In her pleasure-addled state, she was easy enough to manipulate, pliant and soft and heavy-lidded as I set her feet back on the ground, worked my way out from between her thighs, and stood before her. Towered *over* her, one hand planted to the door, the other fiddling with the droopy silk bow at the base of her throat.

Hooded amber swept across my mouth, my chin—across flesh forever stained with her climax. To her credit, Alecto didn't shy away from it, nor did her blush darken when I wiped it all away. Instead, I could have sworn pride shimmered back at me, unfazed by her own pleasure, so unlike past lovers who hated to see their desires and needs painted across my face.

And that only made my cock strain harder to get at her.

"On your knees, fury," I whispered hoarsely, haphazardly undoing her bow tie before dropping my hand to my trousers. The implication was clear, but the pop of a button and hiss of a zipper certainly solidified things. Alecto's eyes narrowed, and when she made no move to sink before me, the hand braced on the door snapped to her throat. Squeezed hard enough to make her eyes widen and her pulse flutter. Then steered her down, down, down to her knees, which she settled on almost sweetly—like she belonged there, at my feet, eyes rebellious and lips quirked.

Stars *above*, how had I ignored this perfection? All for the sake of not double-dipping…

Stupid.

Prideful.

Idiot.

Teeth gritted, I freed my aching cock, the bead of precum smearing across her lower lip as it zeroed in on her mouth. Alecto bucked back into the door, hands resting primly on her thighs, and her gasp resonated through my otherwise silent office when I fisted her hair and roughly tipped her head up for me—

Then seized her parted lips by thrusting between them. Lashes fluttering, my bratty fury sat straighter to accommodate, coughing when I nudged at the back of her throat. A heartbeat later, however, she *moaned*, long and low, the sound vibrating up my shaft and coiling in my gut. I hissed, pleasure taking over, all sharp and unfamiliar and very much welcome.

As soon as her eyes found mine, I saw the challenge in them—the dare to dominate. Even with my cock in her mouth, even as she knelt at my feet, Alecto Clarke had such power over me. Swallowing hard, mind already stupid with desire, I planted my forehead on the door and threaded my other hand into her hair, both buried deep in her curls.

Slowly, achingly, I eased out of her. Let her drag those full lips my entire length. Cocked my head and arched an eyebrow, prompting her to flick her tongue at the silky head, circle it as I had done her clit. Then, just when those audacious ambers met my weathered greys, I thrust.

Deep. Hard. Forced her to take me even as she sputtered and smacked at my thigh.

Smirking, head on the door and cock buried to the hilt, I fucked her face—no sympathy, no coddling. I met her challenge head-on and *took* her, made her mine as drool dribbled down her chin and tears gathered in her eyes.

And she fucking *loved* it.

Alecto opened her mouth wider to take me deeper. Moaned when my cock allowed it, her interest buzzing in my belly and making my balls clench. In those moments, she smirked, even with her mouth full, knowing *exactly* what she was doing to me. I gripped her hair harder. Thrust faster. Did my best to throw her off.

Then nearly blew my load down the back of her throat

when she slipped her hand between her thighs to play with herself.

"*Fuck.*" I withdrew on the verge of implosion, cock throbbing, every muscle stretched taut and about to snap. Alecto panted and gasped, chasing her breath, glowering up at me with the same frustration and want I hurled down at her. That mischievous hand stilled between her thighs, and as soon as I let go of her hair, she slumped and wiped at her face, drying under her eyes and around her mouth with the hem of her blouse.

It would have been easy to just lose myself. To take. To be the selfish bastard like always.

But for the first time in a long time—since *her*, actually—I didn't want it to be over just yet.

Didn't want things to end with my pleasure alone.

Didn't want her to go.

Please don't leave me here alone.

Of course, I let none of that show, exuding my usual take-it-or-leave-it attitude as Alecto shuffled around at my feet. However, the moment she slithered up my body, brushing my cock in passing, and pressed her mouth to mine, I was gone. *Fucked.* All take it and no leave it, an arm around her waist so that her curves crushed against me and she couldn't run even if she tried. Alecto responded by gently cupping my cheeks, our kiss unusually soft—in stark contrast to the way our mouths had brutalized and been brutalized by each other only moments earlier.

But the minx showed her true colors as soon as those devious fingers smoothed along my jaw, down my neck— and locked around my tie. My eyes snapped open to find hers impishly staring back, and she tightened the knot with no warning, collaring me—*choking* me—with my own attire.

Which simply wouldn't fly.

Snarling, I fisted her hair again and tore her away. My

fury went with a cry, all smiles as I dragged my tie off and threw it onto her instead, opening the loop enough to get it over her mane, then sealing it around her beautiful throat. Leashed, she stumbled forward at the first sharp tug, and I marched her across my office, kicked aside the twin chairs in front of my desk, and then tossed her against it, bent her over the cruel edge by the back of her neck.

Cock harder than it had ever been in its whole fucking life.

And the backs of her thighs still glistening triumphantly from her climax.

"Tell me, fury," I whispered roughly, stroking her wayward curls, a little faux tenderness before the main event. "Are you a back-door kind of girl?"

She stilled—and then, much to my surprise, *snorted*.

A snort that turned into a full-blown gigglefest, the mood shattered, the tension gone as her whole body shook with laughter.

"Oh my *gods...*" Alecto peered back with tears and incredulity in her eyes, lips stretched into a smile bright as the sun—whereas mine had thinned considerably. "*What* did you just say?"

Suddenly much too hot, I stood behind her with my trousers around my ankles, briefs halfway down my thighs, and shirt tented over my hard-on. "I—"

"Was that your fucked-up way of asking if I like anal?" she demanded, eyebrows creeping up her forehead when I blinked back at her, stunned at the turn of events.

"I... You—" I shook my head and motioned to the witch bent over my desk with both hands like that explained everything. "The line was *fine!*"

Alecto giggled, propped up on her elbows and ass in the breeze. "It was the worst thing I've ever heard, but okay."

Jaw clenched, I lashed out with a playful, albeit firm,

spank to her backside, which only made her laugh *more*. Quite the strange response to pain and discipline, fury. Sighing harshly, I stepped aside and waited for her to taper off, arms crossed and expression stern. Fortunately, embarrassment didn't seem to faze the ramrod-straight traitor reaching for her; he was ready to go no matter what she said or how she said it.

"Well?" I growled as she brushed her knuckle under her eyes. Alecto chuckled softly, then popped her chin onto her fist, eyeing me over her shoulder.

"Well, what?"

I scoffed and pointed to her ass, my handprint a pale pink across both cheeks. "You really want me to say it again?"

She rolled her eyes. "Say it *better*."

"Fury," I growled, patience running thin for this charade. It all felt too intimate, like we had tripped over each other and fallen into the murky seas where friends and lovers collided. We had never struggled for conversation before, talk coming cheap and easy for Alecto and me, even if most of it involved insults and anger, but this…

I didn't know how to feel about *this*. Teasing and filthy talk and giggles and—

This was uncharted territory, and while my heart didn't seem to mind, my head remained wary.

And my cock just wanted to get on with it either way, so I suppose that meant we were in a fucking deadlock.

"You got any lubricant?"

Determined to focus on what I *could* handle rather than what sent me into a tailspin, I shuffled around my desk, opened the top left drawer, and grabbed the half-empty bottle of lube at the back.

"Always," I drawled, planting it on the desk right in front of her face. Alecto snorted again as she picked it up and examined the label.

"Of course." She shot me a look, eyebrows up. "Only you would have lube in your office desk."

That smart mouth was going to get her in trouble one day —and I so relished the thought of *punishment*. Smirking, I crossed back around the desk while she scrutinized the bottle, then snatched the silky loop around her neck and wrenched it up. Alecto squealed as I dragged my tie up and over her chin, then tightened it between her parted lips. At first, I considered keeping the knot at the front, just for the added girth, but quickly turned the whole thing around so I could hold the tail like a leash when I fucked her.

"*Much* better," I purred, cock resting on her backside as I leaned over, making sure to put my full weight on her as a reminder who had the power here, and grabbed the lubricant from her hand.

And again she let me.

Sure, she glared, eyes narrowed, brows knit, shooting daggers over her shoulders with my tie gagging her saucy mouth.

But she stayed put. Folded over my desk, Alecto stayed even when I stepped back to lube up my shaft, generously applying layer after layer, coating the damn thing thrice over until I'd used up most of the bottle. I saved the last bit for my fingers, the pair I cautiously probed into her puckered hole. *Then* the glare died, replaced by fluttering lashes and stuttering breath. With a soft, strained moan, Alecto lowered herself fully onto my desk, hands splayed over the wood, offering herself to me as I readied her.

"Good girl," I whispered, tossing the bottle aside and smoothing my free hand up her back—all the way to her neck, which I gripped lightly and pushed down farther so she knew to *stay*. My fingers then worked into her hair, her curls with a gravitational force of their own, beckoning me home.

"Look at that... You can be so *good* when you want, can't you?"

When she peered over her shoulder this time, Alecto was all sugar and a hell of a lot of spice, batting her eyelashes at me purposefully, her smirking mouth negating any of the good girl charm.

No one had ever really challenged me during sex before. They all took whatever I doled out like they were *grateful*. Even fae women were... subdued. Not on the battlefield, and, honestly, their subservience was court dependent, but Alecto was the first lover of mine to fight back.

Test me.

Push me.

Force my hand to be rougher.

I rather liked that.

And from the arousal coating her thighs, her cunt still swollen and slick from her first orgasm, so did she.

Once I had experimentally fit two fingers in that little hole, right down to the hilt and back again, I replaced them with my cock. Naturally, even the head was far larger than two measly fingers, and Alecto dropped the bratty charade as soon as I nudged the first inch in, her cheek to my desk, fingers coiled over it and breath catching. For now, I dismissed the brute, instead taking my time to let her adjust.

No fun if it was all pain and no pleasure.

Bit by bit, I filled her, pushing, waiting, lights flashing in my eyes as her body clenched around me. Stars *above*, this was tight.

And so fucking perfect.

Eventually, I worked up to little thrusts, studying her body language, using her response to speed up or slow down as necessary.

Honestly, I ought to get a fucking medal for this—for

taking my time with a lover so divine and not charging ahead like a selfish bastard.

But for Alecto Clarke, just for tonight, I showed great care in her comfort.

In making her feel safe with me.

Until she finally relaxed. Until the resistance was just a touch less. Until her palms met my desk, hands flattened and breath coming faster.

Then I fucked her like I wanted to. Pumped my hips so that the globes of her backside jiggled with every thrust. Knotted the tie around my fist and arched her up, obsessed with the bend of her back, the look of her ass when my hip bones pistoned into it with bruising force, cock vanishing down to the hilt.

Owning her. Savagely. Beautifully.

Her moans and cries mingled with my grunts and snarls. While my office was no stranger to wanton acts of carnality, this was different.

This was... intimate.

I *liked* it.

And for the first time, I surrendered to something that terrified me without question—indulged in my own desires, ceded power to my heart and shut off my ever-ruminating mind.

Having a cock that was already at 99 percent when it claimed her ass, pacing myself was fucking torture—but I did it. I took Alecto with purpose, determined to squeeze another climax out of my fury before the night was through. As soon as she slipped her hand around and down, settling between her thighs, I slowed to an almost painful grind—for me, certainly not for her judging by the way my muffled name dripped from her tongue in long, desperate moans. Eyes clenched shut, she focused on her clit with a determined expression that nearly sent me over the edge.

Finally, I released her hair and folded over, bracing above her with both hands on the desk, grinding, watching, waiting for her to come apart all around me.

And when she did, I swore I saw stars.

Every single fucking star in the galaxy. Alecto surrendered to bliss with a breathy cry, her whole body shuddering and jerking, her ass snapping around my cock like a bear trap. I smacked at the desk, hissing, snarling, a savage beast caught in her thrall—forced to endure her pleasure whether I wanted to or not.

She clutched at me through every delicious shock wave, and I literally couldn't move until she relaxed enough to allow it.

Frankly, it was the hottest thing a lover had ever done.

Teeth gritted, I clamped a hand around the back of her neck again and *fucked* her, pounding into her ass until the pleasure dragged me under. Every inch tightened—and then explosion. Detonation of nuclear proportion, my climax ripping through me like a hundred steel-tipped arrows, pain twining with pleasure, all-consuming.

Destruction in its finest form.

Incoherent babble tumbled from my lips as I twitched and spilled myself inside her.

This was better than any high, even if I felt less in control now than I did totally buzzed out on wolfsbane. I relished the free fall, crashing into her back with a groan, burying my face in her curls.

Wrapping my arms around her and crushing her to me.

Never wanting to let her go…

I did, of course.

When the pleasure ebbed and my vision returned, no longer swirling galaxies and dancing stars but an almost painfully in-focus view of my office, I released her. Alecto trembled beneath me, both of us chasing our breaths, hot and sweaty and stinking of lust. While I flopped onto her as I almost always did in the aftermath, I did so with care, my weak arms braced on the desk so I wouldn't smother her.

Cock still buried to the hilt, I was just about to move, mind veering down dark and dangerous paths—and then she reached for me. Tie out of her mouth, my fury twined her fingers into my hair, soft and gentle this time, before smoothing her hand down to cradle my cheek.

Everything went quiet then. My mind stilled. My heartbeat slowed. My eyes closed, and I leaned into her touch, into her warm palm that felt so oddly reassuring.

No, I—

I cracked open one eye to find her shyly peeking up at me, and when our gazes tangled, there was no animosity this time.

Just… quiet.

Alecto licked her swollen lips, then pulled me closer, steering my head to hers with that cupped hand on my cheek.

She took the leap—closed her eyes and sighed, forehead nuzzling at my temple.

Eyes shut, I followed soon after, embracing the free fall.

And dreading the landing.

22

ALECTO

"Make yourself at home, why don't you?"

"Well, you were gone a thousand years..." Seated bare-ass on Gavriel's huge leather office chair, I exited the tab I'd been using to watch public freak-out compilation videos for the last—oh, yikes—forty minutes, and then gently closed his laptop. "It was either watch humans lose their shit or snoop through yours. Pick one."

"Are you part praying mantis?" the fae demanded as he shuffled back into the room. "Is this when you rip my head off—now that I've brought sustenance?"

Sustenance *indeed.* I glanced up to find his arms overflowing with brown paper takeout bags from the kitchen, bringing with him a scent cloud of grease and salt that made my heart sing and my stomach roar. My giddy little finger-clapping had him rolling his eyes as he kicked his office door shut, and I pushed everything aside, clearing a space on his desk for the haul.

Post-sex, I hadn't wanted to go back to my empty flat and Gavriel wore this *look* that said he didn't want to be alone, either—even if he would never admit it. He had pushed for booze, a nightcap to wrap up the evening, while I demanded food.

And now we had food.

The smug fae had folded and gone hunting for his mate.

Which, in a way, was oddly satisfying.

After he had slipped out to forage, fully dressed in those slightly hideous yellow trousers and crinkled dress shirt, I tidied around the office, magicking away any bodily fluids and righting files that had slid off his desk in the ruckus.

Then got bored waiting for him, so, wearing nothing but his suit jacket, the garment a smidgen too big and smelling strangely like earth, I had distracted myself on his laptop—

Just as Gavriel had distracted me from Benedict, from the way I still felt his disgusting mouth on my hand days after he showed up in my greenhouse to try and publicly bully me into a date. Initially, my heart told me to go to Jack; even though it was a bit fucked-up to get off on pain, to find peace in the sting of his hand and the brutal bite of a flogger, it was actually one of the healthier coping mechanisms I'd tried over the years. I mean, everything was carefully negotiated and consensual, and when it was all over, he made me feel safe.

That was essential.

Given our history, Gavriel hadn't always made me feel safe—or good, or wanted, or cherished.

I really *had* planned to keep things strictly platonic between us. But then Jack and I already had another playdate scheduled next week, and my new Dom was a stickler for rules. They seemed to give him the same peace pain gave me, and I was trying my best to respect that. Showing up on his doorstep—again—and springing a scene on him seemed rude, maybe even disrespectful toward the boundaries we had carefully set for ourselves.

Bjorn had also dipped out for the night, unable to partake

in our usual grading and reality-TV marathon because a friend was passing through the highlands on the way to Iceland. So, my more-than-friends roommate was off on a vamp-only pub date in the village. Jack needed his space. And everything around me had just felt so lonely and empty, and Benedict wouldn't get out of my brain...

So I had ended up here.

The plan hadn't been to show up for sex, but there hadn't really been a plan at all. It had just... happened.

And this time felt different.

He held me when it was over.

Well, *I* held him first, but then we just... lay together, wrapped in each other's arms, quiet and contemplative. Calm and settled. No sneering. No teasing. No thinly veiled insults.

I wasn't flying high or anything, but in some weird way, Gavriel *did* make me feel safer than I would have alone in my room tonight, trying and failing to fall asleep. On top of that, the fae had been a great distraction, and being able to disconnect and live in the moment with someone who made my heart race was... progress.

Sort of.

No guilt—not about the sex, anyway.

Maybe a *tiny* bit of shame for backsliding into Gavriel's arms, roping us both into something unhealthy when we could have just had a conversation.

One that probably would have ended in a fight.

So, win-win, I guess?

"Right..." Gavriel dumped the takeout bags and rooted through one for a tinfoil-wrapped bundle. "Bacon cheeseburger for the lady—extra bacon, extra cheese."

"Good sir," I gushed, pressing a hand to my chest with a dramatic gasp, jacket open just enough to show off a pebbled nipple that caught Gavriel's eye, "however did you know?"

"Shot in the dark, really," the fae told me as he unpacked

the rest. I set my burger aside with a squeal when I spotted what my heart *really* lusted after.

"Oh my gods, *yes*, I love curly fries!" They were good everywhere, but the Root Rot kitchen crew were pros at making them *just* right, crispy on the outside, soft on the inside, not overly potato-y and salted to perfection.

"Uh, those are mine."

I smacked Gavriel's hand away when he went for the cardboard container with that telltale curly-fry squiggle on top in marker, and he retaliated by grabbing my wrist and literally throwing my hand aside. He then snatched the container and flopped into one of the visitor chairs on the other side of his desk, popping it open in his lap with one hand while the other undid the top few buttons of his dress shirt.

All under my withering glare. Eyebrows up, Gavriel pointed to another rectangle container.

"I got you fucking regular fries and made you come twice," he growled as I picked through the takeout bags. "Leave me alone."

Lips pursed, I ripped into the bag with chilled plastic bottles inside—then made a face when I pulled one out.

"Diet Coke?" I held it up for him, nose wrinkled as I poked through the other bottles he must have stolen from the kitchen staff's breakroom while they were busy making our burgers and fries. All diet. "For real?"

Gavriel's eyes narrowed as he chewed a mouthful of curly fries, swallowing hard and rolling his eyes while I cracked open the bottle with a wildly unimpressed look on my face.

"*You* get the food next time, then."

"I godsdamn will if these are the decisions you make under pressure." Ugh, *diet*. Nothing like a mouthful of aspartame to take the fun out of a fizzy drink. Still, it was *just* soda-like enough to pair with a greasy meal, so fine. He was off the hook—for now.

"Hardly under pressure," Gavriel muttered, setting his curly fries on the desk and hunting around for his burger, which, when it came out of the takeout bag, was double the size of mine. Triple bacon and cheese? Quadruple the greasy patties? I liked his style. The fae sniffed at it as he peeled open the tinfoil. "Just... tired and spent. Bit cruel to ask a man to do anything after he's blown his load."

"Ugh, gross."

"What?"

"*Blown his load*," I repeated, mimicking his lofty fae accent. "Fucking gross."

"Just eat your burger, fury."

I rolled my eyes again, grinning. "Useless."

Gavriel's gaze snapped to mine, all serious and vaguely insulted, but the moment those beautiful greys plummeted to my mouth, his instantly split into a crooked half-smile that gave me butterflies.

Weird.

Because while I had no idea how to feel about *this*, the effortless back-and-forth, the constant teasing and prodding of each other's buttons, clearly my body was totally cool with it. Why else did this smile taste so permanent?

Back when I had said we could be friends, I meant it. Not only was it better for both of us to not use rough sex— possibly verging on *hate* sex if we weren't careful—to fix our problems, but Gavriel struck me as a man who needed a friend. Someone to just *be* with him, warts and all.

And I got that. Really. I spent so much time at Root Rot pretending, and it was such a relief to let loose—like taking off your bra at the end of a long day so the ladies could finally *breathe*.

Plus, there was something so freeing about being able to

insult someone, to act like a total dick, without worrying about hurt feelings and rumors flying, about a ruined reputation or some twisted version of the truth circulating the castle.

Did that mean I... *trusted* him?

I...

I took a cautious bite of my burger, perfectly cheesy, bacon crisped just right, and frowned at the fae across from me as he picked the pickles off his late-night snack.

Trust... *him*?

I... No.

I rolled my eyes when he started digging out the onions as well, all huffy and pretentious in the way he flicked the offending bits off his finger.

Maybe. Maybe we were both damaged just enough that opening up to him wasn't as scary as it was with everyone else.

"Tell me, fury," Gavriel rumbled, staring at me over his mutilated burger while I popped a stupid, boring, *regular* fry into my mouth, "what makes you fuck to forget?"

Right. Forget everything about it being easier to open up to him. I coughed and thudded a fist against my chest, fry stuck in my too-dry throat. Meanwhile, Gavriel's eyes lit up like tree lights on Yule, ever the predator, even here, even *now*, surrounded by our greasy post-sex feast. As the jolt of panic in my belly settled, heart rate slowing, I tipped my head to the side and went for my burger again.

"What makes you drink to forget?" *Right back at you, dick.*

Gavriel chewed thoughtfully for a moment, and when he finally swallowed, he flashed a smarmy grin that had me sighing. "Show you mine if you show me yours."

Yeah, expected that. "No."

"You just let me fuck your ass," he said with a scoff, eyes

narrowing as I chomped down on a much-too-big burger bite, "but you don't trust me with your secrets?"

I shrugged and, through a mouthful of half-chewed burger, mumbled, "You first."

Then, to add insult to injury, I wiped my fingers on his chair's armrest, smearing grease and hoping to piss him off enough that he would drop it. Instead, Gavriel lunged forward so swift, his movements so fluid, that I almost jumped out of my skin, then let out a huff when he grabbed a handful of napkins from one of the takeout bags and tossed them my way.

"No," he remarked once he was slumped back in his chair. I kicked up one shoulder again, readjusting the tinfoil around the bottom of my *scrumptious* burger so that I didn't lose one tasty morsel.

"Then I'm not saying anything."

We stared at each other for a long beat, both of us munching slowly through another bite, and Gavriel eventually tossed one leg over the other, ankle on his knee, and stretched his arm out along the back of the other chair beside him.

"Fury, dearest darling," he purred, lashes aflutter and silvery eyes cold, "I thought you wanted to be *friends*."

Indignation clenched in my chest at the way he sneered it.

"Can you stop acting like that's some huge insult?" I snapped back at him, burger set aside and fingers on the prowl for a ketchup packet. "You *need* a friend like me."

His eyes narrowed, that glare almost offended—*wounded* even. When I finally located the little condiment packet, I shook it back and forth, then ripped open the top with my teeth.

"Chill." I spurted the red goop into the corner of my fries container, knowing I'd need three of these—minimum—but not wanting to be a ketchup hog from the get-go. "I need a friend like you, too."

In a blink, that bleeding heart look vanished, replaced with something annoyingly smug. Gavriel sank into his chair like a petulant king settling deeper onto his throne.

"You fancy me."

Maybe.

Probably.

I stabbed a pair of fries into the ketchup. "You fancy *me*— or we would have been a one-and-done situation and you know it."

Gavriel flipped me off from across the desk, and I hoisted a middle finger right back.

"Stop trying to distract me from the matter at hand," the fae growled, regaining some composure by straightening up and setting his half-eaten burger aside. I motioned to his container of glorious curly fries with a scowl.

"Oh my *gods*, just eat your fries." Seriously. I would have demolished the whole thing by now. "If you let them get cold and then just throw them out, I'm going to be pissed."

As if to prove a point, Gavriel shoved a massive handful of curly fries into his mouth and chewed with it open while I stared. Honestly, this guy. Why *this* guy? Shaking my head, I went back to my meal, plowing through most of it in the silence that followed, both of us eating and drinking to avoid the landmine we had almost walked right over.

Until—

"You know, if we play show-and-tell," Gavriel mused, crumpling his tinfoil and tossing it onto the desk, narrowly missing one of the ripped-open brown takeout bags, "it could be under the promise of mutually assured destruction."

I gulped down the last of my drink with a grimace. "Sure. I mean, those would be my terms."

"Good." The fae leaned forward and offered his greasy

hand for a shake. Clearly he needed to unload something, maybe even just *talk* without fear of judgment or scrutiny.

And how nice would it be to hash out the Benedict situation with someone sworn to secrecy after spilling his own guts, someone who had just freely offered me leverage.

Like it had a mind of its own, my hand went for his, and when I tried to retreat, horrified, Gavriel just gripped tighter and held me in place. We shook on it in silence, neither willing to let go first, until finally the grease let me wriggle away and wilt into his high-backed leather chair.

Gods, what had I done?

"So, you first," Gavriel urged, motioning for me to start with a dramatic flourish. My eyebrows shot up, and I crossed my arms with a snort.

"Nope."

"Fucking really?"

"Fucking *really*. This was your idea."

"Yeah, but—"

"Then I rescind my handshake—"

"For fuck's sake, *fine*." Gavriel grabbed two napkins and hunkered down to clean his fingers, every last bit of fryer grease gone, looking oddly serious—and a bit deranged—as he focused on the task. When he finally finished, tossing the used napkins aside with a scowl, he swept both hands through his hair, back and forth, wasting time.

Fidgeting.

Scared, maybe. Bundled up in his jacket, I leaned forward, about to tell him he didn't need to do this—that we could each take a rain check and try again another day.

But then he sighed, lifting heavy grey eyes to mine, teetering on the brink. My little nudge, the poke that sent him over the edge, came as I settled back into his chair and zipped my lips, a wordless promise not to interrupt.

"My father was a low-born fae," he admitted hoarsely.

"And his father before him, his father before him, all the way up the fucking family tree."

Shocking, given the air of royalty he always carried himself with, but I kept that to myself as promised. When his gaze flicked almost shyly to me, I just nodded, expression neutral, ears open and lips firmly shut.

"I came from dirt, but refused to live there forever," Gavriel said slowly, frowning, busying himself with his fingers, nails neat and trimmed. "I wanted to better the family name, so I joined the Ash Court army. And... I was really good at it."

I straightened somewhat: the armor in his closet. Suspicions proven: he had once been a soldier, and now he was... *this*.

"Rose through the ranks, gained the trust of my fellow warriors, did my duty beyond reproach," he growled, almost telling the story to himself rather than me. "Decades down the line, I had my own battalion. I had victories to my name and supporters at my back. When a position became available, I took it... and I wanted to become a commander. Highest rank there was. Most respected. I'd have a place at the king's table eventually, possibly even a seat on the court's war council.

"Then some noble's son swept in to take the job I'd *earned*. High-born idiot who just wanted the medals, the title, the prestige. Fucker could barely hold a sword, never mind command an army. It caused a huge uproar with the men— massive dissent, threats of mutiny and rebellion. They called me in to meet with the war council and find a way to quash it, said that I *deserved* the promotion and the rank, but it was all political in the king's court.

"So, they offered me an assignment—reclaim an old Ash Court fort fallen into enemy hands. We lost it centuries ago, and that had nearly started a civil war. At the time, it stood in no-man's-land between our court and the Amber Court, and they assured me it was abandoned. If I could reclaim the fort, the nobles would have no choice but to promote me on the proper merit.

"I put together a squadron of my best warriors, fae I'd fought alongside since the beginning, who had sworn their lives to me. It... It was supposed to be easy. Simple. Kill the few guards stationed at the fort and toss a flag on the tower."

Gavriel went for his soda bottle, and from the disdain on his face, he probably wished it was whiskey. Vodka. Tequila. *Anything* strong enough to blur the memories.

"It was a disaster," he rasped, soft and strained. "The place was heavily armed—total ambush. We stayed. We fought bravely for our court... and I was the only one to make it back. Broken, beaten, I dragged my best friend's body home to his wife—they burned the others before I could reach them."

I pressed a hand to my mouth, shaking my head, eyes stinging with tears I refused to shed. This was his sorrow, not mine. "Oh, gods, Gavriel—"

"The nobles spun it like I'd gone rogue—that I knew the place was fortified with the best the Amber Court had at their disposal," the fae snarled, grey gaze a million miles away. He slumped into his chair and tipped his head back with a sigh. "They ran this propaganda campaign that turned even my own men against me. I mean, on my watch, their best and brightest had died. In the end, they gave me a dishonorable discharge. I can never serve in the army again —never don my armor in battle. Never carry the king's banner. Nothing. Two long centuries of war and conquest for *nothing*."

He sounded numb.

Disconnected from the trauma.

I had only heard the stories of my parents' deaths; I

couldn't imagine the horror of witnessing people I loved die right before my eyes—and not a peaceful death at that. A violent one, brutal and bloody. Warriors were brothers to the end, and they had stripped him of everything.

All for what—politics? So some rich asshole's kid could play general?

No wonder he drank.

"I'm so sorry, Gavriel," I whispered after a long stretch of silence. "I can't even imagine what you've been through."

"Still wanted the influence and power, to get out of the dirt," he muttered, pinching the bridge of his nose briefly before sitting back up, "but after everything, I planned to make changes from within the viper's nest—show the king what his sycophants have done, how they will one day be the downfall of the Ash Court with their greed."

"Right." I reached for my fries, barely lukewarm but salty enough to hit the spot, and shoved a few in my mouth with a frown. If he wanted to make a difference back home, why was he *here*, at Root Rot of all places? Why would a warrior want to be a librarian? "So, you—"

"So, I came here," he mused, cutting me off with a thin smile. "Traveled to this realm and made a deal."

I blinked back at him, thrown for a loop again—because fae were experts at deals. Hell, I had considered hiring one of the fair folk to find Benedict initially, but ended up going with a djinn because he couldn't screw me over once I had him in my service.

Fae were tricky that way, always ready to take advantage of a loophole.

Apparently.

I'd never made a deal with one, and after Gavriel, the likelihood of ever doing so was down to zero.

"You made a deal," I said slowly, working out the

mechanics piece by piece, hand hovering over my fries, "with a... demon?"

Who else could give a fae the unattainable? Gavriel's smile split wider.

"With *the* demon." He nodded when my eyes rounded. "Lucifer himself took my case, but not for my soul. I owe him one hundred souls for Darkwell Academy—"

"*What?*" I shot up, heart in my throat and temper at a twelve, then slammed my hands on his desk and shoved the takeout bags aside. "Gavriel, I—you... You did *what?*"

"Simmer down, fury." He waved me off with a more genuine grin, unfazed by my anger. "I can't force students to do anything they don't want to do. I can persuade them that Darkwell is the best post-graduate option for their skills, but they need to be accepted on their own merit. I'm basically an admissions scout at this point. In three years, I've only had *two* of my selections accepted. Fucking *two.*"

Hand pressed to my forehead, I collapsed into his chair before my knees gave out. Gavriel was here to... prey on my kids? No. That couldn't be right. He wouldn't... He...

"Not going very well," the fae grumbled, fiddling with his nails again. "Quite frustrating, actually. Who knew the Devil had such high standards?"

Gods. Brain fogged over and a buzz between my ears, I couldn't process this—any of it. The warrior part, all the death and betrayal and dishonor, made sense. That explained the drinking, the screwing his way through the entire female faculty—anything to numb himself to his past. But *this?*

Making a deal with Lucifer?

I—

"Now you."

"W-what?" I managed, struggling to claw out of the stupor he had put me in. Gavriel leaned forward, dragging his chair with him, until he was *right* up against the other side of the desk.

"Now *you*," he repeated, motioning for me to spill my guts everywhere, mix them in with his.

Fucking laughable, really.

"Gavriel, we need to talk about this," I argued. Yeah, he might not be kidnapping students and shipping them to the academy sponsored by Satan, but he *was* preying on a vulnerable population. These kids were here to better themselves, not to be told they were fine as is and, hey, the Devil might have a place for you in his army on Earth.

No. Absolutely not.

"I gave you my secret," he insisted, plowing straight through my objections. "Death, betrayal, shame, dishonor, and a deal with the Devil. Your turn."

I shook my head. No. I couldn't just... carry on like everything was normal. It wasn't. I couldn't look at him the same—not tonight, anyway.

"Don't break my heart, fury." Gavriel might have sounded like his usual teasing self, that sinful mouth crooked and handsome as ever, but none of it reached his eyes. In that layered grey gaze, I saw fear. Hesitation. The expectation that I, like everyone else, was going to screw him over.

And the point of this was mutual self-destruction. Give as good as we got. Be in each other's debt, carrying each other's reasons for drinking and fucking to forget.

How good will it feel not to drag this burden around alone anymore?

I swallowed thickly, throat like sandpaper, anxiety sluicing through my veins, numbing my fingertips, my toes.

Gavriel had just revealed his ugly side. Hell, *he* had suggested it—because maybe he too was sick of lugging the past around all by himself.

And if we were both exposed, both out in the open and in

the know, we might stop falling back on unhealthy shit to make ourselves feel better.

Maybe we could just... talk.

Then have sex because we wanted to, not because we needed to forget some ancient horror.

Fuck it.

"Ash Cedar's real name is Benedict Hammond," I said slowly, forcing every word, body rebelling against the confession and locking up tight. Gavriel's expression flatlined to shock, and he just blinked back at me from across the desk, uncharacteristically mute as I added, "And when I was three, almost four, he butchered my parents in our home —then set it on fire and left me to burn."

Oh.

Gods.

What had I just done?

What would he—

What if he—

Godsgodsgodsgodsgodsgodsno.

"So..." Gavriel leaned forward and steepled his fingers, unnervingly serious with those furrowed brows. His eyes flitted back and forth like he was working out some complex mathematics equation. He motioned to me, palms up, fingers splayed, then steepled his hands again. Struggling. Failing to find the words. "I... What—the fuck?"

At that eloquent prompting, I opened the floodgates. Sure, it was only the bullet points—he didn't need the fine details of how I struggled for years, looked for love and comfort in all the wrong places, acted out, cried, screamed, tried to perform summoning rituals to call my mom and dad's souls back to this realm...

You know, just to *talk* to them.

By the end, Gavriel was the only one in this castle, this continent, this *world*, maybe, who knew that a neighbor had pulled me out of my burning childhood bedroom. That my grandparents raised me far away from the sleepy northern town where the Corwin and Hammond covens had clashed for generations. That no one had ever been formally blamed for the massacre. That my grandpa killed himself in his grief and some drunk driver took my grandma from me a few years later.

That I paid a djinn an exorbitant amount of money to find the real killer.

That I had him manipulate the cosmos to make Atkins retire so I had a legitimate reason for being here at Root Rot.

"And now he's here, and I'm here, and it's been *months* of just... coexisting." I spat the word out and tugged Gavriel's jacket tighter around my naked frame, then folded my leg up so I could hug something sturdy, resting my chin on my knee. At no point did I care that I was flashing my pussy at him—nor did Gavriel's gaze dip down for a quick peek. Not once had his eyes left my face throughout the entire story, like he wanted to scrutinize every twitch of my expression to gauge whether or not this was real. I licked my lips, the meat of my self-loathing and guilt finally coming to the surface. "And I... I'm really struggling. I don't know what to do about him. I feel like I'm letting everyone down, like I'm wasting this opportunity, but I can't just, you know, kill him."

The fae tipped his head to the side with a frown. "Why not?"

Why not? Simple as that. Unlike me, he didn't throw my secret back in my face. He didn't *judge* any of it. He rolled with it, unflinching acceptance in his tone, his body language reading like we were just shooting the shit about academy gossip.

And that felt so—fucking—*good*.

So good, in fact, that tears stung my eyes and soothed my

aching throat. Finally, *finally*, I had someone to just talk to about it.

He'd never, ever know how much that meant to me.

Thievery in the greenhouse last term—forgiven.

For now.

"Because..." My cheeks warmed at his little eyebrow arch. "Because the thought of physically, uh, *killing* him makes me sick. I don't... I don't want to be like him, but I feel like maybe there's no other choice?" I shook my head, deflating at the realization. "I'm scared, and I'm frustrated and angry and floundering. My current plan is to get a taped confession and turn him over to the authorities."

"*Boring.*" Gavriel scoffed, then popped his elbows up on the desk. "D'you want *me* to kill him? I could just do it tonight—smother him in his sleep."

An offer like that should have sent me running for the hills. Instead, it made me all warm and fuzzy inside, the butterflies in my chest aquiver at the thought.

"No," I told him, firm and with a smile. "That's, uhm, sweet, but it needs to be me. He needs to know it was *me*, that I survived and I'm here to ruin his whole life just like he ruined mine."

Gavriel settled back in his chair again with a nod. "Fair enough. So, he thinks you're dead?"

"Pretty sure he thinks Hannah Corwin burned in her bed, yeah. My grandparents and I cut ties with the rest of the family as soon as we moved. Like, they had a kid's coffin at my parents' funeral, so—"

"And now you're..." His brows shot up again, gaze sweeping over me from top to bottom. "Alecto Clarke?"

"I've been Alecto for years," I said with another bob of my head, the anxiety ebbing the more I shared, "but Clarke is new."

In the quiet that followed, Gavriel gave me a longer, more

intense once-over, for once nowhere near verging on a leer or a sneer or a seductive perusal. Instead, it almost felt like he was calculating my *worth* suddenly, and I shifted in his chair, leg down and arms crossed, his jacket covering most of the good bits as a self-conscious blush prickled in my cheeks.

"Alecto suits you," the fae admitted softly, and now it was my time to scoff.

"Right." I forced out a hollow laugh. "Because I'm totally killing it on the whole revenge thing. He hits on me all the time, and I do nothing but pretend to be flattered."

"Because you're playing it *smart*," Gavriel growled, hands clenching over his chair's armrests. "You're playing the long con, fury, and that's the *game*. All the moving parts need to align or you'll fuck it straight to hell—end up like your parents."

My eyes narrowed. "Okay, too far."

His usual impish grin returned, triumphant and genuine as his hands slowly loosened on the armrest, the wood literally groaning as he released it.

"You know, the furies aren't all violence and bloodshed," he mused, tapping his finger on his desk as if to nail the point home. "They have a purpose in this world—creatures of *righteous* justice. They punish those who deserve it, and my darling girl, if you're one thing, it's righteous."

"Wow..." I snorted and went for the fry crumbs left in the container. "What a lovely backhanded compliment. Thanks."

Before he could add to it, I hurled an onslaught of crispy fried potato bits at him, and Gavriel actually dove to catch them in his mouth. The second he snapped up the biggest piece, we both threw our arms up at the same time in celebration—like he had just scored the winning touchdown at the big game.

"Nice," I said through a mouthful of giggles. Yeah. I fancied him. After tonight, I really, really did.

And from the little twinkle in his eye, the feeling was mutual.

Gods, we were so screwed.

Gavriel and me... What a mess.

Maybe Bjorn could balance us out. Hell, with his level head and even temper, maybe he could actually fix us, the ultimate basket cases, the crown jewels of his professional career—

"To secrets among friends," the fae announced out of nowhere, swiping his half-drunk diet garbage and hoisting the bottle high. Sighing, I went for one of the untouched bottles and cracked open the lid.

"Are you sure I can't talk you out of this Darkwell deal?" I asked, trying to sound as nonjudgmental as possible as I held up my hissing drink, bubbles fizzing at the mouth. Gavriel shook his head.

"Not a chance. I'm not hurting anyone, fury. It's all about free will—that's Lucifer's kink, remember."

I ducked my chin as heat exploded across my face at the word *kink*. Because. *Apparently*, I had a few of my own that Gavriel had coaxed out and Jack was all too happy to indulge in.

"Right. Sure. Free will."

"You sure I can't just kill Ced— Hammond?" The question sounded like he was asking if he could crush a cockroach under his boot. "He's *suuuuch* a prat."

Grinning, I leaned forward and held out my bottle so we could clink. "No. I have to do it, no matter what *it* ends up being."

"Fine," Gavriel said with a long, over-the-top groan, "but if it's not done by the end of this school year, I'm going to take him out back and shoot him. Fair?"

If only it was that easy. If only I could have just hired a hitman and got it over with. "Let's play it by ear."

"Righteous bitch," he whispered affectionately. Lips pursed, I lifted my bottle a little higher, exhaustion creeping in as the conversation wrapped and the wee hours of the morning dragged on.

"To secrets between friends," I said back to him, "and mutual self-destruction."

"Hear, hear, fury."

We knocked our plastic bottlenecks together and chugged it all down, eyes locked, goading the other on to finish every last bitterly sweet drop.

Then polished off the last of our greasy feast. Chatted a little more about safer topics. Teased a lot. Groped and kissed and fucked against his office door one last time, serenaded by the three-o'clock bells.

And eventually went our separate ways, to separate beds…

Parting, for the first time, as friends.

What?

Okay. *Fine.*

Parting, for the first time, as a little bit *more* than friends.

23

GAVRIEL

"And now, as one, light your candles and embrace Imbolc."

Bold move to host another sabbat feast featuring darkness and candles, but that was Jack Clemonte: bold and progressive, stubborn to the last, because here we were, on the second day of February, celebrating yet another distinctly *witch* ritual.

Not that it mattered. Lucy Eastwick was long gone, and no one had come *close* to her potential in the long, dreary winter months that followed her expulsion. Was it really a wonder why I drank? *Really?*

The rest of them remained unaware that my potential offering was responsible for the chaos on Mabon, which kept the staff table laughably tense tonight. Still, Jack pushed forward, determined to foist his beliefs and rituals onto the student body, and we all played along, bellies howling and goblets full of untouched wine, lighting candles and waiting for it to be over.

Well, that was *my* approach, anyway. Sandwiched between Ash Cedar to the left and some ancient warlock on my right, I was surrounded by sycophants, biased traditionalists who lived for this type of shit.

Rolling my eyes, I grabbed my green candlestick, the whole dining hall moving in unison after another tedious Clemonte speech about the *meaning* behind all this. Something about the first taste of spring—I'd zoned out a few sentences in. But we were welcoming back the light, the darkest time of the year behind us.

In the literal sense, anyway.

While massive black tri-flamed candles dotted the tables for Mabon, we had white ones tonight—for the purity of spring, or some such nonsense—and bright green candles for personal use. Which we were supposed to... hold after? Maybe? Hadn't been listening.

Mine caught fire the moment I tipped it over the white candle flame, stretched to the left across Cedar to reach our shared fire source.

No. Not Cedar.

Two weeks on and I *still* couldn't believe this boring prat had fooled me. *Benedict Hammond* had pulled the wool over my eyes for years, just the rest of these dullards, and even now, despite my bored expression, it fucking *infuriated* me that I hadn't seen what was going on.

Because now that I knew, bullshit and fakery was all I saw in him, all I smelled whenever he entered a room. With Alecto's traumatic family history shared, her secret safe with me so long as my Darkwell affiliations stayed exclusively with her, the warlock had a great neon sign chiseled into his smooth forehead: *liar*.

In big, blocky, obnoxious letters.

Just before I settled back into my seat, the dining hall erupting with candlelight, the windows charmed to look like a rosy sunset, I caught him looking.

Staring—intently—at her.

My fury.

Down the staff table, she and Bjorn whispered amongst themselves, all smiles as they leaned forward to light their candles. Given her past, I finally understood her aversion to fire—why she had insisted I light her cigarette that night on the beach, so un-witchlike as she shied away from the flames. She did well with it all here, her gaze soft—smitten, even—as she focused entirely on her handsome vampire flatmate.

Did the hairs on the back of her neck stand up, I wondered, the longer Cedar—*Hammond*—burned a hole into her forehead? That black gaze refused to lift, even with his candle lit. My eyes narrowed.

Quite the little train we had going: Alecto gazing adoringly up at Bjorn, Bjorn locked on her, Hammond staring relentlessly at Alecto, and me glaring daggers into the side of Hammond's too-big head.

My grasp tightened around the candle, nails gritting into the wax, and the flame shivered as a strangely unfamiliar urge swelled in my chest.

The urge to... protect.

I'd experienced it before with my siblings, my mother, even the fae in my battalion.

Rarely had I ever felt so inclined to aggressively protect a woman—a *lover*. No one had ever stirred that side of me before, yet when Alecto shared her struggles with vengeance, I hadn't hesitated.

The offer to smother this twat in his sleep had been genuine—and I would have done it in a heartbeat if she accepted. Back then, I hadn't questioned the surge of protectiveness, the need to eliminate a threat.

As annoying as it was to consider, even worse to accept, *obviously* I had a soft spot for Alecto Clarke.

Corwin. Alecto *Corwin.*

My fury. My girl. My *friend*—apparently.

It was the last one that stilled my hand. Above all else, I understood the need to exact one's *own* revenge. Benedict Hammond had hurt her, destroyed her life, cut down her family tree and set it ablaze before she had the chance to watch it grow. She needed to be the one to swing the axe, and while I predicted it would be something boring—taped confessions were such a *snooze*—I still crossed my fingers for a bloody, violent showdown where my girl could stand over his charred corpse, triumphant and finally free from her past.

For now, I held my tongue.

Forcefully, sometimes, because not only did I smell bullshit anytime this lying sack of shit entered my orbit, but she had opened my eyes as to how he treated her.

How he *looked* at her—like he owned her.

Whether he suspected she wasn't who she claimed to be remained to be seen, but Benedict Hammond had eyes for my fury, bold in his flirtations, aggressive in asserting his claim at Sunday staff meetings.

Hell, he had literally shoved one of the shifter professors aside to sit next to her at the last one, and not only had I been seconds away from scalping him just because, but Bjorn had glowered at him so venomously from across the table that it was a miracle he hadn't turned to stone.

If Alecto allowed it, on her day of righteous vengeance, I'd like to break his hands. Both of them—all the fingers, too. Because he had touched her more than once in my presence.

And now that I knew the truth, now that I had begrudgingly accepted that stupid soft spot, his hand on her body—anywhere—fucking pissed me off.

I wouldn't kill him, of course.

But I'd like to see him suffer, even if she eventually chose boring over bloody.

All of that meant something.

More than friendship, I cared for *her*. Her safety, her well-being, her heart and her mind and her feelings.

Ugh. *Tedious.*

But, tiresome as it was, as big a distraction from my overall goals, clearly *this* was the path my heart had embraced—against my consent and without my knowledge. While I had denied it from the beginning, Alecto had always intrigued me, excited me. She knew how to push my buttons and soothe my temper. She called me on my shit and took my mind off everything—Darkwell, the nightmares, the betrayal, the horrors dwelling deep in my own history.

That night, spilling our secrets, embracing mutual destruction, had bonded us, forged a tether between our hearts that, if broken, could destroy everything.

I glanced down the table again. Strangely enough, Alecto wasn't the only creature here with whom I suddenly shared a bond. Despite the miserable winter weather, Bjorn and I had enjoyed many a drunken night on top of the staff tower, each nursing a flask, each offering a part of ourselves with the other.

War stories.

Some good, some bad.

Reliving them out loud might have brought back the nightmares, possibly even made me drink more, but to thrust them onto someone who so intimately understood that life was... a relief.

No judgment.

No fear.

No squeamishness. Bjorn took tales of brutality and bloodshed, conquest and expansion, without batting an eye.

For he had been just as brutal, just as bloody, just as obsessed with land grabs and material gain.

A lifetime ago for us both, we donned armor and cut down foes on the battlefield.

Today, we connected over trauma and failure.

Two people in this castle knew me. Bjorn remained in the dark about my deal with Lucifer, but he had seen my ugliest scars—only to show me some of his own.

The rest of the supernatural ilk seated at this table were totally oblivious to who we three were...

Just like they were with Hammond.

Head cocked, I stayed still as a statue, watching him watch her, even when Jack dove headlong into the second half of his sabbat feast speech. My eyes narrowed when Hammond grinned, the flash of teeth like a match to gunpowder—the spark that ignited the hatred in my heart over the way he looked at her, smiled at her, thought she belonged to *him*.

Hit on her.

Made her feel small and uncertain and furious, wrathful with no outlet.

With a sniff, I tipped my hand to the left as I eased back into my chair, angling the newly lit candlestick *just* right—

So that his sleeve caught fire. So that his stupid, poufy, Tudor-esque traditional warlock robe-jacket-*thing* tasted the inferno he had left Alecto to die in as a child.

Then, for good measure, I willed just a *touch* of my innate power, the air sizzling with my influence, so that the flame spread rapidly from his wrist to his elbow.

"Good gods, man!"

Another of our colleagues noticed before Hammond, but the second the warlock glanced down, he leapt from his chair with a shout, making Jack flinch and trail off mid-speech.

"Stars above, apologies, old boy," I drawled, blowing out the offending candle and setting it on my empty plate, then snatching my napkin to help smother the wildfire on his sleeve. "Wasn't paying attention—"

"You *filthy* little..." Hammond left it at that, mouth

twisted in a snarl as we two battled the flames made to dance by fae magic. By the time we put it out for good, the entire hall buzzed with whispers and nervous giggles, security on the prowl between the tables and den mothers struggling to quiet the student body.

Jack looking ready to strangle us both with his bare hands.

"Goodness," I said with a chuckle, tossing my burnt napkin aside and shaking my head. "Cheap fabrics really just go up in flames, don't they? Hope they put a warning on the label."

Red-faced and flustered, Hammond collapsed into his seat and faced forward in a stormy silence. Hands up in a contrite—fake—apology, I slowly sank into my chair and tucked back in, motioning for Jack to continue with a little chin thrust toward his audience, all of them hanging by a thread and desperate for drama. Scowling, Jack slowly turned around at his podium, then took a few moments to collect himself before restarting his spiel.

Yeah, that little display might have just earned me my first Clemonte lecture. Fabulous.

I stole a glance at Hammond's flayed sleeve, flesh peeking through the ruins of the dress shirt below.

Worth it.

As I went for my goblet, feeling rather *alive* all of a sudden, I caught Alecto out of the corner of my eye doing the same. We glanced toward one another, her expression straddling the line between admonishment and affection. I smirked, pleased that I could decipher the nuances of her mood lately with almost as much skill as I played her body. While there had been no further late-night rendezvous in my office, I'd joined her and Bjorn for the odd meal in this hall over the last few days. Nothing serious, mind you. I had no intention of charging headlong into best-chums territory just because we bared our souls in the shadows—but it was something.

Something *different*, something I hadn't experienced within the Root Rot walls since my contract started.

Something I hadn't felt since before that failed raid, the Amber Court decimating my closest companions and the Ash Court burying me while I grieved.

Camaraderie. Connection.

Understanding.

I didn't hate it.

And if this continued, feeling *alive* and selfless for the first time in ages, like I had done a good deed for someone who mattered—like I could just be the hero, not the hero *and* the loser at the same time...

Well, Benedict Hammond had better watch his back.

Because there might be more *accidents* in his future.

His very *near* future.

24

ALECTO

"Professor Clarke?"

Ugh, gods, just let me fucking eat.

Eyes heavy and smile strained, I slowly looked up from my steaming bowl of minestrone after only slurping down *one* measly spoonful. February 29—the extra day of a leap year. Final day of term exams. The day every major assignment was due across all classes, leaving me with a literal mountain of grading to tackle over the upcoming spring break, most students headed for home tomorrow morning while the rest of us recovered.

But even if they got to leave, the entire castle was just fried at this point in the school year. I had chosen a seat at the far end of the staff table—alone—to just enjoy my massive bowl of soup with the three fresh-baked crusty bread loaves I'd snagged from the dining hall's buffet table. No one to talk to. No students to fight with. No den mothers to snipe at me over portion control. Just—peace and quiet.

This would have actually marked the first meal I'd eaten alone in weeks, and as much as I adored Gavriel and Bjorn's company, on good days and bad, I needed the solitude to decompress. Bjorn skipped dinner to prepare for his final classes of the term this evening, while Gavriel had been barricaded in his office for the last two days on a never-ending interview spree to pad the library ranks after a mass walkout two weeks ago.

No one knew why they left.

But half his staff vanished one night, along with a handful of the new security hires who, frankly, weren't cut out for this academy from the start. So, in more of a mood than usual, the fae popped in and out of my bubble a few times in the last forty-eight hours, mostly to grab coffee or food, grouse a bit about what horrendous candidates he had to entertain, then disappear in a snit.

Jack rarely ever ate in the dining hall with the rest of us outside of sabbat feasts. He was the only one I'd entertain right now of the three weirdly consistent men in my life, if only to listen to his soothing aftercare baritone, the one that lulled me to sleep during our last playdate. Unfortunately, we had both been so busy lately that one Saturday in February was all we could swing.

Another trip to that crumbling fort.

Another early morning strung up and spread open, vulnerable and at a sadist's mercy. Another hour of bliss and pain, totally disconnected from the outside world.

Jack had used a paddle this time, which sucked *way* worse than the flogger. It hurt. A *lot*. A dull, achy, constant throb across my ass and down my thighs—and I'd loved every second of it. We both did, his huge erection impossible to ignore even if I wasn't allowed to do anything about it. No touching him without permission. No kissing. Those were the rules, and my Dom was a stickler for them.

Which, just, *ugh*—Jack's obstinance *did* things to me, made me *feel*, made the butterflies in my chest surge and swarm despite the warped circumstances.

That session had stayed with me for over a week, our filthy secret inked across my skin during classes and meetings and meals. Infatuated with the slow burn of natural healing, I had refused to take a potion to dull the pain or use a balm to mend the bruises.

Of course, everything was gone now, leaving me hungry for another session, a glutton for punishment and an addict for Jack's brand of cuddly aftercare. But lately I was too tired to even consider playing, and just the thought of jogging all the way out to the fort made me want to crawl into bed and never come out.

"Jennifer—hi." I did my best to keep the annoyance out of my voice, the desperation to sit in silence and shove perfectly seasoned soup into my mouth grating my nerves. Standing before me was one of my fifth years, a badger shifter with legitimate herbalism career aspirations after she graduated at the end of the year. Quiet and focused, Jennifer Howard kept her academy uniform neat and was one of the few people who could rock a bright blonde pixie cut without looking like a try-hard. I had no idea why she was at Root Rot Academy—because she was leagues ahead of her peers in my class, both in aptitude and attitude—and I had never bothered to ask. I didn't need to know her previous crimes to like *or* teach her. "What's up?"

"Uh, this is for you?" White-blonde brows furrowed, she held out a weathered envelope with my name scribbled across the front in a shaky cursive, then stamped shut with a red dot on the back. No emblem or artistic seal in the wax. *What—the hell?* I set my spoon down, frowning as Jen added, "Someone, like, slipped it under my door while I was packing for break. No idea what it is or why it came to me."

"That's really weird." Apprehension skittered down my spine suddenly, and I went for the envelope as calmly and coolly as I could. "Nothing strange happened when you touched it, right?"

For all either of us knew, the envelope could have been hexed. Even if it didn't give off a magical aura, you never really knew for sure: hexes were tricky like that, some so subtle they left no supernatural signature in the ether.

"No." Jennifer shrugged, glancing along the staff table with a sniff, about a third of the faculty present and all just as haggard-looking as me. "Doesn't smell off, either, so I've just been looking for you... Maybe someone made a mistake?"

"Or they know we spend time together," I muttered. Not only was Jennifer one of the shining stars in my lectures, but she had volunteered on the Samhain committee and regularly harvested with me during the week. Still, it wasn't her issue anymore. She had done the right thing coming straight to me, and I mustered up the best carefree smile I could as I tapped the envelope against my palm. "I'm sure it was just a mistake. Thanks for bringing it to me."

"No problem."

"Off you go—back to packing."

"Have a good evening, Professor Clarke."

"You too," I said, waving her off as she descended the steps off the elevated staff dining platform. "And have a great break if I don't see you before then."

Out of the corner of my eye, I caught her grin and wave, but Jennifer and spring break were officially the furthest things from my mind. Nudging dinner aside, I set the envelope down flat, then slipped my wand out of its holster.

"*Ipsum revelare.*" Even a basic revealing spell unlocked most charms and undid glamors. While a soft pink light washed over the worn parchment, nothing came of it. For all intents and purposes, the thing was clean.

Maybe.

Someone still could have hexed it—maybe the same

person who conjured all those snakes during Mabon. *Fuck*. Nervous sweat gathering on the nape of my neck, palms cold and heart pounding, I flipped it over and ripped through the wax seal.

Which wasn't tough by any means.

Newly set, then. Someone had done this recently.

Despite the envelope looking aged, thick and luxe and rustically stylized, inside was nothing more than a lined sheet of notebook paper.

Oh gods.

The second I unfolded it, I recognized the handwriting. My eyes narrowed and gut bottomed out.

Alice, what are you doing?

Now it made sense why she would slip this under Jennifer's door: not only did Alice harvest with us, but Jennifer had sort of taken her under her wing a few months back—almost out of pity. They weren't friends, per se... More like gardening club acquaintances.

Alice didn't have any friends.

No one in her corner but me and—

"Fuck."

Dear Professor Clarke,

I know you don't approve, but I've found my soul mate. Brin and I are fated. I understand your reservations. You care about me and my well-being. So does Brin. He wants the world for me, and he promised to give me that and more if I was his wife.

I pressed a hand to my forehead, hunched over the table and reading every horrible word with a sinking feeling. "Fuuuuu*uuuuuuck*."

He found a way to reopen the portal after security sealed it, and on Valentine's Day, he proposed. It was the most beautiful, special moment of my life, and of course I said yes. Tonight, we become husband and wife in front of his entire clan. Little girls dream about their mom and dad being there on their wedding day—but mine sent me here. To them, I'm a disgrace. To Brin, I'm a miracle.

And to you, I'm a friend... I hope.

It would mean the world to me if you were there to witness our union. 7 o'clock sharp, through the portal behind blessed Clíodhna. No plus-ones, unfortunately, but there will be cake!! Double fudge —your favorite!

See you there... Maybe?

xoxo

Alice

Fucking useless security goons.

"Shit, shit, shit, shit, *shit*," I hissed, shooting up with both the envelope and the letter crushed in my panicked fists. Ignoring the curious, marginally irritated side-eyes from my colleagues, I then sprinted out of the dining hall like I had the hounds of hell nipping at my heels, headed straight for Jack without delay.

Hoping we weren't too late to stop this.

JACK

"I can't believe you didn't say something sooner."

Try as I might to keep the conversation between Alecto and me civil, my growl still reverberated harshly down the northwestern stairwell. While empty, there was no telling who was listening from the shadows—and what they might take from whatever words exchanged. Surrounded by the echoes of our thundering footsteps, we raced round and round, charging from the administration wing on the third floor into the bowels of the castle, Alecto's news still ringing in my ears like earth-shattering alarm bells.

When she first burst into my office with a fuming Iris at her heels, I had no idea what to expect—but not this. Never this. A secret portal in *my* academy. A student at risk, smitten with some siren. Initially, my temper had spiked because of Alecto's breach in decorum; she might have been my submissive now, but she couldn't pull rank in front of the others, *especially* Iris Prewett. Outside of scenes, she needed to respect her limitations as a professor and nothing more.

Then, when she had blurted the news about Alice behind a firmly closed door, I'd nearly lost it. This was now the second time she had withheld crucial information from me for the sake of others: first with Bjorn, now with a student, and if we weren't careful, tonight could be an even graver disaster than Samhain.

After all, neither of us believed a siren, one of the most alluring creatures in our world, would marry a teen witch— who *still* couldn't cast—out of the goodness of his heart. With the hour looming and most of the castle's occupants either in class or in their dorms, there simply wasn't time to round up the security squad or call for backup. As it stood, Alice's life depended on Alecto and me—and here I was, starting to question whether I could trust the witch barreling down the stairs at my back.

Worst of all, I couldn't punish her for this, for keeping secrets from me.

Because she hadn't kept a secret from her Dominant, but from her headmaster. This wasn't a scene. This wasn't kink. This was the real world, which was unfortunately a great deal muddier, full of grey areas and questionable boundaries.

"I told security *immediately* after I found out about it," Alecto insisted breathlessly, sounding just as frantic and panicked as I felt. Unlike her, I kept it hidden beneath a granite mask of authority and control. I rolled my eyes at the statement, both of us crossing below the castle's main level and into the underground, the air noticeably cooler. Even if she had run straight to security, these new hires were terrible —and Iris was taking her bloody sweet time to replace them. Above the thunder of our footsteps came Alecto's hand grazing the stone wall, keeping her balance as we sprinted down the dizzying stairwell. "I promised Alice *I* wouldn't tell you, but those idiots said they would file a report."

Typical—and expected, given the scope of this miserable year. Could nothing ever go right? As I barreled through the wooden doorway and whipped around into Clíodhna's alcove, I could feel my tenure here, my professional career and personal reputation, slipping away like sand through my fingers.

Whoever on the administration side of things knew about this and hadn't told me would be fired before midnight tonight—that much was clear. Security. Admin assistants. Den mothers. Iris herself, even. A portal leading directly into my academy was a security breach of epic proportions that I should have been told of *instantly*.

Hell, I should have been there when they sealed it.

Because *obviously* whatever useless incantations they used had failed. Once we had Alice back, even if I had to throw her over my shoulder and bulldoze through a dozen sirens to do it, I would lock the portal shut so tight *no one* could ever breach it again. Already countless spells, hexes, and charms percolated in my ever-racing mind, archived appropriately by type and the necessary focus required. As usual, I thought five steps ahead—but I was needed here and now.

"Here," Alecto muttered, jogging around me and headed for the love goddess's statue. "Let me go first—"

"No." I grabbed her around the elbow before she had made it two strides forward, then reeled her back. Light as a feather, my submissive was so deliciously easy to manhandle, but from the look on her face, the narrowing of her eyes, Alecto appreciated it far less here than she did in scenes. Well. Tough. "Definitely not, *Miss* Clarke."

Her cheeks flashed bright red, and I ignored the dart of guilt in my chest. I so preferred *little one*. Even her name, that of a fury, a creature of the old world, gave me a visceral thrill to whisper aloud. But she was in trouble—I couldn't punish her as I'd like, so she got that. *Miss Clarke.* Let her know she was in the doghouse for all of this, even if it wasn't strictly her fault.

And… And she had done the right thing coming straight to me with the letter.

Maybe just one *Miss Clarke* for the night, then.

Adrenaline buzzed in my fingertips, and I surveyed a stone Clíodhna with a grimace. How the bloody hell was I supposed to fit behind that? As if reading my thoughts, Alecto cleared her throat pointedly, but that only forced my hand. Dressed in my customary fitted three-piece black suit, I strode forth and squished behind the statue—then fell clear through the wall even though I had barely touched it, like unseen hands dragged me into the ether.

The first thing that struck me on the other side was the salty sea air.

Then the unnerving quiet.

Having fallen through backward, I was met with a massive stone wall creeping up overhead, limestone steps at my feet, and when I whipped around, a domed cave with black-blue water sloshing up the stone dock that stretched out from the foot of the stairs.

And sirens.

Dozens of them, beautiful and lovely predators, nude torsos bedazzled with shells and pearls and sea glass visible above the surface. Illuminated by what might have been romantic mood light in other circumstances, countless floating orbs cast the space in light and dark, a warm yellow to soften the harsh features of what looked like an entire clan of man-eaters.

Something was off.

My adrenaline skyrocketed.

Nothing about this looked like a wedding—not even remotely like the siren ceremonies conducted far from the coast that I had read about. Outsiders were seldom welcome. Land brides were always taken by force.

So many eyes on me, calculating, intense—hyperfocused.

I drew my wand immediately, jaw set, expression just as severe as those around me.

This is wrong, Jackie boy.

Run.

I spun around, about to stop Alecto from walking into what was clearly a trap, but my submissive came plummeting through the portal hard and fast, stumbling into me with a grunt.

She wasn't dressed for a fight: thin black leggings and a shapeless floral dress that cut off just below her knees and hit her exquisite curves. Leather boots with a low heel and thick wool socks bunched above them. Hair in a messy bun.

At least it was out of her face.

As if assaulted by the wrongness of the scene, Alecto whipped out her wand and leveled it at the sirens creeping closer to the walkway on either side, each one armed with spears and blades.

A sob cut through the oppressive quiet. Dead ahead, hovering there in the water, was the bride-to-be.

Clutched in a siren's death grip, a dagger to her throat, Alice looked like a drowned rat, soaked to the bone, her usual storm of curls tamed and her makeup running down her cheeks in black tracks.

Beneath the surface, white flared around her.

A wedding dress.

She had found a way to—

"Brin," Alecto barked, stalking around me with a snarl that gave a few of the nearby sirens pause, "you fucking *bastard!*"

I hooked her by the waist and hauled her back. We needed to stay together, vastly outnumbered by a clan of sea warriors who had magic of their own. Paltry, weak, muted magic compared to the bottomless wells inside Alecto and me, but they were armed and dangerous; no sense in starting a fight just yet.

Can't put Alice at even greater risk.

"Lower your wands, witch, warlock, or the girl dies."

Floating around Alice and this Brin character, the siren who spoke did so with true gravitas, a heft in his voice that resonated in me. From the tattoos snaking up his arms, across his chest, ancient symbols I barely recognized, he must have been the clan leader. Broad-chested, muscular but scarred, he appeared weathered compared to the sirens around him, still dangerously handsome but aged, his sun-kissed blond mane shaved at the sides and braided at the back. He brandished a golden trident that I assessed with some concern.

Even if it wasn't a magical conduit, those prongs could tear straight through flesh and bone, then strew our guts around this very cave.

"What is this?" I lowered my wand as requested, stepping in front of Alecto and blocking her from the roving eyes of the sirens in front of us. She still had those on the sides to contend with, warriors flanking us to the right and left, but I shielded her from the siren with the most authority. This time, she let me maneuver her around, lingering in my shadow, her aura prickly and scattered at my back.

Focus, little one. Center yourself.

The tattooed siren sized me up as he swam closer to the helm of the limestone walkway.

"Welcome, Jack Clemonte," he rumbled with the smallest of bows. "Headmaster of Root Rot Academy, warlock of high esteem... I am Rìgh, king of the Domhainn clan. Tonight, you must make a choice."

My eyebrows shot up. "No." The weight of the word rippled through the entire clan, whispers and hisses filling the cavern, and over my shoulder, I caught Alecto's wand arm shoot up, her weapon drawn to counteract the few raised spears to my right. "No, Rìgh, king of the Domhainn clan, I will be taking my student into custody, and then we will leave this place in peace."

Rìgh's laughter had a beautiful singsongy quality to it, his smile barbed and bitter, his mouth full of teeth sharpened to deadly points.

"I'm afraid you're mistaken," he informed me, calm and in control even as our invisible antlers clashed in battle—two old bucks fighting to come out on top. "Tonight, my kin and I will walk on land, and either your blood or your witch's blood will make that possible. Tonight, we complete the ritual passed down by our forefathers, or—"

"Fuck you," Alecto snarled, peering around me to glare and growl and flash her teeth.

A fury, through and through.

"*Or*," Rìgh thundered, his words bouncing off the walls and stirring his fellow sirens to close ranks, falling into battle formations around us, "the girl here dies. Right now. Simple. And if she dies now, you'll *both* be sacrificed."

"Easy, easy." I patted the air, keen on deescalating things as dark water sloshed up the sides of the walkway, sirens creeping closer. "There's no need for violence... Surely you can find another sacrifice? A *willing* sacrifice, even."

Unlikely, but whatever it took to get all three of us out of here—or, at the very least, Alecto and Alice—I'd say it.

"*She* was our sacrifice," Alice's captor sneered, shoving his blade's tip under her chin, "but she's not a witch. Not a drop of magical blood in her!"

More hisses erupted around the lake, but Alice's panicked wail rose above all else. Everything in me tightened, fight or flight engaged, mind silent and thoughts singular.

"Alice, I'm here," Alecto called. "It's okay. You're going to be fine. Just stay calm—"

"So, Headmaster Clemonte," Righ boomed, gesturing between us and Alice with his trident. "What will it be? You, the witch—or all three of you?"

Alecto gripped the back of my arm. "Jack, don't be stupid—"

"Me," I said without missing a beat. I needn't consider it, not for a second. Outnumbered by a clan of carnivores, the choice was clear. The odds of *me* getting Alice and Alecto out in one piece were slim to none, but if I could keep the sirens busy long enough, distract them with this ritual, then at least Alecto could rescue Alice. Save an innocent. Get the *child* under my care back to Root Rot, no matter what became of me.

Alecto's breath hitched, her wounded gasp busting the dams, fear coursing through my veins like icy raging rivers.

Right now, she was terrified.

But she was strong—stronger than she thought. I'd known that from the moment I first set eyes on her.

Trust restored.

Had it ever truly faltered?

No.

I had faith in her.

"*Jack*," she whispered frantically, clawing at my sleeve as she skirted around in front. "Sir, please don't—"

"Your wands." Spear-wielding sirens closed in on the walkway, a few tattooed like their king, many scarred and ravaged by war. If they were demanding them, then perhaps they were unaware that witches and warlocks didn't *need* a conduit to cast. Wands only neatened the spellwork, but we were perfectly capable of charming and hexing with hands alone so long as we could get out the incantation.

It would be messy.

Bloody, even.

But powerful—*raw*.

I held Alecto's amber gaze as I handed my wand over to a siren with his hand outstretched, fingers webbed and talons sharp. She had it in her to be bloody, powerful, and above all else, raw.

Stubborn as ever, my submissive kept her wand trained on the surrounding sirens. No matter how many raised their spears and knives to her, she didn't flinch, didn't budge, unwilling to surrender the weapon many of our kind relied on all our lives.

But then Alice shrieked, her cry shrill and pained and *horrid*, not a sound I ever wished to hear from a child again. Brin had sliced her cheek wide open, red gushing down her face and pooling in the water around them. Eyes shimmering with unshed tears, cheeks stained with rage, Alecto hurled her wand at the lake, then held up her empty hands as further proof of her submission.

All the while seething at Brin, her aura no longer prickly and panicked, but strong and centered.

Determined.

Good. She needed that mindset if any of us were to survive the next hour.

But when our eyes met again, she faltered. Gone was the warrior woman, the fury hell-bent on burning this place to the ground. In her stead was my little one, struggling, confused, desperate for my guidance.

Not this time, little one.

"Jack," she whispered shakily, eyes wide to keep the tears from cascading down her face. "Please… I need you. I-I can't do this without you."

Her uncertainty cut deep, the panic, the fear stirring every Dom instinct inside me to *fix*, protect, and defend.

Maybe it wasn't just the Dominant in me who felt that way for her.

Maybe… Maybe it was just me, Jack Clemonte, warlock,

297

headmaster, *man*, who couldn't stand to see this witch—*my* witch—in distress.

And maybe it was just sentiment, the calm before the storm, reveling in a connection, in what could have been, before it was brutally severed.

"Get in the water, Headmaster, and swim for the altar," Rìgh ordered. Over Alecto's mop of wrangled curls, I finally spotted the altar in question. Barely visible, an onyx platform rose *just* above the sloshing dark water, smooth and glossy and unassuming. When I didn't immediately react, one of the nearby sirens jabbed his spearhead at my calf, its bite jagged and cruel, its tip slicing open my pant leg.

Alecto shook as she glowered down at the guilty siren, her jaw clenched so tight every muscle flared, and I grabbed her by the chin—rough and harsh, as I might in a scene. The contact shattered her concentration, and just for a moment it was her and I locked in each other's gazes, trust paramount above all else.

"Save Alice," I told her, Dom-voice engaged—if only to calm her. She blinked up at me, tears glistening on her lashes like diamonds, and then as the siren jabbed at me again, she nodded. Her head barely moved and she didn't say a word, but she understood the objective.

We didn't matter anymore.

The only one who mattered was already bleeding, terrified and trapped with a monster.

Alice had to get out of here alive—we were inconsequential.

That was our lot in life, at the core of this profession.

And I...

I was fine with that.

For myself.

Not for her. *Should have shoved her back through the portal when you had the chance, old boy.*

"We're wasting a leap day," Rìgh growled, hisses and snarls reverberating through the cave. "*Move.*"

An eerie calm washed over me—acceptance—and I gave Alecto's chin one last squeeze. Her hands snapped around my wrist, but she wasn't strong enough to keep me. She tried, clinging tight as I withdrew, and when we finally broke apart, the whole world came crashing down around me, ears stuffed with cotton, a low whine screeching between them.

Head held high, I marched to the end of the walkway with all the dignity I could muster, then eased into lake water so cold it sucked the air out of my lungs. At the sight of a few sirens smirking, accustomed to the frigid temperatures of the Atlantic, I steeled myself and pushed off the walkway, then front-crawled toward the floating black platform in the middle of the lake.

Swam toward my death.

And their salvation.

Gods, help us.

26

ALECTO

"Get in the water, witch."

"I'm fucking *going*," I snarled, panic making my words sound fiercer than I felt. Trembling, I crouched at the side of the walkway, then slowly slipped into the—holy fucking *gods* —frigid siren-filled lake. All the air whooshed out of my lungs as soon as I was in waist-deep, and I choked down a breath, fear ramping up.

Mind muddled with a million racing thoughts, it all just blurred to white noise. I'd been brain-dead since I woke up this morning, exhausted from the term, from exams and projects, from crack-of-dawn harvesting and the roller coaster that was my personal life, but this shoved everything aside. The fear should have centered me, two people I cared about at risk—

No. That felt... too simple. *Two people I cared about.* Callous. A young woman who had so much potential, wooed and tricked by a siren, was *this* close to having her throat slit. The warlock I depended on, looked up to, *felt* so deeply for that his absence felt like losing a part of myself, was about to be sacrificed in some batshit ritual.

And I couldn't breathe.

Couldn't think.

Could barely *speak*.

The second I let go of the limestone edge, my wand fuck only knew where, the nearest siren—male, bare-chested and muscular, dangerously handsome with jet-black curls and seaweed-green eyes—snagged my wrist and yanked me into the open water. My leather boots, already crap in a high-stakes situation, had started to harden against the cold, which made treading water feel like doing egg-beater kicks in syrup.

Like Alice, my captor yanked me flush against him, his flesh nearly as cold as Bjorn's, his teeth just as sharp, and then held a knife to my throat. I flinched with a sharp gasp, knocking the back of my head into his chin just to get away from the metallic kiss of silver, and he snaked an arm around my waist to prop me above the surface. Below, his black tail beat in slow, even back-and-forth movements, effortlessly cutting through the murky water and keeping me from drowning.

It would be so easy for him to do it—kill me. Slit my throat in a second. Shove me down and hold me under until my lungs filled with freezing liquid and I just... faded away.

No.

Fuck no.

If they thought I'd just sit here scissor-kicking like some meek, cowed victim—they had chosen the wrong witch. Nobody was having their blood drained tonight for some stupid ritual. Brin would never touch Alice again, never make her scream and cry and beg.

We were getting the hell out of here.

We...

Gods, adrenaline was so not helpful in life-or-death situations—not unless you just needed to run. Here, as I tried to think, plan, *focus*, it left me shaky and scattered, but as Jack hauled himself onto the altar in the middle of the lake, I did my best to center everything.

Because he was actually going through with this—for us.

So we could get away.

A willing sacrifice...

Nope. No, the world wasn't about to lose a treasure like Jack Clemonte just so some siren freaks could grow legs.

Fuck these guys.

Teeth gritted to stop them from chattering, I scanned my surroundings and focused on my breathing, on slowing my hammering heart.

Okay, Alice was there, in front of the altar with Brin.

That Rìgh guy was on his way over, trailing after Jack like he had all the time in the world suddenly.

After a few frantic glances left and right, I estimated maybe fifty sirens total in the cave, most situated on either side of the walkway.

Might take me—my eyes narrowed, scrutinizing the distance from this spot back to the limestone, an above-water home base that I could claim and defend—maybe six or seven strokes to get over there?

Okay.

Okay.

Tentative plan brewing—

Alice squealed, and even at a distance, her panic bled into me. My eyes snapped in her direction, mama bear mode fully engaged, and I found her gawking in horror at the platform —at Jack on his back, splayed out like he was already a corpse.

And the sight broke my heart. Jack was infallible in my eyes—always had been. A strong protector. A thoughtful intellect. A caring man who genuinely wanted to do what was best, what was *right*, for the kids in our supernatural communities who were struggling.

I might have grown into a healthier, more functional adult without years of drinking and screwing around if I'd had a Jack Clemonte when *I* was a struggling kid, heartbroken and forever grieving the loss of parents I barely remembered.

This was wrong.

So fucking *wrong*—

"*No!*" A shriek ripped up my throat, carrying with it my fear, my outrage, when Rìgh rose from the depths, ripped open Jack's sleeve—and slit his wrist with a trident prong. Up and down, straight as an arrow, he slashed at flesh, tore it apart, and let his sacrifice's life force drip all over the altar.

Then he was on the move again—headed for the other wrist.

And I lost it.

Careful planning went out the window, and its ashes paved the way for instinct to take charge. For raw, untamed *rage* to drive me.

I spun around in my captor's arms, knife be damned, and clamped onto his rugged jawline.

"*Everto!*" The ejection curse pounded out of my palms in a surge of bright green light, one that ripped him away from me and hurled him clear across the cave. Before I could take my first stroke, however, a hand snapped around my ankle, clawed fingers gritting in deep, and dragged me below the surface.

All the pent-up aggression teenage-Alecto had always imagined unleashing on the monster who left her to burn sparked to life, and even though I couldn't see in the black nothingness, I could *feel*. Teeth bared, I folded over and latched onto my attacker, slashed at exposed skin with my nails and climbed along his steely body until I found his face.

The siren dragged me deeper, down, down, down until my ears popped.

Until I thought I might die.

Until I found his eyes.

I didn't hesitate: I stabbed my thumbs into the sockets as far as I could go, screaming bubbles at him, fueled by a lifetime of fury. Benedict Hammond hadn't killed me that night, and some fucking siren wasn't going to now. Even when something sharp slashed across my arm, then into my waist, I pressed through the pain until I was down to my last knuckle, thumbs-deep in the bastard's skull.

The second he loosened his hold on me, I was gone, kicking hard for the surface, guided by the shimmer of floating yellow orbs. A few feet from salvation, my lungs were about to burst, but I fought on, determined not to die tonight.

I barely processed the first breath, gasping as soon as I breached the surface, on autopilot as I gulped down just enough air to spit it back out at the hazy outlines of sirens closing in. Even with black spots dancing across my gaze, I fired off hexes, defensive spells, curses that I would never dare utter under ordinary circumstances.

We all knew them, but civilized witches and warlocks never went this dark—unless their lives were on the line.

And mine was.

Alice, Jack—they were worth the smudge on my soul, the marks left behind by breathlessly shrieking incantations to tear flesh and split skulls and burst eardrums. When I had enough space to move, I did, exhaustion weighing me down almost as effectively as my stupid boots.

But I *pushed*. Kicked and splashed, focused on the limestone walkway, vision completely tunneled, unable to hear anything above the crash of water all around me. The second someone entered my eyeline, I fired off a few more *everto* spells, hurling sirens all over the cave.

By the time I reached the walkway, I barely had the strength to swim anymore, let alone drag my body out of the lake. Sure, I did it—*no other choice, little one, keep fighting*—but I did so with a sob and a groan, rolling onto dry land to gasp and pant, to feel my heartbeat slamming between my ears.

To paint the white stone red with my blood.

Ugh, *gods*, the cut on my side was really starting to sting—

Light-headed, I rolled over with a groan, the gash just above my right hip feeling like it was being ripped open even more with the slightest movement. Difficult as it was to focus, I did my best and scanned the lake for my people, and while Alice was nowhere to be found suddenly—*shitshitshit*—Jack was still on the altar.

Limp.

Head lolled to the side away from me.

That gave me the strength to push up on shaky legs. All around me, warrior sirens had started to regroup, swimming closer to the walkway, spears up and expressions grim.

At this new height, I saw him better.

Saw the blood pooling in four distinct spots: around both wrists and both ankles.

My heart cracked in two, visceral and very real pain gripping my chest, squeezing tight with no intention of ever letting go. Tears mingled with the lake water dribbling from my hairline, and I raised both arms, palms out on either side of me, righteous fury in my veins and a lifetime of hate in my blood.

"*Interficio!*"

An incantation I never thought I'd cast.

A curse to murder—violently.

Illegal.

Spoken so naturally now, hurled at my enemies with a malice that actually scared me.

Red surged from my palms like a tidal wave, washing over the water in either direction—massacring any sirens who dared stand in its way. As soon as my magic struck, bodies exploded. Literally. Chunks of flesh and bone and viscera pinwheeled around the cave like fireworks, the untouched sirens by the altar suddenly shrieking—scattering. Even good ol' Rìgh hightailed it away from Jack's body, darting underwater, the surface ripples showing the clan fleeing for small slits in the cave wall.

They had honestly thought taking away my wand was enough.

That removing a conduit killed the magic in my marrow.

Fuck them.

Teeth gritted, I surveyed the carnage floating around the walkway almost dismissively. *Hope it hurt, assholes.*

Without an intact siren to be found, my fight or flight flatlined. Such a powerful curse took more than it gave, and I crashed to my knees, panting, aching, dizzy and on the verge of emptying my guts.

Jack.

I lifted my head, even though it weighed as much as a fucking mountain.

Alice.

I crawled to the end of the walkway, a bloody trail in my wake, my wounds on fire.

It isn't over.

Not by a long shot. I slipped into the freezing water like a seal, instantly regretting not taking my boots off, then shoved my body beyond its limits as I kicked off into a front crawl. It wasn't graceful by any means, arms everywhere, water splashing around me like thunder. It wasn't pretty—

but I got to the altar while Jack still drew breath, his chest rising and falling slowly.

Too slow.

Gods.

It took two pathetic attempts to hoist my body out of the water, the altar slick with blood, not a handhold to be found. In the end, I had to grab at Jack's unconscious body just to haul myself up. He didn't move. Didn't respond. Head to the side, eyes half-shut, they had left him to bleed out on the onyx—as intended. The magic in his blood was supposed to... do something.

How?

On my knees, panicking, I took it all in with wide eyes and quivering lips. His life force wept all over the stone and into the water. Nothing around to collect it for a ritual— unless offering it to the water *was* the ritual.

This couldn't be legit. These fucking idiots had been grasping at straws here—

Blinking hard, I went for his wrist and lifted it, the cut deep and oozing.

"*Coeo.*" I wasn't a healer by any stretch, even if I had a brain full of useless information about healing herbs and medicinal plants. But all professors had first-aid training, a certificate we were required to renew every three years. The *coeo* incantation merely sealed the wound and stopped the bleeding long enough to get the injured party to *real* help. With a flash of buttery-yellow light, my magic did the trick.

For now.

Incision closed tight, his black skin turned waxy and fresh—tender, the slightest nudge capable of tearing it open again. Growing more frantic by the second, I moved on to his other wrist, constantly watching his chest for movement, needing to see he was still breathing just to go on. Once I finished there, I moved down to his ankles.

They had slit his Achilles tendons.

The agony he must have felt, and not once did I hear him scream—

I stopped holding it back, stopped trying to be brave. With a sob, I mended those, too, sealing the slit skin but hardly healing the torn tendon. Too complex. Too difficult. I couldn't—

Tears blurred the shadowy world around me when I finally sat back on my heels, and I grabbed at his shin for...

For...

Support.

To feel his sturdiness and his might, to hold his steely muscle and pretend *I* was just as strong.

Still chasing my breath, I snapped upright when the hairs on the back of my neck rose in alarm. The cave had fallen unnervingly silent, the water's surface smooth and dark, the orbs flickering, their magic waning. Soon, the farther those sirens swam from this massacre, the orbs would go out entirely, plunging us into pitch-black.

Perfect time for a counterattack.

I mean, I didn't know for sure, but I suspected sirens had solid night vision.

How do I get him out—

Wait.

Not just him.

"Alice—"

While the water was mostly still, something bobbed at the surface a good ten feet from the altar.

Something dark at the top—and white all around.

"*Alice!*" I tripped over Jack's body in my haste, which sent me tumbling into the icy depths, limbs flailing and adrenaline soaring. Lungs rebelling against the cold, I barely managed to keep my head above water as I paddled over, hoping, praying to all the gods and their ancestors, that it wasn't the worst-case scenario.

That I was seeing things.

But she was real—vivid and bone-chilled, her eyes hooded and vacant, her body bobbing, then sinking somewhat when I reached her.

"No, no, no, *no*." For such a little thing, Alice weighed a ton in the water, so much so that I could only get her head and neck above the surface, legs kicking furiously to keep us both afloat. Struggling, I clapped a hand over the gaping wound on her neck and uttered the sealing spell.

Not that it mattered.

She had no pulse.

"Alice, *no*," I whispered, heart on the verge of pounding out of my chest. "No, I'm sorry, I'm sorry—give me a s-second. I'm here. I'm h-here with you. It's okay. I-I've got you. Just... Hold on."

Brin had slit her throat and... left her there to die.

Alone.

Always alone, my Alice.

Shaking violently and taking in water, I sealed the gash on her cheek, then smoothed her matted curls from her face. The color had leeched out of her skin, lips blue, and if I didn't support it, her head flopped forward, backward, side to side, whatever direction I let it fall.

Sobbing, terrified of what might be lurking below, I rotated her onto her back and hooked an arm around her, then started the slow, desperate swim back to the altar.

The cave growing darker by the second.

Jack unconscious.

Alice...

No.

"H-help me," I croaked, freezing water sloshing up my nose, into my mouth, my limbs like lead and my toes numb.

Despite kicking as hard as I could, paddling forward with one arm, we barely moved, every inch claimed an inch *earned*. Another strangled cry cut up my throat, tears blurring this awful place into darkness. "Somebody, please..." I sucked in a deep breath to scream it. *"Help me!"*

27

BJORN

Even as a gentle thunder rumbled in the distance, the black clouds held firm, keeping the storm at bay, as if sensing that Root Rot Academy had dealt with enough calamity in the last twenty-four hours—and now we needed rest, only if for a night.

Having discovered yet another of Alecto's regular haunts empty, I shut the door of the smallest greenhouse firmly behind me, darkness alive and well in the three rectangular buildings, then stood tall amidst the chill. Silence and tragedy ushered in the month of March, the first day a gloomy one, most students home for their break and those who stayed kept within their towers while the administration sorted out recent events.

Jack unconscious in the infirmary.

Alice's parents en route to retrieve their daughter's corpse.

Alecto... Nowhere to be found.

Until now.

Hands in my pockets, I grinned when I finally spotted what I was after: fireflies dancing in the conservatory.

Charmed to keep the tropical plants happy, it was the only place on campus where you could find the little light bugs all year round, impervious to the winter rains and the brief stretch of summer heat. Like them, the elements didn't bother me. I strolled toward the domed building unfazed by the cold and the wet, dark damp hanging around campus even as we inched toward spring. All that mattered was finding her—making things right.

I would never forget the crazed look in her eyes for as long as I lived, stumbling into my classroom last night in the middle of my final lecture for the term, panting, gasping, sobbing, bleating for help. Soaked to the bone. Bleeding all over the floor. Everything crashed to a halt right then and there, and while a few students I trusted were sent to raise the alarm, I followed Alecto into the abyss.

Helped her haul Jack's unconscious, half-drained body back to the shores.

She wouldn't let me touch Alice.

Wounded and bloodied, Alecto insisted on swimming the girl back herself.

Even on the other side of the portal, in familiar corridors, surrounded by familiar faces, it had taken loads of coaxing to make her release Alice, threats from Iris falling on deaf ears, same as my gentle words of encouragement, pleas from the girl's den mother.

Alecto wouldn't let go.

As if holding her would bring her back to life.

They separated eventually. Seamus had patched her up, her wounds substantial—but they paled in comparison to Jack. In a potion-induced sleep, Root Rot's headmaster would survive, but he had a rocky road to recovery ahead.

Same as my girl.

And she was all that mattered to me at the end of the day. We may not have kissed yet, may not have formalized whatever we were, but she was mine and I was hers. Even with an uncertain future for the academy, I couldn't think of anyone but her.

The moment I saw Alecto's hunched outline through the conservatory's tinted glass walls, I finally slowed, relief coursing through my veins like a fire through kindling. Fixed on her silhouette, I let my feet guide me on the path I had walked many times before—with nurses and professors and librarians, the ones who used me on a dare or because some witch magazine told them you hadn't *lived* until you climaxed from a vampire's bite.

Never had I nudged through the double doors at the entryway with someone I truly cared about. Someone who made me feel *alive* again—who made my heart dance and sing and somersault from her scent alone.

Someone who made me feel less alone in the world.

I had been waiting for the weather to turn before asking Alecto to take *me* on a tour of the conservatory. Let her talk my ear off about all the green darlings, each and every one, long into the night while I melted at the sound of her voice— and then I'd kiss her beneath a full moon, amidst flickering fireflies and the tropical heat.

Tonight, the sauna hit hard, same as always, the cacti and palms happy as can be, and the fireflies scattered as soon as I shut the door, my presence an intrusion. Fronds folded overhead in a thick green canopy. Tropical blooms thrived, flora arranged along the perimeter of the huge circular structure, then throughout to create winding walkways.

I found Alecto in the center of it all, in the heart of her Root Rot kingdom. Seated on a bench beneath an overhang of reaching flowery vines, hands limp in her lap, eyes down, she looked defeated. Dressed in a pair of black leggings, the ones she lounged around the flat in on weekends, she drowned in all that unflattering plaid, sporting one of those

313

flannel shirtdress things that had been all the rage a few years back. Curls wild. Face drawn and pale. From the smell, her wounds hadn't reopened since Seamus sealed them. She shivered when I stopped a few feet from her, my boots entering her line of sight, and I glanced at the massive tartan shawl bunched up beside her on the bench, then sighed.

With her hiding spot discovered, Alecto slowly shifted on the bench, no longer slumped forward over her knees but hunched back against the wood panels. Her amber gaze soared to mine a moment later, tinged red with grief.

"Hi," I offered, tone soft and kind and nowhere near pitying. The corners of her mouth kicked up halfheartedly.

"Hi," Alecto croaked back. If it wasn't obvious from her eyes that she had been crying for hours, the strain in her voice was proof enough. I understood the sorrow, of course, the guilt of carrying someone's death on your shoulders. Hundreds of souls tainted mine, centuries of bloodshed and slaughter leaving scars in my icy flesh no one would ever see but me.

"It's not your fault."

She blinked up at me, once, twice, then folded over again to sob into her hands. Of course that would trigger her, but she needed to know that unlike me, she hadn't *intentionally* stolen a life. The distinction mattered.

Jaw clenched, I swooped in and dropped to my knees before her. While it would have been easy to grab her wrists and pry her hands from her face, I let her struggle against my grasp, let her fuss and pull and fight to hide from the world.

"Alecto—"

"Stop," she rasped, lowering her hands just enough to peer over her fingertips, the liquid gold waterlogged and bloodshot. "I'm a-all snotty."

My heart whumped an extra drumbeat at that. Grinning,

I finally dragged her hands aside, then tugged my taupe sweater sleeves up to my palms.

"I don't care," I assured her, wiping her cheeks dry with the twill as a mama cat cleaned an unruly kitten, even dragging my forearm under her—yes—snotty nostrils. Alecto battled me the entire time, squirming and wincing and shoving uselessly at my arms. But in the end, she let me take care of her, dry her tears, and wait for her breath to settle. In time, her pulse came close to even, the anthem of anxiety and panic settling into a beat I recognized.

To the one I preferred, frankly.

Still, even if her heart had stopped racing, Alecto sat before me with rounded shoulders, utterly drained from last night's ordeal, from her injuries, from her loss. Despite my hands curved over her knees, a touch I had hoped would ground her, she looked up at me sad and shaky, way beyond my reach no matter how hard I tried.

"It's my fault," she muttered, hand flying up as soon as my lips parted in protest. "No, stop, it is. I-I should have gone straight to Jack—"

"You filed a report with security ages ago." She had kept this little Alice drama a secret for months, but as Seamus patched her up last night, her legs dangling over the edge of an infirmary bed, eyes wild but body weak with blood loss, she spilled everything. The head healer and I learned about Brin, about Alice's infatuation, about the portal and who exactly she spoke with on the new security squad. All things considered, she had done what she needed to: security had failed Alice. Period.

Of course, Iris had probably made my girl feel like it *was* her fault—that she had misjudged the situation and fucked up royally somewhere along the way. While Jack slept off his near life-threatening blood loss in the infirmary, his second-in-command sat in his office today, in his very chair, and no doubt sneered over her spectacles while Alecto made an official statement about the incident.

Oblivious to how that went, I assumed from the look of her now, and knowing Iris Prewett as I had for the last six and a half years—*not well* was the understatement of the century.

"You did what you were supposed to do," I argued, drawing her trembling hand to my mouth and kissing the underside of her wrist. Immediately her skin erupted in little chilled bumps, and I let go, ashamed that my frost might extinguish what little fire she had left, and then waited for her to retreat into her sleeve. Instead, Alecto's hand fell to her lap, and I gave her thighs a little squeeze, firm enough to force her eyes back to mine. "You made security aware so the portal could be sealed. You told Alice not to go back to him under any circumstances. Alecto… You did everything you could."

"But I should have saved her," she whispered. Anguish dripped from every word, breaking my smitten heart piece by piece. With a sigh, I shuffled closer and shook my head.

"Alecto, you were in an impossible situation. No one can prepare for that, no matter what hindsight tells you now." I brushed a curl from her face, one that stayed put for a moment before stubbornly falling back into place, dangling over her eye and caught on her watery lashes. "You did what you could, and Jack is alive because of it."

Sniffling, Alecto ducked down as if to fold in on herself again—and I couldn't have that. Without a word, I cupped her chin and forced her back up, using my strength against her, and once again her skin erupted in gooseflesh.

Too cold. She's touched enough death already—

"Sorry," I muttered, withdrawing to tug my sleeves up for some added protection against the ice in my veins, "wait—"

"No." She caught my forearms with speed impressive to

even a vampire, clutching at me and drawing me in so I had no choice but to cradle her face with both hands, cheeks slick beneath my palms. Alecto sniffed softly, golden gaze plummeting to my lips as she murmured, "I... I like the way you feel."

A first in my lifetime.

A compliment so rare it stole away what little breath lived in my lungs.

Blinking back the shock, I surrendered to the fire burning beneath her skin, all-consuming and distinctly *alive*. When our eyes met this time, we both tripped, me into molten gold, her into a frosty blue that made others so obviously uncomfortable.

Fireflies winked out of the corner of my eyes as Alecto and I accepted the free fall.

"I'm here for you," I promised, hating the breathy quality my words took. Alecto nuzzled into my palms in response, the lift of her full lips authentic this time, not forced.

"I know." Her hands crept along my arms, settling on my biceps like she needed them for balance in a world that wouldn't stop spinning. "You always are."

Now wasn't the time.

This wasn't what I had imagined, what I had *planned* since we acknowledged that we were more than friends, the shift in our connection these past weeks subtle and beautiful. Our first kiss wasn't supposed to come in the fallout of death and tragedy, but I couldn't help myself.

Couldn't stop.

Couldn't resist the lure of my girl a second longer.

Ensnared by her mouth, I pushed up just enough to close the distance between us, my lips pressing gently to hers in an innocent peck. No pressure. No force. No expectations.

Only my heart had never beat so soundly.

Kissing a woman had never felt like coming home. Above

the clashing scents of tropical blooms, Alecto's natural vanilla reigned supreme, wafting over me, enveloping me, making me *hers*. Dark eyelashes fluttering shut, she leaned into me with a gasping moan, lips softening against mine.

For a while, it stayed like that: soft and sweet and a little wet. Time stood still just for us. All those months, all the conversations and flirtatious banter and frustrated rants while we brushed our teeth before bed—everything had led to *this*.

More than friends. More than flatmates.

Soulmates, maybe.

Yes.

I liked the sound of that.

Lovely as it was, kissing Alecto stirred something deep inside—something caged and controlled. Bloodlust. The *monster* loved her. Wanted to claim her. Bite her. Plunge fangs deep into her thigh so she squealed and writhed and ripped at my hair. That side of me remembered the brutality in my bones, the ancestry of violence and conquest attached to my family name.

My heart insisted Alecto could stand all that and more, this fiery witch who took no shit and fought off an entire clan of sirens alone.

But not tonight.

Tonight was for this—for the *first*. For comfort and acceptance and change.

Only Alecto was the one to take the next step. After drawing in a sharp breath between her plump, parted lips, she deepened the kiss. Flicked her tongue into my mouth— over my fangs. Made the monster *snarl*. Her fingers found my hair as the bloodlust surged, threading through the white-blond locks and tugging insistently.

I always preached self-control to a full classroom of bored teenagers—yet I nearly came undone at her hungry moan, nearly threw all my tried and tested wisdom out the window against her frantic mouth, her body crashing to mine as she slipped off the bench and into my arms.

Refusing to let so much as a speck of dirt from the floor touch her, I secured an arm around her waist and stood. My girl giggled ever so softly, hands growing bolder in my hair, her weight nothing as I held her like I'd always wanted to. We came together like a lock and key, the perfect fit, and Alecto hooked her legs around me, ankles crossed at my back, while my hands smoothed the undersides of her thighs.

All the way back to her exceptional ass, the kind artists tried and failed to perfect on seductive marble statues for centuries. Little did they realize, they hadn't been working with the right model, because this goddess could have changed the fucking *world* with her curves.

This was more than I could have asked for, cock thick with need, the monster snarling in my chest, starving for a taste of her. Alecto rocked her hips, ground herself against me with breathy little moans that left me weak in the knees, her kiss progressively rougher, our mouths descending into frenzied territory a little too easily.

When her hands abandoned my hair and went for my sweater, ripping at it, tugging, desperate to wrench it off even if that meant peeling it away piece by piece, my carefully cultivated control returned.

Unwelcome as it was, my conscience had a point: this wasn't the time for us to come together. Sure, our first kiss had some flexibility, but the first time I fucked her, ravished her—bit her and made her climax over and over again— would *not* be overshadowed by the death of a student.

No.

When she wouldn't let me retreat, chasing my lips every time I tried to pull away, too much a temptation to resist, I uncrossed her ankles and set her down.

But the shift in positions gave her better access to my sweater, and before I could catch her, Alecto had the twill yanked halfway up my torso, undershirt exposed.

"Alecto—"

"No," she hissed, twisting out of reach when I went for her wrists. "Just let me—"

"*Alecto.*" Her name thundered through the conservatory with a monster's edge, snarly and rough. Even if *I* was the one pumping the brakes, this wasn't easy for me. Being around her all these months and only *just* kissing her now had been painful; to stop on the cusp of something beautiful was torture. But we would regret it in the end, and I had enough regrets in my long lifetime. Alecto wasn't about to become another.

When I finally claimed her hands, I cuffed them together in just one of mine, and her golden gaze shot up with a wild energy that echoed in her aura, that magical charge buzzing angrily all around us—scaring the fireflies away.

"Not tonight," I told her, restraint tenuous and control wavering the second her lips wobbled. A breath later, she came apart again, doubling over with a wail. It would have been easier just to carry on as we were—to fuck her with the savagery I craved.

But *no*.

Fangs gritted furiously into my lower lip, I dragged her close and trapped her in an embrace she couldn't escape. The stubborn creature fought it at first, but then surrendered faster than before. Arms folded between us, Alecto snuggled into my chest, ear to my dead heart, and huffed as I smoothed my sleeves over her tearstained cheek again.

"You're too good for me," she croaked, then buried her face against me when I stilled.

"No, I'm not." Honestly, she had no *idea* the baggage I came with. Six years at Root Rot Academy hardly made up for the devastation of Bjorn the Brutal. Alecto nodded, head bobbing at my sternum, body nudged up against my still *very* erect cock.

Torture. Fucking *torture*.

"Yes," the little witch insisted, voice muffled, "you are."

Frowning, I caught her under the chin and tipped her head back, losing myself in those watery orbs as I said, "We're good for each other. That's all I'll accept out of you."

"I'm a m-mess." She snorted back a nostril-full of snot, cheeks flaming a beat later. "Like, too much of a mess... I'm fucked-up and broken, and I—"

"Alecto Clarke," I growled, my once gentle hand sliding down from her chin to her delicate throat and gripping hard enough that her eyes rounded, her lips the perfect shocked O. "Please stop insulting the woman I adore above all others." I loosened up when her eyebrows arched, her pulse skyrocketing right along with them, then grinned and booped her on the nose. "Or I'll need to put on my no-nonsense voice and set you straight."

She blinked up at me, almost in disbelief, then dissolved into a fit of exhausted chuckles, her face buried in my chest again. Grinning, I wiped at her cheeks, dried her off, and then tucked her under my arm and steered us both to the bench. When we settled, we did so together, Alecto nestled tight to my side, my arm draped across her curves protectively.

Maybe even a little possessively, especially with my chin atop her head, every part of my body language snarling *mine* to onlookers.

Only there were no onlookers in here.

For once in this castle, we had absolute privacy outside of the charged space that was our flat. No curious eyes tonight save those of the fireflies, who eventually trickled out from behind palm fronds and reaching vines,

321

shimmering around us in the heart of the conservatory. Even as the winds picked up outside and the first tentative raindrops splashed across the domed ceiling, we stayed warm, dry, and together, just Alecto and me cuddled up on the bench, her legs folded and knees on my thighs, her eyes shut.

Like we were on a date.

A real date—the kind I had pictured for months now.

Yet grief tainted everything.

Everything.

"Bjorn?" Including the way she eventually said my name, tentative, hesitant, soft and unfamiliar, like her tongue was tasting it for the first time.

"Hmm?" I rumbled back, my hand curved over her elbow, cradling it. Alecto sighed deeply, then tensed, and just when I thought she was about to push away, she nuzzled in deeper.

"I have to tell you something," she said, words once again muffled against my sweater-clad torso. I slowly walked my fingers up the bend of her arm, along her shoulder, and into her hair to fiddle with the rogue curls I loved so much.

"Go on."

"Something important." Alecto finally sat up, though she didn't try to shrug me off, just pushed off my thigh so she could look me in the eye. Her hand remained there, dangerously high and comfortably firm—beyond distracting.

"Uh, right. Important. Sure."

"I haven't told anyone..." She licked her lips, heart fluttering at the lie. "Actually. No. I told Gavriel, and I told him because—"

"Because you like him," I remarked, figuring I should state the obvious—get that out of the way already. I'd known since before Samhain that those two were dancing around each other, flirting with fire, like two brawling alley cats who hissed one minute and snuggled the next.

"Because we're both fucked-up," Alecto countered with a wince, "and... we shared why."

Jealousy plucked at my heartstrings. Not a tidal wave of feeling, of course, but as soft and persistent as the beginnings of the storm on the conservatory rooftop. Clearly she and Gavriel had something she found lacking in me. No surprise there. The fae and I were different creatures, and for Alecto's heart, that was a *good* thing.

Still.

It left me a *little* green-eyed.

"I just don't want to hurt your feelings that I didn't come to you first." She sighed softly, and I gave her a moment when it seemed like she was collecting her thoughts—maybe even gearing up to make the monster *more* possessive than he already felt. "I..." Alecto's gaze fell to her hand on my thigh. "I was scared to tell you."

"Alecto, you're scaring me now." What could be so awful that she feared sharing it with me? My past was all blood and gore, brutality and selfishness. Whatever she had lurking in her heart paled in comparison. Nothing she could say or do would send me running. "Just spit it out... I'd never judge you."

"I know, I just—"

"Come on, *elskling*." I caught her under the chin by my knuckle and brought her back to me. "Sharing is caring."

"My name isn't Alecto Clarke," she blurted, cheeks flaming and heart pounding out of nowhere. My hand fell away from her face, and my little witch reared back. "It's Corwin. I... I chose Alecto for myself when I was a teenager, but I was born Hannah Corwin. And... Ash Cedar killed my parents."

Well.

That.

Was unexpected.

My brain short-circuited, and the best I could manage was a frown and a nod. Alecto released a shaky breath, and when she spoke again, she sounded less frantic—but no less heartbroken than before.

"His name is actually Benedict Hammond..."

I listened to the whole grisly tale in silence. The coven feud. The shattered peace treaty. The murder and the fire and the rescue and her grandparents—

Their untimely demises.

The djinn.

The new name.

His obsession with her eyes—her mother's eyes—and his pathetic attempt to bully her into *something*. She claimed it was a relationship; I suspected Hammond's courting came with more sinister intentions.

Ash Cedar.

Benedict Hammond.

I'd never liked the bastard, and as Alecto trailed off now, voice hoarse and gaze concerned, it took everything in my power, decades of practice and meditation, not to blitz back to the castle and just kill him. Find the fucker and snap his neck.

I cracked mine instead, twisting this way and that for a satisfying *crrrrrick* on either side. Alecto swallowed hard, the dance of her throat catching my eye, and her pulse quickened.

"I... You... We..." She retreated somewhat, untangling herself from my arm and giving me space she must have thought I needed. "I needed you to know before we moved forward."

Right. *Get yourself under control, you ancient fuck.* Splitting oneself open and spilling your guts took courage—courage I had always known Alecto to possess, but this was different. This was deeply personal, scars from her past and secrets that belonged to her. I had no claim on them. Not now, not in the future. They were hers to share when the moment was right.

Never was an option, too.

"I... appreciate that," I told her, slow and careful, mindful not to startle the little fawn and send her scampering into the dark forest alone. "Thank you for sharing." I snatched up her hand just as it balled and retreated into her sleeve, fanning open her fingers to thread with mine. "Alecto, it's very meaningful for me—to know you."

Tears greeted me again when our eyes finally met, but the lift of her lips told me they were happy tears—thank *fuck*. With a thick gasp, she flew into me, grabbed my face tight for a closed-mouthed kiss that started firm and hard, then slowly melted into soft and serene. I let her steer the ship this time, confident that she wouldn't push us too far off course. When she eventually broke away, leaving my lips buzzing with the memory of hers, she stayed close, her forehead against mine and her lashes splayed across her flushed cheeks.

"Thank you," she whispered, and the best I could do was nod, not trusting my voice, knowing it too would wobble with emotion. After all, she needed me to be strong—solid. We were each other's stability when the world crumbled, and this time, Alecto needed *me* to hold back the landslide.

"Of course, *elskling*."

"*Elskling?*"

Hearing her speak my native tongue roused my cock again, but I focused on her face, brushing the curls from it with a contented rumble.

"Darling," I told her, to which she blushed and pulled back, lower lip snagged between her teeth and heart dancing for me.

"Oh."

I raised an eyebrow. "Do you like it?"

"Very much," she murmured with a shy nod. Good. It suited her, though I had a few alternates waiting in the wings. But the moment her brows knit and her expression darkened, I knew now wasn't the time for pet names and sweetness.

"Say it."

"I..." Alecto shook her head, rolling her eyes skyward. "I came here to ruin him, Bjorn. I came here for vengeance after what he did to my family, and life keeps getting in the way. Work and the kids and..." Her pointed glance at me said more than words could. "I don't know if I should just kill him, or—"

"Don't." My certainty seemed to throw her, expression faltering and hand retreating from mine. As much as *I* wanted to cleave Benedict Hammond's head from his shoulders and drop-kick it into the sea, it wasn't something I wished on Alecto—on a witch who knew nothing of war. Besides, death lasted a minute, an hour, a day. If she got him locked up, publicly tarred and feathered in their community, then he had a lifetime of suffering ahead.

Far more preferable.

"But he killed my parents," she said slowly, as if I'd forgotten that bit. I stretched my arm out along the back of the bench.

"And bloodying your hands changes that?"

She sat up straighter, frown deepening. "No, but—"

"It will change *you*," I stressed. "I promise. You'll live with that warlock *forever* if you take his life."

"Yeah..." She glanced down and fidgeted with her shirtsleeves, with a frayed string on the left cuff. Contemplative, suddenly. Right. I could work with that. Alecto fell silent for a long beat, then huffed. "I mean, yeah, I guess you have a point."

"Listen, I'm not excusing him." I twisted in place to face her properly, one leg propped over the other, fingertips toying with her curls. "But time also changes people."

Once again, Alecto blinked up at me, but gone was the surprise, the shock, the flattered flutter of her lashes. Instead, disgust and outrage flashed back at me, and I knew I'd made a mistake.

"What the fuck is that supposed to mean?" she demanded just as my lips parted for a correction. I pressed them together to regroup. We all had a past, myself included, and of all the men in her life, I suspected *mine* was the bloodiest.

Gavriel came at a close second.

Jack Clemonte had... wealth. Maybe some political backstabbing.

I had raiding and burning and torture, serenaded some days by my victims' screams...

"Well—"

"Are you saying I should forgive him?" Alecto readjusted her position, feet planted firmly on the ground and eyes hurling daggers. "Like, everyone makes mistakes—is *that* what you're saying?"

I withdrew my arm and held up both hands, defenseless. "No, I—"

"He *murdered* my family." She snapped it like I couldn't grasp the concept, all fire and wrath—what was meant for him shot squarely at me. "He tried to burn me alive. Benedict Hammond needs to pay for that."

"All I'm saying," I pressed, refusing to rise to her level and escalate things further, "is that a man's history doesn't always define him."

"Wow." Alecto stood, arms crossed, everything about her suddenly screaming *fuck off*. "Just... *wow*."

"Alecto, I'm not really talking about *him*."

"I'm going to check on Jack."

327

"Stop." I caught her shapeless plaid thing before she could slip away. "He's sleeping—and this is ridiculous."

My *elskling* whirled around, though not with enough venom to rip her dress out of my fist. "I share a deeply personal part of myself with you, and your big takeaway is that *time* changes people?"

I let go, trusting that she wouldn't storm off. "Right, poor choice of words—"

"Then what?"

Staring up at her flushed face, that golden gaze accusatory and forlorn and *begging* me to just get back in her good graces—to rewind the clock back to when we were cuddling on the bench, surrounded by fireflies and the first whisper of rain.

But there was no going back. We had left friendship behind for something more meaningful. She had shown me a scar, exposed herself—and then I hurt her. Inadvertently, but that didn't matter. We should be able to discuss this, heated or not, and come to a satisfying resolution.

And I...

I owed her my thoughts. My feelings.

I owed her a scar or two.

"Alecto," I said softly, leaning forward to rest my elbows on my thighs, head hanging at the memories, "I too killed families once." When she didn't immediately bolt, I peeked up, ashamed of my past but refusing to bury it—not when it shaped me into the vampire I was today. "I burned whole villages to the ground. I tortured and murdered and did as the bloodlust commanded. I was selfish. Violent. Vengeful, even against those who were innocent. And I am only *now* beginning centuries of penance for all I took from this land." With a shake of my head, I stood, arms at my sides, totally open to her. "I... I could very easily be in that bastard's shoes, and you..."

Fuck, where was that train of thought headed? I hesitated, unsure if I could be *that* honest with her. Alecto, meanwhile, seemed to pick up on precisely where things were going. She sucked in her cheeks for a moment, then brushed her finger under each eye with a sniffle.

"Are you saying I'm a hypocrite if I excuse your sins and not his?"

She looked up at me, hope flickering in the amber—hope that I might deny it.

"I… don't know."

Maybe?

Alecto nodded, eyes watery again. "Right. Okay. I need to just… go." She gave me her back. "Excuse me."

"Alecto." *Don't go. Talk to me. Yell at me. Vent and let me do the same.*

She held up her hand, sounding more exhausted now than when I'd first found her as she said, "Bjorn, I get it. I… get where you're coming from. I just need some time to think."

Fair enough. I watched her disappear into the nearest overgrown walkway in silence. If we weren't going to be productive, if the dialogue now only made things worse, then fine. *Go.* But this wasn't over, nor would it be the last time we discussed the issue. No more hiding for Alecto and me. No more acting like a coward, like space and silence would fix our problems.

I tabled it for another night, another headspace, and plopped back onto the bench. The wood buckled beneath me with a creaky groan, barely holding its shape. A few moments later, the sound of the door whooshing open to the storm and clicking shut again had me slumping into the backrest. Shortly after that, the fireflies swarmed—whether to punish or comfort, I had no clue.

Either way, I was alone again.

In a fight with my *elskling*.

About to get rained in.

The memory of our first kiss tainted by... this.

By everything.

I pinched the bridge of my nose and shut my eyes tight with a groan.

"Well... Shit."

28

ALECTO

Ugh.

Overreaction City—Population: me.

Chin tucked and shoulders up, I scaled the hillside stone steps two at a time. Even though the clouds had looked like they might hold off until later, rain hammered the Root Rot grounds in huge, angry droplets.

The perfect reflection of my mood today, honestly.

Dark and stormy and bleak, the weight of it all cutting down to the bone.

Of course during my dramatic storm-off I'd forgotten my shawl, every inch of exposed skin now riddled with gooseflesh, my teeth chattering as I trudged up to the castle.

The literal second after I walked away from Bjorn, I knew I'd overreacted. Unfortunately, it was just how I had felt in the moment—and instead of bottling it up, I let it out.

Ripped off the cap so the fizz exploded all over both of us.

Ughhhhhhhhh. I grimaced at the memory, the conversation playing on a constant loop, paused only when I slipped on one of the stairs near the top, heart launching into my throat and arms shooting out for balance.

"Fuck's *sake*," I grumbled. It had started so perfect, cuddly and romantic, just what I needed after yesterday with Jack and Alice...

And that *kiss*.

Then I'd tried to ruin it, take things too far too fast.

Had it been Gavriel in the conservatory with me, he might have given in. The sex would have been awesome as always, but my mood wouldn't have improved. The feelings would still be there, churning away.

It was healthier to talk.

Harder, too.

The risk of a blowup greater.

And that was *exactly* what had happened, with Bjorn of all people.

Of course he wasn't telling me to be BFFs with Benedict fucking Hammond. He had barely gotten his point across, but in the heat of the moment, it had certainly *felt* like he was proposing I, what, accept that Benedict might be a different warlock now?

Ugh times a million.

We could pick up the conversation later—again, the healthier, more difficult, more adult thing to do—after I had cooled off.

Petty and selfish and childish as it was, I needed the space to calm down and leave Overreaction City behind for Logic Central and Rational Thinking Junction.

Or, you know, whatever.

"Silly girl..." I stilled a few feet from the stairs, the ice in my veins hardening at the sound of that fucking *voice*. "Get in here and out of the wet."

Arms folded, rainwater dribbling down my forehead, I slowly glared over at Benedict motherfucking Hammond blocking the nearest door into the castle, propping it open for me with a patronizing smile and beckoning me through with a wave of his huge hand.

Traditional warlock robes fluttering in the chilly breeze, coal-black gaze assessing me from top to bottom, lingering where my wet oversized sweater-dress stuck to my curves.

This fucking guy.

After everything, not just Bjorn but *everything*, I so wasn't in the mood for his crap tonight.

Patience razor thin, I wasn't in the mood to *pretend*.

Jaw clenched, I barreled by him, muttering a rough *thanks* in passing. One stride over the castle's threshold and Benedict showed his true colors, clamping down on my arm and wrenching me back.

"Wait a minute," he said, his tone somehow both light *and* threatening, "a proper thanks is always appreciated for chivalrous—"

"Let *go*," I snarled, whipping around and jerking my arm free, air crackling with my aura.

I seldom ever felt my aura; like you never *really* knew how your own voice sounded, it was just easier to get a read on someone else's energetic charge, the magical force shimmering out of sight, out of mind, in the ether. But, really, no surprise mine was at a twenty tonight: still fired up from the conversation with Bjorn, heartbroken about Alice, worried for Jack... I was a ticking time bomb, and it was just better to be alone until I got a grip on my emotions.

Benedict must have sensed it right away—because the asshole *laughed*, like setting me off was so wonderfully droll.

"Whoa, whoa," he crooned, patting the air like I was some dumb, startled calf. The magical well inside me went from a simmer to a boil, power sizzling through my limbs, adrenaline surging right alongside it. Benedict merely cocked his head to the side, either oblivious to my mood or totally reveling in it. The cruel twinkle in his eye suggested the latter. "Calm down, sweetheart. I was just being a nice warlock—"

"*You...*" This whole nice-guy façade made me want to rip off his ears and shove them down his throat. I pointed a rigid, trembling finger at him, all the rage I had with Bjorn finally directed at the proper target.

But then reality tickled the nape of my neck.

I needed this shitbag.

I needed him to confess at some point, on a recording or in front of witnesses, so I could nail him to the wall in a court of witch law—and watch him suffer for the rest of his miserable life in a hole with no windows below the council courthouse.

"No," I whispered, forcing my arm down, the rest of me shaking—from the cold, the unbridled anger, the roller coaster of *feeling* from the last twenty-four hours threatening to drag me under. I shook my head and turned away, hoping that was dismissal enough. Even one of my kids could tell from my body language, my tone, that now wasn't the time for a fucking conversation. *Nothing* about me said I wanted to shoot the shit in some dimly lit back corridor. "No. Never mind."

Hoping this douchebag could accept that and knowing full well he wouldn't, I started off down the stone hallway, the ceiling arched overhead and stamped with recessed lights. Not a part of the castle I gave much thought to before, but I *had* broken up my fair share of canoodling couples on my way to the greenhouses here in the last few months, den mothers nowhere to be found and *good* security a distant memory.

"I have a gift for you, Alecto." The wooden door finally clicked shut, noisily blotting out the early spring thunderstorm. "One that I think will finally change your mind about me—about that *pesky* rule regarding dating coworkers."

I stopped abruptly and closed my eyes with a deep, centering breath. Clearly he hadn't just been walking by and decided to hold the door open for me: Benedict Hammond had on been on the hunt with some stupid *gift*, ever the fucking stalker.

Time to squash this—peacefully.

Swallowing hard, I faced him again with a thin smile and raised brows. "Is that so?"

Seriously, dude. What about making a rain-drenched witch stand around in some drafty corridor while you pontificated on rules and gifts seemed like a good strategy to court her?

Unless the intention was to court badly.

Piss me off.

Make me hate him even more.

Then, you know, mission accomplished.

Benedict lifted a finger, motioning for me to wait, while his other hand plunged into the depths of his deep purple warlock robes, his cloak thick and stitched with gold filigree. So pretentious. A moment later, he produced a black velvet ring box, and my gut bottomed out, my mouth suddenly painfully dry while my throat ached with thick, hot dread.

Smirking, the warlock cracked the little box open, angling it so the piece inside caught the light.

He...

That...

I lilted into the wall—it was either that or drop to my knees while my heart stopped and lit on fucking fire.

That—was my mom's wedding ring.

I'd recognize it anywhere from all the photos, the keepsakes littered around my grandparents' house in vintage frames. A shimmering oval ruby on a rose-gold band, diamonds by the dozen, patterned beautifully like shooting stars on either side of the main attraction. The story went that it had cost half a year's salary for a jeweler to design it, one of a kind, deeply personal and straight out of my dad's head.

That ring... was a Corwin family heirloom.

No one had ever found it in the rubble of our ancestral home.

He—

This fucker—

He—

"Overwhelming, isn't it?" Benedict mused, shifting the ring box to make every diamond sparkle under the lights. And they did. They danced for me—just as they must have danced for my mom the first time Dad cracked open the original ring box it had once sat cushioned in. Benedict chuckled, staring straight into my eyes as he said, "Consider it a token of my affectionate—"

I launched myself at him with a banshee screech. No wand. No burst of magic from my palms—just pure, uncut, unadulterated physical *rage*. The attack seemed to have caught him off guard, because I was on him in a second, slashing my nails across his face, painting his grey stubble red. There was no plan. No forethought. Fists and fury rained down on him, ten times stronger than the storm brewing outside. I punched and raked and kicked and shoved my knee into his fucking groin so he folded over with a wheeze, ring box clattering to the ground just before his back slammed into the door. Finally, with a little support behind him, he managed to grab my shoulders and shove me so hard I staggered backward—right onto my ass.

Pain bloomed up my tailbone, but I barely felt it, barely acknowledged it, magic and adrenaline twining together into something dangerous.

"I *knew* it," Benedict snarled breathlessly, bracing on the door and glaring down at me like I was literal pond scum. "I'd know those *eyes* anywhere!"

"*Fuck* you!" I shrieked as I shot up, logic and reason out the window, all those cautious plans ashes at my feet. We both drew our wands at the same time, his from a hip holster and mine from the leather strap around my forearm. While mine shook, Benedict's stared me down evenly, the warlock more in control of the moment. Still, I stood tall despite the chaos swirling inside, the one that made my knees knock and my pulse pound. "Give me back her ring, you *fucking* psychopath."

Benedict kicked the ring box in my direction; it sailed by and bounced down the hall, and as much as I wanted to dive for it, I stayed perfectly still, wand trained on his seething face.

"The one I bought her was *much* better," he sneered. Once again my body wanted to crumble, peter to the left and crash into the wall.

I let one knee buckle, my full weight on the other, and nothing more. "*What* did you just say?"

He flashed his teeth, that smile *all* predator. "So, you survived the fire, Hannah? I'd always wondered—"

"My name is Alecto, *Benedict*."

We glowered at each other, wands crossed, the air alive with not just my aura, but his, too, the pair colliding like two charging armies.

"And here I thought the Corwin line had finally died out," he muttered, chin jutted so he could sneer down his nose at me. For the first time since I'd heard his stupid fake voice carrying over the rain, I smirked.

"Nope." The smirk shifted to full-blown grin when his eyes narrowed. "You fucked up, dirtbag."

"Trust me, it won't happen again," he fired back. "You may

have your mother's eyes, but you have your father's arrogance..." His black gaze crawled across my face, then up and down my figure so that I really *felt* it. "And you stink of Corwin mediocrity."

"Fuck you."

"There's that Corwin eloquence," he spat. "I can't believe I considered you on par with her—"

Even though I managed to knock his wand aside, Benedict saw this attack coming. He braced for it, brute force driving me hard enough that I slammed him into the door again, only this time he fought back. It would have been cleaner to cast, to fire off a disarming incantation or a stunning hex—*something*. But the fury inside craved blood, driven by fire rather than fear.

And I just wanted to rip him apart with my bare hands.

Bigger than me, physically stronger, Benedict wasn't the same fighter he was the first time around, and it seemed the only way I'd get the upper hand was with the element of surprise. Because in an instant his arms were around me, hurling me into the wall. I elbowed him hard in the ribs, forcing out a satisfying grunt, but a second later he grabbed my hair and slammed my forehead into the grey stone. Agony ripped through my skull and stars danced in my eyes, but even in a daze, my body had its own agenda. I kicked back with everything I had, nailing him *right* in the knee so that something *cracked*.

"Little *bitch*," he hissed, and I grinned again, sporting a little savagery of my own even as blood oozed down my forehead and into my brow.

"It's less than you deserve, asshole."

"I'll *give* you what you deserve—*oomph*."

My elbow finally said hello to his mouth, and even though it hurt, it felt pretty fucking fantastic, too.

Just as his grip tightened in my hair, wrenching my head

back, a soft throat clear had us both stilling, going from panting combatants to rigid statues.

At the end of the little corridor stood Iris Prewett, dressed in the same dark grey hoopskirt as this morning, the same busy blouse with its frills and ruffles, the same painfully tight bun and disapproving frown.

"Professor Cedar," she said sharply, her hawkish gaze sliding from his face to mine. "*Professor* Clarke. Might I remind you where you are right now—and that brawling is unbecoming of witches and warlocks. We're not *dogs*."

Benedict immediately released me, and I clawed up the wall, needing to grit my nails into the grout for support. Had she heard our conversation? Did I have a witness? Even one as patronizing as Iris Prewett would do.

"He—"

"Miss *Clarke*." Iris held up a hand to silence me—not that she needed to. The way she sneered *Clarke* told me loud and clear that she had heard everything, that even if she didn't know the whole story, she knew enough to determine I was a liar. My gaze darted back to Benedict, but he was busy furiously wiping the blood off his cheeks, oblivious to the fact that we had been caught trying to tear each other apart in an academy hallway.

Iris, meanwhile, strolled toward us slowly, a witch in total control, her massive skirt swaying side to side with every step. She paused briefly to glance down at the ring box, open and on its side, my mom's wedding ring still mercifully set in the silky bedding.

Material reminiscent of her coffin, actually.

My heart skipped a beat at the thought.

He wouldn't—

He ripped Mom and Dad into literal pieces.

He would.

"There are changes coming to Root Rot Academy in the

next few days," Iris remarked, her crisp, nasally voice jostling me out of a huge downward spiral. She sniffed and sidestepped the ring box like she was above it, thin, waifish hands threaded together and resting on her hoop skirt. "Changes you may not be entirely comfortable with."

I stared back at her like an idiot, head pounding, thoughts muddled.

"Let me be the first to offer you a generous severance package, effective midnight tomorrow."

Right after the usual Sunday staff meeting.

"W-what?" I stammered. Jack's unconscious, bloody body flashed across my mind's eye, and my heart dropped *again*. Had he—had something happened? Last I heard he was on the road to recovery, long as it might be. "No, I—"

"Let me be clearer," the witch said primly, finally stopping a few feet away. Benedict pushed off the wall and meandered over to her, squishing around her massive skirt and using it like a cotton-crinoline shield. Blood streaked his face, a trio of bright red lines courtesy of my nails shining like beacons in the night. Despite that, he peered down his nose at me, smug, gloating, glaring—bleeding. Iris, on the other hand, barely acknowledged him, her yellow-grey gaze pinned on me like she was enjoying this. "Substantial changes are coming to Root Rot *Reform* School, changes you may not be entirely comfortable with—and you may not *survive*."

Shock echoed through me.

"No one would blame you for walking away, Miss Clarke," Iris added, tone kind but everything else about her overtly cruel. "Just a little food for thought. Not everyone is cut out for this line of work."

She then twisted back to check on Benedict, scratching some of the blood from his stubble with her thumbnail. Shock seemed to reverberate through him, too, but he recovered faster, oozing from stiff to pliant at her touch, the pair swapping private grins like I wasn't even here.

What—the fuck.

"As with all my staff—" Iris slowly rotated around, struggling to maneuver her massive skirt but clearly trying not to show it. "—I encourage you to think about yourself—to do what's best for you and your... future."

She then flashed a smirk over her shoulder and left, heels clicking down the corridor. Benedict pressed up against the wall to let her pass, then faced me again with a look that could peel flesh from bone in a different magical reality. A shiver cut down my spine, the hairs on the back of my neck standing on end and self-preservation demanding I bolt.

I held my ground.

Stood taller.

Glared down my nose at *him*.

And he stalked after Iris without a word—like a good little puppy who had found a new mistress, an ally in his game of lies, murder, and psychopathy.

I waited until the click of their shoes faded off entirely, then slid to the ground with a stuttering gasp. Head in a world of hurt and blood still dripping down my face, I crawled for my mom's abandoned ring.

Grabbed the box with both shaking, numb hands and clutched it to my chest, panting, on the verge of hyperventilating.

Held it tight—then closed my eyes and *breathed*.

Long inhale. Hold. Longer exhale.

Over and over again, forcing my body to settle, breathing out the shock of—*that*.

"Gods," I rasped when I finally felt more in control, glancing skyward with a scowl, "what is *happening*?"

No one would answer, same as always, but this time my ask was rhetorical.

I knew *precisely* what was happening, what awaited the academy on the cloudy horizon.

A coup.

A return to the old ways.

And those of us who didn't approve could either shut up or ship off.

And Jack... Gods, I had no idea where Jack was or what had happened, but I wasn't going anywhere without him.

Or Bjorn.

Or Gavriel.

Nor would I abandon a single one of my students to that fucking hag and her psychotic new lapdog.

Shivering, I yanked Mom's ring out of the box, then hurled the velvet square down the empty corridor with a cry. While too small for my pointer, it fit just fine on my right hand's ring finger, the ruby glistening beneath the overhead lights.

Shimmering like blood.

Which—was weirdly empowering.

I brought my fist to my chest and closed my eyes, Iris's words still ringing in my ears.

The threat was clear: get out of her way or be crushed under her heel.

My eyes snapped open. No. I wouldn't stand for this, and no one else would, either. Jack would raise hell. Bjorn would *never* strike a student. Gavriel would... Well, he'd complain a lot, but knowing his past, that he had a history of *wanting* to do what was best for his people, I was sure he would choose the right side in all this, too.

Beyond all that, Benedict now knew I had survived, that a Corwin walked the halls of his sanctuary.

He'd come for me. Find a way to silence me so I couldn't expose him.

The easiest thing *would* be to leave. Take a chunk of cash and get out with my life.

I snorted weakly.

When had I ever gone for the easiest option?

I knew what it meant to stay.

Fuck you both.

I knew the risk. I knew the consequences. I knew how the game would have to be played going forward.

Make all the threats you want...

I peered down at my mom's ring, her strength blossoming in my chest and my dad's stubbornness igniting in my heart.

I'm not going anywhere.

TO BE CONCLUDED...

COMING SOON!

It's conclusion time!

Root Rot Academy: Term 3 ~ March 31, 2021

AVAILABLE FOR PREORDER NOW ON AMAZON! xo

.

ACKNOWLEDGMENTS

First and forever, thank you to my editorial queen Amanda! You read through all my first draft nonsense with poise and tact, and no one gets me more hyped up to push forward when I feel like crashing — thank you. I'd be lost without you. Just like I'd be lost without the awesome proofreading skills of Sandra at One Love Editing, and my phenomenal typo-checker Linda. You ladies rock my world with every new release!!

Thank you to all the readers who fell in love with Alecto and her men in the first term. Thank you for taking a chance on my first trilogy, and thank you for continuing this journey with me!

Huuuuuge shout out to my amazing reader group on Facebook!! I have so much fun with you pretties, and even when I'm exhausted, you pretties make me laugh and want to keep going. xoxo

To my Sun and Stars, you're my everything. Thank you for your kindness and your constant support throughout this crazy author journey.

Shout out to my mom, my #1 fan no matter what filth I write.

See you in *Root Rot Academy: Term 3*!! If you enjoyed the second term, feel free to leave a review on Amazon or Goodreads. Reviews help indies thrive — even the one-stars. #nervoussweat

xoxoxoxo
Rhea

ABOUT THE AUTHOR

Rhea Watson is a Canadian reverse harem author who loves a good paranormal romance. She writes layered alpha heroes with rough exteriors who melt for their strong, independent soulmates.

In her spare time, Rhea babies her herb garden, bows to her cat's every whim, and flies through Netflix shows like it's her day job.

Also by Rhea:

ALL THE QUEEN'S MEN SERIES
(Standalones, Same Universe)
Reaper's Pack
Caged Kitten
Haunt ~ October 2021

ROOT ROT ACADEMY
Term 1
Term 2
Term 3 (March 2021)

BLOODLINE TRILOGY
Book 1 (May 2021)
Book 2 (June 2021)
Book 3 (July 2021)

RHEA WATSON WRITING AS EVIE KENT:

To Love a God (Lily of the Valley, #1)
Surrender: A Lily of the Valley Novella

FACEBOOK READER GROUP
WEBSITE